PRAISE FOR *THE SEA[RCH PARTY]*

"A chillingly complex, well-crafted web. . . . [characters walk] mon Lelic's pages as if they are standing right next to you."
—Jane Corry, bestselling author of *The Dead Ex*

"Clever and atmospheric, with shades of *Stand by Me*."
—Mark Edwards, author of *Here to Stay*

"A brilliantly tense tale of teenage frustration, lost souls, and sibling love, with an atmosphere as tense as the end of a summer storm that threatens throughout the book. Plus a whirlwind of an ending that's like riding a roller coaster."
—Araminta Hall, author of *Our Kind of Cruelty*

"I've spent every free moment of the last few days feasting on *The Search Party* . . . a bloody good read and the very definition of unpredictable. Twisty, creepy, brilliantly paced, and with a denouement I never saw coming." —John Marrs, author of *The One*

PRAISE FOR SIMON LELIC

"An intricate, powerful, and deeply unsettling thriller about the profound ways in which cruelty can change its survivors, and the creeping fear that nothing—not your home, not love, not even your own mind—is as rock-solid and impregnable as we all want to believe."
—Tana French, *New York Times* bestselling author of *The Trespasser*, on *The New Neighbors*

"Highly recommended!"
—Karen Dionne, author of *The Marsh King's Daughter*

"I'm such a fan of this author and can't wait to see what he has in store next." —Criminal Element

"Lelic slow[...] [...]ike your stori[...] [...] is one you w[...] [...]ter

THE
SEARCH
PARTY

Simon Lelic

BERKLEY
NEW YORK

BERKLEY
An imprint of Penguin Random House LLC
penguinrandomhouse.com

Copyright © 2020 by Simon Lelic
Penguin Random House supports copyright. Copyright fuels creativity, encourages diverse voices,
promotes free speech, and creates a vibrant culture. Thank you for buying an authorized edition of
this book and for complying with copyright laws by not reproducing, scanning, or distributing
any part of it in any form without permission. You are supporting writers and allowing
Penguin Random House to continue to publish books for every reader.

BERKLEY and the BERKLEY & B colophon are registered trademarks of Penguin Random House LLC.

Library of Congress Cataloging-in-Publication Data

Names: Lelic, Simon, author.
Title: The search party / Simon Lelic.
Description: Berkley trade paperback edition. | New York: Berkley, 2020.
Identifiers: LCCN 2019055349 (print) | LCCN 2019055350 (ebook) |
ISBN 9780593098332 (trade paperback) | ISBN 9780593098349 (ebook)
Subjects: GSAFD: Suspense fiction.
Classification: LCC PR6112.E48 S43 2020 (print) | LCC PR6112.E48 (ebook) | DDC 823/.92—dc23
LC record available at https://lccn.loc.gov/2019055349
LC ebook record available at https://lccn.loc.gov/2019055350

Viking UK trade paperback edition / August 2020
Berkley trade paperback edition / August 2020

Printed in the United States of America
1 3 5 7 9 10 8 6 4 2

Cover art by Robert Norbury / Millennium Images
Cover design by Mumtaz Mustafa
Book design by Alison Cnockaert

For my family

[phone call]

Operator: Emergency, which service please?

Caller: Hello? Hello?

Operator: Do you need fire, police or ambulance?

Caller: I can't . . . Hello? Is anyone there?

Operator: I can hear you. Can you hear me?

Caller: Yes, I . . . Thank God. Please, help us. Please.

Operator: Can you tell me what's happened?

Caller: Hello? She's gone. I can't . . .

Operator: I'm here. I can still hear you. Where are you?

Caller: I don't know. In the woods. Somewhere, I . . . Please. We need an ambulance.

Operator: Right. An ambulance. Can you tell me where you are? What can you see?

Caller: Oh God. Oh God.

Operator: You're in the woods, is that what you said?

Caller: Yes. Yes. Near . . . a building. A house, or . . . [*inaudible*]

Operator: A house, you say? Do you know the address?

Caller: There isn't one. It's empty. Abandoned. But . . . Please. Just come. Quickly. Please. Just—

[call ends]

DAY **SIX**

THE BLOODY RAIN. For twenty-four hours it had fallen, flaying the banks of the river with a tropical fervor. Except it was cold. Granted the summer was officially over, but just two days ago the volunteers had been wearing shorts, while Fleet had stood sweating in his thinnest suit. Since the weather had broken, the water had struck like winter hail. Hard, pitiless, icy. A month's rainfall in barely a day, so they said. Fleet didn't know about climate change, all that, but he knew when something wasn't right. And this weather? It was freakish. As messed-up as everything else that was going on in this town right now.

He paused in the doorway of his hotel to light a cigarette, taking almost as much pleasure from the brief burst of warmth as he did from the nicotine itself. He exhaled a cloud of smoke that was immediately doused by the tumbling rain, then took two more drags and tossed the cigarette into the gutter, knowing it would be ruined anyway the moment he stepped into the torrent.

That's fifty pence down the drain right there, said a voice inside his head. His wife Holly's, unmistakably, and Fleet felt a pang from somewhere in his gut. It was like an ulcer, this constant twinge, and he hadn't yet found a way to stop it hurting.

He thought of home. Was it raining like this there?, he wondered. Because it felt biblical. If he were to get into his car and drive the three miles to the parish limits, would he find himself confronting a ring of blue sky, a rainbow bridge to the world outside?

You heavens above, rain down my righteousness . . .

What was that? Genesis? Isaiah? The quote came unbidden, as powerfully evocative as a familiar smell, and it made him want to light another cigarette.

"Detective Inspector Fleet?"

Just as he'd been about to dash toward his company Insignia, Fleet turned. It was the hotelier, a woman in her late forties to whom Fleet had taken an instant dislike on first meeting her, only to later reverse his opinion completely. She dressed primly, rarely smiled, and wore her hair in a skin-stretching bun. Fleet had marked her down as yet another disapproving gossip, in a town with far more than its fair share, but she'd proved discreet, generous and obliquely loyal. In many ways, she was the closest thing Fleet had in this town to a friend.

"There's a call for you," said Anne, as she pointed over her left shoulder. Her expression was apologetic. She was familiar enough now with Fleet's business to know the news he received was never good.

Fleet checked the screen of his mobile. There were no missed calls, but there was also no reception. The entire town was pocked with dead spots. Which seemed as appropriate an analogy as any.

He followed Anne back inside. The hotel wasn't luxurious, but it was a luxury. Fleet lived only an hour or so along the coast, but rather than traveling back and forth he'd taken a room here, at the Harbor View Hotel. For convenience, he'd told himself. The Harbor

View was no more or less than your typical seaside-town B&B, and Fleet might have picked any one of the dozen or so guesthouses that were clustered beside the harbor. All would have had space, and Anne was the only thing that set this one apart. She cleaned his room, fried his breakfast and—now—fielded his calls. She did so much it made Fleet feel guilty, to the extent he'd started making his own bed. Not that he used it much anyway. Most nights, since checking in just under a week ago, he'd sat up gazing at the harbor, imagining what might be hidden beneath the water.

Anne showed him to the little office behind the reception counter, and gestured to the receiver lying unhooked on the desk. She nodded when Fleet offered his thanks, and then closed the glass door to give him some privacy.

"Robin Fleet," he announced into the receiver.

"Boss? It's Nicky."

The line was poor, the reception wherever Nicky was clearly only a fraction better than it was in the black spot that covered the area around the harbor.

"What's up, Nicky? I was just on my way to the river."

Detective Sergeant Nicola Collins took a breath. Even through the crackle she sounded excited about something.

"We've found them," she said.

Fleet straightened. "You did? When?"

"Just now. And, Rob? Brace yourself. It's a fucking shitshow."

So much for the rainbow bridge.

Fleet had to follow the river inland to get to where he was heading—passing the current search site on the way—and though something inside him lifted when he reached the final dilapidated houses of the town itself, the clouds did not. The sky was gray to the end of the world, and on the roof of Fleet's car the rain persisted with its relentless beat.

As the last few buildings disappeared from his rearview mirror, Fleet found himself in countryside. The forest thickened, obscuring the river. And although Fleet remembered the area far better than he would have liked, he twice took a wrong turning. He blamed the sat-nav, which was insistent that he should cut across a field. He switched it off, turned up the radio—the local station, playing modern pop tunes, teenage stuff, until he dialed to something classical instead—and relied on memory, together with the directions Nicky had given him at the end of their patchy phone call.

It took him half an hour longer than he'd expected, and in the end even the radio signal gave out. Had they really come this far? This deep inland?

The Insignia wasn't built for country lanes, even less for muddy fields, so he had to park it short of the pair of police Land Rovers. Nicky was waiting for him, wellied and dripping. Somehow, though, DS Nicola Collins always managed to look like she was fresh from a good night's sleep and her second cup of coffee. It was those frost blue eyes of hers, clear and crisp against the frame of her short black hair. Also, she was young. Twenty-six? Twenty-seven? A decade younger than Fleet, and Fleet's true age, he always felt, was his own plus the number of cigarettes he'd smoked that day.

But what Fleet had mistaken for excitement in Nicky's voice when he'd spoken to her on the phone was something else, he quickly realized. It was adrenaline, yes, but Fleet could see she was rattled. And DS Collins didn't rattle easily.

"Boss," she said, in greeting. She looked down at his shoes, which were already sinking into the mud.

Fleet flipped the hood of his anorak over his head. "You can al-ways give me a piggyback if I get stuck," he said. Fleet was six-three, and at least fifteen kilos overweight. Nicky was trimmer than a grey-hound, and weighed about as much. Even so, Fleet had no doubt she could have managed it. She was tenacious as hell, which was part of the reason he'd given this particular assignment to her. Others would have seen it as being sidelined, but Nicky seemed to appreciate how crucial it was likely to be.

"If it carries on raining like this, we'll both be swimming soon anyway," Nicky said.

Which might actually have suited Fleet better. When he'd been a teenager he'd swum competitively, and even though it was years since he'd been in a pool, these days he'd probably still show more grace in the water than he did on dry land. Wasn't body fat supposed to help with buoyancy, after all?

They started across the field toward the woods.

"How far have we got to go?" Fleet asked.

"Far enough," Nicky answered. "Especially in brogues. But they were closer to the edge of the forest than they apparently realized."

"They were lost?"

"To be honest, I'm not sure. When they called, they struggled to pinpoint their location. On the other hand, I've got a feeling they knew where they were heading. But their stories are . . . garbled. Which is understandable, given the circumstances."

Fleet turned, but could see only the tip of Nicky's nose past the solid yellow wall of her hood.

"You said they called in," he said, prompting her.

"That's right. About two hours ago. It took us an hour to find them. Would have been longer if we hadn't already been on their trail. The ambulance is apparently on its way, but I guess it got stuck behind a tractor or something. And . . . Well. There's no rush." She looked at him meaningfully.

"Sadie?" Fleet asked. It was all he could say, all he needed to.

But, "No," said Nicky. "Not Sadie."

They passed through the tree line. Even at the edge of the forest the foliage was dense, but there was something like a path cutting through the undergrowth.

About a mile in, they reached a clearing, and Nicky moved to one side. Unlike most of the cops assigned to the investigation, she'd worked with Fleet before, and she knew him well enough to appreciate that the time for commentary had passed. It was important to Fleet that he be able to make his own assessment. When he wanted more from Nicky—or from anyone—he would ask.

The first thing Fleet noted was how well Nicky had preserved the scene. Unexpectedly, this far from the road, there was a clutch of buildings on the other side of the clearing—all long abandoned, by the look of them. There was a small cabin, as well as two large barns, presumably for crops or farming equipment, not that anything was being cultivated out here now. All the structures had been taped off, as indeed had the entire area. Patches of the open ground between Fleet and the buildings had also been marked, and covered with tarps to protect them from the rain. *Footprints?* Fleet wondered. *Or blood?*

He skirted the edge of the clearing, as the rain on his hood struck a steady patter—only interrupted every so often by a heavier drop from the branches overhead. Fleet pulled the hood back to release himself from the distraction.

Half a dozen steps from the access path he saw them. While they'd waited for the ambulance to arrive, Nicky and her three colleagues had herded them under cover, beneath the roof of one of the barns. The four kids were seated on the ground, wrapped in silver blankets, and Fleet noted they were even more poorly prepared for the weather than he was. They had on trainers, T-shirts, shorts, and all were soaked to the skin. They looked like Glastonbury-goers on a come-down, long after the music had stopped.

Fleet's attention moved on, his eyes sweeping the shadows in the outbuilding.

And then he saw it. The body at the base of the tree. It was beyond the view of the kids in the barn, but from the way the teenagers were facing, it was obvious they were aware it was there.

"Jesus Christ," Fleet muttered. He looked at the kids again, and then the body.

You heavens above, rain down my righteousness.

For the first time since he'd been a teenager himself, Fleet felt the urge to cross himself.

DAY **SEVEN**

ABI

WE SHOULD NEVER have been out there in the first place. We should have . . . I don't know what we should have done. What the hell *do* you do in a situation like that?

Did he really . . .

Is he really . . .

I mean, we didn't make a mistake or anything? That's all I'm asking. Like, maybe it wasn't as bad as we thought it was, or the ambulance people got to him in time, and—

No.

No.

I know.

I just . . . I can't believe it, that's all. I mean, I can see it, literally see it, right in front of me, every time I close my eyes, but even still it . . .

Oh God. Oh Jesus.

We just . . . we should never have been out there. We *shouldn't*.

But it was about the act of looking. That's what it was. The not just doing nothing while you lot dredged the river, and searched the allotments, and the old railway cutting, and all the other places that could have hidden a . . . that Sadie might . . . that . . .

Sorry.

I just . . . I didn't expect it to be this hard. I thought I could . . . that I'd just . . . To be honest, I don't know what I thought.

Do we really have to go through it all again? I mean, you know how it ended. How he . . . how he died. And I told you I didn't *see*. It all happened so quickly, and I . . . I mean, I'm tired, and . . . and there's so much I don't remember, and . . .

Right. Of course.

No, I . . . I get it. I do. Let's just . . . let me just . . . I'm fine. It's fine.

I was saying . . . What was I saying?

Right.

We had a choice, we figured. Sit around waiting for a call or a text or whatever, or for someone to come knocking on the door, with news you knew was going to be a fist into your stomach. Or go out and join in the search. Not the actual search, where you lot were. We knew you wouldn't let us within fifty meters, not a bunch of sixteen-year-old kids who you'd basically already accused of being involved somehow.

But the *search*. Bigger picture. The Search for Sadie Saunders.

It's like, our mums and dads were out there helping you. And most of them didn't even know her. Not properly. Obviously Sadie's parents did, but . . . Well. I say that. Although I guess they didn't really know her either.

But my point is, *we* knew her. And me, personally, the whole time I was waiting for news, all I could do was nothing. There was WhatsApp and Facebook and stuff, which helped at first because it felt like you were in touch with what was going on. Not what was

actually going on, though, and after a while that became the problem. You realized that nobody had any better idea than you did.

And it started getting nasty. It didn't take long. It was stuff about
Mason, mainly. Which I suppose was to be expected, not that it
made it any easier to see. And later—not even that much later—it
was stuff about the rest of us as well. And some of it I know exactly
who was responsible. You do too, you must do, but has anyone done
anything about it? Of course not. Which is exactly why people think
it's OK. They know they can say whatever they like if it's not out
loud. Worst case, they'll get put in Twitter jail or something, not
actual jail, which if you ask me is where some of these people, people
like Lara fucking Sweeney for example—

Sorry.

It's just . . . I get so . . . It's everything, you know?

Poor Sadie. And she's still out there! *Somewhere.* I keep thinking
about the last time I saw her. The *very* last time, I mean. We were
sitting in my room and she was listening to me bitch about my dad.
Just, like, about how much of an arsehole he can be. How *mean.*
Because I needed a new blazer for school, for sixth form, and that
turned into him asking me why I was bothering taking A levels in
the first place. He said it was a waste of time. That I wasn't smart
enough to pass. That I'd be better off just getting a job at the supermarket, because that was probably where I was going to end up anyway. And it didn't matter what I said back to him, he'd just shake
his head at me, sneer at me, the way he always does, and there was
nothing I could do to . . . to just . . .

It doesn't matter. The point is, I'd texted Sadie, and ten minutes
later she was at my house. Just because she could tell I needed some
company. You know? Which was typical Sadie. And all evening I
was just sitting there talking about myself, about *my* problems,

while Sadie listened, and told me not to pay any attention, that I should follow my heart, that I was capable of accomplishing *anything*. Which obviously I didn't believe, but the point is she was there for me, the way she's always there, except . . . except . . .

Except now she's not.

No, really, I—

Unless . . . I don't suppose you have a cigarette, do you? I mean, I know that technically I'm too young and probably you're the last person I should be asking, but I just thought—

No. No. I get it. It's fine, really. But, um. Don't tell my parents I asked, will you? They'd kill me. My dad would. And I don't usually smoke, not all that often anyway, but at the moment, it just feels a bit like, screw it. You know? Talking about what happened . . . it's not easy. Especially when I think about how it all began. Our search, I mean. Our *adventure*. That's what Cora called it, if you can believe it. And the rest of them were hardly any better.

Because that's the thing, you see. They made out like they were doing it for Sadie, but that wasn't what was going on at all. They were lying. Every one of them. Cora, Fash, Mason, even Luke, probably— they were lying right from the start.

CORA

WHAT DID THEY say? The others. What did Abi say? I bet she made out she had nothing to do with it, didn't she? I bet she's trying to blame it all on one of us.

It's fucking typical. Abi's such a faker, it's no wonder nobody likes her.

Was my friend. Not anymore.

I bet I know exactly what she told you. I knew what she'd tell you the very second after it happened. I could see it in her eyes. And I'm not trying to make out I'm any less to blame than she is, that I don't deserve what's coming to me, too. All I'm saying is, Abigail Marshall, she's not as innocent as you think.

Nothing, nothing. I don't mean anything, OK?

Look, just . . . just tell me what more I'm supposed to tell you. I don't *know* how it happened. It was all such a blur. All I know is it had nothing to do with me.

Fine. Whatever. But I don't see how going over and over the same old stuff is going to help. You know how it ended. What does it matter how it began?

OK, OK.

The start, then.

It was Fash who said why didn't we. Fareed, I mean. Fash is what everyone calls him. Other than his mum, obviously.

But Fash came to my house. Three days ago. So day four, I suppose you'd call it. We did. Not in a big-deal kind of way, with a great big display or something somewhere, but we all knew exactly how much time had passed since Sadie had gone missing. Although, by counting up, it was also like we were counting down to something. It was like . . . like watching a sand timer. Do you know what I mean?

In fact, that's mainly what I'd been doing: lying on my bed, staring at the hands going round on this old watch. Not just any watch. It used to be Sadie's. It's stupid really. Just this stupid pink thing. I'm surprised it still even works. But she gave it to me, like, years ago, in return for one of my old dolls. Back when I played with shit like that, this was, so we can't have been more than seven. And me and Sadie, back then, we were best friends. Like, *proper* best friends. The way only little kids can be, before all the bullshit like school and stuff gets in the way. You know, boys and stuff.

Anyway, the idea was I gave her my most precious thing, and she gave me hers in return, which turned out to be this watch. And the thing was, until she went missing, I could never bring myself to look at it. Because I'd cheated her, you see. I knew for a fact she treasured that watch more than anything, but I lied about which doll I loved most. And that's what I couldn't stop thinking about. As I lay there staring at the second hand, I couldn't help wondering if that's why Sadie had gone missing. Because of me. Because I'd broken some sacred bond.

It's stupid, I know. Don't think I don't realize how it sounds. But that's basically what I was thinking about, until Fash showed up at my door.

I could tell it was him from the fact he knocked. He's always been polite like that. Too polite, mostly, which is what we keep telling him. But it's basically us versus his mum, and I think we all know who's going to win *that* battle.

But what I mean is, the others, they tend to just climb up the pear tree outside my bedroom window and scare me half to death by rapping on the glass. Or, sometimes, by actually climbing right inside. Mason, one time, he hid inside my wardrobe. This was back when me and him . . . when we were closer. And my heart literally exploded. Not literally, obviously, but if it had it would have served him right.

It took Fash a while to convince me. I think that surprised him. I mean, that's obviously why he came to me before the others, because he thought I'd be the easiest sell. But at first I couldn't see the point. Where would we look, for one thing? And why did we have a better chance of finding Sadie than anyone else? But Fash had answers prepared for both of those questions. Which, had I thought about it, should probably have rung alarm bells at the time.

But what he said was, Sadie might still be out there. Alone somewhere, hurt maybe, and for all we knew, everyone else was looking for her in the wrong place. Why weren't they looking in the woods? We knew Sadie liked to go walking there. We all did. When we were young the woods had basically been our playground—we'd climb trees, play manhunt, all that—and Fash's point was, we knew them better than anyone.

And the other thing he said was, why *not* go? You know? Because the alternative was to keep doing what we'd been doing, and Fash made out he was as sick of waiting around as I was.

So I agreed. And Fash grinned, all relieved and that. Which should have been another clue. But at the time all I was thinking about was how long it had been since I'd last seen *anyone* smile. And Fash, he's kind of funny-looking anyway. Not ugly, I don't mean that. He's tall and he's dark, obviously, and he's got nice eyes, but he's also a bit . . . gangly. Like his bones are a size too big for his body, even in his face. You've seen him, you know. So all I'm saying is, when Fash smiles, it's almost impossible not to smile back.

"So what are we waiting for?" Fash said. "Let's get going." We were in my room, and Fash was sitting on my bed. He patted the rucksack he'd dropped onto the mattress. It was his schoolbag, so I hadn't really noticed it until then. I should have, I suppose, seeing as it was still the summer holidays.

"*Now*, you mean? But what about . . . I don't know. Our parents. Your *mum*."

Fash's expression sort of clouded. Fash's mum . . . she doesn't hit him or anything like that. She's not like Mason's dad, for example, and she's not an arsehole like Abi's. But even so, she's got this control over him. I mean, *strict* is putting it mildly. She's protective, is what it is. If she could, she'd put him in a box, and only bring him out on special occasions.

"I told her I'm staying the night at Mason's," Fash said, and I could see how bad he felt about having lied to her. "And your parents are out, right? Which, the way I figure it, gives us until teatime tomorrow. And, anyway, the day after that, we're supposed to be back at school."

Which I'd almost forgotten about. Going back to school. Starting sixth form. Or, actually, I didn't forget. The truth is I'd been trying not to think about it: the idea of going back to school without Sadie. Without even knowing what happened to her.

So I started packing. I did what Fash did, and used my schoolbag. He told me he would have brought something bigger, but chances were we'd be spotted by someone on our way out of town, and he didn't want people to start asking questions. What he meant was, he didn't want anyone spreading rumors. Even *more* rumors, that is.

That's the problem with living where we do. When I'm old enough I'm going to move to Australia. Arizona. Some place with no rivers, no woods. No crappy fairgrounds and cheap-arse tourists. No wash-out summers. No . . . no frigging ice cream vans. Seriously, how many ice cream vans does one town need? No caravan parks. No caravans, full stop. No wind. Nothing above a gentle breeze. No Harvesters. No sodding Morrisons. No net curtains, either, or people who know your name. Nobody who knows your business when you don't want them to.

No woods. Have I said that already?

Well, anyway, it's worth saying twice.

Lots of people. Hundreds of thousands of them preferably. Millions. Or, failing that, none at all.

The population here is supposed to be, I don't know, ten thousand or something, more in the summer obviously, and yet you always end up seeing the same faces. Literally, wherever you go. And people always end up seeing *you*. Watching you. They smile and they talk about the weather and the wind and the seagulls— people are always going on about the sodding seagulls—but really all they're doing is looking for some petty scandal to fill their sad, pathetic little lives.

Anyway.

It took me about thirty seconds. Packing, I mean. I would have taken longer over it if I'd known we'd be gone for two whole nights, and if I'd known what was going to happen with the weather. But it had been dry for so long, it seemed like it wouldn't ever rain again. Hard to believe now, right?

Next up was Abi. And I swear to God we had to stop her from

packing her hair dryer. She didn't take much convincing, though, and I remember being impressed at the time. I guessed her dad was probably on one, and she was desperate to get out of the house. Abi's dad is always giving her a hard time about something. She's too fat, too thin, too ugly, too stupid. He's basically the opposite of my parents, who are so wrapped up in their own shit, they probably wouldn't notice if I did just move to Arizona. I'm talking about my mum, really. Chris, my stepdad, doesn't really count, because he's barely any older than I am. He's like, twenty-nine or something stupid, which is why my mum married him in the first place. Because she's in denial, basically. That she's forty, not twenty-fucking-four. She pretends to herself I'm, like, her little sister or something, because she can't accept that she's old enough to have a teenage daughter.

But anyway, with Abi I assumed that was what it was, and that she was as upset about Sadie as she said she was. Because that was the other thing: she made out like it was such a big relief to finally be doing something other than sitting around waiting for news. But really she was just like all the rest of us. The truth is she only came because she had to. Because she was worried about what we'd find.

Luke was trickier. We went to him next—me, Fash and Abi. And with Luke, it . . .

God. If only we'd . . .

No, I'm not fucking OK. Why the hell would I be OK? About *any* of this?

I keep seeing him lying there. Just . . . lying there, and . . . and none of us able to do anything, except . . . except . . .

No, it's fine.

I said no, OK? A break's not going to help anything.

What I was saying was, with Luke, when we went to get him . . . it was complicated, that's all. I mean, Sadie was his sister. His twin.

So can you imagine? Not only is your sister missing, presumed . . . presumed all *sorts* of stuff. But your parents are pretty much AWOL, too. Emotionally, anyway, at least in terms of him and Dylan. God, poor Dylan. I mean, for Mr. and Mrs. S it's only ever been about Sadie. They've always been convinced she was going to be this superstar—an actor, a dancer, whatever, because Sadie could do pretty much anything, and they've been pushing her down that path since she was four. Stage school, singing lessons, private coaching, all that. And what that meant was, Luke and Dylan got . . . not neglected, exactly. Overlooked. Which was fine as far as Luke was concerned, because he's always been kind of self-sufficient—just getting on with things in his own way. But for Dylan . . . I mean, he's twelve, so it wasn't the same as when he was younger, but Dylan's always been . . . tricky. Like, not as bright as his brother and sister, for one thing, nowhere near as bright, to the extent his parents were convinced for ages that there was something wrong with him. ADHD or whatever you call it. They had him on Ritalin and everything, until Luke convinced them to take him off it. If you ask me, the only thing Dylan needed was some attention from his mum and dad, and maybe a bit of help at school. But there was fat chance of that. Instead, Luke was basically the one taking care of him. Sadie helped, too, when she could, but most of the responsibility fell to Luke.

And Dylan was there when we stopped by. That day, I mean. The day we left. We knew their parents wouldn't be. They'd basically spent every day since Sadie went missing down by the river. But I guess we forgot about Dylan, and it was because of him that Luke refused to come with us. Well, what he said was, he couldn't.

"What am I supposed to do with Dylan?" he said. "Just leave him here on his own?"

We were standing on Luke's doorstep, and I could see Dylan behind him in the living room, sitting on the sofa. Normally he would have been playing one of his video games, but today he was just staring at the TV. I don't think he'd even registered the doorbell. Up until then I'd barely even thought about Dylan, about how he must have been missing Sadie, too. But it suddenly struck me that he was probably taking it as hard as anyone. Harder maybe, because Dylan worshipped Sadie almost as much as Sadie's dad did, and I doubt he really understood what was going on.

"It'll only be for an hour or two," said Fash. "Your parents will be back soon, right?"

Luke sniffed. "Who knows?" he said. "They might be out all night if someone doesn't give them a shove in the right direction. Although my aunt said she'd come by to make us dinner."

"So there you go then," Fash said, like that settled it.

Luke looked doubtfully over his shoulder.

"For Christ's sake, Luke," I chipped in. "Dylan's not a baby anymore. Do you think your parents would give leaving him alone a second thought? Besides, what's he gonna do, overdose on screen time?"

It's like I said, Dylan spent half his life playing games on his Xbox. *Fortnite*, *Call of Duty*, all that. His parents didn't care, and Luke had given up trying to stop him. Apart from anything, it gave Luke a break from having to look after him. Because Dylan didn't really have any friends, and if he wasn't plugged into something, he spent most of the time getting on our nerves. Sticking his nose in, whining about wanting to join in. Just little brother stuff, really. But it was hard on Luke, is my point.

So, anyway, Luke shook his head. "Sorry, guys. I can't do it. How about I talk to my aunt later and see if she can watch Dylan tomorrow? Then we can all go down to the river in the morning, see if the cops'll let us join in the line search."

"But that's the *point*," Fash said. "They *won't* let us join in, and anyway, they're looking in the wrong place."

Luke narrowed his eyes. "How do you know?"

"I . . . I don't," Fash said. "But it's obvious, isn't it? Otherwise they would have found her by now."

"Not necessarily," said Luke. "The tides, the reeds . . . you know what it's like down there. And anyway, that's where they found Sadie's bag."

Which shut everyone up for a second. Because that was the thing. You could tell yourself that Sadie was just lying hurt somewhere, just like Fash had said. Or that maybe she was on a plane to Goa, or diving at the Great Barrier Reef. But then you remembered about her bag, the one you lot found down by the riverbank. Her rucksack, with her phone in, her wallet.

Everything.

"Come on, guys," said Abi. "He's said he can't. We shouldn't force him." And she gave Fash a little tug.

"Come on, man," Fash said, still looking at Luke. "Come with us. Last time I'm gonna ask, I promise."

Luke stared back at him, sort of frowning. "You're really gonna go?"

Me, Fash and Abi all looked at each other. We shrugged.

"And you really think . . . I mean, you reckon there's an actual chance? That we might find her?"

Fash smiled with one corner of his mouth. "There's always a chance, mate."

Luke looked over his shoulder at Dylan, who was still staring at the TV.

"Aw, sod it. Wait there."

Luke shut the door in our faces. Six minutes later he opened it again, his school rucksack hooked across his shoulder. "I've told Dylan I'm going to the shops. And I'm not his babysitter, right?"

"Right," said Fash, grinning his grin, which got the rest of us all smiling and that, too. We weren't happy. It wasn't that. For me it was mainly relief, I suppose. I felt anxious as well, but in a good way, like we'd finally taken back control. And we were doing it *together*. You know? After days of never feeling so alone.

It lasted as far as the footbridge. The buzz or whatever you want to call it. The sense we were setting off on an *adventure*. Because that's when Abi said what we were all thinking, even if it was only at the back of our minds.

"What about Mason?" she said, and that was the point it basically turned to shit.

"A SEARCH PARTY?"

"That's what they're claiming, sir," said Fleet. "We started interviewing them at the station first thing."

Fleet was with Superintendent Roger Burton on the banks of the river, watching the divers as they surfaced amid the reeds. They were only half a mile or so from the estuary now, already within the ragged fringes of the town. They'd started farther upriver, close to the point Sadie's rucksack had been discovered, and the going had been slow. As the river emerged from the woods, the undergrowth along its banks was thick and wide, and the tides were among the most treacherous on and around the entire south coast. Initially they'd been lucky with the weather, but now even that had turned against them. The rain was one thing, churning up the water and washing away any clues that might otherwise have been picked up by the line searches. But it was the light that hampered them most of all. It was barely September. Three days ago there had been sunbathers on the beach. Yet with the cloud cover and the fog of rain, it was now perennially 4 p.m. in deep December. Literally, meta-phorically, they were floundering in the dark.

"At the station?" said Burton. "You're treading carefully, I hope?"

"The doctors have given the four that made it out the all clear. Abigail Marshall, Cora Briggs, Fareed Hussein and Mason Payne. They had a few cuts, some bruises, in one case a badly damaged knee. Only two of them had to stay in the hospital overnight, but they're coming in later this morning. And we've got appropriate adults lined up."

"Not the parents?"

"We're trying to discourage it. In light of events . . . Well. There are potential conflicts of interest."

They'd interviewed Sadie's friends before, of course, several times over, but since their excursion into the woods, the situation in terms of Sadie's disappearance had moved on. Quite how, Fleet was yet to decide. The stories the kids had so far told about what had happened out there were garbled, just as Nicky had said. Though when Fleet had spoken to them in the woods, it was entirely prob-able they'd been in shock.

"A search party," Burton muttered, shaking his head. "Did they not stop to think about how it would look?"

Burton was a tall man, prim, wearing pristine Wellingtons and waterproofs. He was a politician policeman, with a wife he was prob-ably fond of, but kids Fleet had a feeling his boss would struggle to identify in a lineup. Maybe that was unfair, and it wasn't as though Fleet was one to judge. But it was family men who went furthest in the force these days, and everything with Burton was about how things might look.

"With respect, sir, they're teenagers. I don't imagine they cared. And anyway, it turned out to be something else entirely."

Burton sniffed. "You're not kidding. A funeral procession, is what it turned into. How the hell does one of them end up dead?"

"That's what we're trying to find out. But they're all claiming they either didn't see or they can't remember."

"Can't remember?"

"I know how it sounds. But when it happened, it would have happened fast. And if there was a tussle, it's entirely possible there was a lot of confusion. Maybe no one actually meant for it to happen."

"You mean it was an accident?" said the superintendent.

"I didn't say that. All I'm really saying is, it doesn't look to be as straightforward as we first thought."

"Christ, Rob. The last thing I need right now is complications."

Fleet bit his tongue. A missing girl. Her brother dead. The search continuing along the river, and—what? A new search out in the woods? At what point during recent events had the superintendent assumed there wouldn't be complications?

"We'll get to the bottom of it, sir. It will take a bit of time, that's all. It doesn't help that they're minors."

The superintendent grimaced in apparent frustration. He shook his head again. "It's the parents I feel most sorry for. First Sadie, now this. I spoke to them this morning, you know. Mr. and Mrs. Saunders."

The parents. It was *always* the parents that people felt most sorry for. The assumption seemed to be that because the parents were grieving, they could be absolved of all responsibility. Which wasn't how it worked in Fleet's book.

"We haven't given up on Sadie yet, sir," Fleet said. "She's still out there somewhere." Although he thought of something one of Sadie's friends had said, about watching a sand timer. And there was no question it had just about run out. After disappearing from her house in the middle of the night, Sadie had now been missing for seven days. They had no leads, no firm suspects, and no evidence that didn't complicate the picture further. Christ, they weren't even sure yet what kind of case they were working.

Burton looked at him intently. "Have they given you *anything* to go on in terms of Sadie? Why were they looking for her in the woods, twenty miles from the river?"

"That's partly what I was trying to say. I'm not sure they *were* looking for her. Maybe one or two of them thought they were, but . . ." Now Fleet was the one to shake his head. He was talking in riddles, his own uncertainty undermining the clarity he knew the superintendent prized. "Bottom line is," Fleet went on, "they're saying that they still don't know where Sadie is, or what happened to her."

"And do you believe them?" asked Burton.

"I . . . No," Fleet said. "I don't know. To be honest, I'm not sure what to believe. But, as you're aware, I've had a feeling they've been holding back on us from the start."

The superintendent thought for a minute, then exhaled deeply. He lifted his face toward the rain. "Come on," he said, turning to Fleet. "Let's get some coffee. All we're doing out here is getting wet."

It was Burton's walk that had taken him to the superintendent's office, Fleet often thought. Wherever he was going, whatever the route, he moved with purpose. He strode, in fact, and Fleet had to exaggerate his own step to keep up. Someone watching would more likely have assumed Burton had been called to a phone call with the prime minister than to an appointment with a pot of coffee. Although coffee, of course, wasn't really the point. The man was mingling, showing his face—to the troops, to the volunteers, to the cameras. That was why he'd driven down here on such short notice. He couldn't not, after the debacle in the woods. Already the media attention was more intense than ever, and the brass had to be seen to be in control.

Fleet might have been resentful at the implied affront—he was the one who was supposed to be running things, after all—but the truth was he didn't much care. Burton could give the orders if he wanted to, so long as he didn't stop Fleet from doing his job. In fact, the more Burton flounced about in front of the cameras, the less Fleet was obliged to do it, and the more time he had for proper police work.

They headed toward the Overlook, a café-cum-visitors'-center that had become the de facto headquarters for the search. Volunteers were being fed and watered in the main restaurant, while the police had been given access to a large back room to allow them to coordinate activities beyond the media's glare.

Fleet didn't want any coffee. For the past week, it had felt like he'd subsisted on nothing but. It was just as well, though, because Burton seemed to have forgotten that's what they'd come in for. After spending ten minutes pressing flesh with the volunteers, pausing every so often for a camera flash and obliging Fleet to do the same, Burton led the way behind the counter, into the squad's makeshift command center. TVs, telephones and computers had been set up on foldaway desks, and the floor was a potential lawsuit of power cords. There were three officers seated at the workstations, and when Burton strode in, they stood up.

"Give us the room, please, ladies and gentlemen."

Fleet tried to hide his surprise: that anyone would actually use that phrase outside a Hollywood movie; and that Burton had something to impart that he hadn't foreseen. Whatever it was, it was unlikely to improve Fleet's day.

"How's Holly?" Burton asked him, once the junior officers had filed outside.

"Holly? She's . . ." Clearly Burton hadn't heard about the split. Not that he should have. Fleet and his wife had kept their troubles to themselves, their separation a yearlong secret. It would all come out when the divorce went through, obviously, but Fleet was happy to delay the inevitable outpouring of bogus sympathy for as long as he could. "She's well, sir," he finally answered. "Thank you."

"Any potential new recruits on the horizon?" Burton pressed, out of politeness or lack of tact, Fleet could not have said. "Children, I mean," the superintendent added, unnecessarily.

"I . . . No, sir. I would say not."

Burton looked mildly affronted. "Well, don't leave it too long. We're none of us getting any younger." He seemed to glance at Fleet's belly—unless that was Fleet imagining things. *Jesus, Rob, if your weight's starting to make you paranoid, maybe it's time to do something about it. Start running. Take up swimming again. Anything.*

Burton pulled out a chair from under a nearby desk and settled on the seat as though deflating. Fleet hadn't noticed when Burton had been preening in front of the cameras, but the superintendent—only just past fifty—*did* look old. Yes, he was slimmer than Fleet, and would have run rings around him on the squash court, but there were lots of different kinds of healthy, as Holly so frequently delighted in reminding him. Maybe Fleet should get more exercise, and maybe he should cut down on the mayo in his BLTs—not to mention laying off the smoking and the caffeine—but Burton was like a high-performance tire that was wearing thin. Sooner or later, the man would burst.

"Another word of advice, Rob," the superintendent said, as though reading Fleet's mind. "Don't go into politics. It ages a man quicker than cancer."

Fleet sat down on a chair opposite him. Screens had been put up to cover the windows, but through a crack he could just make out a group of locals watching the divers from the bank of the river. "I'd say there's very little chance of that either," Fleet said.

Burton's smile flickered, then went out. "Rob, listen," he said, leaning forward.

Fleet braced himself. *Here we go.*

"There has been . . . talk," the superintendent said.

"Talk, sir?"

"People are saying—unfairly, I might add—that we messed up."

The *we* being purely figurative, Fleet assumed.

"This search party," the superintendent went on. "They're saying we should have found them sooner."

"All I can say, sir, is that we *would* have found them sooner. If their parents had informed us they were gone. And if—" Fleet stopped himself. It was true that the kids in the search party had only been reported missing almost thirty-six hours after they had apparently started out, but in his opinion that wasn't the main reason they hadn't been found. As soon as he'd heard the kids were gone, Fleet had wanted to divert some of the resources that were tied up in the hunt for Sadie, but Burton had wielded his veto. He'd justified it in all sorts of fancy ways, but the message, boiled down, was that it *wouldn't have looked right*. There was a significant police presence in the woods now, of course, but to Fleet's mind it was a clear case of shutting the stable door after the horse had bolted.

The superintendent had recovered his posture. "It's easy to be wise in retrospect, Detective Inspector. And it's unbecoming to crow 'I told you so.'"

Once again Fleet was obliged to hold his tongue. The joke among Fleet and some of his peers was that, as a copper, you were forced to hold your tongue so much, you might as well have one hand tied behind your back.

The superintendent softened his tone. "Look," he said, "I'm on your side, Rob. I am. That's why I wanted to have this conversation with you. In private. Before things have a chance to escalate."

Fleet waited.

"All I'm trying to convey," Burton went on, "is the urgency that now applies to this situation. We need results, and we need them quickly."

"A teenage girl has been missing for a week," Fleet responded. "Nobody's been sitting on their hands."

"*I* know that. And I know your strengths, Rob. There's not a doubt in my mind that you're the best person to lead this investigation. That's why I appointed you in the first place."

But? thought Fleet.

"But the perception is, things are spiraling out of control. We don't even know what we're really dealing with. *Two* searches now, rather than one? Two *murders*, potentially—assuming we ever find Sadie. Added to which, there have been . . . complaints."

"Complaints?"

"From the local community. A feeling has been expressed that you may be using this investigation to settle old scores. To do with that business between the locals and your sister."

Fleet shifted, not trusting himself to speak.

Burton sighed. "We're caught in the middle here, Rob. Half the town is asking why we didn't charge these kids when we had the opportunity, if we were really so certain they were involved in Sadie's disappearance. The rest of the community—not to mention the press—has decided that we put too much pressure on them. That it was our fault they set off in the first place. Which makes it our fault what happened out there in the woods."

Fleet opened his mouth to respond, and Burton raised a hand.

"I know it's bullshit, Rob. If I'd had any concerns about your history here, I wouldn't have brought you in. You're a bloodhound. You pick up a scent and you follow it. All I'm saying is, if it turns out we've been on the wrong trail, and there's no pot of gold at the end of it . . ."

"The bloodhound will be in for a kicking," Fleet finished.

Burton looked at him coldly, as though Fleet were the one making his life difficult. He breathed, and Fleet got a waft of what the superintendent had eaten for breakfast.

"There are two ways to look at this, you know," Burton said. "The fiasco in the woods, I mean. We can view it as the failure the press are already saying it was, and allow ourselves to be pilloried by the public. Or, we can see it as an opportunity."

"An opportunity, sir?" *Really?*

"To move things on. To get a result."

"An arrest, you mean. Someone to blame. If not for Sadie, then for everything else."

"Or perhaps, in an ideal world, for Sadie as well."

Fleet frowned. "I'm not sure I'm following you, sir."

"This Mason boy. The boyfriend. You've always liked him for Sadie's murder."

Careful, Rob, Fleet told himself. *Be very careful.*

"I always suspected him, sir. Of *something.* Just as I've always had my suspicions about the rest of them. But there's nothing to say conclusively that Sadie was murdered, let alone that Mason was the one to do it."

"But he's your prime suspect. Correct?"

"I . . . Correct."

"And he *was* out there in the woods with Sadie's brother and the others? His prints everywhere, blood all over his shirt?"

"They all had blood on them, sir. I told you, it's a mess. We don't yet know the full story. Which is what I've been trying to get across. The search party . . . it changes things. What we're trying to work out is *how.*"

"So a lesser charge, then. Possession, intent, *something.* Just for the time being, until we have enough to prosecute for Sadie."

"But at the risk of repeating myself, sir, we don't even know for certain that Sadie's dead."

"Oh, come on, Rob. This is me and you now. We're seven days in. We've just been watching divers dredging the river. This sort of story, it's not going to have a happy ending. You know that as well as I do."

Fleet did know. And he was surprised at himself for wanting to deny it.

"Plus," the superintendent went on, "it would at least show the community that our focus on these kids—on Mason in particular—has been justified. It would answer some of that criticism I mentioned, mitigate some of our responsibility."

Now Fleet bridled. *Mitigate some of our responsibility?* It sounded almost like a threat.

"This wouldn't be about money, would it, sir?" he found himself saying.

"Excuse me?"

Hold your tongue, Rob, said a voice, even as a louder one egged him on. "The dive teams are barely five hundred meters from the estuary," he said. "And it's expensive, mounting this kind of operation, especially for the sake of one girl. What happens when the divers reach open water? Do they have permission to turn around and start again?"

The superintendent reddened. "Careful, Detective Inspector."

"But if we make an arrest based on what happened in the woods," Fleet pressed, "even if it eventually comes to nothing, you'll at least have the cover to scale things down. Pull the divers out, the uniforms, the *bloodhounds.* Shut up shop and shrug your shoulders and move on."

Burton rose to his feet. He was the color of a heart attack, Fleet thought, even as he marveled at his own capacity to self-destruct.

THE SEARCH PARTY   39

There was a knock.

When the superintendent didn't respond, Fleet did. "Come in," he called, his eyes never leaving his superior's.

A constable poked his head into the room. "Sir?" he said, addressing Fleet first. "Sorry to interrupt, but—" He hesitated, as though he'd registered the expression on the superintendent's face.

"What is it?" Fleet prompted.

"I . . ." The PC forced his attention back to Fleet. He straightened. "The dive teams, sir. At the river. They've found something."

MASON

SO—WHAT? YOU'RE going to start listening to me now? And I'm supposed to trust you? Like, I tell you what happened and this time you promise to believe me?

No way, man. You're forgetting, I know how this works. I've seen it. You put me through it. I'm not falling for the same thing twice. You twist things, try to trap people, even when they haven't done anything wrong.

But that's how it starts, isn't it? *Just run us through it,* you say, and the next thing I know I'm being accused of murder.

Four times you had me in here. That's twice more than any of the others. You only didn't charge me because you didn't have any evidence. But do you think that makes any difference out there? Do you think anyone believes it when you say I was only "helping you with your enquiries"? Or do you think that maybe they draw their own conclusions? Just like you, in fact. I mean, look at you. You're sitting there watching me in exactly the same way you were before. You *still* think I'm responsible. Don't you?

You know what? Don't even answer that. Don't even bother. Because I know exactly what you're doing. And I know *why*. I mean, *Fleet*. You might at least have thought to change your name. It took me a while to put two and two together, I admit, but after I realized, I did a bit of digging of my own. Turns out I knew most of the story anyway—everyone round here knows the story—I just didn't think to connect the dots. So my point is, don't bother trying to play games. You're out for revenge or something, retribution, and step one, for obvious reasons, is you trying to pin it all on me.

So, with all due respect and everything, go fuck yourself.

FASH

FIRST OF ALL, I just want to say how sorry I am. My mum, she . . . she told me it was important I made that clear. And I am sorry. So, so sorry. Truly. About what happened. About . . . about everything.

But I know being sorry isn't going to bring him back.

The hardest part is, I think I knew something awful was going to happen from the start. I don't know how. I just did. That's partly why I was so reluctant to go in the first place. I . . .

What?

Who told you that?

Oh. Right. Well, I . . . I mean, yeah. Yes. It *was* my idea. But . . . I wasn't sure. That's what I meant. I knew we had to do *something*, that we couldn't just carry on sitting around waiting. But at the same time, I was in two minds. That's all I'm saying. And I think I was hoping one of the others would talk me out of it. Maybe that's why I went to Cora first. I knew she'd be the hardest one to convince, you see. Except Luke, maybe, because of Dylan, but he . . . he . . .

Sorry.

Sorry, I . . .

I just . . . I can't get my head around what happened, that's all. I can't get the picture out of my brain.

No. Thank you. I'm OK. And you want to know, right? And my mum said I should tell you what I remember. And I promised her I would, so I will.

Not everything she tells me to do, no. Why? Why do you ask? People think she's strict, and she is, I'm not saying she's not, but that doesn't mean . . . it doesn't mean anything. It's just the way she is.

No. Never. I mean, not like *argue* argue. I'm not saying I don't disagree with her sometimes. With her way of looking at things, the fact that she's always constantly going on about . . .

Nothing. It doesn't matter. The point is, she's only looking out for me, trying to give me the opportunities she and my dad never got themselves. They came to this country with nothing. With literally the clothes on their backs. And my dad, before he died, he worked crazy hours, and now my mum does, too. So it's only fair that I try to be respectful.

Look, is this relevant? You wanted to know about the search party. Didn't you? The day we left? So can't we just talk about that?

Right, that's right. So I went to Cora, and me and her went to Abi, and then Abi suggested we go to Mason.

Right, sorry, that's right; after me and the girls had already been to Luke. And yeah, yes, Luke wasn't all that happy with the idea of asking Mason along. In fact, he wasn't happy at all.

No effing way, is what he said.

He didn't say *effing*, obviously.

Oh, OK. Well, if you're sure. My mum doesn't like it when I swear, so I try not to, but I suppose if I'm only telling you what other people said, it doesn't really count.

But Luke, the way he reacted. It was because of all the rumors, I suppose. I mean, you basically as good as told the world that you thought Mason was guilty. That . . . that he'd killed Sadie. That's what everyone was thinking, anyway. Not me. Not Cora and Abi. At least, I don't think so. But Luke . . . I guess he wasn't sure. With everything that was going on, I suppose he didn't know *what* to believe.

"Come on, Luke," said Cora. "Mason's your friend."

And that's one of the things I've been struggling with most of all. Like, how did we get to the point where we all just suddenly turned against one another? After we'd always been so close? Because I know we're all kind of different, and you're probably wondering why we were even friends. But the thing is, we basically grew up together. We went to the same nursery, the same schools, all the way up to Harbor Park. I was always best friends with Luke, and Cora was best mates with Sadie. That was when we were younger. But then Mason started being mates with Luke, which meant Mason and I became friends as well, and then Abi started hanging around with Cora and Sadie. Abi fell out with her old friends, I think. In primary school, this was. They were basically always mean to her, and Sadie sort of took her under her wing. She was like that, you see. Even when she was younger. She's always been kind, and generous, and . . . just . . . just a genuinely nice person. And it wasn't because she was so talented or so . . . so pretty that everyone liked her. She always just seemed to be able to get on with people. In a way I've never really . . . I just admired that about her, that's all.

So Sadie—her and Luke—I suppose they were the link that held the rest of us together. And actually the fact that we're so different is one of the things that in the end made us so close. Plus, like, none of us has ever really fit in with anybody else. There's me with my skin, Mason with his music and his boots, and Cora with her clothes like she's planning to put on weight. Like a skater, basically, apart from the fact she's never been on a skateboard in her life. Abi's normal, sort of, but even so, she's never been liked. She just . . . she tries too hard, I think, always posting pictures of herself on Instagram, or going on about saving the world. Not like Sadie, who was popular without even trying, but what I think is, us lot were like an antidote for her. When she was with us, she could just be herself, just the person she'd always been. She didn't need to be the star of the show, or top of the class, or whatever else people were expecting her to be. And for Luke it was the same sort of thing. If Sadie had the pressure, Luke had all the responsibility. With Dylan, mainly, but also in terms of looking after himself. It's like, he never got the attention from his parents that Sadie did, for example. Nowhere near. And again, when he was with us he could just forget. Particularly when Mason was around, because Mason's got this way of making you feel like what other people think doesn't even count. Which, again, I've always admired. He never lets anyone give him any shit. It's like, with me, I do OK at school and that, but it doesn't seem to count for anything. Being smart just makes people hate you, bully you, or else they're on your case trying to push you to do even *better*. You can't win. But Mason has never bought into any of that. I *wish* I could be like him.

I remember this one time—we must have been about thirteen— we were all hanging about in the woods. We had this place we used to go. Like a base, you know? It was near the stream, our favorite climbing tree was nearby, and there were these old stumps in a sort of circle you could use as seats.

Anyway, we were all there—everyone except Abi. And when she turned up she didn't say anything, and it was obvious she'd been crying. And the weird thing was, she had on this hat. Like, a woolly hat, which came right down over her ears, even though it was the middle of summer.

"What's with the tea cozy, Abi?" said Mason.

Which maybe wasn't exactly the most sensitive way to say hello, given that Abi was obviously so upset. But with us lot it was just the sort of thing you came out with, although admittedly Mason more than most. But what I mean is, because we knew each other so well, none of us ever tried to hide anything. Nobody ever made out they were cooler than they were, and if something shitty had happened, you just admitted it. You didn't try to pretend everything was OK, not the way we all had to do at home.

So Abi took off her hat. She still didn't say anything. But the thing was, she didn't need to. Because her hair, which was normally sort of mousey, was bright green.

"Whoa!" said Mason. "What the hell, Abi? What happened?"

Abi burst into tears. But slowly it all came out. She'd had her hair cut, apparently, and she'd been feeling all brand-new, until she'd got home and her dad had started laughing. All, like, "How much money did you waste on that?" and "I don't know why you even bother." Just to make her feel bad. And apparently what he said was, "You're a five, Abi. On a good day. You'll never deserve a higher score than that. Look at your mother if you want someone to blame." And Abi was distraught, but what she also thought was, *I'll show him.* And her dad's always liked blondes, which for some messed-up reason means Abi's always wished she was blonde, too. So she bleached her hair. Herself. And whatever she used . . . Well. Obviously it hadn't quite worked.

"He's gonna laugh at me for the rest of my life!" she wailed. "*Everyone* is. The entire school!"

"So what?" Mason said, grinning. "*I* actually think it's awesome."

"It's not awesome," said Abi. "It's *hideous*. There's no way I'm going to school tomorrow. I'm never showing my face in public ever again!"

And that's when Mason got all serious. "Screw that, Abi," he said. "I'm all for bunking off school and everything, but only for the right reasons." And he made her swear. I mean, it took about an hour, literally, but he wouldn't let it drop until Abi promised she'd turn up the next day at school. And then what he did was, he got the rest of us all together that evening. Him, me, Luke, Sadie and Cora. And he'd got hold of this bottle of hair dye. And none of us even had to think about it. I mean, my mum didn't talk to me afterward for about a month, and Sadie's dad practically had a stroke. But it didn't matter. We'd have dyed our hair green even if it had meant getting expelled. For Abi's sake, you know? For *ours*.

And that's what I mean. That's how it was with us before.

But then I guess something changed. Probably around the start of the summer. For me, I . . . I was concentrating on preparing for sixth form, I suppose. That's why I didn't always go out when the others asked. And anyway, me and Mason, we . . . I don't know. It's like I said, I was always mainly friends with Luke, and just lately, with Mason . . . it had been a bit awkward, I suppose. Not just for me. For everyone. Because before Mason and Sadie got together last year, Mason had been with Cora. So Cora was dealing with that, plus the fact Sadie seemed to be hanging around with Abi more, when before, Cora and Sadie had been inseparable. So it was all just . . . just different, that's all. And then, after Sadie went missing . . . Well. To be honest, the rest of us have hardly spoken.

But Luke.

I was telling you about Luke.

"You've heard what they're saying about him," he said, talking about Mason, about how he didn't want us asking him along. "You know what they're saying he did."

"They're saying stuff about the rest of us as well, just in case you hadn't noticed," said Cora. "And anyway, are you really going to listen to a bunch of rumors? In *this* town? You know what people are like. You know what the *police* are like. They always think it's the boyfriend. The husband, the lover. If they had any actual evidence, they would have arrested him by now. The fact that they haven't—"

"Means they haven't found it yet," said Luke. "It doesn't mean Mason didn't do it. That he isn't secretly some kind of psychopath."

"A *psychopath*? Really?" Cora threw up her arms and turned away. Abi looked slightly afraid.

"Dude," I said, stepping forward. We were at the footbridge, the big one near the caravan park, where the river's at its widest. Not far from where you lot began the search. "Mason isn't a psychopath," I said. "My *mum* is a psychopath. To give you a frame of reference."

For a moment Luke just stared at me, and I was worried I'd said the wrong thing. Like, joking. Was that still OK? Because we hadn't. It didn't feel like we had. Not since Sadie had gone missing.

But then Luke laughed. It was only a snort, really. But it was like something suddenly lifting.

Luke looked ashamed. Ashamed or afraid or just upset, really, I suppose. And tired. You know? Just really, really tired. Which we all were, I think. I don't know about the others, but I hadn't slept more than a couple of hours at a time since Sadie had gone missing.

"Yeah," Luke said. "Yeah, OK. Sorry."

Cora gave him this broken little smile.

We had to backtrack to get to Mason's house. He lives with just his dad now—his mum left home when Mason was small—and they aren't particularly well-off. None of us are, but in this town it basically goes in rings. If you live by the water you're considered rich, even though most of the flats round there are usually empty. It's Londoners who own them mostly, people who come down to go sailing, or play golf at the course along the coast. Then, round the high street, it's mainly families. A long way from being rich, but doing OK.

That's where I live; Sadie and Luke's family, too. Cora and Abi are in the next ring, just before you get to the trading estate. The houses there are bigger, a bit, but scruffier. It's not rough exactly, but me, personally, I don't like walking there at night.

As for Mason, he lives in an area that's basically one step up from the caravan park. The houses are all bungalows. Not even bungalows, really. I don't know what you call them. They look like the class-rooms on the field at school—the temporary ones, the teachers call them, even though they've been there since the 1980s.

When we got there Mason's dad was round the side of the house. I couldn't see what he was doing, but whatever it was he didn't seem to be enjoying it, because he was just standing there with his hands on his hips. Then again, Mason's dad isn't the kind of person who seems to particularly enjoy anything. Mason can't stand him. He blames his dad for his mum leaving home. Which from what I've heard is probably fair, to be honest, because he drinks, he doesn't really work, he's basi-cally what my mum would call a—

Don't tell him I told you this, will you? Please? I'm just trying to be honest, that's all. And he hates me enough as it is.

Because I'm brown, obviously. Why else?

Anyway, we managed to slip past him, and Cora was the one who knocked. Luke was hanging back, and Abi was holding his hand. I stood off to one side. In the end we had to bang on Mason's window, because it turned out he had his music on.

He came out a minute later. Black jeans, black T-shirt, white ear-buds dangling around his neck. It was no wonder he hadn't heard us—I could hear the drums from where I was standing. I heard my mum's voice, then, from the day she threw my headphones in the bin. *They'll make you deaf,* is what she said. But I know what both-ered her really was not being able to tell what I was listening to.

"Hey," said Mason, sort of suspicious. It struck me that it was the first time we'd all been together since day one, since the day Sadie went missing. I'd seen Cora, and Abi, and Luke once, but not at the same time, and I hadn't seen Mason at all. And it turned out later that Mason had been on his own the entire time.

"Hey," Cora said back. Me and Abi nodded. Luke didn't say anything. He only moved to let go of Abi's hand.

"What's up?" Mason said, into the silence. He looked at me, Cora and Abi in turn, and then his eyes locked on Luke's.

Luke stepped forward then, and I suddenly had a feeling that it was a huge mistake. Mason, the search party, everything.

But Luke surprised us all, I think. He said, "We're forming a search party. For Sadie. Wanna come?"

Just like that. Just like we were asking Mason if he wanted to hang out at our old base.

Mason didn't answer right away. He looked at us, at our bags, at what we were carrying. At the sky, I think, and then over our shoulders toward the woods. And then he looked at Luke.

"I'll pack my stuff," he said. And he went back inside. And I guess that's when he decided to get the knife.

CORA

WHAT DO *YOU* think?

No, I didn't know he had a knife. *Obviously*. Do you think I would have gone with him if I had? Into the woods. At night. With nobody else around. Or thinking there was nobody else around, anyway.

Of course I wouldn't have. None of us would.

I keep, like . . .

I keep *seeing* it. You know? Just, like, flashes. Out of the corner of my eyes. I even dreamed about it. Last night. It was in my hand and I couldn't let it go.

And then, afterward, the way it was just lying there. Just . . . fucking . . . just *lying* there. All covered in . . . in . . .

Fuck.

I need a cigarette. I'm sorry but I do.

I'll tell you one thing first, though. Mason deserves everything that's coming to him. And you can tell him I said that, by the way. I don't even care anymore. I *don't*. I can't believe I ever did.

To think I slept right next to him. And all the time his rucksack was just right there. He even used it as a pillow. And maybe his hand, the entire time, was holding the knife. I keep imagining him in the middle of the night, touching the knife against my throat. Watching me. *Deciding*. I keep imagining him using that knife on Sadie.

MASON

I TOLD YOU, I'm not going to explain myself to you. Not again. Not anymore. Just ask yourself this: what would you have done? *I* knew I was innocent. *I* knew I hadn't killed Sadie. But if it was true what everyone was saying, that basically meant someone else had. And as far as I knew, that person had just turned up at my house, asking me to come for a little walk with them in the forest.

So go on. Tell me. What would you have done?

"SIR? THEY'RE HERE."

Fleet nodded to the uniform who was poking his head through the door, and turned back to the interview room table. He indicated for Nicky to stop the recording.

"Let's take a break," he said.

He led Nicky into the corridor outside. They were in the local police station, where all the interviews with Sadie's friends were being conducted.

"You want some backup on this, boss?" she said, when the door had closed behind them.

"More than anything," said Fleet. "But there's no sense you getting caught in the cross fire. Go and grab yourself a cup of coffee."

The DS couldn't hide her relief. "I'll put a pot on," she said. "Guard it till you get out."

"I imagine by then I'll need something stronger. A shot of cyanide should do it."

Nicky smiled. "I'll see what I can pillage from the evidence locker."

They parted, and Fleet headed toward the room that had been cleared for him to use as his office. In reality it wasn't much more than a storeroom. It had a window, but it was paned with security glass, and it was positioned too high for anyone less than eight feet tall to be able to see out. Otherwise the room was no more comfortable than any of the interview rooms he'd lately become so familiar with. Gray walls, gray furniture, gray floor. To think people these days were painting the walls in their homes a similar color. Or so Nicky had told him. Interview-room chic, she'd called it. "We should go into business, boss," she'd said to him. "No one knows shades of gray like an ex-copper." Which was true enough, Fleet thought—the irony being that the law itself was so black and white. True or false. Innocent or guilty. Alive or dead.

Fleet knocked before he entered. He'd gone for polite, courteous, but the noise his knuckles generated sounded weak to his ear, almost cowardly. It was a nothing sound, when the news he bore warranted a warning siren.

When he stepped inside, the first thing that struck him was the hope. He could see it in their faces, in their eyes, in the way they rose the instant he walked in. It came off them in waves, like a force field driving him back.

Yet he stepped through it, and at the same time punctured it completely.

"You've found her. Oh God. Oh God. Oh please God, no."

Alison Saunders, Sadie's mother, collapsed backward into her chair. She was a thin woman, lost in the dripping shell of her raincoat, yet the chair scraped on the concrete floor from the momentum of her weight. The noise carried all the way up Fleet's spine and into his teeth, which he realized were already clamped tight.

He raised a hand consolingly. "Sadie is still missing, Mrs. Saunders. The search is ongoing." Gently, he closed the door behind him.

"You've found something though, haven't you?" Ray Saunders, Sadie's father, was a tall man bent short by his grief. He was using the chair back to hold himself upright. Seeing him up close for the first time in several days, Fleet found himself questioning why he didn't feel more sympathy for the man. He and his wife had just lost their son. The daughter they cherished had been missing for a week. If Fleet had been standing in their shoes, he had his doubts he would be capable of standing at all.

So he respected them, there was no question about that, and he couldn't begin to comprehend their heartbreak. Even so, he couldn't warm to them. And although there was no direct evidence linking them to Sadie's disappearance—nothing, at least, that Fleet and his team had been able to find—Fleet couldn't shake the feeling that they'd played a role in their daughter's disappearance *somehow*.

And of course there was the question of their responsibility for what had happened out there in the woods . . .

"Take a seat, Mr. Saunders. Please." Fleet gestured to the chair Sadie's father was clutching. Like a blind man feeling his way, Ray Saunders lowered himself into it.

Fleet moved a third chair to the same side of the table, careful not to drag it on the floor. He sat down himself, so that the three of them formed an awkward triangle.

"First of all, I'd like to express my deepest condolences," Fleet began. "I know you've spoken to Superintendent Burton, but I haven't personally had a chance to—"

"Please," said Sadie's father. "Just tell us. What's happened? Why did you ask us here?"

For a moment Fleet held Ray Saunders's eyes. The only thing he saw in them was desperation.

"We found Sadie's jacket," Fleet said.

He noticed Alison Saunders's hands tighten around the seat of her chair.

"We'll need you to confirm it was hers, naturally," Fleet went on. "But it matches the photograph you gave us. And I should warn you . . ." He looked at the father. "There is blood."

Sadie's mother let out a keening sound, so inhuman that Fleet's first instinct was to think something had found its way into the room. Sadie's father slumped forward, so the back of his head was level with his shoulders. Fleet had thought of the man as being black-haired, but in just the past few days he seemed to have turned predominantly gray.

Fleet waited.

Ray Saunders said something he didn't catch.

"I'm sorry, Mr. Saunders. Could you repeat that?"

Sadie's father looked up. "How much blood?" he said, his voice broken.

Fleet's gaze flicked briefly to Sadie's mother. She had a hand over her mouth and her eyes screwed shut. She sat so still, Fleet couldn't even be certain she was breathing.

"The jacket was found in the river," Fleet said, "a considerable way downstream from where we found her rucksack. Forensically speaking, therefore, it presents something of a challenge."

Ray Saunders was looking at him as though he were speaking a foreign language. "How much blood?" he repeated. It was like he was stuck. Like he couldn't move on until his question was answered. Perhaps he was feigning his reaction, but if so, he was doing it well.

"Some," Fleet said. "That's all I can tell you. What I can't say is how much would have been washed away by the water."

"And is it . . . it's definitely Sadie's?"

"It is her type," Fleet answered. "We're sure of that much, at least."

Sadie's mother made a movement with her right hand, as though she were describing something in the air. Her husband interpreted the gesture before Fleet could, and folded his wife's hand between his. Alison Saunders was forced to stretch, and she teetered on the edge of her seat.

Sadie's father cleared his throat. It took him three attempts.

"What, um . . ." He coughed again. "What state was her jacket in?"

Fleet frowned slightly.

"Was there . . . I mean, was it torn? Were there signs of violence?"

"The jacket is intact," Fleet told him. "The blood is largely on the hood."

He watched for a reaction, but all Ray Saunders showed was confusion. Again, if he was acting, he was extremely convincing. Fleet wondered how long it would take for either one of Sadie's parents to show they had worked out what the blood being on the hood implied. Because if Sadie had been wearing the jacket, and the blood was hers, it would almost certainly have flowed from a wound to the base of her skull.

"I wish I could offer you better news," Fleet said. "But there is no reason yet to give up hope. There is still the possibility that—"

"Was it him?"

Alison Saunders's voice stopped Fleet short. She was in the same precarious position on her chair, her eyes raw and her shoulders hunched, but she was facing Fleet now, confronting him, and her tears had dried on the sudden fire in her cheeks.

"I'm sorry, Mrs. Saunders?"

"Was it *him*? Mason Payne. And the rest of them. Those . . .

children. My daughter's so-called friends. They're here somewhere, aren't they? What have they said? What aren't you asking them? If they know what happened to Sadie, why won't they tell you?"

Fleet paused before answering. His training dictated that he should stick to the company line, that he should assure Sadie's parents that he and his colleagues were making progress, but that it would take some time, and that obviously he wasn't at liberty to divulge specific information relating to ongoing interviews. But that was bullshit, and Sadie's parents would have smelled it. And although Fleet had his doubts about them, he felt that, on balance, they deserved better.

"Sadie's friends haven't been able to tell us anything yet that might lead us to your daughter," he said. "They're . . . confused. Understandably. And I have to stress that they are here voluntarily, and that there are limits on how much time we can spend with them. But rest assured—"

"Voluntarily?" spluttered Sadie's father. "You haven't arrested them?"

"No one has been formally charged, no."

"Why the fuck not?"

Fleet flinched at the profanity. It wasn't the word itself, but the fact it had come from Ray Saunders's mouth. So far, from day one, the man hadn't so much as raised his voice. But everyone had a breaking point, Fleet supposed. And he had no doubt that his own would have come much sooner.

"Because, to put it frankly, Mr. Saunders, we lack evidence. It would be an egregious error to make an arrest if we couldn't back up our assertions in court."

Egregious? Jesus, Rob. So much for plain speaking.

"So what you're telling us is that you've been barking up the wrong tree," said Sadie's father. "This whole time you've been looking in the wrong direction, just like everyone's been saying."

Fleet had been watching both of Sadie's parents closely, but like the confusion he'd shown before, the anger Ray Saunders was exhibiting seemed authentic. There was nothing to suggest he hadn't genuinely come to believe what he and his wife had been hearing from their friends and neighbors. That Sadie's friends perhaps weren't to blame after all. That Fleet had been blinded by some personal vendetta. That *he* was at fault for what had happened in the woods, and that he'd allowed whoever was really responsible for Sadie's disappearance to get away.

The irony in the sudden reversal of popular opinion hadn't escaped Fleet. At first the community had been only too eager to interpret the police's interest in Mason and the others as proof that Sadie's friends had been involved. But now, after what had happened in the woods, opinion had flipped. People in the community were closing ranks—exactly as they had in the past.

"Mr. Saunders," Fleet said, "Mrs. Saunders. I can assure you that we have been pursuing every line of inquiry that has been open to us. If you know my personal history, as I'm sure by now you do, then you'll understand that there is *nothing* I want more than to find your daughter."

Ray Saunders stood, pulling his wife up with him. Sadie's father appeared too angry to speak. Alison Saunders was shaking her head, fresh tears tracking the makeup that scarred her cheeks.

"You're too late," she said to him. "Whatever you do now, whatever you say . . . it's already too late."

"Mrs. Saunders, I—"

"I hope she haunts you," said Sadie's father, and Fleet recoiled as though he'd been slapped.

"Excuse me?" he managed.

"My little girl," said Ray Saunders. "Your sister, too. I hope they both do."

"One lump of cyanide?" said Nicky. "Or two?"

She had a cup of coffee waiting for him in the kitchenette. Outside, the open-plan office was strangely quiet. Most of Fleet's team were either down by the river or up in the woods. If you were a visitor, you wouldn't know you were standing in the nerve center of the biggest missing-person inquiry the south of England had seen in the past twenty years. Fleet didn't want to think about how a journalist might paint the scene.

"Give me all you've got," said Fleet, in response to Nicky's question. "Just make sure it does the job. And I'd take quick over painless."

Nicky clicked a single Canderel into the mug. The sweetener sank meagerly into the tar-colored liquid.

Fleet frowned. There was a perfectly good bowl of sugar on the sideboard.

"Just following orders, sir," said Nicky, seeing his scowl, and Fleet recalled how he'd asked her at the start of the investigation to refuse to put sugar in his coffee no matter how much he begged. It was a token gesture toward a healthier diet which, at the time, Fleet didn't think he'd notice.

"Besides," said Nicky, wincing as she sipped from her own mug, "not even the good stuff could improve the taste of this shite."

Fleet gave half a smile. He was staring vacantly at the liquid in his cup, his mind already back on Sadie. *I hope she haunts you . . .*

"Do you know he barely mentioned his son?" he said.

"Luke, you mean? Or Dylan?"

That was one of the things he'd learned to appreciate most about working with Nicky. She could follow his non sequiturs almost as well as Holly could.

"Either. Both. For Ray Saunders in particular, it was all about Sadie. He didn't even ask what was happening out in the woods."

"But that's been the theme," said Nicky. "Hasn't it? Of Sadie's entire life, from what we've gathered. Sadie's the one they worshipped, Luke the one they tolerated, and Dylan the one they wished they'd never had."

"Quite," said Fleet, bobbing his head. He looked up. "There's been no further news, I take it?"

"No, boss. Nothing from the woods, other than complaints about the weather. And nothing from the river since they found Sadie's jacket."

Fleet sank again into his thoughts. "What have we got, Nicky?" he said, after a moment.

"Boss?"

"With the case. Give me your take."

Nicky exhaled. "We've got a search area the size of a small country, a bunch of guilty-looking teenagers telling us stories, the superintendent breathing down our necks, and a press like a pack of wolves—not to mention a town that's decided we dropped the ball. At best, we're guilty of incompetence. At worst, there's blood on our hands."

A mouthful of coffee caught in Fleet's throat. It was nothing to do with the rancid taste.

"Jesus, Nicky. You're really not into sugarcoating things this afternoon, are you?"

Nicky shrugged. "You asked, sir."

He had, it was true. And they both knew what he'd really been fishing for. To Nicky's credit, she'd done him the favor of not mindlessly regurgitating what Fleet so transparently wanted to hear. That they were on the right lines. That he wasn't responsible. That he hadn't fallen into the trap of using current circumstances to try to wash away the past.

Plus, that they weren't wasting time by trying to piece together different strands of the same story when they already knew how it ended.

"Would you do something for me, Nicky?" Fleet said. "All these rumors that have been flying around online. Round up any extra pairs of eyes you need, and see if you can find out where they originated."

"The rumors about Sadie, you mean? Or Mason?"

"Forget about Mason for the time being. There was always going to be gossip about his involvement." *No thanks to us,* Fleet didn't add. "But the rumors that were floating around about Sadie before she went missing. And the more recent ones about her parents—the inference of sexual abuse."

Nicky showed her curiosity. "Do you think there's something in them? I thought we'd discounted those stories already? There's nothing in Sadie's history to suggest even the slightest possibility of sexual abuse. No strange behavior, no teachers or other parents who claim to have had concerns."

"Can you trace them back though? Find out where the rumors originated?"

There was the slightest hesitation before Nicky answered. "We'll do our best, sir."

Translation: it'll be like looking for a needle in a haystack. Or mapping the infection route of a virus. Backward.

"I know you will. And one more thing. Sadie's financials. Could you gather together any printouts for me? Bank statements, wage slips, whatever we have."

"Sure. That won't take long. It's pretty thin reading."

"No, I know. And, to be honest, I think I know the figures off by heart already." Fleet set down his coffee.

"Are you heading out, boss?"

Fleet nodded. "Have someone take care of Sadie's friends. Give them something to eat if they want it, all the . . . I don't know, fizzy pop or whatever they can drink. I'll be back shortly, but in the meantime keep them talking. And obviously make sure they know to come back in the morning. Ask, though. Don't tell. Run it past their parents if they're here."

"Kid gloves. Right?"

"Right. For the time being."

"What are you going to do?" Nicky asked him.

Fleet exhaled. "I'm off to break the habit of a lifetime."

ABI

I'LL BE HONEST, I had my reservations from the start. About Mason, I mean. About even inviting him along. Because it was obvious you lot suspected him, and you wouldn't have without good reason. Right? And when Luke called him a psychopath, I suddenly . . . I just had this feeling, that's all. A *bad* feeling. Like, what if he was right? What if Mason *did* kill Sadie? I mean, he's always had a temper. *Always*. To be honest, if it wasn't for the others, I'm not sure me and him would have even been friends. But he was mates with Luke first, which meant he hung out with Sadie, which meant if I wanted to hang out with Sadie too, I didn't really have much choice. I guess with us lot it's always been a bit like it is in a family. Like, the way you don't get to pick. I mean, don't get me wrong. Mason can be funny and everything, and he's the most loyal person I've ever known. But at the same time, he can also be cruel. To me, because I can tell he thinks I'm stupid. To Fash, because he's always so nice. Plus, Mason's always been so intense, you know? About music, for example. Or films. Me, I like to watch a movie without having to think about it. But Mason has to analyze them frame by frame. He pauses them and rewinds them and watches them over and over. And with Sadie, when Mason talked to her, he always had that same expression in his eyes, just as though he was talking about his favorite movie.

So, yeah, I wasn't sure about asking Mason along. But Cora was all like, "He's our friend, don't call him a psychopath," that sort of thing, just basically taking Mason's side. Which is hardly surprising, considering their history. You know, the fact she's never got over Mason dumping her so that he could be with Sadie. If you ask me, he only went with Cora in the first place to try to make Sadie jealous. Which maybe it worked, or maybe it didn't. I mean, him and Sadie didn't get together for another six months, but it was obvious Mason had fancied her all along, at least to the rest of us, and just as obvious that Cora never stopped fancying *him*. Not even after they broke up.

Plus, the other thing about Cora is, she always has to get her own way, which is exactly how it turned out this time.

Although the weird thing was, after we picked Mason up and started heading back toward the footbridge, I have to say, I felt . . . it felt . . . OK. It's odd, but sometimes seeing people is all it takes. It makes you realize how much you've missed them. Do you get that? Sometimes it goes the other way, too, like the way it does with my mum and her sister at Christmas, but I'd basically been in this bubble since Sadie had gone missing, not really talking to anyone, just watching what was going on through my phone. Reading the rumors, all the stories, not knowing what to believe. But then, getting everyone together, it was actually like this huge relief. It even felt good seeing Mason. Not good exactly, but not as creepy as I thought it would feel. And rather than being scared of him, I actually felt a bit sorry for him. At the time, I mean. There was the way he looked at us when we turned up at his front door, for example. It's like that thing my mum always says about spiders.

Spiders, right.

Like, Mum always goes, *They're more scared of you than you are of them.* Which is obviously bullshit. I mean, they've got eight legs, and eight eyes, and they're all, like, hairy and gross, whereas we, you and me, we just look normal. Right? So how is it remotely possible that a spider would be more scared of you than you are of it?

But with Mason that was the phrase that came to mind. He looked like he thought we were about to attack him. And then afterward, as we left, we got spotted by his dad. Who'd been round the corner. Painting, I thought, until I realized he was standing there going over and over the exact same spot.

"Mason?" said his dad. "Where the hell do you think you're going?"

Mason ignored him. He kept walking, away from the house, so the rest of us just had to follow him. Although, personally, I couldn't help looking over my shoulder.

"Mason!" his dad said again. "*Mason!* Get back here!"

Mason stopped. He waited for a second, then he turned. Like, *what*? You know? But he didn't say it.

"I asked you a question," said his dad.

"I'm going out," said Mason. "What does it look like I'm doing?"

"Out?" his dad repeated, like it was the most ridiculous thing he'd ever heard. "You're going out. With your friends. While I'm slaving away out here, trying to get rid of"—he stabbed his thumb into the air above his shoulder, and half turned around toward the wall—"*that.*"

I had to lean to get a better view of it. Of the wall, I mean. The graffiti. URDERER, it said. Without the *M*. The first letter was just a splodge of red now, where Mason's dad had gone at it with his bucket of suds.

"I told you to leave it," Mason said. "Someone'll only come back and do it again."

"Leave it," his dad repeated. "*Leave it*. That's your solution to everything, isn't it. Just shut yourself in your room and stick your headphones on."

Mason gave this little shake of his head. "Which is it, Dad? Have a go at me for staying inside, or shout at me in front of my friends when I decide to go out? You don't get to do both."

His dad was holding the bucket he'd been using in one hand, a big yellow sponge in the other. He squeezed that sponge so hard, water dripped down all over his shoes. It was red from the paint, and it looked like blood.

"Come on," Mason said, talking to the rest of us. "Let's go." And he turned away from his dad and started walking. This time when the rest of us followed, I didn't dare look behind me. I kept expecting to hear a shout, or for Mason's dad to come charging after us. It's what my dad would have done, I reckon. I mean, he'd *kill* me if I ever spoke to him like that.

"Jesus Christ, Mase," said Cora, once we were safely down the lane. "What was all that about?"

Mason shrugged. "He thinks I did it," he answered. Just matter-of-fact. You know, like, *Ho hum, my dad thinks I'm a murderer.* No big deal.

Just like that.

The rest of us exchanged these little glances. I looked at Fash, who looked at Cora. Then all three of us looked at Luke.

Luke didn't say anything for a second. Then he said, "I told you the graffiti would be overdoing it, Fash. And you could at least learn to spell. 'Murderer' begins with an 'M.'"

Which, for a second, was like . . . is that even funny? You know?

And then I noticed Fash's face. About the same time Cora did, I guess. Luke and Mason, too.

And suddenly, from nowhere, we burst out laughing. All of us. Together. Fash maybe slightly behind the rest of us, but in a way I hadn't laughed since the start of the summer, when all six of us—Sadie, too—had taken some speakers and a bottle of wine each down to the sand dunes, and Fash had got so drunk he kept insisting he could light a fire using only his eyes.

It was just the sudden release of tension, I suppose. All the worry and stuff that had been building up inside us. The fear, too. The irony is, even as I was laughing, I kept thinking to myself, what if somebody sees us? Laughing like that, when Sadie was . . . when she was still missing. Like, how would that look?

To be fair I was thinking mainly about Mason's dad. I kept checking behind to see if he was following us. But we kept laughing all the way to the footbridge. We'd try to stop, one of us would, and it would quieten down for a sec, but then someone would snort and get us all going again.

Which is what I mean about it being ironic. Because when we got to the footbridge, guess who was sat there waiting? With this smile that said, *Well, well, well.* You know? As though, by laughing the way we were, we'd just proved everything people had been saying about us all along.

CORA

LARA FUCKING SWEENEY, that's who. Arse on the railing, arms propping up her tits, and hair so dry from the peroxide, I was surprised it didn't catch fire in the sun.

We were laughing until we saw her, I can't even remember why, and then, just like that, we stopped. Lara kind of has that effect on people. She could suck the atmosphere from a rain forest.

"Hey, gang," she said, loud enough that anyone within a hundred meters would have heard. "Off to bury another body?"

She was standing in the middle of the bridge, these two sixth formers beside her. Sam Powrie and Ian Nolan. I didn't know them, but I knew their names. Lara's always got some horny sixth former in tow, rarely ever the same one twice. They don't give a shit about her, just like she never gives a shit about them. All Lara cares about is looking popular, and the sixth formers only hang around with her on the off chance she'll let one of them cop a feel. Or both of them at the same time, knowing her.

"You're not doing it right, Lara," I said to her. "Trolls are supposed to wait *under* the bridge."

"For the fat little piggies to come traipsing across, you mean?" she said, running her eyes top to toe over me and Abi.

"Goats, you mean," chipped in Abi, looking all superior until it dawned on her what she'd just called herself.

That smirk of Lara's widened. "Whatever you say, Scabby."

That's what Lara calls Abi, on account of the fact Abi had eczema literally about a decade ago, when the lot of us were all in primary school together. Lara was a bitchy little cow even then.

The boys just watched on mutely, gauging their chances if it turned into a fight, I expect. It was three against five, not that Lara would have got her hands dirty, but it still didn't look good. Mason's handy enough, obviously, but Luke would have tried making peace even as he choked to death on his broken teeth, and Fash . . . Fash is just Fash. He's been in more scrapes than any of us, probably even more than Mason, but only because of the color of his skin, and with Fash there's never any need to ask about the other guy.

"Seriously," said Lara. "What's with the Sherpa look? If I didn't know better I'd say you were heading out of town. Running away, even." Her sharp little eyes had taken in our rucksacks. Abi's in particular was stuffed to bursting.

Sam and Ian had moved either side of Lara in the middle of the bridge. They were both a head taller than her, so they looked like bodyguards. The three of them were blocking our way.

We walked onto the bridge ourselves, stopping a couple of meters away from them. You could see the river through the cracks between the boards. I didn't like that. It's like when you're standing on the pier down on the seafront. It always feels as though you're going to slip through. And even though the river wasn't flowing particularly fast, on account of the fact it had been so dry, I guess, everyone knows how dangerous it is. If you grow up in this town, it's basically the first thing anyone tells you. *Stay away from the river—the currents will carry you out to sea.*

"You *don't* know any better, Lara," said Mason. "But don't be too hard on yourself. Personally, I blame the parents. Maybe one of them dropped you when you were a baby."

Lara's parents are almost as bad as Sadie's are. You know, just in terms of the whole *my little princess* thing. That's probably where the rivalry came from. Between Lara and Sadie. Not so much about grades and stuff, and not that Sadie ever bought into it, but at some point someone had told Lara that life was basically a popularity contest, and that if you weren't winning, you were losing.

I laughed at what Mason had said. "It would explain the snout," I said, pushing up the tip of my nose.

Lara's got this thing about her nostrils. I heard from Poppy, this girl in my class, who heard from Hanna, Hanna Crawley, who heard from one of Lara's mates that Lara's been saving up for a nose job. Which doesn't surprise me at all. Talk about vain. She's worse than Abi. And the difference is, Lara likes looking in the mirror because she's *convinced* she's beautiful. Abi only spends so much time fussing about her appearance because she's paranoid she's ugly.

Plus, the thing about Lara's nose is, and for God's sake don't tell her I said this, but it's not even that bad. She only looks like a pig now and then because she spends so much of her time looking down at people.

For once, though, Lara didn't react. Normally if you talk about her nose, you can pretty much rely on her to turn the color Mason's dad did back at his house. Instead she just batted her eyelashes.

"Blame the parents," she said, all sweetly. "Now that's an idea." She looked at Luke.

I stopped smiling then. Mason did, too.

"What's that supposed to mean?" Luke said.

"Haven't you heard what people are saying?" Lara answered.

I was just about to reply, but Abi piped up from across my shoulder.

"No one here's interested in what people are *saying*. Especially when all the rumors that are flying around were started by *you*."

She was talking about all the stuff online. The stuff about Sadie before she went missing. The stuff about Mason and us lot afterward. And obviously the shit about Sadie's parents.

Lara gives us this *who me?* look, which to be fair she's world champion at. It's like, she *never* gets in trouble at school. She always manages to blame someone else, or casts just enough doubt that the teachers believe her. Or choose to, anyway. It helps that Lara's mum is chair of the school governors.

"You'd have to be pretty sick to make *that* stuff up," she said. "Right, Luke?"

I caught Luke's eye and gave him this little shake of my head. But I guess he couldn't help himself.

"What are you talking about, Lara?"

Lara feigned surprise. "You haven't heard? Did your friends not think they ought to fill you in?"

Luke looked at me and I sort of shrugged. It was supposed to be an *I have no idea what she's going on about* shrug, but I winced at the same time, and Luke could tell right away what it meant. Because I did know. Of course I did. Luke had messaged us to say he was deleting his accounts—Facebook, Instagram, all that—because he realized none of it was helping, that it was all just making things worse, but I'd sort of kept an eye on things. Not like Abi, nothing like Abi, who can't go to the cinema without ducking underneath her coat every twenty minutes to check her phone, but I wanted to know what people were saying. Just . . . just because. So obviously I knew exactly what Lara was referring to. I mean, you lot must monitor all that as well, right? So you must have seen the stuff about Sadie's parents, too.

But Luke—he obviously hadn't.

"What's she talking about, Cora?"

"It's nothing, Luke. It's bullshit, that's all. Just more of the same twisted bullshit they've been saying about the rest of us. That they were saying about Sadie before she disappeared. And Abi's right. It probably all came from Lara in the first place."

"Twisted is right," said Lara. "Poor Sadie," she added, shaking her head.

"For the last time, Cora," said Luke, "what's she talking about? Tell me what people are saying!"

Lara answered before I could. "The theory is, your dad loved Sadie a bit more . . . intimately than was strictly legal. And, well. That your mum helped."

"Shut the fuck up, Lara!" I shouted.

She took a step back, raising her hands in the air. I looked at Luke, who was basically frozen in place, like a computer when you give it too much to think about.

"I'm not saying I believe it," said Lara, all innocent. "Although you have to say it makes a certain amount of sense. You know, in terms of motive. And opportunity. And the fact that your little brother is so . . . well, *weird*." She shook her head. "The things he must have seen . . ."

Luke came out of his trance. His jaw snapped shut, and his fingers curled into fists.

"But no," Lara went on. "Personally, I don't quite buy it. I'm not saying it didn't happen. But I've got my own theory about who killed Sadie."

This time she looked directly at Mason, then slowly at the rest of us, one by one.

"You know what, Lara?" I said. "Maybe *you* killed her. You could never stand the fact that Sadie was more popular than you. That she chose to hang out with the likes of *us*."

"Yeah," said Abi. "And unlike you, Sadie didn't have to go shagging her way round the entire school just to make a few friends."

Lara laughed. "You see?" she said. "You *are* out of touch. Because again, that's not what I heard."

Mason went red.

"Guys," said Fash. "Everyone! Let's just go. OK? Why are we even standing here listening to this?"

"You're not going anywhere, Paki," came a voice, and Ian Nolan stepped up and gave him a shove. And I didn't know this until afterward, but apparently Ian was one of the kids who always gave Fash a hard time at school. Or after school mostly, in fact. Whenever him and his mates could catch Fash on his own.

But fair play to Fash. He didn't back away. Instead he turned around and shoved Ian right back. I guess he must have been more angry than I realized. "I'm not a Paki, dickhead," he said. "I'm English, and my parents were born in fucking Qatar."

Ian made to retaliate, but Mason stepped into his path.

"Back off," he said. Not loud, just sort of quiet. But if you know Mason, and you've seen him lose his shit, you would have known to do what he said.

But Ian didn't. Instead, he said, "What are you gonna do about it, *murderer*?"

And that's when Mason finally flipped. Seriously, he just . . . he lost it. And I don't know if he'd made some sort of mental connection—if he'd decided it must have been Ian who'd graffitied his house—or whether it was just what Lara had said before, but he grabbed Ian by his T-shirt and he smashed his fist right into his nose.

It was just . . . it was horrible. I mean, I've seen boys fight loads of times, but usually it's like watching some stupid dance. Lots of shoving, and name-calling, and then maybe someone gets someone else in a headlock, and everyone ends up on the floor. But this . . . it was like Mason didn't care. Like all the things that would have usually held him back just . . . just didn't count anymore. And after he hit him, he hit him again—once, twice, three times. And Lara started screaming, and Sam, the other sixth former, was standing there openmouthed, just gawping at what was happening like the rest of us.

And I remember thinking, *We should have gone around*. Just that, over and over: we should have gone around. Not that there was another bridge within half a mile—nothing but the old pipeline bridge on the edge of the woods, which we wouldn't have been able to cross, even if we'd been stupid enough to try. But from teasing Lara about her nose, I couldn't believe what was suddenly happening. I guess none of us could. That's why nobody moved to stop it, until Mason made to throw Ian into the river.

Ian was fighting back by this point, landing some punches of his own. But you could see that first punch had left him dazed, and even though he was bigger than Mason, Mason was stronger. Or maybe not stronger. It was his rage that was letting him win, that was all. And as Ian was swinging his arms, Mason ducked his head and started driving Ian toward the railing. And suddenly the water down below didn't seem to be flowing so slowly after all.

"Mason, don't!"

By the time I yelled, Mason had Ian up against the handrail. Ian was still swinging his arms, but Mason had a hand up under his chin, and was forcing him over the side.

I rushed forward. We all did. And for a minute it was one big scuffle, all of us trying to pull the two of them apart. Luke took an elbow to the face, and someone's heel came down on my foot, so hard I figured they must have broken my toe.

But in the end we managed to get between them. Luke and Fash dragged Mason off. Lara was clucking over Ian, who'd dropped to his knees. There was blood all dripping from his nose, and he looked as angry as Mason did. About the fact he'd just been beaten up by a kid a year younger than him, probably, and about what his mates would say when word got around.

"Are you crazy?" Abi yelled at Mason. "You could have killed him! He could have drowned!"

Which was the moment Mason finally stopped struggling, as though it had dawned on him what he'd been trying to do. Because Abi was right. If Mason had managed to throw Ian into the water, Ian would have gone under. No question. He was dazed from that punch, like I said, and it was a three-meter drop to the water's surface.

"I wasn't going to do it," Mason growled. "I was just trying to scare him, that's all." He wriggled until Fash and Luke let him go.

Ian was staggering to his feet. "You . . . you *psycho*. That's what you are. A fucking psycho!" He kept touching the top of his lip, looking at the blood that came away on his hands.

"Come on," said Luke, pulling Mason away, toward the other side of the bridge. "Mason, come *on*. Let's just go."

Mason allowed himself to be led. Ian was yelling all sorts of stuff by this point, but Mason didn't even look back.

I did, though. Me, Fash and Abi had fallen into step behind Mason and Luke, sort of on autopilot. We were in shock, I guess—stunned—but even so I couldn't help turning around. And that's when I caught Lara's eye. She was crying, but by now she looked almost as angry as Ian did.

"You'll pay for that!" she yelled. "All of you! Just you wait and see!"

FLEET SAT IN his car staring at the familiar green door. It was long overdue a fresh coat of paint. It clearly hadn't been touched in the time since Fleet had last seen it, other than by the abrasive sea air. Not a lot about the rest of the house appeared to have changed either. It was a bungalow much like the others in the close—roomier inside than it appeared, with a heavy, concrete-tile roof that made the building look like a neckless man wearing a hat made of lead. The only real change was that the weathered paintwork suggested the man had developed a skin condition. It was no wonder he didn't look happy.

Fleet had parked his Insignia at the entrance to the street: close enough that he could see the building clearly; far enough—he hoped—that he wouldn't be spotted from one of the windows. He adjusted his seat to create space between him and the steering wheel, and for a moment he reclined and closed his eyes, listening to the sound of the rain. Then he reached to gather the folders that were piled in the passenger-side footwell.

What have we got? he'd asked Nicky, and though she hadn't

given him the answer he'd been hoping for, she'd summed it up neatly enough. In short, they had nothing. Or not nothing. What they had was worse than nothing, because everything they did have seemed to point in different directions, to the extent that they still didn't know what kind of case they were working, at least in terms of Sadie. Although perhaps, as of this morning, that had changed. From a missing-persons inquiry, there seemed no question they'd progressed now to murder.

In truth there'd never really been any doubt—not in Fleet's mind, anyway. He'd hoped with all his heart that Sadie had simply run away, and for a while he'd almost allowed himself to believe it. Everyone who'd known her had claimed it would have been out of character, but Fleet knew all too well what growing up in this place could do to you. The small-town atmosphere was so oppressive, the distant horizons felt like walls, the open skies like a ceiling that was pressing in. And that Sadie was such an overachiever—grade-A student, top billing in the school productions, and what must have felt like the expectations of an entire town on her shoulders—would in Fleet's estimation only have made things more intolerable for her, particularly as she'd got older. Plus, throughout the summer there had been rumors flying around about Sadie online, focusing mainly on her alleged promiscuity. None that Fleet or his colleagues had been able to verify—it was innuendo mainly, verbal winks and knowing nudges, which Sadie's friends had claimed were flat-out lies—but the SadieSlut hashtag couldn't have failed to have taken its toll on her mental well-being.

But if Sadie had run, why hadn't she taken anything with her? Clothes, photographs, her favorite soft toy? And why hadn't she been picked up on CCTV *anywhere*? Why had nobody come forward with any credible information, despite a nationwide appeal? People didn't just disappear, not in this day and age, and not when the net that had been cast to find them extended so far and so wide—not unless they were already dead.

Suicide, as such, was a plausible explanation as well. There'd been no note, no message, but a couple of the investigators on Fleet's team had argued strongly that Sadie had thrown herself in the river. But that, to Fleet, *did* seem out of character. Perhaps teenage suicides often did, but Fleet still didn't buy it. Didn't? Or couldn't? Had he simply refused to face the possibility? The reality was he'd never had to answer that, because on the second day after Sadie had been reported missing, they'd discovered her rucksack.

It had been found by a dog walker on the bank of the river, two miles from the estuary. And right away Fleet had felt certain that something wasn't right. On the face of it, the discovery of Sadie's bag—containing her wallet, her mobile, her house keys: everything she would have carried on her person—suggested she may have suffered an accident. Perhaps she'd slipped, fallen, and been caught by the current. The tides in the river here were vicious, something Fleet knew all too well.

Except he didn't buy that explanation either.

The dog walker who'd found the bag had showed Fleet the exact spot in which it had been located, and to Fleet's mind it had been too high on the bank, too close to the bridleway, for it to have genuinely been washed up by the water. Perhaps Sadie had dropped the bag *before* she'd suffered her accident, but if that were the case, why had the contents been soaking wet?

No, Fleet had decided, something about the rucksack was definitely off. Rather than a clue to Sadie's disappearance, it felt more like a red herring, as though someone had tried to make it *look* like Sadie had suffered an accident. And the discovery of Sadie's blood-soaked jacket that very morning all but confirmed his initial instincts had been right. Sadie wasn't responsible for her disappearance. Someone else was. Someone who, between the hours of midnight and 11 a.m. on Friday 31 August, had managed to either entice Sadie from her house or force her from it, and then taken her to some secret location. There, they'd either killed Sadie or held her captive, and kept her hidden from a search team that at its peak had matched the size of a small army. Further, they'd left behind no evidence, beyond what had turned up in the river. It was no mean feat. In fact, it would have been nigh on impossible without some degree of cooperation from Sadie herself. Which is why, after everything, Fleet had come to the conclusion that Sadie had been murdered by someone she'd known.

Sitting in his car with his case notes on his lap, Fleet flicked through the transcripts of the interviews he'd conducted with Sadie's friends.

Abigail Marshall.

Cora Briggs.

Fareed Hussein.

And finally, of course, Mason Payne.

You've always liked him for Sadie's murder, the superintendent had said, and it was true Fleet had been leaning Mason's way. He'd had his suspicions about the rest of them, too, mainly because he'd been convinced right from the start that Sadie's friends were hiding something. Collectively or individually, he wasn't sure. Was that enough, though? Had his focus on Sadie's boyfriend in particular really been justified?

The only alibi Mason had been able to offer for the period during which Sadie had disappeared—which Fleet and his team had established as being somewhere between the point Sadie's parents and her oldest brother had gone to bed, and the time the next morning the mother had checked Sadie's room to find her daughter gone—was that he'd been at home, asleep. Then again, that was the only alibi almost everyone had been able to offer, from the neighbors, to Sadie's teachers, to Sadie's parents themselves.

On the other hand, the circumstantial evidence against Mason was more compelling than it was against anyone. The local sex offenders register had been checked and rechecked. *Everyone* had been checked and rechecked, Sadie's parents most thoroughly of all. In the end, it was Mason who'd emerged as having both the means to kill Sadie and the most credible motive. Fleet didn't pay much attention to rumors, not when rumors were all they were. Take the instance of Sadie's parents, for example, and the inference of sexual abuse. The rumors might have counted for something, if Fleet or anyone else had been able to come up with the slightest evidence that they were true. But what Fleet *was* interested in was the effect any rumors might have had, and the stories that were flying around about Sadie's promiscuity could well have tipped Mason over the edge. He had a volatile personality anyway. He had a history of getting into trouble at school, and instances throughout his childhood of low-level violence. If Mason had allowed the rumors to influence him, if he'd come to suspect Sadie really was cheating on him—how might he have reacted?

And there was one other piece of evidence implicating Mason—the thing they'd found in Sadie's bedroom. Again, it was hardly conclusive, but it certainly didn't help Mason's case.

At the end of the day, though, hadn't it all been mainly supposition? A degree of desperation as well, to tie someone—anyone—to Sadie's disappearance? Was it true what people were now saying, that Fleet had allowed past events to influence the present—that he'd been driven by some misguided compulsion to right an injustice, twenty years too late?

The ringtone of his mobile jolted Fleet from his thoughts.

When he saw who was calling, he hesitated, contemplating letting the call ring out. But really there was no question about him answering.

"Are you fucking kidding me, Rob?"

The voice of his wife—soon to be ex—came blaring through the earpiece the moment Fleet swiped the screen.

"Hello, Holly."

"Don't fucking 'hello, Holly' me. After all the shit you've put me through. You're there. You're part of it."

"Calm down, would you? What are you talking about?"

"You know full well what I'm talking about. I spotted you last night on the news. I'm talking about you, and the girl, and whatever the fuck happened with her friends. Have you been there all this time? Since the beginning? Skulking around in the background, letting your boss cover for you in front of the cameras?"

Fleet sighed. He was careful to do so away from the microphone. He had an urge to light a cigarette, but Holly would have heard that, too.

"I've been here since the beginning, yes," he said. "But I haven't been . . . how did you put it?"

"*Skulking*," his wife spat.

"Right. That. I've just been getting on with the job. I haven't been trying to hide, from you or anyone else."

The lie came easily, perhaps because he'd half managed to convince even himself. He looked again at the green door.

"*The job*," Holly echoed. "Jesus Christ, Rob. Since when was self-flagellation part of the job?"

Holly lectured on English literature at the university. She used these words to rile him.

"Self-what? Remember I don't speak Chaucer, Professor."

Holly sniffed. *"Self-flagellation.* It's a Catholic thing. Which I know you claim you're not, but you aren't half good at it sometimes."

It was another attempt to get a rise from him. Fleet stayed quiet, conceding the point, and eventually the silence softened.

"Seriously, Rob. What are you playing at?"

Fleet pictured his wife pacing the kitchen at home. *Her* home now, he reminded himself. Fleet's home, if you could call it that, was a shitty little bedsit in a block he remembered being called to more than once when he'd been a PC working the night shift. He could afford better, a bit. He just didn't want to commit to anything longer than a week-by-week contract. Not yet, he told himself. The same thing he'd been telling himself for the past eleven months.

"I'm not playing, Holly. They asked me. That's all. What could I say?"

"You could have said no."

"I could have. I suppose. But . . . you know." A bloodhound, the superintendent had called Fleet, and like it or not, that was his reputation. He found people. He didn't always himself know how. Holly's theory, meant more as a criticism than a compliment, was that it had something to do with Fleet knowing so intimately what it felt like to be lost. But whatever it was, finding those who'd gone missing had become Fleet's main remit now on the force, to the extent that he no longer really fitted into the central command structure. He went wherever he was needed: from being seconded to a remote Scottish island, where a trail of lies and cover-ups in the local community had led Fleet to discover a priest's body buried under a cairn, to—most recently—an investigation run by the Met into the identity of a torso found floating in the Thames.

There was silence for a moment at the other end of the phone line.

"Have you been back?" Holly tested.

"Back?" said Fleet.

"You know what I mean. Back home."

"No, I . . . I've been staying away."

"Good. Keep it that way."

Fleet glanced again at the green front door.

"I'm serious, Rob. Don't even think about it. This isn't the same. Even I can tell from here, it isn't the same."

"No, I know. I *do* know, Sprig, I promise."

Sprig. When was the last time he'd called her Sprig? It was a silly nickname, one he'd never used other than in private. He couldn't even remember when he'd started using it. But Holly, sprig of—it was stupid, but at some point it had stuck.

"What are you eating?" Holly asked him, and Fleet had to laugh.

"I've been sticking mainly to a liquid diet," he told her.

She knew he wasn't much of a drinker. "Coffee, you mean? It's battery acid, Rob. Especially that stuff they brew at police stations. I know. I've tasted it."

"I've cut out the sugar," Fleet said, resting a hand on his ample belly.

"Meaning you're basically running on empty."

Jesus, thought Fleet. He couldn't win.

He smiled.

"I'm fine," he said. "Seriously, Holly." Because he knew that was really what she was calling to check, even if her initial mind-set had been kill rather than cure. And the tone they'd settled into now showed Fleet they'd made progress, of a kind, since their separation. Before, the instinct had always been to pick a fight, on both sides. Their conversations lately reminded Fleet of the time when they'd first started dating, when Holly had lived up in Cambridge and Fleet had been down on the coast. They'd spoken for hours sometimes, deep into the night, the distance somehow drawing them together. These days their conversations were briefer, because irrespective of the cessation of hostilities, it never seemed to take long before matters came to touch on the very thing that had driven them apart. It remained like a chasm between them, wider than any gap that could be reckoned in miles. He could forgive her, and she could forgive him, and still they could never be together.

"You don't sound fine, Robin," Holly said, slipping into the use of his full name. In the past she'd deployed it as a sign of affection, because she knew exactly how much he hated it. Or had, once, before Holly had turned it into something good. "You sound . . . thin," she went on. "Like a ghost of yourself."

Fleet would have dismissed the description as pointless poetry—another consequence of Holly's love affair with language—if, as was her habit, she hadn't summed up the way he was feeling so precisely.

"Look, Holly, I'd better go."

And somehow, with a sentence, Fleet ruined it. He managed it every time. He was like a clumsy oaf with five thumbs, trusted to look after a house of cards.

"Right," said Holly, in a tone Fleet recognized all too well. "Of course you do. Take care of yourself, Rob."

"Holly, wait. Listen, I . . . Thanks. You know, for—"

But the line had already gone dead.

Calling, Fleet thought.

He stared at the screen of his mobile, which blackened and then showed him his shame. He tossed it onto the seat next to him, then raised his head to stare through the windscreen. He lit that cigarette, exhaling the first cloud of smoke through the crack he'd left in the driver's-side window.

That door was still out there waiting for him.

Don't even think about it, came Holly's voice.

And she was right. Always, about so many things, Holly was right. So if he knew it, why did he never listen?

He pulled the car keys from the ignition and unbuckled his seat belt.

"HELLO, MUM."

Fleet was unprepared for how old she looked. He'd warned himself, braced himself, and yet the face that confronted him when the door opened was as worn and weathered as the faded green paintwork. His mother's hair, once blonde, was now gray, her posture buckled by the weight of years. And not only that, probably. There were some things, Fleet knew, that aged you quicker than the passing of time: politics, the superintendent had claimed, was one; grief, clearly, was another. If Fleet hadn't known his mother was only sixty-one, he would have guessed her to be a decade and a half older.

But even as he tried to keep the shock from his expression, another thought struck him. The last time he'd seen his mother he'd been seventeen years old. He was now thirty-six. If she looked old to him, what must he look like to her? Flecks of gray had started appearing in his own hair of late, and he was a long way from the beanpole he'd been as a teenager. On the contrary, his middle-aged spread had kicked in early.

There was a pause, long enough for Fleet to wonder whether his mother recognized him at all.

Then, "I was wondering how long you were going to sit out there," she said.

That voice. It had been roughened by the years and the cigarettes, just like her skin, but underneath, it was as familiar to Fleet as the voice inside his own head.

Fleet hadn't cried since the day he'd left home. The urge to do so came upon him now, seizing him as violently as a sudden cramp.

What was he doing here? Why the hell hadn't he taken Holly's advice?

"I suppose you're deciding whether to come in," said his mum. "Me, I'm deciding whether to let you."

Which cured Fleet of the urge to cry, at least.

"I suppose one of us needs to make a decision," he said. "Otherwise we could be standing here for another nineteen years."

His mother looked beyond him at the weather. Somehow it seemed to make up her mind for her, though she didn't appear best pleased with the decision.

She turned her back.

"Wipe your feet," she said, retreating into the house. "And make sure you close the door properly. It—"

"Sticks when it's raining," finished Fleet. "I remember."

There was a glitch in his mother's movements, but she didn't turn around. Fleet watched her as she veered into the sitting room, caught the slight stiffness she showed on every second step. A knee, perhaps? A hip? Another reminder of time's false promise. It didn't heal. Not always. Often it simply found new ways of inflicting hurt.

Fleet closed the door, shoving it in the end with his shoulder, and found himself alone in the hallway of his childhood home. For a moment nothing seemed real. How often he'd dreamed of this place. When he had nightmares, which was frequently, this house was invariably the setting. Which on the face of it made no sense. Fleet's childhood here had been safe, secure, dull—right up until the day it hadn't been. And at that point Fleet had been weeks away from moving out forever. The house, as a setting, had barely featured. Then again, after what had happened, everything about Fleet's upbringing had become tainted. He didn't believe in counseling, therapy, all that sitting around excavating old bones, but even he would have agreed that the house had become a symbol. On the one hand, it was a cradle. On the other, a coffin.

He found his mother standing by the fireplace, her back to the doorway and her fingers holding the crucifix that had always hung around her neck. When she looked at him it was via the reflection in the mirror on the chimney breast.

Fleet noticed the pictures on the mantel. They were all of him. Every one of them. As a newborn, as a toddler, as a boy, as a teenager. At the oldest he would have been about fifteen.

His mother saw him looking. "My son," she said, as though introducing the image to a stranger. She turned, and pulled back her shoulders.

They were all of him. Every one of the pictures was of him. There was not a single photograph of his sister, Jeannie, not even from when she'd been a baby. It was as though she'd never existed. Never lived, never laughed—never felt compelled to take her own life.

Fleet felt a surge of anger, and in that moment he was seventeen again, his coat on his back, his bag at the door, his mother standing in exactly the same place she was now, holding her crucifix in exactly the same way. The only difference, then, was that she'd been crying.

Fleet forced himself to take a look around the room, using the opportunity to breathe. What had he expected, after all?

There was nothing that surprised him. The same flowery sofa, the same pale yellow walls. The TV was new—not new; different—but probably only because the last one had finally broken down. Even the potpourri on the windowsill was as he remembered it, and for a second he thought he detected the familiar rosewater smell. But it was a ghost, probably. A phantom. The potpourri, by now, would only have smelled of dust.

"I should go," said Fleet. "I'm sorry."

His mother laughed out loud: a single, bitter bark.

"What I mean is, I should never have come," he explained.

"So why did you?"

He hesitated. She was asking him what he was doing here, at her home, but also why he'd come back at all. Why, when he'd left town, had he not just stayed away for good?

"How did you know it was me?" Fleet said, instead of answering. "Out there. In my car." He peered over the top of the net curtains, out into the road. "You couldn't have seen me from here."

"I saw your car. Nobody round here drives a car like that. Like a businessman's car or something. And I saw the smoke coming out the window. As if you were deciding." She shrugged. "As if you couldn't."

His mother took her own cue, and pulled a tin from the pocket of her cardigan, gray like her hair. From the tin she extracted a pre-rolled cigarette, like the ones Fleet's father had smoked before he died. His mother, when Fleet was younger, had always smoked Rothmans. Five a day. One before breakfast, one after dinner, and the others at times of need in between. Unless his mother had changed her habits, Fleet gathered this was one of those times.

She saw him looking at the tin.

"Economizing," she said. "It's not a choice."

Once again Fleet felt a tightening within him, from his toes through his gut into his jaw. *It's not a choice.* It was one of his mother's mottos. A phrase she used to disavow her responsibility. Like the pictures on the mantel. *It's not a choice,* she would have said. As though she'd been left with no other option.

She lit her cigarette and put the tin back in her pocket. Her free hand went once again to the symbol around her neck.

"I want you to know," Fleet said, choosing his words, "that I didn't come back because of anything apart from Sadie Saunders. I'm doing my job, that's all. That's the only reason I'm here."

"Your job," his mother answered on her out breath. "You couldn't have been"—she rolled her smoking hand—"a teacher. A traffic warden if you wanted the uniform." She sniffed. "Although I suppose it was predictable enough that you'd join the police."

Fleet ignored her. "Also, I wanted to say . . ." *Sorry?* But that wasn't quite true. In fact, it was a long way from true. "I wanted to let you know that I'm aware of what people are saying. I hope . . . I didn't want you to have to deal with any repercussions, that's all. Not on my behalf."

His mother's face puckered as she smoked. She exhaled, sucked, blew out again.

"I thought you were leaving," she said.

In his car Fleet forced himself to start the engine. If he hadn't been aware his mother would still be watching, he would have given himself time to calm down. He felt drunk on something, inebriated, to the extent his hands were shaking.

He pulled away too fast, and only realized when it was too late that he hadn't checked the road behind him. But the movement that had caught his eye was only a car pulling out from the side road opposite, turning in the other direction. Fleet eased his foot from the accelerator, slowing the engine and attempting to slow his heart.

He drove. He wasn't ready yet to return to the station, but he knew that if he stayed on the roads he would find himself heading out of town, from lack of anywhere else to go as much as anything—and if that happened he had his doubts he'd have the willpower to turn around. So he went to the river, and parked on the rise behind the Overlook. Below him, the search for Sadie Saunders went on.

I'm doing my job, Fleet had told his mother. *That's the only reason I'm here.*

It might even have sounded half-convincing, if he hadn't been standing in his mother's living room when he'd said it.

So why kid himself? Why *test* himself? Unless the test was the point. Was that why he'd gone to see her in the first place—to see if his motives when it came to Sadie were really as distorted as people were saying? It was possible, Fleet supposed. Probable. Except now, looking down at the river, he didn't know whether he'd passed or failed.

Abigail Marshall.

Cora Briggs.

Fareed Hussein.

Mason Payne.

And Luke Saunders, if only they could have asked him.

The truth lay buried in their stories somewhere, Fleet remained convinced. But he was missing something, clearly. How was what happened in the woods linked to Sadie's disappearance? Was there cause there, or only effect? Or was the truth another shade of gray, a blood-flecked mixture of one and the other?

And if Sadie's friends had really played no part in her disappearance, why did they continue to behave as though they had something to hide?

One of the divers surfaced and headed toward the riverbank. A second followed close behind. The dive teams had progressed a fair distance since Fleet had seen them that morning, and it wouldn't be long now before they reached the estuary and the superintendent decided their job was done. Another day, perhaps. Two at the most. And then the search for Sadie would be scaled back, to a fraction of the manpower it had currently. Burton would see to that, Fleet could be sure, because although it was technically still Fleet's investigation, political and publicity considerations were now uppermost in Burton's mind—meaning the sand in the timer had begun to gather pace. Fleet didn't even know how much longer he'd be able to hold off on pressing charges against Mason, nor whether he was justified in wanting to wait.

Perhaps he wasn't. Perhaps his instinct—that Mason's involvement was, at most, only part of the story—was leading him astray. And perhaps, in terms of the dive teams, it didn't matter either. Because as Fleet's eyes swept the final stretch of river, there was one thing he was suddenly sure of. If the divers were still hoping to find Sadie, they were looking in the wrong place.

FASH

I HAD NO idea how much time we'd already wasted. Rounding up the others, all the stuff with Lara by the bridge, not to mention the detour we took after that to make sure she didn't see where we were heading. By the time we made it into the woods, it was already gone lunchtime, and it was only when we started to think about what we were going to eat that we realized we hadn't brought any proper food with us.

It was my fault, I suppose. Seeing as I was the one to get everyone together. I should have . . . I don't know. Been more prepared. That's what the others thought, anyway.

"What do you mean, you didn't bring anything?" said Cora, when someone suggested we stop for lunch. Abi, I think, even though we'd only just got started. We can't have been more than half a mile into the forest, although to be fair it definitely felt like farther. We'd lost sight of the outside world a hundred meters in, and the canopy above us was like a ceiling. The forest is mainly beeches and oaks, and the leaves were already turning coppery. Some had even started falling, but the foliage on the branches was still so thick you wouldn't have known that it was sunny.

"I just . . . I didn't bring any," I answered. "I guess I forgot. I brought a blanket," I added, hoping that might help make up for it.

"Oh, great," said Cora. "A blanket. Just what we need in this heat. I don't suppose you brought a scarf, too, did you? And maybe a thick winter coat?"

Cora gets crabby when she's hungry. She's crabby most of the time, if I'm honest, but when she hasn't eaten it goes up a notch. Several notches. And I could tell she was still rattled by what had happened on the bridge. We all were, I think. That feeling we'd had when we'd been laughing after Mason's house—that sense of togetherness, just like it used to be between us before Sadie went missing—had pretty much evaporated, and it got worse the moment we stepped into the woods. It was the reality of it, I think. The realization that we were actually doing this, and remembering why we were out there in the first place.

And anyway, to be fair to Cora, she had a point. We were all standing there in shorts and T-shirts, apart from Mason in his Doc Martens, and I could feel the sweat beneath the shoulder straps of my rucksack. So maybe a blanket shouldn't have been first on my list. I just thought—to lie on. That's all.

"Seriously," said Abi, "we really haven't got any food? What are we going to eat?"

"We could kill a bear," said Mason. "Eat that."

Which didn't help with the Abi situation at all. She looked at Mason wide-eyed, and he just stared back at her, flexing his knuckles. I guess those punches he'd landed had started to hurt.

"Shit," said Cora. "Some search party we turned out to be. We might as well just turn around now."

Mason shot me this look.

"Wait," I said. "Have we really not got *anything*? I think I . . ." I slipped my rucksack off my back and crouched down next to it. "I did! Look." I pulled a Snickers bar out of the front pocket. I'd bought it a couple of weeks before, after football training, but it had been too hot to eat it at the time.

"One Snickers bar," said Cora. "Whoop-de-doo."

"It's a Duo," I countered. I didn't mention it had melted in the heat.

"I brought Pringles," chipped in Abi. "They were for snacking, but . . . Well." She sucked in her tummy, smoothed her hands down the rear of her shorts. "Maybe limited rations would be good for us."

"You're not fat, Abi," said Cora, rolling her eyes toward Mason.

"What? Who said I was?"

"Lara Sweeney did. She called you a piggy. And you haven't stopped thinking about it since."

"She called us *both* piggies, actually," said Abi. "And anyway, I wasn't even listening."

Another eye roll from Cora.

"What flavor?" said Mason.

"Huh?" said Abi.

"What flavor Pringles?"

"Does it matter?" said Luke.

"Well, if they're barbecue I'd rather eat my own vomit."

Cora snorted. "The more for the rest of us," she said.

"They're salt-and-vinegar," said Abi. "Obvs. Barbecue make your fingers smell of cat's poo."

There were nods of agreement. Personally, I'd have taken barbecue over salt-and-vinegar any day of the week. But at least they weren't sour-cream-and-onion.

"So, one tube of salt-and-vinegar Pringles," said Cora, "one Snickers bar—"

"Duo," I said.

"*Duo,*" she conceded. "Is that it? Has anyone got anything else? What about water? Did everybody at least bring a bottle of water?"

We had, all of us. Which was something. And it turned out that, as well as Pringles, Abi had also brought nuts. And sunflower seeds. And a massive bar of Dairy Milk chocolate. All for snacks, she said, which is why she didn't mention them at first when we were talking about food. Mason had Rizla, rolling tobacco and Fruit Pastilles. Luke had a sharing bag of Doritos and half a packet of Jelly Babies he'd saved from the cinema and had meant to give to Dylan. Cora had cigarettes and gum.

So the food situation wasn't even that bad, either.

"What else has everybody got?" said Cora. "I mean, aside from the midnight feast and Fash's blanket." She looked at Abi first, because Abi's rucksack was the fullest. "No, wait, don't tell me," Cora said, when Abi opened her mouth to speak. "Let me guess . . ." She shut her eyes and held out a hand, like Luke Skywalker trying to use the force. "You brought . . . your makeup kit. And your hair straighteners. And the *Love Island* special pullout section from last week's *Heat* magazine."

Abi glowered. "It's mainly clothes, *actually*," she said. "Apart from all the food that everyone else completely overlooked. And you're welcome for that, by the way." She looked in her bag. "And I brought this, because I knew you lot would all forget to bring one as well."

She dangled a plug by its lead.

"A phone charger," said Cora. "You brought a phone charger."

I saw Mason give something like a smile. "Nice one, Abi," he said. "And you're right. I completely forgot to pack mine."

Abi took that as a victory, and shot Cora this look.

"What about you, Cora?" Mason said to her, because it was obvious Cora was about to burst. "What have you got in your bag?"

Cora's bag looked the lightest.

"I told you what I brought," she said. "Water, fags and gum. And a groundsheet from my stepdad's camping gear for us to sleep on."

"A groundsheet?" I said. "How is that any different from a blanket?"

"Duh," said Cora. "Groundsheets are for the ground. Blankets are for on top. It's like the difference between a hat and a pair of shoes."

My mouth was open, but I didn't say anything. It's like, if Mason had brought a blanket, I bet Cora would have said it was the smartest idea in the world.

"I brought a torch," said Mason. "Two torches, actually. My iPod. And some portable speakers. Battery-powered," he added, with a glance at Abi.

"Cool," said Cora.

You see what I mean?

Obviously Mason didn't mention anything else he'd brought. Maybe I should have been paying closer attention at the time.

"What about you, Luke?" said Abi. "What did you bring?"

Luke was sitting on the ground.

"Luke?" said Cora, gently.

"Sorry, I . . . Nothing much, I guess. A torch, like Mason. Dylan's old army compass. And some . . . some stuff of Sadie's."

Nobody spoke. The rest of us looked at each other over Luke's head.

Cora crouched down beside him. "What kind of stuff?" she said.

Luke looked sort of ashamed. "Stupid stuff. Just . . . a jumper she liked. Her hairbrush. A book. An old one. About some girl. She used to read it over and over. Not recently. But when she was younger."

"*Anne of Green Gables*," said Abi, kneeling down, too. "Right? I remember it was always her favorite. She kept it face out on her bookshelf so she could always see the cover."

Luke nodded. "When you came by, I just . . . I dunno. I grabbed some of the stuff I thought she'd like. That she might . . . need."

I met Cora's eye, and we both looked down.

Luke got to his feet.

"But it's a waste of time. You all know it is. I should never have come in the first place. None of us should have. I should be at home, looking after Dylan. Who's he got left now if he hasn't got me?"

"He's got your aunt, remember?" I said. "And your parents will be back soon. They'll make sure he—"

"Fuck them," snapped Luke, bitterly.

He looked at the rest of us, all staring at him in shock. "Seriously, fuck 'em." He looked down again, started scratching at the ground with a twig. "It's like, all that stuff they're saying about them online? The stuff Lara was going on about? I wouldn't even be surprised if it was true."

"Luke!" said Cora.

"What?"

"You can't say that. You shouldn't!"

"Why not? If you ask me, it's more likely they had something to do with whatever happened to Sadie than . . ." Luke stopped himself. His eyes flicked toward Mason.

"Than me, you mean?" said Mason. "It's all right. You can say it. And actually, I happen to agree."

"For Christ's sake, Mase," said Cora.

"What? It's true. I *know* I had nothing to do with it. Which means, as far as I'm concerned, *everyone* else is more likely to have killed her than me."

"Shut up!" said Abi, springing to her feet. "Just . . . fucking . . . *shut up*, will you? We don't even know she's dead! I mean, that's why we're out here, isn't it? To try to find her? So why would you say that?"

Mason didn't even flinch. He looked at Abi and tilted his head.

"Look," I said, with a glance at Luke, who was staring out into the woods now. "Let's not talk about it. OK?"

"It's a search party, Fash," said Mason. He was still looking at Abi. "What the hell else are we supposed to talk about?"

"No, I know, but . . . let's not talk about it like *that*. Let's just . . . I don't know. Work out how we're going to do this."

"What do you mean?" said Cora.

"Well, we agreed we'd give ourselves till tomorrow evening, right?" I said.

"Who agreed that?" said Mason. "I don't remember agreeing to that." He looked at me sharply.

"No, I . . . It's just what we thought," I said. "Me and Cora."

Mason looked at Cora, who shrugged.

"And besides," I said, "if we're gone any longer than that, they'll send a search party out looking for *us*."

"Not my parents," said Cora. "They won't even notice I'm gone."

Luke gave Cora a grunt of sympathy.

"If you ask me," said Mason, "we should stay out here as long as it takes. If we're serious about doing this, I mean."

"Well, however long we stay out here," said Cora, "we need a plan. A system, just like Fash said. Otherwise we're just wandering in the forest. And I know we know the parts around here, but in case you hadn't noticed, it goes on for miles. If we get lost . . ."

"We're not going to get lost," said Mason. "We know the woods better than anyone."

Cora looked at him then, and sort of frowned.

"That's right," I said, quickly. "We do. These parts at least, just like Cora said. So how about we stick to the area we know? We work north, but at the same time weave from east to west. Like . . . like Snakes and Ladders. And we walk in a row. A couple of meters apart. The way they were doing in the line searches along the banks of the river. That way we won't miss anything."

"Miss *what*, though?" Abi said. "And why are we looking *here*? The police already came this far, before they turned around and started focusing on the river. Which must have been for a reason, right? They've got to know what they're doing better than we do."

Mason gave a snort. "The cops haven't got a clue. Trust me. They've been searching the river for days now and all they've found is Sadie's bag."

He looked at Abi again, the way he was doing before.

Abi swallowed.

"I don't know, guys," she said. "I mean, what if Luke's right? What if we're kidding ourselves? What if it *is* all just a waste of time?"

"It's not a waste of time," I said. "You were right what you said before. We *don't* know Sadie's dead. And Mason's right, too—we don't know the cops are looking in the right place. Not for certain. Maybe . . . maybe Sadie came out here to get away from it all. Just for a walk or something. We know she liked to do that, right?"

I looked at Luke, who nodded.

"So maybe she got hurt somehow. Like, twisted her ankle or something. And she's lying out here waiting for someone to come and find her."

I know, I know. But you hear stories about people surviving in the wilderness all the time. Like that guy in the Grand Canyon, who got his hand stuck underneath a boulder. Was it the Grand Canyon? They made a film about it. Me and the others, we watched it together. Except for Abi, who doesn't really count, because she spent most of the time staring at her phone.

But my point was, why did it have to be murder? Why was everyone—the police, our parents, the entire town—assuming the worst? It *could* have happened the way I said. I'm not saying it did, but . . . I don't know. At least it was better than thinking about the alternative.

But Abi didn't look convinced. She folded her arms across her chest.

"For Christ's sake, Abi," said Cora. "I thought you were up for it."

"I am," Abi said. "I was." Her eyes kept flicking toward Mason. "I am," she settled on. "I guess."

I turned to Luke then. We all did. Because it felt right that Luke should have the final say.

"Luke?" I said. "What do you reckon?"

He looked at me for a minute, then out again into the woods, before lifting his eyes toward the treetops.

He hooked his rucksack over his shoulder.

"I reckon we should probably get going," he said. "Before it starts getting dark."

CORA

AS WE WALKED I kept thinking about what Mason had said. You know, that as far as he was concerned, when it came to Sadie, *everyone* was a suspect.

And I started to wonder.

About Sadie's parents, a bit. Because those rumors *could* have been true. You know, that they did stuff. To Sadie. Or at least that her dad did. You'd never have guessed it, looking at her, or based on anything she ever said. But Mr. S has always creeped me out a bit. He's just so . . . obsessed. Obsessive. Which I have to say, I used to be jealous of. Having a dad, to start with, not a stepdad who doesn't even count. But also a dad who actually cares what you're doing, and always wants to show you off. A mum, too. Not like my mum, who's basically at the opposite end of the scale. It's like I told you, I could have been out in the woods for a week already, and she wouldn't have noticed I was gone. Or if she noticed, she wouldn't have done anything about it. It's like, God forbid she take on some fucking responsibility. God forbid she start behaving like a *grown-up*.

But then, the more I thought about it, maybe what Sadie had

wasn't so great after all. I mean, it wasn't normal. Was it? And her parents were never like that with Luke and Dylan. So what made Sadie any different? The fact that she was good at stuff? Or maybe, for her dad, that she was a *girl*?

And then I started wondering about other people, too. Like Mr. Prior, at school, who everyone goes on about being a pedo. And I know for a fact there's a pedo who lives on Bay Street, because there was that whole demonstration there when people found out. Or maybe he wasn't a pedo in the end. I can't actually remember what happened, other than he got beaten up. But my point is, this town is full of weirdos, and those are just the ones you *see*. Because with people, you never really know, do you? What they're hiding. What they're lying about. What it is they might have done.

Which is how I also started wondering about *us*.

Take Luke, for example. I feel bad now for even saying it, for even thinking it at the time, but my mind just started working by itself. And with Luke I was thinking, how would *I* feel? If I had a twin and my parents loved my sister more than me. If they spent all their time and attention and their money on her, and treated me like I was nothing more than the live-in help. *Look after your brother, Luke. Go see what Dylan wants. For Christ's sake, will you tell your brother to be quiet?*

You know that Dylan was an accident, right? Sadie's parents only didn't get rid of him because of their beliefs. Because they're Catholic, basically. And Luke always said he was an accident as well. He was like the toy in the packet of cornflakes, he reckoned. The buy-one-get-one-free. He never acted like he blamed Sadie, though. What I always thought was, him and Dylan loved her just as much as she loved them. More even. And Luke and Sadie were twins, you know? They couldn't read each other's mind or anything, but they were closer than any brother and sister I've ever known. They hung out together, for a start, and what brother and sister do you know who do that?

But the thing is, deep down, who knows what might have been going on in Luke's head. Maybe there just comes a point. I mean, all brothers and sisters argue, right? And maybe, the calmer things are between them generally, the more explosive the fights turn out to be . . .

So, yeah, watching Luke forge ahead through the trees, swinging a stick he'd found from somewhere at the leaves, I started imagining him swinging something at Sadie. Just . . . snapping. Not necessarily on purpose. But for Sadie the result would have been the same.

And then there was Fash. He was walking behind Luke, not even trying to catch up. He kept looking over his shoulder. Maybe he was just being paranoid the way I was, because I kept checking to see where Abi was, too. But the more I watched him, the more it looked like he wanted to be on his own. He looked worried about something. Guilty. As though there was something that was playing on his mind.

And the other thing about Fash, the thing you probably don't know about, is that he always had sort of a thing for Sadie. He would never have admitted it, obviously, and he'd deny it if you asked him about it now. Especially now. Jesus. But if you hung out with them both, and you paid attention, you noticed it more and more. Fash would watch her, just little glances, and then he'd look at Mason to see if he'd noticed. And when Sadie touched him, like on the arm or something—Sadie was always touching people on their arms—Fash would go all tense. Just for a second, as though he'd been touched by a wire and a little jolt of electricity had shot through his body. And OK, *everybody* had a thing for Sadie. But maybe, with everything else—with Fash's mum, and all the shit he put up with on a daily basis—things were just building up. Like with Luke, I guess, except different. Like in that movie, the black-and-white one, the one Mason has a poster of on his wall. Where that bloke kills the woman in the shower. Which on the one hand sounds completely ridiculous, comparing Fash to a psycho with a knife . . .

Psycho. That's what I meant.

But in a way that's the whole point I'm trying to make. Nothing makes sense. None of it. Why would *anyone* want to kill Sadie, is what I'm saying. So why should one explanation seem more unlikely than any other?

And fucking Abi. I didn't like her trailing along behind me. At least with Fash and Luke I could *see* them. And Abi was acting guilt-iest of all. She didn't want to be there, clearly. She didn't want any of us to be there. I mean, she wasn't even looking, for Christ's sake. Every time I turned around, all I saw was her staring at her phone, shoving sunflower seeds into that gob of hers when she figured no-body was watching. Which was another clue. Because when Abi stuffs her face like that, it's a sure sign she's feeling nervous.

And Abi's always been jealous of Sadie. *Always*. She would never have admitted it, obviously, but Sadie's was the life she wished she had. She would have given anything to look the way Sadie did, for a start. To be blonde rather than brunette, to have blue eyes instead of plain brown. To be as popular as Sadie was, too. As talented. As loved, I guess, is the sad part, particularly when you think about Abi's dad. So who knows? Maybe Abi had just had enough. Like, it must be exhausting trying to catch up all the time, so instead, maybe what she thought was, rather than trying to catch the leader I'll knock the leader out of the race.

Shit.

I don't know. The truth is I didn't know then, and I'm not sure even now.

The ironic thing is, before the search party, I suspected Mason least of all. I'm not saying he didn't have a temper, that he couldn't be a bit full-on. You only have to look at what happened on the bridge. But that was just . . . it was just everything boiling over, that was all, and anyway, Ian had it coming. That's what I told myself at the time. Mason wasn't *dangerous*, not the way people were making out. And that's why I was walking beside him. Because, out of any of them, at that point, it was Mason I trusted most of all. More than Abi, more than Fash, more than Luke even.

Can you believe that? Given what happened?

I was walking next to Mason because he made me feel *safe*.

ABI

I HATED IT. Every step.

It's like, the others might have known where they were going, because they still went out into the woods all the time. Not to climb trees and that anymore, just to smoke, to drink sometimes, to hang out without worrying about anyone bothering them. Me, I tended to make up some excuse, or try to convince them to go to the quay instead. It was always way better down there anyway. We could blag our way onto the fairground rides in the summer, or take over one of the benches and talk about school, or our parents, or even just the people passing by. The tourists, Lara Sweeney and all her lot, the weirdos who ran the rides. We were never cruel or anything, except maybe if we were talking about Lara. We were just having a laugh, passing the time. But out in the woods it was never as much fun. *I* never thought so anyway. For some reason, out there, things always seemed to get all deep and meaningful. Like, in a depressing way. You know? Probably because it was so depressing being surrounded by all those trees.

So yeah, the truth was, I hadn't really been out in the woods much, not since we were younger, and I'd never liked it even then. It was just so creepy. If you caught the trees at the wrong angle they looked like people, and you could never be sure you were really alone. Sadie used to go into the woods by herself sometimes, just when she needed to clear her head, she said, but there's no *way* I would have gone out there without someone else with me. Not if you paid me a gazillion pounds.

So I hated it anyway, is what I'm saying. Every single step. And that was before you consider why we were out there. Because the thing was, as we were walking along, I kept imagining I'd seen her. Sadie, I mean. Parts of her. A shirtsleeve that turned out to be a root. A flash of blonde hair that was really just a patch of dead grass. At one point I almost screamed out loud, because for a second I could have sworn I'd almost trodden on one of Sadie's hands.

But it was just a leaf.

I don't know if the others were thinking the same, but me, personally, all I wanted to do was go back. I couldn't believe I'd gone along with Fash's plan in the first place, that I thought being out there might actually make things better.

"Guys?" I said, after we'd been walking for what felt like hours, weaving back and forth the way we said we would. "Has anyone else got a signal?" I was holding my phone up in the air, as high as I could get it to go.

"Nope," said Mason.

"Uh-uh," said Fash.

Because that was the other thing about being out in the woods. The signal on my phone had given out when we'd crossed the river, and if everybody else's phones were the same, that meant we had no way of contacting anyone. If it got to the point we needed help.

"Seriously," I said. "You'd think we were in the middle of nowhere, not a couple of miles from the center of town."

I noticed Cora making a face. "Like, *hello*?" she said. "The center of town *is* the middle of nowhere. And what do you expect when we're surrounded by all these trees?"

"Sor*ry*," I muttered. "I was just trying to check if there was any news, that's all. If the police had found anything in the river."

"And they said they'd text you, did they?" said Cora. "And anyway, you're supposed to be looking for Sadie, not trying to get a signal on your phone. This is a search party, remember?"

"But if they *have* found something, there'd be no reason for us to be out here, *would* there?" I told her. "Besides, I—"

I stopped moving. The others turned and stopped, too.

"What is it?" Fash asked me.

"What the hell was that?" I said.

"What the hell was what?" said Cora.

"That noise. I swear to God I just heard a noise."

And then, as I stood there listening, I heard it again. I'd been trailing behind the rest of them and I went rushing to catch up, scraping my arm on a tree.

"Ow! Shit!"

"Calm down, Abi," said Cora. "Jesus."

I ignored her and focused on the others. Luke had come back from up ahead and I went and stood next to him, on account of the fact he was holding a massive stick.

"Seriously," I told them. "I heard a noise."

"A noise?" said Cora. "In the woods? Well, there's a fucking surprise."

"Fuck *off*, Cora!" I snapped back at her. Just because I'd had enough. You know? Of her constant bitching.

"Jesus," said Luke. "What is it between you two at the moment?"

I looked at Cora, daring her to answer, but for once in her life she kept her mouth shut.

"You're bleeding," Fash said to me.

I pointed my elbow at him so I could see the underside of my arm. And there was, there was a massive scrape. Look. See? You can still see the scab. And even though I knew Mason had been joking when he'd mentioned bears, all I could think was that if it was a bear or something I'd heard, it would be able to smell my blood. Like sharks do. Is it sharks? Who can basically tell when something's bleeding from half the ocean away. I saw *that* in one of Mason's movies once, and I haven't gone swimming in the sea ever since. It's like, what if you're *on*, you know?

"What was it you heard, Abi?" said Mason.

"I . . . I don't know. Just . . . something. In the trees." I checked behind me. "Are you *sure* there aren't any bears out here? Not wild ones maybe, but . . . I don't know. Couldn't one have escaped or something?"

"Escaped from where?" said Cora. "A traveling circus?"

"Or a *zoo*, perhaps?" I said.

"The nearest zoo is in London," said Cora. "What do you think, it took a train from Paddington Station? A suitcase full of marmalade sandwiches?"

I shot her evils.

"There aren't any bears, Abi," said Fash. "I'm pretty certain of that."

"Fash is right," said Cora. "There aren't any bears." She paused for a moment. "It's the *wolves* you want to be watching out for."

And then, when I turned to her, Mason put his head back and let out this enormous *howl*. And Cora started wetting herself, obviously, like it was the funniest thing she'd ever heard. And even Fash was smiling, and Luke was looking down toward his feet. Like it was all one big joke to them. Like *I* was, you know, just because I'd got scared. It was like the way they always laugh when I say something stupid. Which I can't help sometimes. It's not *my* fault. The words just start coming out and then, by the time I hear them, it's too late to take them back. It doesn't mean everyone always has to constantly take the piss. And anyway, I couldn't see what was so funny. For me, personally, when Mason howled like that—it made my skin crawl.

What could I do, though? They didn't believe me. But I bet they're wishing they'd listened to me now.

CORA

IT WAS GETTING dark by the time we reached the stream. In the summer holidays, when we were younger, we'd sometimes go to the stream to splash about. You couldn't swim in the river, obviously, and the beach was always crammed with tourists. So the stream was like our little secret. A place we knew no one else would come.

"Do you reckon here's a good place to stop?" said Luke, when we came within sight of the bank.

I don't think I've ever been so relieved. I mean, I would have been fine if it hadn't been for Abi. Not *fine*, obviously, but it was only because she was acting so jittery that I'd started to get freaked-out myself. Not because of bears. I mean, seriously. Fucking *bears*. What planet was she even on? But she was constantly looking over her shoulder, and after a while I started checking behind me, too. And obviously the darker it got, the harder it was to see. It had got to the point that, from imagining I was seeing Sadie in every shadow, I probably wouldn't have spotted her if she'd been swinging right in front of me from a tree. I—

Jesus.

I can't believe I just said that.

I just meant . . . You know what I meant. Right? I didn't mean to imply . . . I didn't mean anything, I swear. I'd just . . . I'd been trying to make sense of it, you know? Walking along, trying to figure out how we'd got to the point where we were doing what we were doing. As in, searching for our best friend in the middle of the woods, and praying we wouldn't find her dead. I was comparing it to the beginning of the summer, to that night we spent on the beach, the day we finished our exams. The start of the evening anyway, before Mason threw a Mason and ruined it for everyone else. But at first, as we were passing around the bottles of wine, nothing else seemed to matter. Not school, not exams, not our parents, not being stuck in this shithole of a town. Nothing except being out there in the sand dunes with our friends. And it wasn't like we were setting the world to rights. We were just . . . having a laugh. That's all. And what I couldn't work out was why couldn't life be like that all the time? Why did all the bullshit have to come along and ruin things? And when I thought about that, I had to bite down to stop myself crying.

So yeah, when Luke suggested we stop, I was the first one to agree. But nobody objected. The others were obviously flagging as well, which wasn't surprising given the heat. Because there was no breeze out there. No oxygen, it felt like. Just this thickness in your throat, like the air was something you could have chewed.

There was a clearing by the stream, and without anyone saying anything, we dumped our bags and collapsed down next to them. I had no idea how much ground we'd covered, but it felt like we'd walked for miles. And it was tough going in the forest. The ground was hard because it had been so hot, but there were still lots of twigs and stuff underfoot. It was as tiring as walking on sand.

Abi was trying her phone again, and the boys began feeding

themselves sips of water. I'd caned half of my bottle already, so rather than wasting any more I figured I'd take a drink from the stream. I splashed my face first, and the water was deliciously cool. I made a scoop with my hands, and brought the water to my lips— but then Luke appeared out of nowhere and batted my hands away.

"Hey!" I said, turning.

"You can't drink that," he said.

"Why not? It's clear."

"But it's barely running. And anyway, it doesn't matter what it looks like. It's what's in it that matters. Like, microbes and stuff. You'll make yourself ill."

"He's right," said Fash. "Here." He tossed me a full bottle of water. "I've got plenty if you're running low."

I fumbled the bottle, but caught it before it rolled into the stream. I looked down at the water and, rather than clear, this time the stream looked like it had turned black. It was just the light, I expect, or lack of it, but it made me think of something in a fairy tale. One of the old ones, the type that always gave me nightmares, where people drown, or have their eyes pecked out, or end up being eaten alive. It gave me the creeps, and I crawled back up toward the others.

We laid out my groundsheet and Fash's blanket. Compared to elsewhere in the woods, the ground was weirdly soft. It was because of the stream, I suppose, and seeing as it was going to be our bed for the night, I guess I should have been glad. But the ground being so spongy felt wrong somehow. Sort of . . . rotten. Like touching a piece of gone-off fruit.

Nobody spoke much after that. We were all exhausted, and not just from the day we'd spent searching. It was everything catching up with us, the sleepless nights since Sadie had gone missing. If you'd asked me before we got there, I would have pretty much guaranteed we'd have sat up talking all night. The way we would have when we were younger. But Luke just rolled onto his side, so that his back was toward the rest of us. Fash started snoring almost the second his head hit the ground, and soon enough even Abi fell asleep. Her phone screen went dark, anyway, which was as much of a sign with Abi as you really needed. She was sharing Fash's blanket, whereas Luke was off lying on his own. I ended up being next to Mason, slightly apart from the others.

We lay in silence for a bit, but I could tell Mason was still awake.

"Mase?" I said, keeping my voice down. "Do you really think . . ." I paused.

"Think what?" he said.

"Just, that Sadie's . . . that there's a chance we'll find her?"

"That's why we're out here," he answered. "Isn't it?"

I wriggled uncomfortably. There was something weird about his tone of voice. It was sort of . . . bitter. Cold. "Sure," I said. "I guess."

For a moment there was just the sound of the others breathing.

"I never believed what people were saying, you know," I said eventually, because I figured maybe that was why he sounded pissed-off, and also because I'd been wanting to say it for a while. "Not even for a minute."

"What part of what people were saying?"

I was lying on my back, staring up at the canopy, which looked like cracks in the dark blue sky. I glanced toward Mason, and realized he was looking right at me.

"Just . . . that you had anything to do with it," I said. "With whatever happened to Sadie." And I meant what I said, at the time.

"Yeah?" said Mason. He didn't sound convinced.

"Yeah," I told him. "And none of the others did either. Not really. Not even Luke."

Mason didn't respond.

"Do you . . ." I turned slightly away. "Do you miss her?" I asked him.

It was stupid, really. I'd only carried on talking because I wanted to hear someone's voice, and because I was worried about everyone else falling asleep before me. And I don't know what I expected Mason to say. Not what he came back with, anyway.

"Do *you*?" he said. Although maybe it wasn't what he said, more the way he said it. Sort of accusing, you know? Which, looking back, should have been, like, a clue or something. My first hint about what he was really up to.

"What's that supposed to mean?" I said.

"I was just asking," said Mason. "That's all. The same way you asked me."

"Yeah, but . . ."

"But what?"

I paused again. "Of course I miss her," I told him. "How could I not?"

Mason didn't say anything, and I was beginning to wish I hadn't started the conversation in the first place.

"I wouldn't have wished this, you know," I said. "If that's what you're thinking."

I turned toward him. He was still looking at me, watching me, and I didn't like the expression in his eyes.

"Mase? *Truly*. I wouldn't have."

Now he was the one to turn away.

"Anyway," I said. "Don't you think . . ."

"Think what?"

"That Sadie had changed," I said, because I'd been dying to say that, too. "Just lately, I mean. Over the summer in particular. Since that night on the beach."

I meant that night I was talking about earlier, with the wine, in the sand dunes, when Mason and Sadie had ended up having an argument, and Mason had stormed off in a strop.

"Changed?" said Mason, and I could tell he was suddenly all ears. "Like how?"

"Just . . . I don't know. She didn't seem different to you?"

"No, she didn't seem different. She was just Sadie. Just the same Sadie she's always been. As beautiful, as kind, as funny . . ."

His voice kind of trailed off, and I could hear how much he loved her.

"Yeah, well," I said, knowing I should shut the hell up. "Maybe you didn't know her as well as you think you did."

I rolled away, and I could feel Mason watching me again. I kept waiting for him to say something, to ask me what I'd meant. But instead he just stayed quiet.

I don't know how much time passed after that. I'm pretty sure I heard Mason get up, but I refused to turn and look. Instead I just lay there listening, because the woods had suddenly come alive. There were all sorts of noises in the undergrowth. Up in the trees, too. Owls and stuff. Bats. All the other things that only come out at night. I wouldn't have minded so much if Abi had been awake, because I knew she would have been more afraid than I was. As it was, it was just me and my imagination, and I was convinced I'd be lying there the entire night.

I wasn't, of course. I fell asleep soon after. I remember thinking about Sadie, and that stream, and thinking the sound of it was like the sound of Sadie's voice. But then I guess I drifted off. At one point I woke and thought I saw a figure watching us from the tree line, but when I rubbed my eyes and looked again, there was no one there.

Then, later, I was sure I heard someone crying, but that could just as easily have been a dream.

In the end I guess I slept more deeply than I realized. I didn't feel the cold, and I didn't notice when the dark gave way to the morning gray. In fact, I'd probably have slept longer, if I hadn't been woken by a scream.

FULL DARK, NO stars. Just the rain slashing at the curtainless window, the light from the streetlamps along the harbor walkway refracting sharply in the broken beads of water.

Sitting in one of two chairs positioned in the alcove, Fleet turned his wedding band over between his fingers. The color of the metal wasn't dissimilar to the fiery glow that was leaking through the window, though the ring itself was more scratched than Fleet had realized. As a symbol of his and Holly's marriage, perhaps it was fitting that it should be so scarred. Even the shape of the ring seemed emblematic. The loop was supposed to represent eternity, but futility, in their case, seemed more fitting. Hadn't their arguments always gone round in circles? And no matter how many times they'd sought to resolve things, they'd always ended up precisely where they'd started.

"Detective Inspector?"

Fleet turned, caught unawares by the voice at the open door. He sat up straighter, and slipped the ring back onto his finger. Another futile gesture, it occurred to him.

"Anne," he said. "Sorry, I didn't mean to wake you. And it's Rob, please."

The hotelier was wearing pajama bottoms and a hoodie, her hair loose across her shoulders. It was such a change from her customary primness, Fleet almost hadn't recognized her. Certainly she looked younger than he'd assumed her to be. Perhaps early rather than late forties. Her coloring—dark hair, gray eyes—was similar to Holly's.

Anne took a step into the room. Her feet were bare, Fleet noticed. She had a tattoo that might have been a feather at the fold of her left ankle—another surprise.

"You didn't wake me," she said. "I didn't even hear you come in. Would you like a light on?" Rather than switching on the overhead light, she moved to a corner and turned on a side lamp. Instantly the room felt warmer. It was the guests' lounge, Anne had informed Fleet when he'd checked in, with half a dozen comfortable armchairs scattered around the room in pairs, and a television in the corner farthest from the door that Fleet had never seen switched on. In fact, he'd never seen any of the chairs occupied either, though he knew there were other guests staying at the hotel.

"What time is it?" said Fleet, even as he moved to check his watch. The hands on the dial showed him it was just before midnight. He'd left the station not long after ten. "God, sorry. I only meant to sit here for a minute."

Anne tucked her hands into her armpits. "Tough day?" she said. Then, flushing, "You don't need to answer that. They're all tough at the moment, I would imagine."

Fleet winced his agreement.

"I actually came down to get a drink," Anne said. "A proper drink, I mean. Would you like one?"

Once again Fleet looked at his watch. "Well, I . . ."

Anne freed her hands and made a flustered motion. "I'm inter-

rupting. And you already told me you weren't much of a drinker."
Fleet had, when he'd checked in and Anne had offered him directions to the local amenities, which in this area amounted to a corner
shop, a café and a pub.

Anne smiled awkwardly and turned away.

"You know what?" Fleet said, as she retreated toward the door.
"I'd love a drink. I could do with something to help me sleep."

Anne studied him for a moment, as though testing his sincerity.
"Really? You're certain you don't want to be left alone?"

"Really," Fleet assured her.

She smiled. "Brandy OK?"

"Whatever you're having."

She wasn't gone long. When she returned she had a tumbler in
each hand.

"May I?" she said, gesturing to the armchair opposite Fleet's.

"Please," he said, making room.

"To be honest, I'm not much of a drinker either," said Anne,
when she was settled. She'd tucked her feet underneath herself on
the seat.

"So what's the occasion?" said Fleet, raising his glass at her and
then taking a sip. He didn't care much for the taste, never really had,
but the burn was exquisite.

Anne gave a lopsided shrug. "The same as you, I suppose. Can't
sleep. I rarely can when the place is empty."

She tested her own drink and gave a slight grimace.

"Empty?" said Fleet. "I thought there was a couple in the room
opposite mine? And I saw a third room key missing from the hooks."

Anne smiled. "Did anyone ever tell you you'd make a good detective?" Her eyes sparkled in the lamplight. "They checked out this
afternoon," she said. "Both couples. The weather, you know?"

Fleet joined her in looking out of the window. If he was honest, he was surprised anyone would want to visit the town in the first place, rain or no rain. But with the weather what it was, and the beach no longer an attraction, there was certainly nothing else to keep them here. Other than morbid fascination, of course, which Fleet didn't doubt would bring its own glut of visitors soon enough.

"Are you missing her?" said Anne, and for a moment Fleet's stomach gave a lurch. "Or him, I suppose I should say. These days, I mean."

Which threw Fleet completely. "Sorry, I . . ."

"Your wedding ring. I saw you playing with it. I'm prying again, I know, but it's either that or ask you about your investigation. Or I suppose we could make small talk about the weather."

Fleet looked down at his left hand. With relief, he realized, because he'd assumed at first that Anne had been asking him about someone else.

"It's a her," he said, with a smile. "And I do miss her. Although I should probably be getting used to it." He looked up. "We're separated. Soon to be divorced."

Anne surprised him with her reaction. She didn't seem concerned that she'd put her foot in it, or offer him the customary condolences. Instead, "I'd kind of figured," she said.

"You had?"

Anne took a drink and shrugged. "I had you pegged as either a divorcée or a widower. My money was on widower."

"What made you think that?" *A widower,* thought Fleet. *Good grief.* Was that really the persona he projected? At thirty-six years old.

"The fact that you're staying here, for one thing," said Anne. "And I field your phone calls, remember? If you were living with someone, I assume I would have spoken to them by now."

Fleet couldn't argue with the logic. "Maybe you missed your calling," he said. "It seems I'm not the only detective in the room."

Anne smiled at the drink in her lap. Sadly, Fleet thought.

"I almost did join the police force, as it happens. A long time ago now."

"Oh?"

"But it was only to get back at my dad. A threat because he was such a bloody crook. Only small fry by your standards, I expect. Although everyone's small fry in this town."

Fleet gave a sniff at that.

"Anyway, my dad—he had a finger in whichever pie was cooking. A touch of fraud, a spot of fencing. He brought the money in, I went to school and ran the household, from the point my mother left us when I was twelve. That was the deal, until one day I came home and found him at the kitchen table with a set of scales and a bowl of white powder."

"I'm guessing he wasn't baking a cake," said Fleet.

Anne laughed. "Now *that* would have been a shock." She ran a finger around the rim of her glass. "I was sixteen by then," she went on, "and I'd already seen what drugs had done to some of my friends at school. Not friends, really, but I knew them, and I wasn't having any part of it. Because I knew my dad, and I knew he'd be looking for me to act as his little gofer. So I told him to flush it down the toilet or I'd go to the police."

"How did he react to that?"

"I went to bed that night with a fat lip. But the next day I came home from the careers office with a brochure and an application form, and left it filled out on the kitchen table for him to find. I was serious, too. I would have joined. And when he confronted me about it the next evening, my dad saw that, too."

"So what did he do?"

"He went straight," said Anne. "To the coach station, that is. Took what he needed to and left. Which is how I ended up here."

Fleet frowned his confusion.

"My grandmother owned this place originally. My mum's mum, who'd disowned my mother when she'd run out on us, and had always loathed my dad. So she was only too pleased to take me in. I had to do my bit—by the end it was just me and her running things—but nothing I wasn't used to doing at home, back on the other side of town. And when my grandmother died, she left the place to me. The mortgage as well, but that's a different story."

Anne took a long swallow of her brandy, almost draining the glass. She winced.

"And that, in a nutshell, is me," she said, clearly trying not to cough. "It's not even the short version, either." She waved a hand. "There are a few car-wreck relationships I could throw in, I suppose, which Freud would probably have found interesting but most normal folk would assume were par for the course. For a forty-three-year-old spinster like me, I mean, whose only excitement these days is an occasional illicit shot of brandy."

Fleet watched her as she finished her drink. He wondered whether it was the alcohol that was making her so open, or—more likely, he thought—the loneliness.

"So, how about you?" said Anne. She set her glass on the windowsill and folded her arms, wriggling to make herself comfortable.

"Me?"

"I've shared my story," said Anne. "What's yours?"

Now it was Fleet's turn to drink. "You must have heard by now," he said. "If you didn't know already."

"I've heard rumors," Anne admitted. "But I've been living in this town long enough not to believe anything that carries on the wind. Mainly because it has a habit of changing direction."

As if on cue there was a gust of rain against the window, the breeze across the harbor gaining strength. Fleet thought about Mason: the way the community, one minute, had been ready to lynch him, but were now up in arms about the supposed incompetence of the police. Although maybe they were right on both counts.

"The stories I heard . . . they were to do with your . . . sister, was it?" said Anne. "Was she older or younger?"

Fleet felt a tightening within him.

"Younger," he said, and that was all.

Anne took the hint. "Sorry. Too far. I didn't mean to open up old wounds. And anyway, I was actually asking about . . ." She tipped her head at his wedding ring. "You know. Unless that's an open wound, too. Shit, just tell me to mind my own business. You probably only had a drink with me in the first place to be polite!"

Ordinarily Fleet would have shied away from both topics, even in the safety of his thoughts, but there was something about Anne's directness that he couldn't help responding to. Holly was direct, too. Painfully so, sometimes. In fact, it was the very characteristic he'd been most attracted to the first time he and Holly met, six years ago now, not long after Fleet had made inspector. He'd been asked to give a presentation on personal safety at Holly's university campus, aimed primarily at female members of staff. She'd come up to him afterward and challenged him on why the police had considered it appropriate to pick a man to deliver the lecture to a group of women. To which he'd had no response, other than to apologize, at which point she'd asked him if he'd let her buy him a cup of coffee. The story they'd come to tell—only partially in jest—was that Fleet had been too intimidated to say no.

"It's fine," said Fleet to Anne. He splayed his hand and examined his wedding ring, then folded it away in his fist. "My wife and I . . . it turned out we were less compatible than we thought, that's all."

Anne waited for him to go on.

"It was my fault," he said. "I wasn't honest, with myself as much as with her."

He sensed Anne shift slightly.

"I don't mean . . . What I mean is, Holly had different . . . expectations. Of what our marriage would lead to. And I guess for a long time I was guilty of letting her live with the misconception."

"I'm not sure I'm following," Anne said.

Fleet looked her in the eye. "She wanted—wants—a child. I don't. Can't, won't, however you want to put it."

Anne raised her chin slightly. There was a gleam of understanding in her eye. She'd clearly heard more details about Fleet's past than she'd let on.

"So really, it's all one open wound," Fleet said, smiling but feeling no humor. "My past, I mean. My marriage. It wouldn't take Sigmund Freud to join the dots."

He finished his brandy in a swallow and, taking his time, set his glass down on the windowsill next to Anne's.

They sat in silence for a moment, before Anne rose and left the room. She returned with the bottle of brandy, and poured them each another measure.

She clinked her glass against Fleet's, still in its place on the sill, then folded herself back into the armchair.

"It's none of my business," she said, testing the silence. "But did you try . . . talking to someone?"

"A therapist, you mean?" said Fleet. He nodded. "Holly insisted, so we went to a couples counselor."

"And what did they say?"

Fleet reached for his drink. "He said it sounded like there was more than one thing going on. That there was clearly a lot we needed to work out." He shook his head. "All very insightful, I'm sure, and Holly was keen to go back, but as far as I was concerned, no amount of talking was going to alter the simple facts. And not having children . . . it was tearing Holly apart."

Anne nodded. "I get that," she said. "I really do."

Fleet looked across at her, even as she dropped her gaze. He wondered about those car-wreck relationships she'd mentioned, about what choices—what sacrifices—she'd had to make in *her* past. And whether, given the life she had now, she considered them worth it.

They finished their drinks. After a while, Anne stood up. She looked out at the rain for a minute, and Fleet watched her reflection in the glass.

"Well," she said, when she turned. "I think I'll go up to bed."

She met Fleet's gaze, and allowed her hand to rest on his shoulder. There was a pause.

"Thank you," said Fleet. "For the company. If it's OK with you I might sit here for a while. This case, you know? It's hard to switch off."

Anne smiled at him. She withdrew her hand.

"Of course," she said. "Don't sit up too late." And she left Fleet looking at himself in the darkened window.

DAY **EIGHT**

"SOMETHING WRONG WITH your neck, boss?"

Fleet was later into the station than he'd intended. Nicky was already at her desk, in the area of the open-plan office that had been cleared to accommodate Fleet and his team. About half of the officers under Fleet's command had been seconded here, just like Fleet himself. The rest were locals, more accustomed to working pub brawls than murder inquiries, but diligent enough, from what Fleet had seen so far. Of them all, Fleet knew only Nicky well. His specialty in finding missing persons meant Fleet himself was something of a stray (a "bloodhound without a leash," Holly had quipped once), but officially he and Nicky belonged to the same branch of CID. He requested her presence on his assignments often, because he knew her work and he trusted her judgment. Plus, unlike him, she was a people person, and she had a knack for smoothing potentially fraught relationships with the locals, who sometimes resented outsiders stepping on their size twelves.

Fleet had a hand cupped around his neck as he walked in, though it was in fact a headache that was bothering him more. Inwardly he'd blamed the brandy, but he was at a stage where it was hard to tell what was down to the alcohol and what was a symptom of his lack of sleep.

"It's nothing," he said in response to Nicky's question. "Fell asleep in an awkward position, that's all." He decided not to mention the armchair, or the fact that Anne had found him there at half past six this morning, his head back, his mouth open, and his brandy glass still balanced on his lap. "At this rate I should probably give you a discount on your room fee," she'd joked. "It doesn't feel right charging you summer rates when you barely ever seem to use the bed." And then, to Fleet's everlasting gratitude, she'd swapped his empty brandy glass for a pint of cold water.

"Sorry I'm late," Fleet said to Nicky. "Breakfast with the super. And, it turned out, the Crown Prosecution Service."

"The CPS?" said Nicky. "I thought lawyers only ate brunch."

"It seems they're happy to get up in time for breakfast if someone else is paying," answered Fleet. "Though I admit it was strange watching one drink something other than blood."

Nicky made a bat face, fluttered her hands like wings. Fleet gave a pissed-off laugh. He didn't mind the superintendent parading before the television cameras, even taking credit that wasn't his due. What he objected to was being asked to run an investigation, and then to find that the very person who'd appointed him had seen fit to undermine his authority. Apparently Burton had taken the liberty of briefing the CPS on everything they had against Mason Payne. Which remained thin, in Fleet's opinion, and he could tell the government lawyer had felt the same. But Burton had obviously bullied the man before Fleet had arrived, and the lawyer had confirmed that the CPS would in theory be willing to proceed with a prosecution. At which point Burton had looked at Fleet as though he'd done him a personal favor, on the level of saving his career.

"As for the situation in the woods," the lawyer had gone on, "I understand the picture there remains hazy. You've got a dead body, and a weapon, but nothing much more conclusive than that. Yes, Payne's fingerprints are on the knife, but there are at least two other sets on there as well, not to mention the prints that are too distorted to identify. And there's nothing definitive to say the crimes are connected. As such, even manslaughter would be a stretch. But if you really want to go down that route, it would be helpful if we could show the jury Sadie's body."

Fleet had left the table at the country hotel willing the man to choke on his granola. But the message from the superintendent had been clear: find Sadie and find the truth, or be prepared to settle for what they had. And he'd spelled out the timing to Fleet as well. The river search would be called off within twenty-four hours. At which point it would be considered beneficial to community relations if Fleet could coordinate the announcement of the arrest. It was a cheap PR trick, and the fact that Fleet had been expecting it did nothing to make him feel any less like a politician's patsy.

"So what did the CPS say?" Nicky asked.

"That there was enough evidence to start proceedings against Mason," Fleet told her.

Nicky showed her puzzlement at his tone. "Which is good news," she said. "Right?"

Not for Mason, Fleet found himself thinking. He glanced toward the corridor containing the interview rooms.

"Is everybody here?" he asked.

Nicky gave an almost nod. "Cora and Abi arrived just before you did. Fareed is in room one. No sign yet of Mason."

Fleet checked his watch. Already it was almost ten o'clock, another reason the superintendent's little breakfast gathering had caused him such irritation—Fleet had lost time he could profitably have spent doing exactly what his superior had asked him to: hunting for the truth about what had happened to Sadie.

"Give him another half an hour, then send a taxi," said Fleet, half wanting to be there to see Mason's reaction when a squad car pulled up outside his house.

"The kid gloves are coming off then, I take it?" said Nicky.

"They are for Mason," said Fleet. "In the meantime, until he gets here, let's make a start with the others."

Nicky rose from her desk. "Before we do, boss, there are a couple of things you'll probably want to see."

Fleet raised his eyebrows.

"Sadie's financials, for one thing," said Nicky, handing him a clutch of papers. "I hope you don't mind, but I took another look at these myself when I realized something was bothering you."

"What did you make of them?" said Fleet, scanning the figures himself.

"Not a lot, to be honest," said Nicky. "Other than to feel slightly depressed at the thought a sixteen-year-old girl had more in her bank account than I do."

"She was saving for university," said Fleet. "That's what her parents said. Sadie paid in almost every penny of the money she got each week for working at the local Harvester. Except . . ." Fleet turned to Sadie's wage slips. "Here. Look. She was working extra shifts over the summer. But almost from the first day of the holidays, the deposits into her savings account stopped."

"So that leaves . . . what?" said Nicky. "About four hundred quid unaccounted for?"

"Literally," said Fleet. "Because it wasn't in her bedroom and it wasn't in her purse."

"She could have spent it. It was the summer holidays, after all."

"Spent it on what, though? Ice cream and candy floss?"

"Cider and cigarettes, more likely," said Nicky.

"Except that's an awful lot of cider. And Sadie didn't really smoke. Only socially, from what her friends have said. And she didn't have any fancy new clothes. No new trainers or anything like that."

"Not that she would have needed to pay for that stuff herself, anyway," said Nicky. "All the things she wanted, her parents bought. She was Daddy's little princess, after all."

"Quite," said Fleet. He tapped the paperwork against his leg.

Nicky allowed him a moment to ponder before she moved on.

"We made a start on the social media stuff, as well," she said. "Trying to trace the source of the rumors about Sadie? I say *we*, but really . . . Well. Maybe you should speak to him yourself."

Nicky led Fleet deeper into the open-plan office. It was as busy as it would be all day, with every one of the dozen or so desks occupied. Soon enough, people would be heading out to follow up on their particular assignments—some to the woods, others to the Overlook and the river—but for the time being they were working the phones, frowning at their computers or wading through hours of almost certainly useless CCTV footage.

"You remember DC Dalton," Nicky said, stopping at the workstation of a detective who, in his baggy suit and spectacles, looked barely any older than Sadie's friends.

Fleet nodded a greeting. Dalton made to stand, but Fleet gestured him back down.

"You look like you've had about as much sleep as I have," Fleet said to him, which he hoped the young man would take as the intended compliment.

Dalton cracked a lopsided grin. "I managed to snatch an hour or two, sir."

Fleet leaned closer to the DC's computer screen, which was tiled with browser windows showing various social media websites.

"So, what have we got?"

Dalton glanced at Nicky over Fleet's shoulder. Fleet sensed, rather than saw, Nicky nod her head.

"Well," said Dalton, flicking between windows at such a rate that Fleet had to blink to keep focused. "This."

On-screen, the DC had maximized a window showing a page with an Instagram header, and a message announcing, *Sorry, this page isn't available.*

"OK . . ." said Fleet, waiting for Dalton to explain.

"You see, what I thought was," the DC said, "if we were going to try to work out where the rumors about Sadie sleeping around originated, simply by following the posts, it would be like trying to untangle Christmas lights. Like, when they get all knotted? And you can't tell the beginning from the end? And *that* made me think of bulbs."

"Bulbs?" said Fleet.

"Bulbs," agreed Dalton. "On the Christmas lights." He nudged his glasses farther up his nose and shifted in his seat, his tiredness evidently forgotten as he excitedly continued to explain. "You know, when one of them blows. And even though the lights are probably fine, the only way to get them working again is to check each bulb individually. My dad used to make me do it every year. It was like a tradition, as much a part of Christmas as putting up the tree. I remember, this one time, years ago now this was, I—"

Nicky coughed meaningfully.

"Right," said Dalton, nudging his glasses again. "Sorry. But my point is, it's like that old story about shovels. You know, the idea that when a man walks into the garden center to buy a shovel, it's not a shovel he really wants. What he really wants is a *hole.*"

Bulbs, shovels—Fleet was losing the gist. He stole a glance at Nicky, whose expression told him to stick with it.

"I'm not following you, Detective Constable."

"Yes, sir. Sorry, sir. All I'm trying to say is, it's not the posts themselves we should be interested in. It's any suspicious activity *around* the posts. Such as a deleted account, for instance."

"The broken bulb," said Fleet, catching up.

Dalton's face lit up, almost as though he were plugged into a power source himself. "Precisely." He turned back to his computer screen. "And of all the Instagram accounts most heavily involved in spreading rumors about Sadie, this is the only one that was deleted after Sadie went missing. Although what the user probably didn't realize is that when it comes to social media, nothing is ever gone forever, not if you know where to look. Or maybe she did realize, but there wouldn't have been anything she could do about it."

"She?" said Fleet.

"Don't get too excited," Nicky chipped in. "The user data associated with the account was all fake, as far as we can tell. But Garrie here uncovered the name of the account itself."

She nodded at Dalton, who flicked to another window on his screen and highlighted a line of text amid the code. "The account's an old one," he said. "It's been active on and off for a couple of years."

"SweeneyTodd2002," Fleet read aloud. It took him a second or two to make the connection. "Sweeney. As in, Lara Sweeney?"

"It has to be a possibility," Nicky replied. "The nature of the previous posts would seem to fit. Sarky comments and stupid jokes, mainly. All very teenage-girl. Garrie here is going to dig a little deeper to see if there are any other ways to identify the user. But the rumors about Sadie definitely originated from this account.

It's much easier to untangle a ball of string if you have an end to start from."

"Or a ball of Christmas lights," said Fleet, letting his hand fall on the young detective constable's shoulder. "Let me know when you have anything more."

"There is one other thing, actually," said DC Dalton. "The stories about Sadie's parents. You wanted to know about those, too, right?"

"Tell me," said Fleet.

"Well, it's pretty much the same story," said Dalton. "Another deleted account, another anonymous user—although my hunch is it's the same person. Same pattern of messages, same syntax, that sort of thing. This time they were posting under Princess_69."

Fleet rubbed a hand across his cheek. A phrase he'd repeated the night before came back to him. Something the couples counselor had said to him and Holly. *It sounds like there's more than one thing going on . . .*

"I'm assuming you're on that, too?" Fleet said to Dalton. "Trying to trace who owned the account?"

"Absolutely," Dalton replied. "In fact, I'm hoping having two leads to follow might make things easier. At the very least it doubles our chances."

Fleet nodded. A bit of good news, finally. "We should talk to Lara," he said to Nicky. "Find out what she has to say for herself."

"Sure thing," Nicky answered. "I'll set it up."

Fleet clapped Dalton on the shoulder. "Good work, Detective Constable. Outstanding, in fact. Keep it up."

"Sarge?"

Both Fleet and Nicky turned. One of the uniforms had appeared behind them. "Sorry to interrupt, guv," he said to Fleet. "But, Sarge"—

he turned to Nicky—"you said you wanted me to let you know when he arrived. The Payne kid."

"He's here?" Nicky asked him.

The officer nodded. "I've stuck him in interview two."

Nicky turned to Fleet, who took a breath.

"Shall we?" he said.

MASON

HERE WE GO again. You really don't give up, do you? Why don't you just arrest me and have done with it? I mean, if you're really that sure I did what you're accusing me of.

There's only one reason you're focusing on me. You know it, I know it. So let's talk about that, shall we? Let's talk about what you found in Sadie's bedroom.

You've said over and over that it gives me motive. But that's bullshit. I *loved* Sadie. She loved *me*. I would never have hurt her. *Never*.

And anyway, this is exactly what I'm talking about. You find something and you call it evidence, but really you don't know the first thing about it. You might as well have found a . . . a packet of condoms in her room. A morning-after pill. Just because you found a *pregnancy test* doesn't mean I killed her.

What, you think I murdered my unborn baby, too? Besides, how do you know the pregnancy test was even hers? If Sadie had been pregnant she would have told me. We would have figured out what to do *together*.

I bet you think you can blame me for what happened in the

woods as well, don't you? Just because I was the one to bring the knife. And, as it happens, that's the only reason I bothered coming in today. I almost didn't. I almost just said to myself, *They never listened to me about Sadie, so why's it going to be any different this time?* Which is what I figured yesterday. What I still believe, even now. But what I decided was, at least if I get my side of things on record, you won't be able to claim that I changed my story later.

So here I am. Reporting for duty.

Seriously, go ahead: ask me whatever you want to know.

Ha. I thought that might throw you. You don't even know where to start.

The scream?

Right. Huh. To be honest, it was more of a shriek. I mean, at first I figured it was my alarm clock. But when I raised my head and remembered where I was, I saw Abi standing in the middle of the clearing, tipping out the contents of her rucksack. There were sunflower seeds going *everywhere.*

"What the fuck, Abi?" I said. Because—and I hold my hand up—I'm not a morning person. I mean, if I ever *was* going to kill someone, it's over the breakfast table I'd probably do it.

Oh, piss off.

Sitting there telling me this is serious? You think I don't know that already?

It's you who's the joke. You, your little sidekick here. Your whole so-called investigation. So why don't *you* get serious for once, and stop wasting time judging me?

I am calm. I was.

Whatever. Do you want to know what happened or not?

Sunflower seeds. Right. So they're going everywhere. And there's only one thing Abi's more obsessed with than food, so right away I should have realized what was up.

"Where is it?" Abi was saying. "Where the hell is it?"

"Where's what?" said someone else. Luke, I think, from the edge of the clearing, sounding even more confused about where he was than I'd been.

"My phone," said Abi. "My sodding phone. It was just . . ." She spun around, pointed at the head end of the blanket. "Right there. I left it *right there*, so I could see the time if I woke up in the middle of the night."

I looked at my watch, and realized it wasn't even seven. The light was sort of milky, and in the sky there was an early-morning haze. They were the first clouds of any kind I'd seen in weeks. Already it felt muggy, like stepping into the bathroom after somebody else has just had a shower.

Fash sat up, blinking. Cora, lying beside me, gave a groan, like she was awake but was still in denial.

"Relax, Abi," I said, getting up. "It probably slipped under the blanket or something." I gave Fash a nudge with my foot, and he half crawled, half rolled to one side. But when I lifted up the top edge of the blanket that he and Abi had been sleeping on, there was nothing under it but grass.

"See?" said Abi. "It's not there. I already looked. And it's not in my pocket before you say anything, and it's not in my bag either. I told you, it's gone!"

"For Christ's sake," I heard Cora mumble. "S'just a phone. Wasn't any signal out here anyway."

"That's not the point!" said Abi. "And it was a brand-new iPhone, thank you very much. Not your shitty old Samsung."

Cora had given up on sleep, it looked like. She sat up, scrunching her eyes against the light. "Now you're just getting personal," she said. "It's not my fault you lost your stupid phone."

"So whose is it then?"

"Seriously?" said Cora, turning. "You're actually trying to blame me?"

"You're the one who was having a go at me yesterday for trying to get a signal!"

"I wasn't having a go at you for trying to get a signal! I was having a go at you for staring at that stupid screen all day when we were supposed to be—"

"Um, guys?" said Fash. "I think mine's gone, too."

He was frisking himself, checking the space around him. He even stood and lifted up the blanket the way I had. Cora's groundsheet, as well, which is what finally forced Cora onto her feet.

I'd started looking around for my phone by this point. I'd emptied my pockets and piled the stuff beside my bag. My lighter was there, my wallet—but not my phone.

"Shit," said Cora, who'd realized by now that hers was missing as well. If anything, she looked more panicked about it than Abi had, whipping the groundsheet into the air and rummaging through the pockets of her rucksack.

"What the hell?"

It was Luke's voice again. I turned—we all did—to see him holding his water bottle upside down. A single drip fell to the floor.

He looked at Cora. "For Christ's sake. I would have shared if you'd just asked me. There was no need to drink it *all*."

"What are you talking about?" said Cora. Luke was still staring at her, and now the rest of us were staring at her, too. "Seriously," she said. "What the hell is everyone looking at *me* for?"

"Your bottle was half-empty," said Luke. "And I wouldn't let you drink from the stream. So you obviously decided to steal the rest of my water while I was asleep."

Abi held out her hand. "Give me my phone back," she said to Cora. "Enough messing around."

"I don't have your stupid phone! And I didn't touch your water, Luke!"

Luke was holding his bottle to his mouth, tipping his head back to try to catch another drip.

"Here," said Fash. "Have some of—"

But when he picked up his bottle, he shook it and it didn't make a sound. Then I checked my bottle, which was lying at the foot end of the groundsheet. It was empty, and so was Abi's.

"What about yours, *Cora*?" Abi said.

Cora was already reaching into her rucksack. Her bottle was still half-full.

"That . . . that doesn't mean anything," she said, seeing the way everyone was looking at her. "I was using my rucksack as a pillow!"

"*So?*" Abi said.

"So whoever messed with your bottles couldn't have got to mine! That's the only reason mine's still full!"

Abi rolled her eyes. She took a step and made a lunge for Cora's rucksack.

"What the hell, Abi! Get *off*."

Abi had Cora's bag by one of its straps, and Cora was trying to keep her from taking it.

"Whoa," said Fash, "what are you doing?"

"I'm going to look inside her bag, that's what," said Abi, giving the strap another yank. "I bet she's got our water in a secret flask or something. Not to mention my phone."

"A *secret flask*?" said Cora. "Seriously? And will you stop going on about your stupid phone! The rest of ours are missing, too!" She was still having a tug-of-war with Abi, until Fash and Luke pulled them apart.

"Everybody *calm down*," said Luke. "Let's just . . . I don't know. Try to work out what's happening."

"It's obvious what's happening," Abi said, and she jabbed a finger at Cora. "*She* thought it would be funny to—"

"All right, all right!" Fash cut in. "Jesus." He pressed the heel of his palm to his head as though he had a sudden headache or something. I watched him for a moment, curious.

"Look," said Luke. "There's no point blaming one another."

"So who else are we supposed to blame?" said Abi. "There's nobody else out here but us!"

I saw Cora open her mouth, her eyes flick toward the trees. But whatever she'd been about to say, she swallowed it.

"Why don't we all have another look around?" said Luke. "For the phones, I mean. The water's not the end of the world. We probably *could* drink the stream water if we boil it."

"How?" said Cora. "I mean, I don't suppose anybody brought a kettle, did they? And a five-mile-long extension lead?"

"We could . . . build a fire or something," Luke answered. "Heat it up over that."

"What, in our hands?" said Cora. "Unless someone's carrying around a saucepan that the rest of us don't know about?"

"Jesus Christ, Cora!" Luke snapped. "I don't know, do I? I'm just trying to be positive, that's all! You're the one who . . ."

"Who what?" said Cora, when Luke abruptly stopped talking. "Who stole the phones? Who tipped out the drinking water? You still think it was me!"

"No one's saying that," said Fash. He wasn't clutching his head anymore, but there was no denying he looked tired. Exhausted even, as though he hadn't slept a wink all night. "Let's just do what Luke suggested. OK? Have another look around. See if anything else has been messed with."

Cora stood fuming for a moment, as did Abi. But when me, Fash and Luke turned to get on with it, they had no choice but to start looking around, too.

We searched for a good ten minutes, but we couldn't find the phones. Or any secret flasks, come to that.

"What about the bags?" said Fash. "Is anything else missing from them?" He'd made a start on laying out his belongings on the ground. Fash is the kind of person who, when he goes to the supermarket, places his stuff on the conveyor belt like he's building a jigsaw. Me, I just upend my basket and hope none of the contents fall on the floor.

"Not from my bag," said Cora. "It's empty already. *See?*" She held her rucksack upside down and gave it a shake. She made a point of staring at Abi.

Abi ignored her, thank God. She was picking up the sunflower seeds, blowing on them one by one, and then dropping them back into the packet.

"Mine's fine, too," said Luke, peering into his rucksack. "It's only my phone that's missing."

I almost didn't bother checking my bag. I was watching the others, for one thing. I wanted to see their reactions. And there was nothing I'd brought with me I gave a toss about. That's what I thought . . . until I remembered.

"Mason?" said Fash. "What about you? Have you got everything you came with?"

I'd turned away and dropped to my knees. I was running my hand around the inside of my rucksack, feeling into every corner. Carefully at first, then faster and faster.

"Mase?" said Fash, when I didn't answer. I sensed the others looking over, too.

I raised my head. "Sure," I said. "Couldn't find my iPod for a sec, that's all." I pulled it from a side pocket of my rucksack and held it up in the air.

"So that's it, then," said Luke, sitting down. "It's just the water and the phones."

Abi didn't answer. She flopped onto the ground beside her bag. Cora, standing, folded her arms. Fash was still surveying his belongings, double-checking that nothing was missing.

"Looks that way," I said to Luke, shrugging. He shrugged back, then made a start on doing up his rucksack. I took the opportunity to sneak another look in mine, even though I knew exactly what was in there. Or, rather, what wasn't.

Because Luke was wrong. It wasn't just the water and the phones.

That knife I brought? The kitchen knife?

That was missing, too.

FASH

"SO WHAT NOW?"

It was Luke who voiced what we were all thinking. After we'd packed up our stuff, we sat munching sunflower seeds in the clearing. We were passing around the bag, each taking a few at a time. Abi had ended up next to Cora, so obviously she'd passed it the other way first. Because they were niggling at each other even more than usual. I mean, they were mates, but they'd never been as close as Abi was with Sadie, for example, or as Cora and Sadie used to be when we were younger. And probably that was part of the problem. I always had the impression that Abi and Cora were sort of jealous of each other, you know? That, when it came to Sadie, they were vying for position. Except out there, in the woods, it seemed to be more than that—unless it was a reaction to Sadie no longer being there. Either way, I figured it was down to stress. A response to everything that had happened.

"I'm thirsty," Abi said, as though in answer to Luke's question. Which I suppose it was, in a way. Because she had a point. We were all thirsty. And we were only going to get thirstier. It was barely eight o'clock, and we were sitting in shadow, but already it felt as hot as it had all summer. And on top of that there was the sound of the stream just a few meters away, which sounded like a little kid's laugh. You know, sort of mocking, like it had something you wanted and it knew there was nothing you could do to get it.

"We're all thirsty," I said. "And breakfast isn't exactly helping much." I quite liked sunflower seeds ordinarily, but they were sticking to the insides of my mouth. It was like trying to swallow papier-mâché.

"Feel free to eat your own food," Abi sniffed. "Oh, sorry, I just remembered. You didn't bring any."

I expected Cora to say something, but she'd gone quiet since she had realized she was in everybody's bad books. Not that I necessarily blamed her myself. I didn't know *who* to blame. Why would Cora—or any of us—hide our phones, or deliberately get rid of our water? On the other hand, it was like Abi had said before. There was nobody else out there but us five. So it *had* to be one of us. Didn't it?

The bag of sunflower seeds came back around, and Abi snatched it from Cora without even looking at her. Then she stuffed it back into her rucksack.

"Well, I don't know about the rest of you," she said, standing, "but I'm not staying out here without water. Without any way of contacting the outside world."

Mason dropped his head between his knees, and gave a sort of sniff. Not a laugh, but not far off. Which, I have to admit, was getting a bit annoying. The way he refused to take anything seriously.

"What?" said Abi. "What's so funny, Mason?"

Mason looked up. *"The outside world,"* he said. "Jesus, Abi. We're not exactly in the middle of the Amazon. And you've only been awake an hour. You can't be *that* thirsty."

"Like, *hello?*" Abi said, and I have to say she was getting pretty annoying, too. But I guess the others would probably have said the same thing about me. It was like I was saying about Abi and Cora . . . We were all tired, and hungry, and, yes, thirsty, so I suppose it was only natural that we'd start getting on each other's nerves. But, *"Hello?"* Abi said. "I haven't had anything to drink for almost *twelve hours*. My pee just now was bright *yellow*."

Mason scrunched up his face. "I thought pee was supposed to be yellow?"

Which made me laugh. Not because it was particularly funny. Just . . . just because, I guess.

"I think your pee's supposed to be white, dude," I said. "Not white, but . . . you know. Clear."

"Seriously?" Mason said, and I couldn't tell whether he was joking or not. Abi was standing there openmouthed.

"Dylan had purple pee once," said Luke. "And not just a little bit purple. Purple like . . . like a lightsaber or something. Like Samuel L. Jackson in *The Phantom Menace*."

"What the hell?" I said, not sure whether to smile or frown. Luke didn't seem sure, either.

"This was like, two summers ago. He started crying the second he saw it, and he ran to find our mum and dad." Now Luke's face set in a scowl. "They totally ignored him," he said. "They were heading out to one of Sadie's shows. I mean, they weren't even late. They had time. They could have . . ." Luke shook his head. "I don't know. But they could have *listened* to him at least. Instead they just left, and told me to tell Dylan to stop making up stories."

I shared a glance with Mason, and waited for Luke to go on.

"He burst into tears again the second they left. So I made him take me to the toilet to show me what he meant. And he wasn't kidding. The water in the bowl was practically neon. So I . . . I took him to A&E. I didn't know what else I was supposed to do. I was worried he might have kidney failure or something."

"What did they say?" I asked. "The doctors, I mean."

Luke sniffed, like what he was telling us should have been funny. "They asked Dylan what he'd been eating. Which, it turned out, included a Slush Puppie. Three of them, actually. Not actual Slush Puppies. The fake kind they sell at the end of the pier, which are basically made of nuclear waste. He'd stolen some money from my dad's wallet and pretended when he bought them that they were for him and his friends."

I gave a snort. I couldn't help it. I noticed Mason grinning, too, and in the end even Luke cracked a smile.

"Man," I said. "What I wouldn't give for a Slush Puppie right now. Cherry flavor, with two fingers of strawberry at the top."

"Raspberry," said Mason. "All the way. But right now I'd settle for lemon-and-lime."

"Or just a Sprite," Cora suggested. "Squash, Ribena, anything. As long as it's cold."

There was a noise like someone being strangled, and we turned to see Abi making fists at her sides. "Will all of you please just *stop*?" she said. "It's like you're deliberately trying to make things worse!" She folded her arms and turned her back.

I caught something in Mason's smile then. I mean, I guess I was smiling a bit, too, but something about Mason's expression seemed . . . I don't know. Different somehow. Cruel.

Cora got to her feet. "So?" she said. "What's it to be?"

"Well," I said, when nobody else spoke. "We obviously have to find something to drink. Except . . ." I glanced at the stream. "There *isn't* anything to drink out here. So I don't see that we really have any choice." I looked at Luke, who dropped his head. He was thinking about Sadie, obviously. About leaving her out there. Not that we knew *where* she was, but there was no getting away from it: going home meant giving up.

"You're kidding," said Mason. "Right?"

The rest of us were already standing. Even Luke, after I'd offered him my hand.

"You're turning tail already?" Mason went on, rising now, too. "Even though we've only just started?" He glared—at me in particular.

"It was always the plan to head back today anyway," I said, giving him a lopsided shrug.

"I told you before, that wasn't *my* plan," said Mason. "That's just what you and Cora cooked up between yourselves."

"Cooked up?" said Cora. "What's that supposed to mean?"

"We can't stay out here forever, Mase," I said, trying to be appeasing. "Apart from anything, our parents will have realized we're missing. My mum will have, anyway."

"I thought you told her you were staying over at mine?" said Mason.

"No, I did, but—"

"So there you go then. She won't start worrying at least until this evening. And none of the rest of our parents are going to panic exactly, are they?"

"How do you know?" said Cora.

Mason rolled his eyes as he turned toward her. "Because my dad doesn't give a shit where I am. Yours and Abi's probably won't even notice you're out of the house, and Luke's—"

"No," said Cora. "I meant, how did you know Fash told his mum he was staying at your place? He told *me* he said that. But at the time we didn't even know you were coming with us."

"He . . . told me yesterday. In the woods."

"When? I didn't hear."

"You were probably arguing with Abi," said Mason, waving a hand. "Jesus, Cora, what's the big deal?"

He turned back to me and raised his eyebrows. Like, *well?*

"I suppose we could keep searching for a *bit* longer," I said.

"What the hell, Fash?" said Cora. "You don't have to do everything Mason says, you know."

"So what's *your* hurry, Cora?" Mason said to her. "Don't you want to find your friend?" He emphasized the final word so that it sounded like it was wrapped in quotation marks.

"What? Of course I do! Why do you think I came out here in the first place?"

Mason smiled, snidely. "And that's the question, isn't it? Why are any of us here? And why is everyone so desperate to hurry home the second there's the slightest excuse?"

I saw Abi shift uncomfortably.

"In case you hadn't noticed, Mason," said Cora, "we're miles from home on the hottest day of the year with nothing to drink but pond water, and with no way of calling anyone for help. That's not an *excuse*. That's a frigging *reason*."

"And whose fault is that?" Mason answered. "The water, I mean. The phones."

Cora turned red. "I told you already! It wasn't *me!*"

Mason stared at her. "Maybe it was," he said, "maybe it wasn't. But it was clearly *someone*." He turned his stare on me.

Cora spoke again before I could. "What's your problem, Mason? If you've got something to say, just fucking say it."

"It's just curious, that's all. Don't you think? That we set out to try to find Sadie, and yet the second we close our eyes, something happens to force us back?"

He was looking at me again, and I swallowed. Because I hadn't thought about it like that. The phones, the water . . . I'd assumed that it was all a prank or something. I didn't imagine it was anything more serious than that.

"As for my *problem*," Mason went on, "my girlfriend is missing and nobody but me seems to want to find her. Plus, the second we get back home, the police are going to do what they're probably wishing they did last week: they're going to lock me in a prison cell and throw away the key."

Cora sniffed. "So that's what this is about for you. The Mason Payne Self-Preservation Society."

Mason whipped around to face her. "I don't give a *fuck* what happens to me! But if the police lock me up, they'll say they've *solved* it, and that'll be the end of it. They'll stop looking and they'll stop asking questions and then we'll never find out what happened to Sadie. *Never.*"

He was breathing heavily, and there was a bubble of spit at the corner of his mouth. It was hard to believe that just a few minutes ago I'd been getting annoyed at him for not taking things seriously.

"Easy, mate," I said. I reached out a hand and touched him on the shoulder. Tentatively, the way I would have tested something hot.

He flinched when I made contact, but after a second his shoulders dipped lower. His eyes met mine, then moved on.

"Luke," he said, turning. "You agree with me. Don't you? You agree we should keep looking?"

I looked at Luke—we all did—and suddenly I felt this rush of sympathy for him. It was everything, you know? Sadie, obviously, but also all the stuff that was waiting for him at home. Like Dylan. Like, how do you deal with something like that? Explaining things to your little brother when you're hurting, too, and you don't even understand what happened yourself? And then there was us. Luke was the one whose sister was missing, and yet every time there was a difficult decision to make, the rest of us turned to him.

"I've been thinking," said Luke. "About the phones and that? And the first thing is, I think we should stop blaming each other."

"*Thank you,*" said Cora.

"Because the thing is," Luke went on, "who's to say it *wasn't* someone else? Just because we think we're alone out here, doesn't mean we are."

Abi's eyes widened. I caught Cora glancing toward the tree line.

I narrowed my eyes. "That noise you heard," I said to Abi. "Yesterday, just before you came rushing over. Do you think . . . Do you think that could have been someone following us?"

Abi didn't even stop to think. She nodded.

Cora cleared her throat. "I heard something, too," she said. "I mean, I'm not sure if I *heard* it exactly, but I saw something. Maybe. In the night. Some*one*, rather. Watching us from the trees."

"What?" Abi said. "Are you *serious*? Why didn't you say something?"

"Because I thought I was dreaming. Or . . . that it was just one of you lot going for a pee. And anyway, nothing *happened*."

"Apart from our phones being stolen, you mean? And all of our water?"

For once Cora didn't have an answer.

Abi's eyes widened even further. "What if whoever's out there had something to do with what happened to Sadie? What if *that's* who's trying to force us back?"

"Oh, please," said Mason.

"*What?*" said Abi.

"First of all," Mason answered, "it probably *was* one of us that Cora saw. And second, even if there is someone following us—and

I'm not for one minute saying there is—but even if there is, it's probably just . . . Lara Sweeney or something. One of those dickheads from the bridge. And the water was them getting their revenge."

Cora folded her arms. "I thought you said it was one of us," she said. "I thought you said it was *me*."

"I'm not saying one thing or the other! What I'm saying is, either way, there's no need to panic!"

There was a silence. Abi wrapped her arms around her middle. Cora dumped her bag on the ground and frisked herself to find her packet of cigarettes. It took her three attempts to fire up her lighter.

"Look," I said, as Cora exhaled a cloud of smoke, "why don't we just take a vote?"

Mason scoffed.

"It's the fairest way," I said. "Surely? And I don't see how else we're going to decide."

Abi nodded. Cora rolled a shoulder.

"So," I said. "Let's start with who votes we go back. Raise your hand if you think we should call it a day."

Abi had her hand in the air almost before I'd finished speaking. Cora put her hand up, too, her cigarette between her fingers, and her arm hinging at the elbow.

We looked at Luke. Even then, even though we were supposed to be voting, it somehow still came down to him.

He focused on Mason. "For the record," he said, "I never really thought you had anything to do with it. With Sadie, I mean. With what they said."

Mason was clearly waiting for whatever came next.

"But the thing is," said Luke, "I can't stay out here. And it's not because of the water, or because of whoever might be out there. It's Dylan. He's hurting, man. A lot. I feel bad enough for leaving him as

it is. And you know my parents aren't going to be looking after him."
He kicked a stone. "Not the way he needs."

I don't think any of us were surprised. Luke hadn't wanted to
come with us in the first place. And when he mentioned Dylan, there
wasn't exactly much that we could say. Not even Mason.

I watched as the others gathered up their stuff. When they started
walking back the way we'd come, I lingered next to Mason in the
clearing. I waited until the others were out of earshot.

"It was always a long shot, Mase," I said, trying to sound consol-
ing. "And who knows, maybe the police have found something
while we've been gone. Something that puts you in the clear."

Mason turned on me then, as though I'd just accused him of killing Sadie myself.

"That was convenient for you, wasn't it? You didn't even have to
vote."

He made to walk off and I pulled him back. "Mase, wait. What
do you mean? I just . . ." Something in his expression made me let
go of his arm.

He sneered at me, and shook his head. "Don't even bother trying
to justify it. I know *exactly* what you did."

"LOOK AT THOSE leeches," said Nicky, as Fleet maneuvered the car through the entrance gates.

Fleet glanced out the driver's-side window. Most of the news vans were either down by the river or up in the woods, the more respectable outlets having—at least on the face of it—honored police requests to show some consideration to the local community, and in particular to stay away from Sadie's school. But there were always going to be a few hacks who pushed the boundaries. Literally, in this case—the school grounds were fenced off from the road, and three or four men were leaning against the wire mesh, cameras in one hand and cigarettes or vape sticks in the other. They'd noticed Fleet's Insignia approaching the school gates, and one or two were tracking it through their telephoto lenses.

"At least they're getting wet," said Fleet, taking in the rain. He was tempted to stop the car and shoo the photographers away, but he knew they'd only flock back again. Less like leeches then; more like pigeons. Plus they were wasting their time, anyway. No editor in their right mind would print a picture from a pap who'd door-stepped a school—would they?

There was a visitor's space free in an awkward corner, and once they were parked Fleet led the way inside the building. There'd been a few modernizations to the school over recent years, but the general layout didn't appear to have changed since Fleet had been a pupil here himself. Harbor Park remained the only major secondary school in town. It wasn't large by city standards, but if you lived within the parish, and unless your parents were rich enough to send you to one of the private schools in the surrounding countryside, this is where you were destined to serve your adolescence. Purely out of curiosity, Fleet had checked the school's Ofsted rating, and hadn't been surprised to discover that, according to the government's inspectors, Harbor Park "required improvement." It was tired, in other words, with the majority of investment flowing elsewhere—a fitting symbol of the town itself.

The head teacher met them in the entrance hall. Ms. Andrews was a thin woman, tall and stooping. She had the look of a long-distance runner, Fleet thought, or perhaps of someone whose primary form of exercise was worrying. In many ways she reminded Fleet of Superintendent Burton, though the comparison did the head teacher a disservice. Rather than being a politician, Ms. Andrews struck Fleet as a genuine crusader, albeit a battle-weary one, only just about clinging to the diminishing possibility that she might one day make a difference.

"Detective Inspector," the head teacher offered by way of greeting. She nodded to Nicky as she took Fleet's hand. They'd all met before, shortly after Sadie had gone missing, but this was the first time Fleet and Ms. Andrews had spoken since events in the woods, and the first time since the school had been back in session. The new term had begun two days before. Sadie would have been entering the sixth form, beginning her A levels—taking her first steps toward a boundless future.

"I'm sorry we're not meeting again under better circumstances, Ms. Andrews," Fleet said, "but thank you for arranging this at short notice. Are they ready for us?"

"They are," the head teacher confirmed. "They're in my office. And they've requested I sit in, if you don't object?"

"Not at all," said Fleet, with a glance at Nicky.

Ms. Andrews led them along the corridor. The smell of the place was disconcertingly familiar to Fleet, as though whatever had been used to clean the floors over the years had seeped into the parquet, and the same food as had been served twenty years ago would shortly be on offer for the pupils' lunch. The pupils themselves were currently between lessons, and they eyed Fleet and Nicky warily as the head teacher escorted them through the building, but parted as Ms. Andrews forged a path. The children wore a version of the uniform Fleet had once worn himself, the gray jumpers and striped ties complemented now by a deep maroon blazer. The kids looked smarter than they had in Fleet's day, there was no denying it. He tried to decide if they also appeared older, shrewder—or whether he was simply projecting what he'd come to believe after the time he'd spent in the company of Sadie's friends.

"After you," said Ms. Andrews as they reached the door to her office. She held it open, and gestured Fleet and Nicky inside.

Lara Sweeney was sitting demurely in a plastic chair, one of four that had been positioned on the visitors' side of the head teacher's desk. Beside her sat a man who couldn't have been anything but the teenager's father. From Lara's perspective, the resemblance was unfortunate: they had the same beady eyes—too small and close together for the shape of their faces—as well as the same upturned nose. The man's hair was darker than Lara's, but only because the teenager's had obviously been bleached.

"Detective Inspector Fleet?" said Ms. Andrews, making the introductions. "This is Lara. And this is her father, Trevor Sweeney."

The man hadn't risen when Fleet and Nicky had walked in. And when Fleet offered out his hand, he could tell Sweeney gave half a moment's thought to not shaking it.

"It's a pleasure to meet you, Mr. Sweeney," Fleet said, endeavoring not to show his distaste as Sweeney took his hand with just his fingers. "You too, Lara. This is my colleague, Detective Sergeant Collins. Nicky, in fact. And you can call me Rob."

The head teacher signaled Fleet and Nicky into the two empty chairs, and then quietly took her own on the window side of the desk. Beyond the fence that enclosed the playground, it was just possible from where Fleet was sitting to see the edge of the woods—and, snaking its way toward the harbor, the depthless gray of the river.

"What's this about?" said Sweeney, getting straight to the point. "What do you want with my little girl?"

Fleet couldn't help but be distracted for a moment by his surroundings. The last time he'd been in this office, he would have been fifteen years old. Him and Thomas Murphy, his best mate at the time, who'd died five years later from a heroin overdose. So Fleet had heard, anyway. Fleet himself had been long gone by then. But him and Tom, standing with downcast eyes before the headmaster's desk, nodding along to Mr. Sternway's lecture about the dangers of failing to adhere to their teacher's instructions when it came to mixing chemicals in the science lab, and trying—and failing—not to laugh. Sternway himself had retired the same year Fleet had left town, and though Fleet had never heard tell of the reason why, he'd often wondered if there hadn't been a connection. Not with Fleet's leaving per se, but with the *reason* he left. Perhaps Sternway blamed himself as much as Fleet did. Or perhaps he'd had as much as he could take. Of children. Of watching their innocence die.

"It's just routine, Mr. Sweeney," said Fleet in response to the man's question. "We're hoping your daughter can help us with a few queries, that's all."

"Is this to do with Sadie?" said Lara. Her eyebrows were arrowed and her forehead was creased. She reached and took her father's hand. "It's so awful, what's happened to her. Just . . . so awful."

"For the moment, all we know about Sadie is that she's missing," Fleet replied. "Nothing more than that."

"No, I know, but . . . it's upsetting. That's all I meant." Lara sniffed and lowered her head, and her father locked his eyes on Fleet's.

Fleet turned to Nicky. They'd agreed beforehand that it might seem less confrontational if their questions came from her, particularly as they'd learned from the head teacher that the girl's father would be present.

"Lara?" said Nicky. "I understand this is difficult for you."

The girl nodded, eyes downcast.

"Were you and Sadie close, would you say?" Nicky asked her.

Lara raised her head then. She looked at Nicky, and clearly sensed the insinuation in the DS's question.

"I knew her, obviously," Lara answered. "*Everybody* knew Sadie." She paused for a moment, then added, "She was like that, you see."

"Like that?"

"Always keen to be the center of attention," said Lara. She smiled, as though fondly.

Nicky showed half a smile back. "I see." The DS had her notebook open on her lap, and she scribbled something on the page.

Lara waited. Her tie was neatly knotted and her blazer buttoned, with an exactness Fleet hadn't spotted among any of the pupils out in the corridor. She'd dressed for the occasion, clearly.

"From what we understand," said the DS, "you were one of the last people to see Sadie's friends before they went looking for her in the woods. Is that right?"

Lara let out the lightest of exhalations, and turned toward her father.

"I'm sorry, Lara," Nicky said. "Was there something you wanted to say?"

Lara's father patted his daughter's hand. "It's OK, princess. You're free to say whatever you want to. They can't punish you for speaking your mind."

"It's funny, that's all," said Lara. "The idea that Sadie's friends *went looking* for her."

"You don't think that's what they were doing?"

"You'll have to ask them," Lara answered. "All I'm saying is, if they were out there looking for Sadie, that suggests they didn't already know where she was."

Nicky gazed back at her impassively. "Did they say anything that would make you think that? That they already knew where Sadie was?"

"They didn't tell me where she was buried, if that's what you're asking," said Lara, and Fleet noticed the head teacher shift uncomfortably behind her desk. "But sometimes it's not what people say, is it? It's how they behave."

Nicky nodded. "Indeed," she said, holding Lara in her gaze a fraction longer than was necessary. She looked at her notebook. "And how were they behaving, would you say? Did they seem . . . nervous? Upset? Agitated?"

"Actually," said Lara, with the assurance of a liar finally drawing on fact, "they were laughing. I remember being quite shocked."

Lara's father gave a disapproving tut.

"And once you'd got over your . . . shock," said Nicky, "did you notice in which direction they headed?"

"They ran off. In a hurry. I didn't notice in which direction."

"So you didn't follow them?" said Nicky, and Fleet watched Lara closely.

"Follow them? Why would I follow them?"

"From what we've gathered you were pretty upset. In the wake of an altercation that had allegedly taken place."

Lara's mask slipped slightly. "There was no *allegedly* about it," she said, bridling. "Mason Payne practically broke Ian's nose. At the very least you should arrest him for *that*."

"Rest assured that any allegation of assault will be fully investigated. But in the meantime," Nicky went on, "and just for clarity, you're maintaining you didn't pursue Sadie's friends into the woods?"

"Now wait just a minute," said Sweeney, leaning forward. "What exactly are you insinuating? Are you trying to suggest my daughter had anything to do with what happened out *there*?" He gestured loosely at the window, toward the trees on the distant horizon. "From what I gather, a boy was *killed*."

"That's right, Mr. Sweeney," Nicky replied. "A boy was killed. And as much as this investigation is focused on Sadie, we're also looking to establish exactly how that happened. As it stands, your daughter is the closest thing we have to an independent witness."

Sweeney smiled and shook his head. "You see?" he said to the head teacher. "This is exactly why I wanted you in here. Talk about independent witnesses . . ." He shook his head again. "Rest assured, officers, that if you start putting words in my daughter's mouth, Miss Andrews will be there at your tribunal to back me up."

Fleet saw the head teacher stiffen slightly, whether at Sweeney's presumption or his failure to use her preferred title, Fleet couldn't have said.

"Come now, Mr. Sweeney," said Ms. Andrews. "I'm sure that's not the police officers' intention. Please try to remember that someone else's daughter is missing. This is about the safety of our children, nothing more."

"I think we all know what this is about," Sweeney said, glaring at Fleet. "*He* screws up. He's got a bee in his bonnet about something that happened almost twenty years ago, and when he takes it out on a bunch of kids, one of them ends up dead. And now he's looking to cover his arse by blaming *my* kid. Excuse my French, princess," Sweeney added as an aside, once again patting his daughter's hand.

There was tension around Lara's lips, as though she were suppressing a smile.

"Please," Fleet said, and he focused on Lara. "Answer the question my colleague asked you. Did you follow Sadie's friends into the woods?"

Lara didn't even blink. "No," she said, turning to Nicky. "I didn't follow them. Into the woods or anywhere else."

Nicky turned the pages in her notepad. She spun it so that Lara could read from it. *SweeneyTodd2002* and *Princess_69* were written and underlined on an otherwise empty page. "Do you recognize either of these Instagram handles, Lara?"

Lara moved only her eyes. "Nope," she said. "Should I?"

"They don't belong to you?" Nicky asked her.

"If they did I probably would have recognized them," said Lara. She exhaled as though suddenly bored, and examined one of her fingernails.

Nicky kept her eyes locked on Lara. "Do you know who does own them?"

"My daughter just said she doesn't recognize them, Detective Sergeant. If she's never seen them before, how is she supposed to know who owns them?"

Nicky ignored the interjection. "Lara? Please answer the question."

"No, I don't know who owns them," said Lara. "Why? What does it matter?"

"It matters because we believe that whoever owns these accounts was responsible for starting the rumors that were circulating about Sadie before she went missing. You are aware of those rumors, Lara?"

Lara's expression, when she looked at Nicky, was a challenge. "You mean the rumors that she was sleeping around? That rather than the goody two-shoes everyone thought she was, she was actually just a common slut?"

"Lara!" exclaimed Ms. Andrews.

Lara looked at the head teacher evenly. "The detective sergeant asked me if I was aware of the rumors, Ms. Andrews. I was only checking to see which rumors she meant."

"Yes, Lara," said Nicky. "Those rumors. You're clearly aware of them. And as I say, they seemed to have originated from these accounts."

Lara was looking at Nicky now with open contempt. "Seriously?" she said. "Sweeney Todd? Do you really think I'd be stupid enough to set up an account that could so easily be linked back to me?"

It was a reasonable point, and obviously one Fleet had considered himself. On the other hand, Lara seemed exactly the type of person who would want *everyone* to know what she was saying, and the Instagram handles might well have been a way of conveying her identity while at the same time shielding her from potential repercussions.

Nicky leaned forward in her chair. "Have you heard of the term 'defamation,' Lara? Are you aware that it is a civil offense to spread lies about a person's character that end up doing them harm?"

"Now hold on!" Lara's father interrupted. "Lara just said she had nothing to do with those accounts. Talk about defamation!"

"And anyway," said Lara, unperturbed, "it isn't an offense if it's true." She looked at Fleet. "That's right, isn't it, Rob?"

Nicky frowned. "Are you saying you know why the rumors started?"

Lara rolled her eyes as she turned her head. "What I'm saying is, *someone* clearly knows."

"Who?"

"Well, from what you're saying, whoever owns those accounts."

For the first time since the conversation had begun, Nicky showed her impatience. "So you don't know what the rumors were based on? And you had nothing to do with spreading any stories about Sadie? Like this one, the post that started it all from what we can gather . . ." Nicky flipped a page in her notebook and read aloud. *"FACT: Sadie Saunders spreads her legs for strangers. Witnessed with my own eyes. #SadieSlut #PoorMason. And this . . ."* Nicky pulled out her phone and showed Lara the photo that was on the screen: a picture taken in the dark of someone who may or may not have been Sadie, with her eyes closed and her mouth open, and a blob that might have been the back of somebody's head obscuring her shoulder. The second figure in particular was so blurred it might have been anyone, but the nature of the act they were supposedly engaged in was clear enough. It was an image that had spawned a dozen memes.

"I might have shared a few posts," Lara said. "But it's like I said, it's not an offense if it's true."

"But how can you make that judgment?" Nicky pressed. "If you didn't start the rumors, and you don't know what they were based on, how do you know they weren't lies?"

"Because I saw her face."

Nicky blinked. "I beg your pardon?"

"I saw her face," Lara repeated. "Sadie's. When I showed her."

"When you showed her?"

Lara lifted a shoulder, then let it fall. "I just felt so bad for her, you know? When I saw the posts for the first time. And from the way Sadie was strutting around, acting the way she always did, it was obvious that she didn't know what was going on. She didn't seem to realize that everyone else was laughing behind her back. So I did what I figured was the decent thing."

"You showed her," said Nicky, and Lara nodded.

"The posts, the memes, the replies. We were in the shopping center, which is where everyone had been hanging out in the holidays. It was pretty busy, so unfortunately quite a few people saw. But I called out to her and suggested she come over, and when she did I showed her on my phone."

Nicky stole a glance at Fleet. Lara noticed, and switched her attention to him.

"And that's how I know, you see," she said. "I could tell from her face. Because it wasn't anger I saw in her expression, or outrage, or anything like that." Lara folded her arms, and came close to showing a smile. "What I saw, when I looked at her, was guilt."

MASON

FIRST OFF, I want to make clear, I had nothing to do with what we found.

You can ask any of them. They'll tell you. It wasn't even me who was leading the way, meaning I *couldn't* have had anything to do with it.

Seriously. Ask them whether I was out in front. And then come back and tell me what they said.

Whatever, man. Ask them or don't. It's your investigation. But me personally? If I need to I can sit here all day.

ABI

I DON'T KNOW. I guess . . . Luke maybe? Because he was the one with Dylan's compass. Unless that was later, after we got lost. Not lost exactly, but . . . turned around.

Maybe it was Cora who was out in front. It could have been Cora.

Why? What does it matter?

Although I keep wondering what would have happened if we'd just kept walking. Or what *wouldn't* have. You know? If I hadn't seen it. Or if I'd just kept my big mouth shut. Or even if it hadn't started raining. Which sounds stupid, probably, but that was important, too. Particularly to what happened after.

Because that's the thing. We almost made it out. All of us, I mean.

Almost.

But in the end, Mason got his way.

CORA

MASON? HE WAS at the back, obviously. Sulking, fuming, whatever. Basically acting like a dick. Luke was next, still swinging that branch he'd picked up the day before. And then, ahead of Luke, it was—

You know what? I've just figured out why you're asking.

Jesus.

You think Mason put it there, don't you?

That night, while the rest of us were sleeping. That he had it with him all along and he used it to keep us out there in the woods. But you're wondering how we would have found it if Mason wasn't leading the way. Except that's bullshit because I can tell you exactly who was out in front. I remember because they started off behind me and then pushed past me in a hurry, like they were on a mission or something.

Fash. I'm talking about Fash. And if it was Fash leading the way, then that basically proves your theory.

What do you mean, you don't understand? Fash hasn't told you yet? About him and Mason?

Seriously? He's still covering for him? Even after everything that's happened?

No fucking way. I'm not getting involved in that shit. If you want to know, then you're going to have to ask him yourself.

FASH

I AM BEING honest! I have been! There's nothing I'm not telling you, I swear to God, I—

Mason? What about Mason? Did he say something? I thought . . . I mean, he told me that it didn't . . .

Nothing. Nothing.

Look, I . . . I need to think. OK? Just give me some time to think.

No, I know, but . . .

Where's my mum? I'd like to talk to my mum.

Please. Please.

I just want my mum.

MASON

WELL? WHAT DID they say?

See? I told you. I was nowhere near when they found it. They all said that, right? Every one of them?

So there you go then. Except . . . why are you looking at me like that? Don't tell me you still don't believe me?

Jesus H. Christ.

You don't, do you? You still think I'm lying.

Fash? I'm not following you. So what if Fash was out in front when they found it? How does that prove anything, other than exactly what I've been trying to—

Oh.

Oh, I get it.

Ha.

I see now.

He blabbed, didn't he?

No, wait. I bet it was Cora. Cora and her mouth. Which I swear is just fucking typical. She knows it's completely irrelevant, that it has nothing to do with what happened, but even so she can't let it go.

So what did she say exactly? Just so I know what I'm being accused of. I mean, I have that right, don't I?

Wait, what? No, that's . . . You *don't* know, do you? You're just . . . you're judging me and you don't know the full story. I mean, do you even know what it is we *found*?

ABI

MY PHONE.

That's what we found.

Except . . . except it wasn't. What I mean is . . . or rather, what I thought was . . .

Right. Right.

From the beginning.

So we left the clearing. And the idea was we go home. Because of the water situation and also because it was a stupid idea in the first place. The search party, I mean. The only thing we'd managed to achieve was to argue, and basically to give ourselves the creeps. In fact, it was worse than that, because it was obvious even then that something wasn't right. It's like, I *know* I heard something out in the woods that time, and that it wasn't some stupid bear. Or a wolf for that matter. And *somebody* must have taken our phones, right? And drunk all our water?

But anyway, we were walking along, and nobody was really talking. We were going single file, Fash up in front, then—

Fash. That's who was leading. I remember now, because I remember the look on his face when he passed me. What I figured was, he must have had an argument with Mason back in the clearing.

After Fash, it was Cora, then me, then . . . Luke, I think? Mason was definitely at the rear.

We were following the stream, which cut diagonally back toward the river. If I'd had my phone I could have seen how far we'd come the day before, but I guessed that, because we'd been weaving back and forth, we couldn't have been more than five miles from the footbridge. The stream met the river farther north, but Fash reckoned it would only take us half as long to get there, just because the way was clearer, and we wouldn't need to hack through the trees.

Personally, I didn't really care which route we took. I just wanted to get home. The sound of the stream was like mental torture, and something weird was going on with the weather. It was still hot, but it had got darker, as though we'd gone the footbridge way after all, right through the middle of the forest. Which was strange, because last time I'd noticed, we'd been walking in sunlight. But when I looked up I saw the sky had turned white. Not white, like, fluffy-cloud white. White like . . . like frosted glass. And even though I was sweating, for some reason it made me shiver.

I felt bad for Sadie, though. Because basically what we were doing was giving up, and I didn't want to leave her all alone. Which is what it felt like we were doing. So I kept looking, is my point. The others didn't, obviously, otherwise they would have spotted it first.

"You guys," I called. "Wait up!"

Cora was just in front of me, and she turned.

"Abi?" said Fash, from up ahead. I'd started down the bank toward the stream. It was dry, but it was still slippery, and I had to grab at the tree roots to stop myself falling in. "Seriously, Abi," said

Fash. "We'll be out in three or four hours. We can get a bottle of water or something then. If you drink the stream water you'll get ill. Didn't you hear what Luke said before?"

I didn't answer because I was trying to concentrate. And I didn't want to say anything until I was sure.

Mason had caught up by then, and I heard his voice from up on the path. "What's she doing?" he said.

"Going for a swim, it looks like," said Cora. And there was the sound of her sparking up a cigarette.

"Abi . . ." called Luke, like a warning, but when I got down level with the water, I surprised them all by hopping to the other side.

"Look!" I said. "There! Do you see?"

There was a pause while the others looked where I was pointing.

"Is that . . ." said Fash.

"It's my phone!" I said. "I'm sure it is."

I recognized it from the cover, you see. It was lying there, right beside the stream, right on the edge of the water, like whoever had taken it had dropped it without knowing, and it had slid from the path down the bank. And the cover was bright pink, so it stood out like . . . like a bright pink thing lying in a patch of mud, I guess.

There were some rocks on the path side of the stream, which is why I'd jumped to the other side, and I had to lean across the water to pick it up. I remember I was grinning . . . right up until the point I felt it in my hand.

"No, wait, this is just . . . shit," I said, because I'd realized the phone wasn't mine after all. It was just some cheap-arse Nokia. A smartphone, but the sort I wouldn't be seen dead with.

"What's the problem?" said Fash, who was standing nearest. He'd started down the bank himself, and when he got close to the rocks, he held out a hand to help me back to the other side.

"It's a phone," I told him, "but it isn't mine." I held it up for him to see. When I did, I realized the case was different, too. It was the same color as mine, but there was also a pattern on it, like little daisies.

"So whose is it?" said Fash. "Is it Cora's?"

But Cora had a Samsung, and obviously she would never have put it in a pink cover. And I knew for a fact it didn't belong to any of the boys.

"I don't know, I . . ." It had taken me a second to work out where the HOME button was, but when I pressed it, the screen lit up. And I swear to God, when I saw what was on it, I almost dropped the phone in the water.

"Abi?" said Fash, when he saw my face. "What's wrong?"

For a moment I didn't answer. But when he said my name again, I turned the phone toward him.

There was a photograph, you see. On the lock screen. You've probably got one on yours. Like, of your family or something. Your kids. Me, I've got a picture I took at the start of the summer, of the six of us sitting on the beach, that time we went down to the dunes. I used a selfie stick, but even so, we're all crushed together. I'm on one side next to Cora, and the boys are in a bundle on the other. Sadie's in the middle, laughing her head off. I love that photo because it reminds me of Sadie when she was happy.

And that's what gave me such a shock. Because the thing was, on the phone—on this Nokia I'd found in the middle of the forest, lying in the mud by the stream—the lock screen was the very same photo.

What I saw when I turned it on was a picture of *us*.

CORA

NOBODY SAID ANYTHING for a good half a minute. After the two of them had climbed back up the bank, I mean, and Abi had showed us the phone. She just held it in her palm in the middle of the circle, sort of balanced, like she didn't really want to touch it. The way she would have held something dead.

"It was seriously just right there?" I asked. "Just lying there down by the stream?"

"*Yes*, it was just right there," Abi answered, as though for the hundredth time, even though it was the first question anyone had asked her. "You heard me call out when I spotted it. You saw me go over and pick it up."

"I know, I . . . I'm not suggesting anything. I'm trying to work out how it might have got there, that's all. Whose it . . . whose it could be."

Abi gave a shiver. "Here," she said. "Somebody else take it. *Please.*"

I lifted it from her hand, and she turned away.

I looked at the photo again, remembering the moment it had been taken. It was right after we'd got down to the beach. The sun was still up, and Mason had just opened the first bottle of wine.

"Can I see?" said Luke. I hadn't noticed him move behind my shoulder.

I nodded and silently passed it to him. When he held the screen up in front of him, his face went the color of bone.

"It's Sadie's," said Mason. "It's got to be."

"*What?*" I said.

"It has to be hers," Mason insisted. "It's nobody else's, right? And she was the only other person who had a copy of that photo."

Which wasn't necessarily true. I mean, Abi had sent the picture to all of us right after she'd taken it, but that didn't mean none of us had forwarded it on. And obviously Abi had posted it on Instagram. She puts her *cornflakes* on Instagram, for Christ's sake.

Plus, the other thing was, Sadie had an iPhone like Abi's, and you'd already found it down by the river. Right? With her wallet and her house keys? So, really, we couldn't be sure *whose* it was.

"Hold on," said Fash, voicing what I'd been thinking. "We shouldn't go jumping to conclusions."

Luke had started tapping at the phone screen. The rest of us watched him to see what he was doing. All of a sudden his legs went from under him, and he dropped arse-first onto the ground.

"Luke?" said Fash. "What's the matter?"

Luke was just staring at the phone, one hand covering his mouth.

I tried to see what he was looking at, but Mason took the phone from Luke's hand. His jaw tightened, and he turned the screen toward us. At first I couldn't work out what the problem was. There was just a bunch of apps showing on the home screen, and the same photo we'd already seen in the background.

And then I realized. He'd unlocked it. Luke had. Meaning he must have entered the code.

"Zero-eight-zero-eight," said Luke, which was all he needed to say. It was Dylan's birthday, the code Sadie used for everything. Her phone, her bank card, anything that needed a PIN.

Mason was looking at the screen. After a moment or two tapping and swiping, his eyebrows joined at the middle.

"There's nothing on it," he said. "No photos, no contacts, no messages. Nothing."

"Are you sure?" said Abi, angling herself to try to see.

"Literally," said Mason, "there's nothing. Just the apps that would have come loaded on the phone."

"So what does that mean?" Abi asked, looking to me now.

Mason turned the phone over in his hand, and then he was the one to go white. "What's that?" he said, pointing.

We all looked closer. I swallowed.

"That's just . . . It's mud," said Fash. "Isn't it?" There was a stain on the corner of the cover, and he reached out with his finger, as though he meant to wipe it away.

I grabbed his arm. "Don't," I said. "Don't touch it."

Fash looked at me. He didn't say anything. He let his arm fall away.

"Oh God," said Abi. "That's not . . . Please don't tell me that's . . ."

"We don't know what it is," I said, because I swear to God she was practically hyperventilating.

"It is, though, isn't it?" said Abi. "It's blood. It's Sadie's blood." She looked like she was about to cry.

"We don't know what it is!" I said again. "Just like we can't be certain the phone is even hers!"

"Oh, for fuck's sake!" said Mason. "Who else apart from one of us would have that photo on their lock screen? And it's Sadie's passcode! That's pretty fucking conclusive if you ask me."

Luke was still sitting on the ground, his thumbs tucked under his chin and his fingers steepled across his mouth. I sat down next to him, and wrapped my arm around his shoulders.

"Mase," I said, quietly. Just like a warning, you know? And I tipped my head slightly in Luke's direction.

But Mason either didn't hear, or he wasn't in the mood to listen. "I told you," he said. "I fucking told you. And you lot all wanted to go back! You were *dying* to go back."

"Mason!" I said again, practically shouting this time. "Shut *up*, will you! Just stop! Just for a minute!"

Luke had started muttering to himself, saying something I couldn't make out.

Mason was shaking his head, ignoring me the way he had before. "Now we *have* to stay out here," he said. "Nobody's going home now."

"Mase . . ." said Fash. "Let's just . . . let's think about this for a second. Let's try to work out what it means."

Mason spun. "It *means* Sadie was out here. That's what it means. It means she's probably *still* out here."

"But why would Sadie have a second phone?" I said, as much to myself as anyone. "It doesn't make any sense."

Mason opened his mouth to answer, but it was obvious he didn't know what to say. "I don't know," he said eventually. "I don't fucking know, OK? But that's not the point. You know as well as I do, that's not the point."

Luke got to his feet. "I need to go home," he said, and I realized that's what he'd been muttering before. "I need to get back."

"What?" said Mason, as Luke swung his rucksack over his shoulder. "No, Luke, wait. We can't go back. Not now. You see that, don't you?"

Luke shook his head. "Dylan," he said. "Dylan needs me. I need to get back. I'm sorry, Mase, but I do."

Mason took hold of his arm. "Luke, wait. Listen. Maybe Dylan needs you, but what if your sister needs you more? What if she's out here and she's hurt? Just like we said before?"

Luke opened his mouth again, but this time nothing came out.

"Guys?" said Fash. "Don't you think . . . I mean, if it is Sadie's phone, shouldn't we . . . I don't know. Tell the police or something? Especially if that's . . ." He gestured to the phone in Mason's hand. "If what's on it isn't mud."

"The police?" said Mason, incredulous. "What are the police going to do?"

"They'll run, like, tests or something," said Abi. "Won't they? They'll be able to find out for sure."

"Find what out?" Mason scoffed. "It's Sadie's phone. We *know* that. All that forensic shit takes days, and anyway, the cops have already made up their minds. They think Sadie's dead, and they think I killed her. If we turn up with this," he said, waggling the phone, "and they discover I was there when we found it, it would be like handing them a written confession. And I know none of you lot gives two shits about what happens to me, and it's not like I give much of a fuck anymore either. But personally, I'm not ready to give up on Sadie. Not yet."

"Come on, Mase," I said. "You know that's not true. You know we care. And you know none of us are giving up on Sadie either."

"So prove it," said Mason.

I glanced around at the others, and it was obvious no one knew what to say. Abi was looking like she was about to be sick. Fash was staring into space. And Luke . . . Luke looked about as lost as I'd ever seen him. I mean, I could only imagine what he was going through. What he was imagining the phone might mean.

And not just the phone.

The blood.

"So what are you suggesting we should do?" I asked Mason. "I mean, if we *did* stay out here."

"We search the area, obviously," he answered. "And we follow the stream deeper inland."

"Inland?" said Fash. "But we just came from that way."

"We did," said Mason. "But was anyone actually looking? Or thinking about anything other than a drink of water since we left the clearing? You and Cora walked past that phone without even batting an eyelid."

I felt myself flush. Fash looked the way he would have had his mum just caught him searching for porn on his computer.

"And anyway," Mason went on, "there's no point carrying on the way we were going. The police already came this far, before they decided to concentrate on the river." He shook his head. "I *knew* they were looking in the wrong place."

"And the water situation?" I said, when no one else spoke. "If we stay out here—if we do as you say—what exactly are we supposed to drink?" I looked at the sky, which at some point had turned from white to gray. "I mean, sun or no sun, it's got to be the hottest day of the year. And the air's so thick I can barely breathe."

Abi nodded vigorously. "Right," she said, and she held her throat. "I'm not kidding, guys. I'm seriously about to die here."

But I swear, it was as though Mason had an answer prepared for that, too. Or someone did, anyway. Because right then, right on cue, that's when it started to rain.

THIS TIME FLEET didn't bother with the satnav. The longer he spent in this place, the more the lie of the land came back to him. And not just that: other memories had come bubbling back, too. Memories of growing up here, of school—of a prevailing boredom, and the stupidity he and his friends had resorted to in order to keep themselves entertained. Drink, drugs, fucking, fighting. He looked back on the person he had been and shuddered at the thought of who he might have become. If he hadn't left. If his sister hadn't died.

Jeannie.

His beautiful, broken little sister. Who had probably saved Fleet's life, just as he had failed to save hers.

He rolled the Insignia to a halt in the same spot he'd parked the last time he'd been out here, past the news vans and just short of the cluster of police vehicles. Nicky was in the passenger seat beside him, a finger to one ear and her mobile to the other, straining to hear the voice at the other end of the line. Fleet had been lost in his thoughts, hypnotized by the sound of the rain and the steady sweep of the wiper blades, and he tuned back in to what was being said.

"Sorry, Liv, can you repeat that? I lost you when we left the main road. Liv? Are you—"

Nicky pulled the handset from her ear and frowned at the screen. Fleet could hear the beeps signaling a disconnect sounding faintly from the earpiece.

"Who's Liv?" he said.

"Olivia. PC Brightman. She's the one who was following up on the phone the kids say they found in the woods. The one they decided must have been Sadie's."

"And? Any joy?"

"We've got confirmation that the emergency call Cora made at the start of all of this came from a number that was registered to a pay-as-you-go. All the search party kids had contracts, so we know it almost certainly wasn't one of theirs. And given that their phones all apparently went missing . . ."

"But is there anything definitively linking it to Sadie?"

"Well, for starters, the number was assigned three days before she disappeared."

Fleet felt a tightening in his stomach, a sense of something clicking into place.

"And we found the shop the pay-as-you-go was bought from," Nicky went on. "The bad news is that the CCTV footage has already been deleted. Plus, the phone was paid for in cash, so there's no record there either. But Liv has been down there talking to the employees. Apparently the kid who sold the phone near shat himself when Liv showed him Sadie's picture. He'd seen her on the news, obviously, and he was terrified he was going to end up in handcuffs."

"For what exactly?" said Fleet.

"Obstruction of justice, I suppose. Failing to respond to our requests for information. Although Liv said the kid also stank of weed. Hence the memory loss, perhaps."

"So he ID'd her? He confirmed he sold the phone to Sadie?"

"He gave a tentative ID. He said it *might* have been Sadie who bought the phone. That was as far as he was prepared to go. But if it was her, he said, she didn't look anything like she does in the picture we've been circulating to the press."

"Meaning she disguised herself?"

"Possibly," agreed Nicky. "Or possibly he was just trying to cover his back."

Fleet considered for a moment. He reached to open the car door. "Either way," he said, "and given what Sadie's friends have told us, we need to work on the basis the phone was hers. I assume it was bagged with everything else the kids had on them when we caught up with them?"

"It was. I've checked in with Forensics, and they're bumping it to the top of the queue. It looks like the phone got wet in the rain, so there was no obvious sign of the blood Cora mentioned, and the fingerprint situation is a mess. But if there's something there, they'll find it."

Fleet nodded his approval and unfolded himself into the weather. He'd come prepared this time. As well as a waterproof jacket, he was wearing a pair of boots he'd bought from one of the fishing supply stores near the harbor, and they sank into the ground the moment he took a step from the gravel onto the grass.

He strode heavily toward the woods, as Nicky checked her mobile again at his side.

"Nothing," she said. "Not even a single bar. It's a miracle those kids got reception out here at all."

They passed several police officers returning from the woods, and Fleet mirrored their salutes.

"You know," said Nicky, "that might actually make sense. A disguise, I mean, even if it was just sunglasses and a ponytail. If Sadie bought the phone, but didn't want to be recognized. And the money. The fact she'd stopped paying her wages into her account. It means she would have had cash—money to spend that couldn't be traced. Plus, there's the fact she bought a second phone in the first place . . ."

"You think she ran away after all," said Fleet, who'd been mulling over the same thoughts himself.

"Maybe she was *planning* to," Nicky replied. "I mean, everyone's been saying it would have been totally out of character, right? That Sadie was prepping for her A levels after getting straight nines on her GCSEs, had already drawn up a short list of universities. But those memes, the stuff online . . . maybe they bothered her more than people realized."

"Because . . ." Fleet prompted.

"Because . . ." Nicky frowned. She shook her head. And then she stopped walking. "Because the rumors that she was sleeping around were true. Just like Lara said."

Fleet stopped walking himself. He raised his eyebrows, then turned and continued on.

"So is that the theory now?" said Nicky, her voice betraying her excitement. "That Sadie ran away? Does that mean . . . Do you think she might actually be alive? Except . . ." She slowed again. "How does that tally with us finding her bag? And her coat, more importantly. The blood . . ."

It was the very question Fleet had been wrestling with, and he didn't like any of the answers he'd come up with. The only one that made sense was barely an answer at all, just the same meaningless phrase that had been going around and around in his head. *It sounds like there's more than one thing going on . . .*

They entered the forest, and this time they ran into a group of at least a dozen officers heading back toward the Land Rovers. Instead of saluting this time, Fleet frowned. "Shit," he muttered.

And then, with a glance at Nicky, he picked up the pace.

Superintendent Burton was standing under a canopy that had been erected in the vicinity of the old farm buildings. Fleet noted the place in the dilapidated barn he recalled first seeing Sadie's friends— looking like partied-out festivalgoers, he remembered thinking. A group of trauma survivors might have been a better description— yet Fleet wondered now what each of them had been contemplating behind their hollowed-out eyes. How they'd managed to get themselves into such a mess? Or how they might get themselves out of it?

"Sir," said Fleet, as he approached. Nicky dropped back a pace, but lingered just behind Fleet's shoulder.

"Ah," said Burton, turning. "Detective Inspector. I understand you wanted to speak with me. It must have been important for you to have driven out all this way."

Detective Inspector, Fleet noted, *not Rob.* "I believe it is, sir."

Fleet had tried several times to contact the superintendent over the phone, only to be told each time that he was unavailable. When he'd finally learned where Burton was, he'd decided to corner the superintendent in person. Yet now that he had the man's attention, Fleet couldn't help but be distracted by the activity around him. All about there were signs of precisely what he'd feared was happening when he'd seen the uniformed officers trooping from the woods. Here, as by the river, the search was being wound up.

"Sir, if I may, I was hoping to convince you—"

"Superintendent? Superintendent Burton? Harry Boxall from the *Sun.* Any chance of a quick word?"

Fleet turned to see a man in a shabby raincoat blundering across the clearing. There was a photographer behind him who was much better prepared for the weather, from the hood on his mountain-grade jacket right down to the rain cover on his camera.

"How the hell did they get through the cordon?" Fleet muttered. Then, raising his voice, he started to wave the two men back. "For Christ's sake, Boxall. You know better than to—"

Burton laid a hand on Fleet's shoulder, and indicated to a uniform who'd intercepted the men to allow them to approach.

"Superintendent Burton," said Boxall, as he drew near, "is the search for Sadie Saunders being called off? And what about the investigation out here?"

"Our inquiries on both fronts remain ongoing," replied Burton, smoothly. "The activity you are witnessing is simply a case of resources being redirected in the most appropriate way. The combined investigation is already the most extensive, and most expensive, in the county's history, and we are satisfied that the commitment in terms of manpower will soon be seen to have paid off."

Fleet turned to his superior. Had Burton really just said what Fleet thought he had?

"Does that mean an arrest is imminent, Superintendent?" said the journalist, who'd obviously interpreted Burton's words in the same way Fleet had.

"It does indeed," Burton replied. "And it means we are confident justice will be served. Now, if you'll excuse me, there is still important work to be done." He signaled to Nicky, who spread her arms and started forward, herding the journalist and his photographer back the way they'd come.

"Detective Inspector Fleet!" Boxall pressed, resisting Nicky's attempts to move him. "How do you respond to accusations that the police are responsible for the death of a minor? That the course of the investigation before the superintendent's intervention led directly to events out here in the woods?"

Fleet noticed Nicky glance toward him, and he heard the photographer capture the expression that fell like a shadow across his face. It was . . . It was a fucking ambush. Burton had set the whole thing up. He'd done exactly what Fleet had accused him of wanting to do the day they'd spoken at the Overlook. He was walking away, opting to protect his precious budget rather than waste any more money searching for the truth. And he was using a tabloid hack to convey the threat he'd implied before: either Fleet made an arrest that justified their focus on Sadie's friends, and in doing so spared the force its blushes, or he'd be hung out to dry himself.

Dimly, Fleet heard Nicky's voice filtering through the rain. "You heard the superintendent," she was saying. "You got what you came for. Now, seeing as we're out here in the woods, let's make like a tree, shall we? That means *leave* in case there's any confusion."

The superintendent was walking away in the opposite direction, toward the barns. Fleet hurried after him. He caught up with Burton halfway across the clearing.

"Sir. *Sir.*" Fleet failed to keep the anger from his tone, and Burton turned to him sharply. The superintendent was in full uniform beneath his yellow waterproof jacket, and the rain trickled from the peak of his cap. In contrast, the water was running straight from Fleet's hair into his eyes.

"I know what you're going to ask, Detective Inspector, and the answer is no."

"But we have evidence, sir. The kids—Sadie's friends—found a phone that places Sadie in the woods not fifteen miles from where we're—"

"I know all about the phone," said Burton. Then, taking in Fleet's reaction, "Don't look so surprised, Detective Inspector. Forensics notified me the moment your DS asked them to shift their priorities. As I instructed them to. And from what I understand, all you have is a mobile without an owner. There is nothing to specifically connect the phone to—"

"There's a photograph, one only Sadie and her friends were likely to—"

"Don't interrupt me, Detective Inspector," said Burton, cutting in himself.

"Yes, sir. Sorry, sir. But if you'll just hear me out . . ."

"I don't need to hear you out," said Burton. "You want me to authorize yet another search of the forest. An area, need I remind you, that spans more than thirty thousand acres, and after we have already committed over a hundred officers over the course of the past eight days. Officers, need I remind you, who are badly needed elsewhere. Although even if I had two hundred officers out here—a thousand—we would barely be able to scratch the surface. As recent results show."

"But the phone . . ."

"The phone proves nothing. All the evidence we have—the evidence *you* gathered, I might add—points to Sadie being somewhere in that river. We have her bag. We have her coat, which you may recall is covered in blood. You were standing right next to me when the divers pulled it from the water."

"Fuck the coat," Fleet said.

"I beg your pardon?"

"I said, fuck the coat. And fuck the river, too. Sadie was never in the river."

Burton drew himself to his full height. "And you know this how, Detective Inspector?"

"Because, for one thing, we would have found her by now. In spite of the currents, in spite of the tides. *Because* of them, in fact.

In case you're forgetting, sir, I have experience here. I happen to know what I'm talking about."

Burton did everything but sneer. "Make up your mind, Rob. Your history in this town is either relevant or it's not. It's not a card you get to play as and when it suits you."

Fleet bit down, hard. "The other thing to bear in mind," he said, doing all he could to keep his voice steady, "is that the evidence has moved on. At first it made sense to focus on the river, to focus on Mason, too, but now, in light of the phone—"

"To coin a phrase," said Burton, "*fuck the phone*. If the phone is all you have, you're wasting both your breath and my time."

"It's not just the phone," said Fleet, tightly. "It's the search party, too. It's what happened twenty feet away from where we're standing."

"The search party? How does the search party change *anything*? A bunch of kids thought it would be a good idea to go wandering in the woods, for reasons known only to themselves, and an argument turned into a tragic accident, leaving one of them dead. We've always known what happened out here, Detective Inspector. The only question is who the public decides to blame."

"I'm not disputing *what* happened, Superintendent. The part I'm questioning is *why*."

"We know why! I've just told you *why*! Because a bunch of misfit teenagers—"

"I agree that's how it looks, sir, but the truth is, I don't think even the kids themselves understand what was really going on out here. And that's what I'm trying to get to the bottom of. And I think, if we can figure that out, we'll also find out what happened to Sadie."

Superintendent Burton's face was as thunderous as the sky above him. "Didn't I tell you not to interrupt me, Detective Inspector?"

This time Fleet didn't apologize. He returned the superintendent's stare.

"You sent me here to find a missing girl," Fleet said, blinking away the rain in his eyes, "because finding people is what I do. If you still want me to find her—to find out what happened to Sadie Saunders—then I'm telling you, we need to search the woods. Again. Properly this time. Not the way we did the first time, before we diverted toward the river. And not the way we've been doing it over the past forty-eight hours, with half the manpower that should be out here and in barely a fraction of the area we need to cover. Methodically, this time. Tracing the same route as Sadie's friends." He took a breath. "It's your operation now, clearly. *Sir*. But if you want to be able to call it a success—to stand onstage and take the plaudits and feel like you actually earned them—then I'm telling you what needs to be done. Budget be damned. *Backtracking* be damned." Fleet shook his head. He knew he'd already said too much, but he couldn't seem to shut himself up. "Christ, Roger, have you been sitting counting figures for so long that you've forgotten what police work actually involves? Sometimes you *have* to change course. It's called following the evidence."

Burton's face had turned from gray, to red, to deathly pale. For a moment, the only sound was the patter of the rain.

"Sir—" said Fleet, and Burton raised a palm. Slowly, he let it fall, and then he stepped so he and Fleet were toe to toe.

"The only reason I'm not suspending you *right now*," he said, his voice low but full of venom, "is because it would be tantamount to admitting we messed up just as badly as everyone is saying we did. As they're saying *you* did, in fact, Detective Inspector Fleet." Burton leaned closer still. "And as much as you deride those little *figures* you believe I'm so obsessed with, you seem to forget that without them, neither you nor any copper out here would have a job in the first place. You'd be swigging cider, sponging from the state, just like every other middle-aged male in this decrepit pisshole of a town." He jabbed a finger at Fleet's chest. "Do not. Fucking. Forget that."

The superintendent opened his mouth to say something more, but stopped himself when a pair of uniformed officers who were crossing the clearing came within earshot. When they noticed the expression on Burton's face, they dropped their eyes and veered away.

Burton took a breath, and exhaled audibly through his nostrils.

"We're wrapping things up," he said. "Here, at the river. The search teams have uncovered all they're going to."

"And Sadie?" said Fleet.

"Will be found, eventually. Probably by a bunch of mushroom pickers a month from now if she's really out here in the woods, or else washed up on a beach twenty miles along the coast. In the meantime, there will be a press conference at the station this time tomorrow, at which you will announce that Mason Payne has been arrested for the suspected murder of Sadie Saunders, and for whatever charge you can come up with that will put a lid on the debacle out here in the woods." Burton pulled back his shoulders and straightened his cap. His tone, when he went on, was dangerously even. "And in case you're struggling with the figures, Detective Inspector, that gives you twenty-four hours to clean up your mess. If you don't, I swear to God . . . you're going to wish you hadn't left me to do it for you."

IT DIDN'T TAKE long for the clearing to empty. By the time Fleet and Nicky had got there, the search itself had already been concluded, and now only a few stragglers remained at the scene. The superintendent was long gone, taking his entourage with him. Even Nicky had headed off toward the cars, to try to get a signal on her phone.

After turning his back on the access path, Fleet was able to picture the group of buildings as Sadie's friends would have seen them when they'd stumbled across them. He had to ignore the POLICE DO NOT CROSS tape sealing off the structures, of course, as well as the boot prints that had turned the area into a goalmouth on a municipal football pitch.

Conscious of the few fading voices behind him, he moved closer to the buildings. There was nothing much to the cabin anymore. The roof was cracked, like an egg caved in by a spoon, and the walls had a drunken tilt. There was nothing inside that Fleet could see through the glassless windows except rotten floorboards and treacherous shadows.

The barns were more substantial. There were two, one set back slightly from the other, and each about the size of a modern block of flats—the type developers slotted into every available space on prime residential streets, with rooms the size of cupboards but plenty of them. Whatever the buildings had once been used to store, they were largely empty now, save for several pieces of broken machinery—a plow in one barn, an engineless tractor in the other—and various bits of junk that had washed up on the tide of passing time.

Beyond the buildings, the forest immediately thickened, so much so that Fleet could barely see beyond the first row of trees. Except . . .

He edged closer, moving between the two barns and into shadow that was almost as thick as night. Amid the rain, water dripped from the gabled roofs in heavy drops, and one found the gap between Fleet's coat collar and his neck. The feeling as it ran down his back was of an ice-cold finger tracing the length of his spine. He shuddered.

On the far side of the buildings, he paused, and checked again toward the trees. Briefly, before, he thought he'd seen movement, and for a moment he could imagine precisely how Sadie's friends had felt out in the woods: Abi when she'd heard something in the undergrowth, Cora when she'd spotted a figure standing over them as they slept.

But there was nothing, just the rain and the morbid light.

Fleet made to head back toward the access path, meaning to catch up with Nicky. But as he turned, it happened again: a flutter at the edge of his vision, accompanied this time by a sound, as well as a distinct, unshakable sensation that someone was watching him.

He spun sharply . . . and almost leaped from his Gore-Tex hiking boots when a hand fell on his shoulder.

He clutched his heart.

"Jesus Christ, Nicky."

Nicky gave a start herself, half-amused, half-surprised by Fleet's reaction. "Sorry, boss. I thought you'd noticed me coming."

"No, I . . ." Fleet glanced again toward the trees. A shrug of air disturbed the leaves on the branches, and then once again all was still.

Keeping one eye on the tree line, Fleet said, "I thought you went looking for a signal?"

"I did. I didn't find one. I had a bar for a moment, but then it was gone. I was trying to get hold of Forensics, to ask them to get a wriggle on."

Fleet shook his head. "It wouldn't make any difference."

"Burton?" said Nicky.

"You guessed it."

"But if they find the blood, and it comes back as a match for Sadie's, or her prints are on the . . ." Nicky trailed off when she noted Fleet's grimace.

"'The search teams have uncovered all they're going to,'" he quoted. "Apparently. We're to rely on a bunch of mushroom pickers instead."

"Mushroom pickers?"

Another headshake. "Never mind," said Fleet. "Bottom line is, if Sadie's out here, we need some other way of finding her." He looked out once again into the trees.

"We could ramp up the pressure on Mason," said Nicky. "Charge him, slam the door, then offer him a ray of light if he points us the way to Sadie's body."

"Careful, DS Collins. You're beginning to sound like the superintendent," said Fleet. Then, turning from the tree line, "Sorry. That was uncalled-for. I'd take it as a mortal insult if someone said that to me." He gave her a conspiratorial smile, and Nicky returned it.

"So, what's the deal with Mason, anyway?" she said, glancing out into the woods herself. "Have we officially gone off him? What's made you change your mind?"

"I'm not sure I have changed my mind," Fleet answered. "In fact, right now, I'd still say Mason is our most likely suspect. On paper, anyway." He angled his head and took a step closer to the trees. He could see nothing, no one, but Fleet couldn't shake the feeling that someone was looking back at *him*. And unless some poor PC had been left behind and was hiding until Fleet left, to cover his embarrassment, there was only one other person it was likely to be . . .

"Boss?" said Nicky, frowning. She'd clearly realized something was distracting him. "What are you staring at?"

"I . . . nothing," said Fleet, in all honesty. "But humor me, will you? Let's take a look around."

"But . . . why?" said Nicky. "This whole area, the buildings included, would already have been swept from top to bottom."

"It would," Fleet agreed. He led the way toward the tree line.

"Boss? Seriously. What are you hoping to find?"

"That's something else I'm not sure of," said Fleet. "But answer me this: if you were trying to hide from someone, where would you go?"

Nicky shrugged. "As far away from them as possible."

"And if that wasn't an option?"

"Well, I suppose . . ." Nicky turned her gaze toward the woods. Her expression when she looked back at Fleet told him she'd finally caught on. "Right under their noses," she said.

The rain continued to fall, and its relentless percussion grew louder as they slipped between the trees. There was marginally more shelter underneath the canopy, but the drops that found them were thicker, heavier, as indeed was the atmosphere more generally in the woods. Amid the undergrowth it was even harder to see than it had been in the clearing, and there was a sense of the gloom pressing in.

Fleet shivered, suddenly feeling the cold. His boots and his jacket may have been waterproof, but his trousers weren't, and the wool clung wetly to his skin.

"What's the point of this place, anyway?" said Nicky, as they wove their way between the trees. "The clearing, I mean. The buildings. Is it a farm or what? Or did it used to be, rather."

"I'm not sure I ever knew it was here," said Fleet, ducking to avoid a branch. "There were barley fields on the other side of the main road back in the day, and the access path would probably have been wide enough then for that tractor. So it was probably a farmer's store or something, if not a farm exactly. Unless it was just somebody's idea of a country retreat." He glanced Nicky's way. "It's probably up for grabs if you're interested," he added.

Nicky shuddered in response.

"What? Not a fan of country living?" said Fleet.

"I don't mind the country. So long as it's paved. With street lighting. And there's somewhere I can get a decent latte. Oh, and there are no cows." Nicky checked across her shoulder, as though on the off chance something bovine might have crept up behind her.

Fleet felt the glitch in his step. "Cows," he echoed. "You're afraid of cows?"

"Not afraid, exactly. Just . . . wary. It's the way they look at you. Like they're planning something."

Fleet laughed. "What is it that a cow might be planning?"

"Exactly," said Nicky, deadpan. "That's the part I don't like."

About ten meters in, they paused. Fleet cast around, and was astonished to see how utterly the clearing was already lost to view. If you leaned to catch the right sightline, you could just about make out the buildings, like icebergs spotted through a fog. But otherwise it was as though they'd stepped through a wardrobe and into a completely different world. The search teams out here must have had a hell of a job.

Fleet tried to recapture that sensation he'd had before, that there was somebody out here watching him. But now, other than Nicky, he would have sworn he was completely alone.

He looked up. "The kids," he said. "Sadie's friends. They talked about climbing trees when they were younger. Right?"

Nicky nodded. "They mentioned it once or twice. Why? Are you getting an urge to reenact your youth?" She looked at the tree that was closest to them, barely more than a sapling, and then, brazenly, at Fleet's belly. "Because no offense, boss, but we might want to look around for something sturdier."

Fleet frowned at her. "Is that a comment about my weight, Detective Sergeant?"

Nicky shrugged ruefully. "There's a reason you've stopped taking sugar in your coffee. And again, no offense, boss, but if you were expecting me to follow you up, and one of those branches were to suddenly give way . . . Well. Let's just say I'm not overly keen on the idea of wearing your arse cheeks as a hat."

Fleet gave a snort. He returned to scanning the branches high above him. "Actually, I was mainly wondering what the view would be like from up there. And how often those search teams would have thought to look *up*."

Nicky looked where he was looking, wincing at the raindrops in her eyes. "Hardly at all, I would imagine," she said. "Especially in this weather. As for the view . . ." She shrugged. "We can take a look for ourselves if it's important to you?"

"I don't think that will be necessary," said Fleet. "To be honest, even if I weren't so . . . calorifically challenged, I've never been the biggest fan of heights."

"Really?" said Nicky. "I didn't know that."

"It's not something I tend to boast about. But there's a reason my bedsit is on the ground floor, and why I always used to insist to Holly, whenever she suggested we go on holiday, that we went somewhere we could drive."

At the mention of Holly, Nicky looked away. Until Fleet had spoken to Anne about his marriage, Nicky had been the only person—at least as far as Fleet knew—who was aware that he and his wife had separated. And even then, Fleet had never discussed it openly. With Nicky, he simply hadn't tried to hide it.

"Well," said Nicky, "for everyone's sake, let's hope we're never asked to find a cow that's gone missing up a mountain."

Fleet smiled. "Knowing cows, it would probably be a trap." He cast around again, all at once convinced that he was wasting what precious time they had.

"See now, look," said Nicky, and she wandered a few meters deeper into the woods. "If you were going to climb a tree, you'd want to pick one more like this. It's practically a spiral staircase. And look at those branches. They're thick enough that they'd probably even hold . . ." Nicky stopped herself, but not before she'd turned in Fleet's direction.

"A cow?" suggested Fleet.

Nicky grinned. "Right."

She began walking around the trunk of the chestnut. Fleet looked at his watch. "You've officially humored me, Detective Sergeant. I think we can probably wrap this—"

"Boss?"

Nicky was on the other side of the tree. Fleet moved to try to see what had caught her attention. "What is it?"

"Look. There. Is that . . ."

Fleet circled the trunk and crouched down next to her. They looked where Nicky was pointing, and then at each other. Nicky struggled with the zip of her waterproof, and pulled out a pen. She used it to nudge what at first glance Fleet had assumed was a leaf.

"A Snickers wrapper," he said, realizing what he was looking at.

"*Duo,*" Nicky added, and she raised an eyebrow.

Fleet stood. He looked up, around, and then back down at the base of the chestnut tree.

"If it had been here before, the search teams would almost certainly have bagged it," Nicky said. "Meaning they either missed it, or one of the PCs dropped it themselves . . ."

"Not likely," put in Fleet.

"Or," Nicky concluded, "someone else dropped it after the search teams had already cleared the area."

Fleet tapped his fingers against his thigh, thinking of the feeling he'd had of being watched; of Sadie's friends wondering whether they were being followed . . .

"Should we call someone?" said Nicky. But even as she asked, Fleet could tell she was thinking the same thing he was. *And say what? Show them what?* If the pay-as-you-go wasn't going to change Burton's mind, a piece of litter was hardly going to do it.

Fleet looked around once more, and had to fight an urge to call out into the trees. He knew it would be pointless. Worse than that, it would be like trying to entice a deer with a rifle shot.

Are you out there? he wondered. *Are you watching right now?*

Nicky was busy transferring the Snickers wrapper into a clear plastic evidence bag.

"Have you got another one of those?" Fleet asked her, as he fished inside his own jacket pockets. He took out one of his business cards and a pen.

"Sure," said Nicky, frowning slightly. She passed him a spare evidence bag.

There was an old tree stump close by, and Fleet turned to it. He bent down, and for a second allowed the pen to hover before he started to write. Then he slid the business card into the evidence bag, and placed it on top of the stump in what he hoped was clear view.

Nicky was watching the whole time, her frown deepening.

"I haven't got a better idea," said Fleet, shrugging. "Have you?"

MASON

NO ONE COULD argue after that. After it started raining, I mean. There were no more excuses, no more petty reasons to give up and go home. Which didn't stop them looking for one—I could see it in their eyes—and I suppose I should have realized they'd come up with something eventually, but in the meantime, what exactly could they say?

"If I were you I'd get out your water bottle," I told Abi, who was staring at me like I'd summoned the rain myself, just to keep her out there. "You never know how long it's going to last."

Which, after a minute, is what she did. It's what we all did. We opened our mouths, too, tipping our heads back and shutting our eyes. It was a proper end-of-summer downpour, thick and heavy, so there was no problem catching the drops. They were big as berries, bursting in your mouth the moment they hit the back of your throat. I swear to God, they even tasted sweet. I'd been so focused on being pissed-off at Abi's moaning, I'd forgotten how thirsty I was myself. I even started grinning. I couldn't help it. And when I'd had my fill, I looked around, and I realized the others were grinning, too. Cora, at least. Fash, as well. Abi was still gobbling up raindrops, her eyes screwed tight and her hair plastered to her forehead, but even Luke twitched a smile when he caught my eye. His hair was stuck to his head, too, the rain all running into his eyes, but it was like, no one cared, you know? Just the opposite. After the heat, and the dust, and fucking *everything* since the start of the summer, all any of us felt at that moment was relief.

"Jesus," said Fash. He had to shout to get anyone to hear him, because the rain was coming down that heavily. "When was the last time it actually rained? And like *this*."

I spread my hands and raised my head again. It was like that scene in that old prison movie. *The Shawshank Redemption*. Have you seen it? There's this bit, when Andy Dufresne crawls through the tunnel of shit, and then he gets out the other side and he realizes he's free, finally, and the rain, it's coming down in ropes, just like it was out there in the woods, and the guy, Andy, who's completely innocent, by the way, he takes off his shirt and he spreads his arms and he's standing there like he's Jesus Christ or something, like it's an actual religious experience he's having. Which I guess is exactly what it is.

But my point is, that was me. Just for a minute. It was as though the rain was washing away all the shit that had stuck to me as well. The shit people had thrown at me since Sadie went missing. The shit *you* started.

And then it hit me. Because with Andy, in the film, it's the beginning of the end. You know, just before he disappears to go and live on a desert island, or on a beach in Mexico or wherever. Me, I was still in the same old place, still stuck in the middle of a nightmare with no prospect of ever waking up. It only took me about thirty seconds to remember that. To realize that the rain wasn't actually going to wash away anything.

"Dude," said a voice at my shoulder. I hadn't noticed Fash move up beside me. "Are you, like, crying?" he said. He spoke quietly, and he'd turned his back on the others, who were busy filling up their water bottles. His hand moved toward my shoulder, like he meant to comfort me or something, and I shrugged it away. Right at that moment, Fash was the last person I wanted trying to make me feel better. And anyway, what did he think he was going to say? Because what I'd realized was, whatever happened from that point on, nothing was ever going to be the same again. Not that my life had ever exactly been perfect or anything, but *some* things were. You know?

Sadie was.

Look at me. For fuck's sake. Fucking doing it again.

Fucking *Shawshank Redemption*. Fucking overrated is what it is.

No, I'm fine.

I said I'm fine.

Christ.

Christ.

So the rain. I was talking about the rain.

So yeah, at first it was as though it had started snowing on Christmas Eve or something. But that feeling . . . that sense of relief I mentioned? It didn't take long to wear off.

"So are we doing this?" said Cora, when all our bottles were full. Which is exactly what I was talking about before. It's like, it had started already. You know? The others all looking for some *other* reason to go home. Because Cora, when she said it, she was looking up at the sky, like we couldn't go looking for Sadie *now*, not if it meant getting *wet*.

And fucking Abi. Because of course she decides to chip in as well. She was looking at the water in her bottle, going, "You aren't supposed to drink rainwater either, are you? Isn't it meant to be full of, like, pollution and stuff?"

"Well, it's too late now," I said, throwing my rucksack over my shoulder. "You've already swallowed the equivalent of half a bucketful. So let's get on with this before the cancer kicks in, shall we?"

I didn't give her a chance to respond, and I didn't wait to see if the others were following me. I started walking back upstream, the way we'd said we'd go before. I went slowly, making a show of scouring the ground around me, and stopping every so often to peer down into the water. Eventually I heard the others fall in behind me. Nobody said anything for a while. There was just the sound of the rain, which had eased off slightly since the clouds had broken, but was still falling heavily enough that there was no particular shelter beneath the trees. I was waiting for the bitching to begin, because after an hour or so even I started feeling the cold. It wasn't the air temperature so much as the fact that I was completely soaked through. And even though Abi was the only one to bring a waterproof, I fully expected her to be the one to start.

Except she didn't. No one did. Instead, after a while, everyone began to spread out. Cora and Luke crossed the stream, and Fash and Abi moved up alongside me, veering slightly deeper into the woods. There was a curtain of trees between us, but that didn't stop me hearing what they were saying.

"Fash?" Abi said, and I could tell by the way she was trying to keep her voice down that she was worried about anyone else listening in.

Fash looked at her, I guess, and waited for her to go on.

"What do you reckon happens when you die?" she asked him.

There was a beat, as though Fash was trying to process what she'd just said. "Bloody hell, Abi," he hissed at her. There was a gap in the trees then, and I saw him glance over, but I couldn't tell if he was worried about Luke overhearing, or me.

"No, I know. But seriously. What do you reckon happens?"

I could have told her what happens if she'd really wanted to know. Nothing happens. Zilch. It's lights out and then it's over. All that bullshit about God and heaven and having a soul . . . if it were true, what would be the point of living in the first place? It's lies, is what it is. A fucking comfort blanket. When you die, you're dead, end of story. Literally.

But obviously that's not what Abi wanted to hear.

"I don't know, do I?" said Fash. "Why are you asking *me*?"

He sounded uncomfortable, like death was the last thing he wanted to talk about. Which I suppose it is for most people most of the time, but even still . . .

"Your mum's religious, isn't she?" said Abi. "So I just . . . I don't know. I just wondered what you thought, that's all."

"My mum's a Muslim, so what? Luke's parents are religious, too."

"Yeah, but I can't ask *him*, can I?" said Abi.

"If you did he'd probably say the same thing as me. That he doesn't know either."

"I know you don't *know*," Abi said. "No one *knows*. But what do you *think*? That's all I'm asking."

Fash exhaled, like he could tell Abi wasn't going to give it a rest until he answered.

"I think . . . I think *something* happens. But I don't know what."

I snorted. I couldn't help it. But I'm pretty sure neither of them heard.

"Really?" said Abi, sounding like someone had just offered her a free iPad. "You really think that? That dying isn't the end?"

"Keep your voice down, Abi, for Christ's sake," said Fash.

We all walked on for a bit, and neither of them spoke.

Eventually Fash gave a sigh. "What I think is . . ." he said, in a whisper, and you could tell he was struggling to find the words. "I think there *has* to be something else. Because . . . I don't know. It's like . . . thoughts. You know? Like, where do they come from? And dreams and ideas and . . . and all that stuff. The stuff that isn't muscle or bone or fat or whatever. The stuff that's us. The real us, I mean. That has to go *somewhere*. Right? And maybe there's no heaven or hell or anything, but there's definitely got to be something. Like . . ." He sighed again. "I don't know. Like the way we can't see infrared. Radio waves. Pollution. Things that are all around us right now. So maybe the afterlife is like that. All around us, but the only thing is, we can't see it. Not until after we die."

At first, when he finished his little speech, I figured he was taking the piss. I kept waiting for him to start laughing, to tell Abi he was yanking her chain.

But he didn't. Meaning he actually genuinely believed that shit.

"Right!" said Abi. "That's exactly what I reckon! And what you were saying about the things that are around us right now. That's what I think about ghosts."

"Ghosts?" said Fash, and I couldn't help but glance across. Abi was about ten meters away, deeper in among the trees. Fash had turned toward her, meaning he couldn't have seen me looking.

"Right," Abi said. "Like, if ghosts exist, there *has* to be something else."

"I guess . . ." said Fash. "Although I'm not sure I believe in ghosts exactly."

"I do," said Abi.

And in my head I'm like, *There's a fucking surprise.*

"I've even seen one once. Of my gran. In her old house. My granddad lived there on his own for a bit, after she died, and until his stroke put him in a home, and me and my mum used to stay with him practically every other weekend. And it was one of those times I saw her."

"You did?" said Fash. "What was she doing?"

"She was in the garden," said Abi, "watering the plants, I think."

I turned away to cover my snort. I couldn't help it. It just slipped out. I mean, seriously. You're dead. You can walk through walls. So what's the first thing you decide to do when you come back? Turn the hose on the fucking hydrangeas.

"Yeah, well," said Fash, who'd glanced my way. "Like I said, I'm not sure I believe in ghosts."

I could tell he wanted to change the subject, but Abi sort of had him trapped.

"But what you were saying before," she pressed. "About there being *something*. Do you reckon, like, with Sadie—"

But that was as far as she got.

Fash turned on her. And he snapped like he never snaps at *anyone*. Not even the dickheads who always give him such a hard time at school.

"I said I don't fucking know! OK? Just give it a rest, will you?"

And he stormed off, leaving Abi standing where he'd left her. She saw me looking over, and she flushed. I couldn't tell whether she was angry or ashamed or what. She turned away, dropping her head, and hurried on as though following after Fash.

We walked for hours, after that. No one talking much, everyone dripping wet. We took shelter under an elm tree at around lunch-time, and polished off Abi's sunflower seeds, as well as most of the sweets, but it was so cold standing around that we all just wanted to keep moving.

By the time it started getting dark, everyone was dead on their feet. I didn't know how far we'd come. Miles, it felt like; deeper into the forest than any of us had ever been before. And we hadn't found anything, needless to say. As the light had begun to fade, the others seemed more worried about looking over their shoulders than at the ground around their feet. The girls, anyway. Fash, too. As though they were thinking about the night before—about whatever had happened at our camp. But again, I didn't know whether they were genuinely worried or they were only doing it for effect.

"What's that?" said Luke, from up ahead.

I looked where he was pointing, but all I could see were shadows along the bank. We'd stuck with the stream all day, and gradually the terrain had begun to change. The banks either side of the stream had got steeper, the water farther below our feet.

"Is that a cave?" Luke said, and he waited for the rest of us to catch up.

I turned on my torch. Sure enough, just in front of us, there was a cavity in the side of the bank. It was as though the roots from the trees above it had opened up a crevice in the rock. It was hard to tell how far back it went, because the torchlight was swallowed by the dark.

"Uh-uh. No way," said Abi. "I'm not going in there."

"Who said anything about going in there?" said Cora.

"Although it would get us out of the rain," said Luke. "And we need a place to sleep, right? Unless anyone was planning on heading home tonight?"

Which was out of the question, obviously. We'd have struggled to make it back to the clearing we'd slept in before daybreak, let alone all the way to the river.

"At the very least, we have to take a look," I said.

"Take a look?" said Abi. *"Why?"*

"What do you mean, *why*? Why do you fucking think?"

"Chill out, Mason," said Cora. "Jesus."

"Well, I'm going in," I said, ignoring her. "Is anyone with me?"

I looked at Fash, who didn't move. Luke shrugged and made to follow me.

"Guys," said Abi, grabbing hold of Luke's arm. "Seriously. I didn't want to say anything before, but I'm pretty sure I heard someone following us. If we all go in that cave, they could . . . I don't know. Trap us, or—"

"Christ almighty," I said. "Here we go again. What did you hear exactly, Abi? When? And why didn't you say anything earlier? It's not like you to hold back if there's moaning to be done."

Cora shook her head, tutting at me, but she didn't say anything. Fash just stared at the ground.

"OK, OK," said Abi. "Maybe I didn't *hear* anything exactly, but I definitely kept getting this feeling. Like someone was watching me, you know? There's somebody out there, I know there is!" She looked around, over her shoulder, and I realized how much light had gone already.

"I wouldn't worry, Abi," I told her, winking. "It was probably just a *ghost*."

And I turned my torch toward the cave, and led the way into the dark.

ABI

HE'S *SUCH* AN arsehole.

And it wasn't just out there in the woods. I told you before, he could be like that even before Sadie went missing. With me, with Fash, with all of us. With Sadie, too. It's like, when he got that way—all sarky and bitter and cruel—I had to wonder why she even stayed with him. Although, if you ask me, she only did because she was worried what he'd do if she tried to split up with him. Take that time on the beach, for example, when him and Sadie ended up having an argument, and ruining the whole night for everyone else. Sadie accused him of being, like, overbearing or something. Is that the word? Of being like her dad, basically, is what she said. Like, always wanting to know what she was doing, what she was *thinking*. And Mason said it was only because he loved her, and Sadie said, *Well, sometimes it's just too much.* And Mason said, *If you feel that way, then why didn't you tell me?* And Sadie said she was telling him, right now, and Mason said, *Fine, if that's the way you feel, I'll leave you the fuck alone.* And he stormed off, and Cora went after him, and I ended up going after Cora, because she had all my stuff in her bag, but not before

Sadie started crying. And then, right away after, she was all laughing and that, but in a sad way, going, *I guess it's true what people say, that girls always end up marrying their fathers.* Not that she meant *actually* getting married. I mean, God, can you imagine? Although Mason used to talk about it, too, and he always made out like he was joking, but you just knew, watching him, that actually he wasn't joking at all. Which I guess is partly what Sadie meant about Mason being like her dad. About wanting to keep her for himself.

So yeah. Arsehole. That's all I'm trying to say.

And obviously I didn't want to go inside the cave. Because I wasn't lying when I'd said I thought someone was following us. *Obviously* I wasn't lying. Plus, the cave itself . . . I mean, I'm not *totally* stupid. I knew what Mason was suggesting. The reason he insisted we look inside. He thought *Sadie* might have been in there. Somehow. And to be honest, I did, too.

"What's that smell?" said Fash, as he followed Mason in. The rest of us were hanging back on the edge of the stream. Cora because she was just as scared to go in there as I was, I guarantee you, and Luke because he was acting sort of protective. The way he does sometimes. Because he knew I was worried about what was out there in the woods, and he didn't want to leave me on my own.

"It's just cave smell," I heard Mason saying. His voice had gone all echoey. "Why? What did you think it was?"

Either Fash didn't answer or I didn't hear.

"Whoa," said Mason, after a minute. The rest of us were peering into the opening, trying to see what they could, but all I could make out was their torch beams. And then one of them swung straight toward us, making all three of us wince. "It's *big* in here," said Mason. "Seriously, what's everybody waiting for? Come on in."

"Shine that torch somewhere else and we might actually be able to see where we're stepping," said Luke, with a hand up over his eyes.

Mason's torch beam swung back toward the dark.

"Have you . . . Is there anything in there?" I called out. I was asking Fash, but surprise, surprise, Mason was the one to answer.

"Not really. There's some kind of altar. A satanic thing, I think. And a statue of what looks like a goat, or a demon or something. And . . . is that a pentagram, Fash?"

"Ignore him," came Fash's voice, sounding about as fed up with Mason's bullshit as I was feeling. "There's nothing to worry about. Come in and get yourselves dry."

I looked at Luke, who nodded. Cora had already started forward, and after hesitating for a moment, I followed her inside. I was fully expecting Mason to jump out and grab me, but instead he was just standing on his own in a corner, moving his torchlight around the cave. And it was hard to tell in the dark, but I'm pretty sure he was smiling.

I moved away from him and stood next to Cora. She was using one of the other torches to look around. We only had three. Torches, I mean. On account of the fact our phones had gone missing. There would probably have been a light on Sadie's Nokia—the one we found, I mean—but I guess none of us thought to check. But maybe it's a good job we didn't, because otherwise it might have run out of battery, like the torches did later that night. And if it had . . . I don't know. Maybe we'd all still be out there.

"You were right," Cora said. "It is big in here. It must go six or seven meters into the bank."

Actually, it was smaller than I'd imagined. But only because I was worrying it would turn out to be the entrance to an entire, like, network or something. With tunnels and, I don't know, caverns and that. Like a whole other world. Like in stories. You know?

But it was basically room-sized, with three walls and a roof. There was space for us all to sit down, to lie down if we'd wanted, and the ceiling was high enough that none of us had to stoop. And yeah, it smelled a bit weird, but only of earth and stuff. Nothing . . . bad.

And the other good thing, I suppose, was that at least it was dry. Because obviously, after eight hours or whatever of traipsing about in the rain, we were all completely soaked through. Even my waterproof turned out not to be. What I wanted to do was change into something dry, but when I checked the clothes in my rucksack, they were just as wet as what I was wearing.

"Can we light a fire or something?" I said, trying to wring out my spare jumper.

The others had finished exploring—it didn't take long—and they sat down and leaned against the walls, sighing like my dad does when he gets in from work and parks himself on the sofa.

Fash put the torch he'd been holding in the middle of the floor, directing the beam toward the ceiling, which was basically a crisscross of tree roots. Cora and Mason switched the other torches off, which left us sitting in this weird kind of half-light, where you couldn't really see other people's faces. The entrance to the cave had turned into a gaping hole, as black as the cave itself had looked when we'd been outside peering in. I didn't like it. I didn't like it at all. I mean, it should have felt cozy. With the rain coming down outside, and being in the dry, and sitting up close to people who were supposed to be your friends. But instead I just felt trapped. Like we'd been cornered or something. You know?

"A fire would be a neat trick," said Mason. He tossed a stone or something through the entranceway, and it made a rustling sound as it landed somewhere amid the trees on the other side of the stream. "What exactly do you suggest we burn?"

"Like . . . wood, or—" But then I realized what he was getting at. I bit down, clamping my lips tight. Mason was directly across from me, and though I couldn't see his face, I could just imagine him smirking.

"Not to worry, though," said Mason. "I've got something to warm us up." I saw him shift, and there was a noise like he was rummaging in his rucksack. And then he held what he was clutching in the middle of the torchlight, like it had been beamed down from heaven or something.

"What the actual *fuck*?" said Cora.

"No way," said Fash. "You've been carrying that with you the whole time?"

"Well, it didn't carry itself," said Mason.

"Why didn't you mention it before?" said Cora. "Jesus, Mason."

There was a rustle and then a popping sound as Mason uncapped the bottle. "Gang?" he said. "Meet Dr. Daniels. Dr. Jack Daniels. Curer of ills. Banisher of chills. The finest healer in the land." He took a swig, straight from the bottle, and made a sound like it was the sweetest thing he'd ever tasted. Then he passed it along.

"Where did you get it?" said Luke as he took the bottle. Again, I couldn't see his face, but it looked like he was staring at the label, as though trying to work out whether it was real. Because we hardly ever got hold of spirits. There's only one place in the entire town where they let us buy alcohol, the little corner shop on the road behind the quay. But Old Man Miller, who runs it, only ever lets us buy cider. Alcopops. Stuff like that. He won't sell us anything stronger, no matter how much we beg. Mason even tried wearing a disguise once so he could bag us a bottle of vodka, but Mr. Miller just laughed him from the store. He—

Wait. You won't arrest him or anything, will you? Mr. Miller, I mean. For selling us alcohol?

No. Right. Of course. *Obviously* you've got other priorities.

"It's my dad's," Mason said. "Was my dad's. He must have blown his dole money at the office. But I figured we'd need it more than he does. In fact, we're doing him a favor. The doctor told him he should cut out the booze."

The bottle had made its way to Cora. She took a swig, and because she was sitting right beside me, I was able to see her grimace. She offered the bottle to me.

"No thanks," I said, and I made to pass it straight to Fash.

"What's the matter, Abi?" said Mason. "Worried about sharing our spit?"

He leaned forward a bit, into the torchlight, and his face . . . It scared me. Not just because of the way the light was shining—you know how people's faces look when they hold a torch up under their chin? But also because of his expression. For the first time since we'd been out there, he looked almost . . . not cheerful, exactly. *Excited*. And that was the reason I didn't want to drink. Because I didn't trust him. Like, why had he even brought it in the first place, that's what I wanted to know. And saved it until that moment? And yeah, OK, maybe I say dumb stuff sometimes, but I can't be *totally* stupid if I figured out he was up to something before it crossed any of the others' minds.

"Have some," said Cora, oblivious. "It does actually warm you up."

I took a sip. A small one. And I passed the bottle on to Fash. From the look on his face, he was clearly wondering the same thing I was—wondering about Mason, I mean—but he only hesitated for a second. He tipped the bottle back and swallowed. "You're right," he said, gasping slightly and screwing his eyes up tight. "It's not as good as a fire, but it's definitely got a burn."

"It does the trick, doesn't it?" Mason said, taking another swig himself. "It's just a shame we don't have any Coke to go with it."

"Stop it," I found myself saying. Just quietly, and I don't think anybody heard me. Except Cora maybe, who turned her head.

Mason had passed the bottle on again, and it was on its way back round. "It's almost like a regular night out," he said, and this time I could hear his grin. "All we need is for some old biddy to walk by and give us evils, and for one of us to start puking in the gutter."

"*Stop it,*" I said again, louder this time.

I saw Mason's shadow turn its head toward me. "Stop what?" he said, all innocent.

"Stop acting like you're enjoying this. Like it's a . . . a *regular night out.*"

He moved forward enough that I could see his face. "Are you not enjoying yourself, Abi?"

"No, I'm not enjoying myself. We're not *supposed* to be enjoying ourselves!"

There was a flash in Mason's eyes then, where they caught the light of the torch.

The bottle reached me again and this time I didn't even take it. I just shook my head as Cora held it out.

But then I changed my mind. All of a sudden, I didn't care anymore. I *wanted* to be drunk. Just completely off my face, you know? So that I wouldn't feel anything, wouldn't have to *think* about anything, least of all what we were doing. *Why* we were doing it. And when it would end. When, instead of sitting in a hole in the middle of the woods, freezing our arses off because of the rain—and because of the fact we were wearing *shorts*—we could just go home and . . . and . . . and I didn't know what. Anything. Nothing. Whatever the hell you're meant to do when your best friend goes missing, and you're basically waiting for her to turn up dead.

I snatched the bottle off Cora as she made to pass it to Fash, and I tipped my head back as I raised it to my lips. I didn't even wipe it first. I just swallowed—once, twice, again, until Fash grabbed the bottle away from me, and I collapsed forward, coughing.

"Jesus Christ, Abi," Fash was saying, somewhere off to my left. "Are you OK?"

"She's fine," I heard Mason say. "Just getting into the spirit of things. Right, Abi?"

I tried to grab the bottle off Fash again. I don't know whether I wanted another drink or just to chuck it at Mason's head.

But Fash moved it away from me. He passed it straight on to Mason.

"How about some music?" said Mason. "I've still got my iPod. Maybe we should listen to one of the playlists Sadie made me."

"Dude . . ." said Fash, glancing at Luke.

"What?"

"Just . . . I don't think we should."

"No," agreed Cora. "No music." The bottle had come round to her again, and she took a gulp. If I'd had to guess, I'd have said she was feeling the way I was. Just, like, *screw it*. You know? Like she was determined to get as drunk as she could.

And that's the way it went. The bottle kept coming round, and we all just kept on drinking. At least, that's what I thought, but the bottle seemed to last forever. And then eventually, at some point—I couldn't have told you when, because I'd completely lost track of time—but at some point the whiskey was gone. Finished. And I didn't feel cold anymore. I barely even noticed that I was still soaking wet.

When the bottle made its way back to Mason, he held it up to the light. Then he stood up, and tossed it into a corner of the cave. It didn't break. It just landed by the entrance with a *thonk*.

Mason smiled when he turned back to us, and he didn't sit down.

"So," he said. "What should we talk about?"

The rest of us just stared. It was like, we *had* been talking. A bit. Just as we drank, you know? Not about anything in particular. About the rain, mainly. About how mad it was after the summer we'd had. About how it felt like an end.

"Abi?" said Mason. "You had a subject, didn't you?"

"Huh?" I said, confused. And more than a little bit pissed. Not happy pissed, though. Normally stuff like whiskey makes me happy. Lively. But sitting there against the wall in that cave, I didn't think I'd ever feel happy again.

"Death," said Mason. "That's what you were talking about earlier, wasn't it? You and Fash? So go on. Why don't you ask the others what they think about the afterlife? About whether they think ghosts are real."

I'd been . . . not dozing exactly. But sitting there in a sort of trance. Letting my brain swim away on the alcohol. All of a sudden, though, it was like a warning siren had gone off somewhere inside my head. Like when you fall asleep in front of the telly and then the phone rings, and you don't know if it's your alarm or your mum's car getting broken into outside or a signal that, actually, the building's on fire and you're seconds away from being roasted alive. You get this jolt, like electricity, telling you to get ready for something bad.

"What about you, Cora?" said Mason. "Do you think, if people die, they find a way to come back to haunt us? Assuming we deserve it, I mean."

"I don't want to talk about ghosts," said Cora, with a glance toward the woods outside. All we could see was the rain, and the slope of the bank on the other side of the stream, and the gray silhouettes of the trees. And I don't know if it was just because of what Mason had said, but to me they looked like people. Like dead men in the dark, closing in.

"No," said Mason. "I don't imagine you do."

Cora looked up at him, sharply.

"So how about a game instead?" Mason went on. "Truth or dare."

"What are we, twelve?" said Fash. "Come on, mate. Sit back down. You're making me nervous." Which he said with a laugh, like he'd meant it to sound like a joke, but all it did was make him sound afraid.

"Let's start with an easy one, shall we?" said Mason, ignoring him. He'd started to pace, meaning from where I was sitting he was moving in and out of the light.

He stopped, and turned to face us. "Which one of you tipped away the water?"

There was silence as the rest of us tried to work out whether he was joking.

"Was it you, Cora?" he said. "Or *you*, Abi?"

"What? No, I . . ."

"For Christ's sake, Mason, not this again," said Cora. "You're drunk. Just sit back down, like Fash said, and let's the lot of us get some sleep. And then, in the morning, we can all go home. We're not going to find anything else out here. Not in this weather. And we should tell the police about Sadie's phone."

I'd started nodding without even realizing.

"I'm not drunk," Mason said. "And I hate to disappoint you, but nobody's going anywhere. Not until we get this straightened out."

He *sounded* drunk. But the thing was, I believed him when he said he wasn't. Whatever was making him act the way he was, it wasn't the alcohol. It dawned on me that maybe he'd only been pretending to drink when the bottle had come around to him. Maybe that was why it had lasted so long.

"Mase . . ." said Luke, and he reached a hand to Mason's elbow. "Come on, man. Take it easy."

"No, Luke," Mason said, pulling his arm free. "You of all people need to hear this." And, as before, he faced me, Cora and Fash across the torchlight. "OK, fine," he said. "Let's cut to the chase, shall we? If you've had enough of playing games?" He moved to his left, and it was only just before he spoke again that I realized why. He was standing in front of the entranceway, blocking the rest of us inside.

And his face changed. Before, he'd been acting as though he was enjoying himself. As though it was all just a bit of a laugh. But now he looked the way he had so far only in flashes. As though whatever he'd been carrying around all knotted up inside him had finally come undone.

He bent down, and he picked up the bottle of Jack Daniels. He gripped it by the neck, and then he smashed it against the wall of the cave.

"So," he said, turning, the broken bottle gleaming in his hand. "Which one of you killed her?"

FASH

I WAS LYING. Before. You were right. I mean, it's all true, all the stuff I told you, except . . . except I didn't tell you everything.

My mum, when I spoke to her, when I asked her what I should do . . . she got mad. I doubt she'll ever not be mad at me ever again. She says I should have been honest with you from the beginning. And I realize that now, I do, but I didn't want to get anyone in trouble. Not Mason. Not the others.

Not Sadie.

And not myself either, I suppose.

But Mum made me realize it's too late for any of that. So I'll tell you, I will—I promised my mum I would. Except you have to believe me when I say to you, I had nothing to do with what happened to Sadie. I swear it. On my mother's life. It's just . . . I mean . . . the truth is, I may know a bit more about what happened than I made out.

And Mason. I knew a bit more about what he was doing, too. At least, I thought I did. But when he stood up in that cave, clasping that broken bottle, I realized I didn't know as much as I'd assumed.

"What the hell, Mason?" said Luke, who had got to his feet first.

None of the rest of us were very far behind. The whiskey had gone right to my head, so when I stood up I almost fell over again.

"This isn't fucking funny, Mason," said one of the girls. Cora, I think.

"Do you see me laughing?" said Mason, pointing the bottle like a gun. "Now answer me. Who was it? Was it you, Cora? Is that why you've been acting like such a *bitch*?"

"Was *what* me? What the hell are you talking about?"

"I'm talking about Sadie! As you well know!"

Cora made a sound like there was something caught in her throat. "You're . . . what? You're seriously suggesting that one of us killed her? That *I* did?"

"Or maybe it was you, Abi," said Mason, turning. "Or *you*, Fash."

"Me?" I said. "You think *I* had something to do with it? What happened to . . . to searching? To trying to find out the truth?"

"What the fuck do you think we're doing right now?" he spat at me. "Although, while we're on the subject, maybe you can explain why you were so eager to help me in the first place. Were you worried about what I'd find if I went without you? Is that why you walked straight past Sadie's phone?"

"But I . . . I didn't see it! Honestly, I . . ."

"*Help* him?" Cora said. "Help him do what? What the hell is Mason talking about, Fash?"

I was standing there shaking my head. I couldn't believe what Mason was doing. "You lied to me," I said to him. "You *told* me you wanted to search for Sadie! That's why you had me round everybody up. To form a *search party*. That's what you said!"

Because that's the thing. That's what I lied about before. One of the things I lied about, anyway. I told you the search party was my idea, that I hadn't seen Mason since the day Sadie went missing. But that's not true. He came to me, you see. On day three, I guess it was.

After he'd been at the station with you lot all day, and people around town had started talking. More than talking. By that point, everyone had pretty much decided. You know, that Sadie was dead, and that Mason was the one who'd killed her. And his dad had accused him as well. Well, not accused him exactly. What he did was punch him in the stomach. He'd come home from the pub and apparently he'd been getting a load of grief from all the regulars, so come kicking-out time he'd stumbled home, and he'd dragged Mason from his bed, and he told him if he didn't own up, he'd throttle him and chuck his body in the river—the way everyone was saying Mason had done to Sadie. And when Mason denied it, that's when his dad put a fist in his gut. Which he's done before when he's been drunk, but this time, apparently, his dad had no intention of stopping there. He made to hit Mason again, with a poker this time, but according to Mason he was so far gone that when he raised the poker he staggered backward, and that's how Mason got out of the house. He barged his way past, and out the front door, and he ran until he reached the river. And that night, when he was out there on his own, that's when he came up with the idea. To form a search party, is what he told me when he came to me the next day. And what he said was he needed my help, because there was no way the others would agree if *he* asked them, not when they probably all thought he was guilty, too. He even suggested what I should say to them: that the police were looking in the wrong place, and that we knew the woods better than anyone—all the lines Cora had noticed him using himself.

But it was a trick. A lie to get me to do his dirty work. He just wanted us all together, away from help and off our guard. Somewhere he could watch us, test us, *trap* us.

"You need to hear this, Luke," said Mason, still brandishing the bottle, and blood dripping from his hand. "You need to listen to what they've got to say for themselves."

"Mason, Jesus," said Luke. "Put that down, will you? You're . . . you're bleeding. And you're going to get someone hurt!"

Cora was looking from me to Mason, and back again. "You tricked us?" she said to me. "You and Mason were planning this from the start?"

"No! I wasn't planning anything, I swear it! Mason came to me asking for my help. What exactly was I supposed to do?"

"But . . . the search party," said Abi. "Does that mean we were never really looking? That the search party was never really real? What about Sadie? About her being hurt, lying out here in the woods somewhere . . ."

Even in the dark, Mason's expression was plain enough. Disgust, ridicule, revulsion: you name it, it was written on his face.

"Sadie's *dead*," he said. "It's *obvious* she's dead. It's been obvious since the day she went missing!"

"But . . . how can you be so sure?" I asked him, whining like a little kid.

"Because I know what the police do," said Mason. "*Remember?* They threw it all in my face. They even sat there and watched me *cry*." He adjusted his hand around the broken bottle, and I realized how badly he was bleeding. How much it must have hurt.

And not just the cut.

"Plus," he went on, in a voice that was barely above a whisper, "if she were still alive she would have let me know. One way or another."

Which, even given everything I was hearing, made me feel kind of sad. That he thought that. That he probably even believed it. He really loved her, you see. Far more than she could ever have loved him.

"So was it you?" said Abi. "All the stuff that's been happening. The phones, the water, the noises we've been hearing in the woods . . ."

"Don't give me that," said Mason, rounding on her. "Don't try and play all *innocent*. Why the fuck would I have messed with the water? The phones, maybe, if it had occurred to me, and if there'd been any reception out here in the first place. But I *wanted* you out here, remember? Why would I give you an excuse to go back? Which, by the way, is all any of you have been looking for since this started. So why don't *you* tell *me*, Abi? Why were you so desperate to go home? What was it you were worried we would find?"

"Nothing! I wasn't worried about anything! It was *me* who found Sadie's phone, remember?"

"Too right I remember," said Mason. "I remember you falling over yourself to pick it up. Because it was sitting there as plain as day, and you knew that if you didn't, either me or Luke would have. And then you wouldn't have had a chance to delete whatever you needed to in order to remove any link to Sadie. But you forgot about the photo on the lock screen, didn't you? The passcode, too. Unless you simply ran out of time. Or maybe you freaked out when you noticed the blood."

"No! That's not what happened! Tell him, Fash! You saw me! I didn't delete *anything*."

I didn't know what to say. I was still busy trying to come to terms with what was happening. With what Mason was doing.

"What happened, Abi?" Mason pressed. "Did you not know Sadie had the phone on her when you killed her? Did it slip out of her pocket when you were getting rid of her body? Or maybe . . . maybe it was never Sadie's in the first place. Maybe you planted it deliberately—to fool the cops, to pull the search in the wrong direction. You bought the cheapest phone you could get, uploaded that photo, changed the code so it was the same as Sadie's, and then—the finishing touch—applied just a dab of Sadie's blood. Except it back-fired. Just when everyone was about ready to give up, you accidentally gave us a reason to keep looking."

"Mason, listen to me," said Luke. "This is crazy! None of what you're saying makes sense. Why would Abi want to hurt Sadie? Why would *any* of us?"

Mason ignored him. "Because you know that's what the police think about Sadie's bag, don't you?" He was looking at Abi, but it was obvious he was talking to us all. "That it was put by the river deliberately, to make it look like Sadie had fallen in. They think the *killer* put it there. They think *I* did!"

Abi went white. I guess we all did.

"You've always been jealous of Sadie," Mason said to Abi. "Of how popular she was, of how *pretty*." He spat the word, and it was as though he were spitting at Abi. "Is that why you started all those rumors about her online? All those *lies*?"

Abi started shaking her head, faster and faster.

"Except it didn't work, did it?" Mason went on. "It didn't make you any less of a leper, and it didn't make your dad suddenly love you as much as Sadie's dad loved *her*. So what happened after that, Abi? Did Sadie find out? Did you argue? Did you kill her just to shut her up?"

Abi's head was still moving from side to side. Her eyes were screwed up tight, but not enough to stop her tears.

"Stop!" she said. "Just stop! I *didn't*. I *never*. Cora, please . . ." She turned to her right, begging Cora for help.

"Make up your mind, Mason," Cora said. "Was it me who killed Sadie? Or was it Abi? Or maybe it was actually Fash, which is what you seemed to be implying before. The truth is you haven't got a clue, have you? You're plucking theories out of thin air, seizing on anything that will deflect attention away from *you*."

"You're right," Mason said to her, with a smile that was anything but. "Maybe it *was* you. Because Abi wasn't the only one who was jealous of Sadie, was she?"

"What the hell is that supposed to mean?"

"*I wouldn't have wished this, you know,*" Mason said, in a voice I guessed was supposed to be Cora's. "*Maybe you didn't know Sadie as well as you think you did.*" He sneered at her, and shook his head. "You think I don't know how much you hated me and her being together? You think it wasn't fucking *obvious*?"

Cora cracked something like a smile herself. And even though I hate to say it, and maybe it was just because of the light, but I'd never seen her looking so ugly. "You arrogant *shit*," she said. "You actually think I'd kill someone over *you*?"

"And Fash," said Mason, ignoring Cora and turning to me. "You're just as bad. We all saw exactly how much you fancied Sadie. So tell us, what happened? Did you come on to her and she rejected you? And you just lost it? It's always the quiet ones, isn't that what they say? Poor repressed little Fash, always the victim, always so under his mother's thumb. Was it getting to you? Had you had as many knockbacks as you could take?"

My mouth fell open, but Luke stepped forward before I could speak.

"Listen to yourself, Mason. You're talking shit! Saying one thing and then the other, just like Cora said." He made a move as though to seize the bottle, but Mason took a step back.

"That's because I don't *know* what happened!" he said, with something between anger and desperation. "I don't *know* who I can *trust*! For all I know, *you* killed Sadie."

Even in the dark, I saw Luke's face go purple. For a second, he looked as though he was going to hurl himself forward, broken bot-

tle or not. "Sadie's my sister," he said. Not loudly. But in as frighten-
ing a voice as I've ever heard. "I'd sooner kill *myself* than hurt her."

The bottle wavered in Mason's hand, and for the first time I saw
him show a flicker of doubt. But then he looked at me, Cora and Abi
in turn, and his whole body seemed to tighten.

"Do you want to hear something, Luke?" he said. "Do you want
to know why the police were so convinced it was me? Because they
think Sadie was killed by someone she knew. Someone she trusted,
who could have lured her out of the house. Which, yeah, puts *me* in
the frame, but also applies to every single one of *them*." This time he
swung the bottle in an arc. Without any of us realizing, I think, me,
Cora and Abi had clustered together. "And there was something
else . . . something they found in Sadie's bedroom. Something anybody here could have planted."

I had no idea what he was talking about, but even so, I felt the
bottom drop out of my stomach.

"They found a test. Hidden away in her stuff. A *pregnancy* test."

All at once inside the cave there was a silence, so heavy that for
a moment it drowned out the rain.

"Sadie was *pregnant*?" said Cora, in shock, or horror, or both.

"I didn't say that," Mason hissed at her. "I said they found a test.
Half a one. A two-pack, with one of the thingamajigs missing. To
make it *look* like Sadie was pregnant. Which gave the police the one
part of the case against me they were missing. It gave them motive.
They think I wanted Sadie to get rid of it, or to keep it, or whatever
she *didn't* want to do."

Even Luke shrank backward as he tried to process what he was
hearing. Me, I couldn't have said anything if I'd wanted to.

"But the thing is, me and Sadie were careful," said Mason. "*Always.*
There's no way she would have had a pregnancy test. She wouldn't

ever have *needed* one. So what I want to know," he went on, holding up the bottle again, "is the answer to the question I asked at the beginning. Which one of you did it? And which one of you tried to trick the police into thinking it was *me*?"

I looked at Luke, hoping that if anyone could get through to Mason, he could. But Luke seemed almost to have shut down. His mouth was hanging open, and his eyes were focused on the floor. Abi was no help either. She was staring at Mason, shaking her head uselessly.

"Mason, listen to me," said Cora. "Nobody tried to frame you. I *swear* it. We're your friends. We're *Sadie's* friends. We would never have tried to hurt either one of you!"

"So where were you, Cora?" said Mason. "If you're my *friends*, how come I didn't hear from any one of you after Sadie went missing? Even you, Fash. I had to come to *you* to ask for help, remember?"

To trick me, he meant. To *use* me.

But on the other hand, I guess he had a point. I mean, I could only imagine how he must have felt. How it might have *seemed* like we'd turned our backs on him. But it wasn't that. Not for me, anyway. The truth is, there was another reason I was staying away. The same reason that, when Mason came to me, I agreed to do what he asked.

"Maybe I didn't come to see you," said Cora, "but I tried to help you. I *did*. I just, it didn't . . ." She was looking at Luke as she spoke, but before she could explain any further, there was movement in the shadows outside. Even Mason noticed from the corner of his eye.

"What the fuck was that?" he said.

I looked at the others, to see if they'd seen it, too. Luke was frowning out into the darkness. Cora and Abi glanced at each other, as though . . . as though they were sharing something. You know? A thought, a realization . . . *something*.

And then there was a noise, like someone running through the undergrowth, and Abi shrank back against the wall of the cave.

"Oh shit," she was saying. "Oh shit, oh shit, oh shit . . ."

Luke darted forward, but stopped when Mason swung the bottle.

"Cut me if you want," said Luke, with the jagged glass centimeters from his face. "Go on. *Do it.* It's the only way you're going to stop me getting past you."

And I guess he must have seen something in Mason's eyes. Capitulation, hesitation, whatever you want to call it. And then Luke was moving again, out of the cave, across the stream and scrabbling up the bank.

"Luke!" yelled Cora. "Wait!" She sounded afraid—even more afraid than she was of Mason, I guess, because she was suddenly running for the woods, too. And by this point I don't think Mason knew *what* to do. In fact, in spite of the broken bottle, he looked about as terrified as any of us.

All of a sudden Abi started running as well. Whether to go after the others, or to get away from whoever was out there, I don't know. And then it was just me and Mason left in the cave.

"Mase?" I said. "We need to go after them, Mase." I edged forward, close enough that I could hear the raggedness of his breathing. "I swear to you, the stuff you were saying . . . it's not true. None of it. But whoever's out there . . . maybe *they* know what happened to Sadie."

The bottle twitched in Mason's hand. He looked at me, out into the darkness, then back into the recesses of the cave.

"*Fuck!*" he suddenly roared. And when he turned to face me, there was so much fury in his eyes, so much frustration, I could have sworn he was about to lodge that bottle in my throat.

And then he was gone, out of the cave and into the rain. Before I knew it he'd been swallowed by the darkness.

I only hesitated for a moment, and then I was running for the woods, too. And I don't know about the others, but the only thing on my mind was to help my friends. I didn't mean for anyone to get hurt, I swear it. All I can think now is that we'd have been better off remaining exactly where we were. In spite of Mason. In spite of the bottle.

We should have stayed and taken our chances in that cave.

FLEET WAS WALKING the estuary when he discovered the inscription. He hadn't been looking for it. He'd had no idea it was there. He'd only come down here in the first place in an attempt to clear his head.

The promenade ran beside the water's edge, funneling the river into the sea. At some point in the past two decades, the council had scraped together enough money to lay some paving, paint the railings, install a few Narnia-style streetlamps—to put just enough gloss on the area, in other words, that any visitors might at first glance consider it a pleasant place to take a stroll. The local tourist board had even planted several pairs of coin-operated binoculars, perhaps in a halfhearted attempt to recoup the town's investment. But just as the railings had started flaking, and every third streetlamp was out, the slots on the binoculars had all been blocked up with chewing gum. Now passersby were denied the dubious pleasure of watching in close-up the tatty fishing boats setting out on the steel-gray water, or the golfers on the course across the river swatting their balls wildly into the wind.

Not that either option would have interested Fleet, even if there'd been enough daylight left by which to see. It had already begun to fade when he'd first come down here. To think, to walk. To make the most of the break in the weather when he'd finally left the station. Now, under cover of darkness, the rain had returned, and Fleet would long ago have gone back to his hotel if, in the dying of the light, his eyes hadn't caught on the words that were etched on the bench.

In memory of Jeannette Fleet, loved and never forgotten.

The bench was the last on the harbor walkway, a final resting place for passing pedestrians before the river washed away into the sea. Fleet could see exactly why his mother would have chosen this particular location—and who else other than his mother could have been responsible? He imagined her sitting exactly where he was now, in the slight hollow he could feel beneath him in the seat. Early mornings, late evenings—it would be as private a spot as was possible to find in an area that was so exposed. The perfect place for Fleet's mother to set aside her shame and, with her eyes on the point the heavens met the water, to quietly allow herself to grieve.

He'd misjudged her. For the best part of twenty years, he'd assumed she'd put religion over family, her god over her one and only daughter. He thought of the crucifix around his mother's neck, as well as the mantelpiece devoid of Jeannie's image—not to mention the accusations Fleet had hurled his mother's way before, as a teenager, he'd stormed from his childhood home. Driven by guilt, undoubtedly, but anger, too. At the fact his mother, after Jeannie killed herself, had chosen to act as though she'd never been alive. If suicide was a sin, he'd challenged his mother, then what was *that*?

But it turned out things hadn't been so simple. He thought of his mother now as being like the very river that had taken his sister's life: cold, inscrutable, but with unseen currents swirling below the surface. Her faith—her anger—tugging her one way; her grief—her love—the other. And he felt ashamed that, after watching her suffer the loss of one child, he'd forced her to endure the same thing all over again.

You heavens above, rain down my righteousness.

Standing, Fleet wiped the rain from his face. He moved to the railing and looked down toward the churning water—at the spot, by the final kink of the river, where Jeannie's body had caught amid the reeds. He heard his wife's voice: *It isn't the same* . . . And it wasn't. Of course it wasn't.

But it scared him how close he'd come to believing it might be.

As Fleet turned to walk back toward the harbor, the wind kicked the rain into his eyes. Perhaps if it hadn't, he might have seen them, though it was hard to imagine afterward how else things might have played out if he had.

"Evening, officer," said one of the men. Tall, broad, gruff. Stepping from the darkness into the pall of a streetlight, like a performer laying claim to center stage. There were three other men around him, hanging back in the shadows like cowardly hyenas around a lion. Fleet didn't need to glance around to know that the rest of the harbor was deserted. The nearest building was back beyond the boats, its curtained windows glowing dimly, like sightless eyes.

"Good evening," said Fleet, and he made to keep walking. The lion—a match for Fleet's height and build—stepped across his path.

Fleet raised his chin. "Can I help you with something?"

For some reason this was considered funny. The men's laughter carried with it a stench of lager. From somewhere nearby Fleet heard a drunken babble of conversation, rising and fading, as though a door had been opened and then shut again. The Hare & Tortoise—the pub Anne had told him about when he'd checked in, and from which the men in front of him had no doubt recently spilled.

Fleet took a moment to survey their faces. Three of them he didn't recognize. One, he did.

"Looking for someone, were you?" said Lion, who to match his status within the group had a mane of unkempt hair, long enough that he would probably have been able to tame it into a ponytail—though Fleet had to wonder what the bloke's mates, who hardly seemed in touch with their feminine side, would have made of that.

Hyena One—spotty and shaven-headed—cackled again. Hyena Two, thickset and bald, belched. The fourth man stood twitching quietly in the background. The one Fleet recognized: Mason's father, Stephen Payne.

Fleet, who'd dealt with plenty of drunks in his time, found Payne's manner difficult to read. Was he nervous? Excited? Afraid, perhaps? And if so, of Fleet's temper—or of whether he'd be able to control his own?

"Shame what happened to your sister," said Lion, prodding his chin toward the river. "It was before my time, of course. Must only have been ten when it happened. When she topped herself, I mean. But Stephen here remembers it. Don't you, Steve?"

Excited. Stephen Payne was definitely excited. He'd started nodding and seemed to be finding it difficult to stop. His pupils were dilated, too, meaning it perhaps wasn't only lager he'd been indulging in this evening.

"Still, some people round here say it was justice," said Lion. "Say that's what happens when you go around telling lies."

"Is that right?" said Fleet, focusing on Payne. "So how come you're still knocking around, *Steve*?"

Which was stupid. But stopped Payne nodding, at least. A memory came back to Fleet, of a situation similar to this one. Fleet had been outnumbered on that occasion, as well, though back then he'd known exactly who he'd been dealing with. Stephen Payne, obviously, a year younger than him, though at the time half a head taller. Nigel Sullivan, built like a postbox, with an intellect to match. Matthew Morgan. Morgue, to his friends—as in, shit with him and he'll happily put you in one. And James Cooper. Little Jimmy Cooper. Wouldn't hurt a fly. Unless that fly happened to be a fourteen-year-old girl he'd taken a fancy to, but who'd made the dubious decision not to fancy him back.

When Fleet had confronted them—thirteen days too late for it to have made any difference; hell, a year too late, it had turned out—they'd kicked the living shit out of him. And Fleet had welcomed it. Self-flagellation: when Holly had used the word, she'd known as well as Fleet did that he knew exactly what it meant.

Looking at Payne now, Fleet saw nothing about the man that came as a surprise. He was tall, and carried weight, but nevertheless managed to look malnourished. There was a hollowness to his cheeks and a pallor to his skin that suggested it had been years since he'd last sat in sunlight, and longer since he'd come within a fork's distance of a vegetable. But none of that made him look weak, exactly. Maybe he would have struggled to lift a barbell at the gym, but in a pub brawl his fists would no doubt land quick and heavy. Or even in his son's bedroom at home.

What surprised Fleet more than Payne's appearance was his own reaction to being in his presence. It was the first time since Fleet's arrival back in town that he had been. Predictably enough, Payne hadn't come to the police station with his son—probably because he'd been worried that if he set foot in there, they wouldn't let him back out. But he'd been on Fleet's mind. Of course he had. And seeing Payne now, Fleet felt an old familiar rage—a readiness to risk his reputation, his career, his freedom, for the chance to rip the man's throat out.

"Different faces, same old story. Eh, Steve?" said Fleet, gesturing loosely around the group. "The only difference now is that people in this town seem to have cottoned on to what a lowlife you are. Is that why the buddies you had back in the day decided to ditch you? Just like your old lady, from what I heard."

"No one *ditched* me," said Payne. "I ditched *them*. Waste of oxygen, the lot of them. Decided it was time to get me a new life."

"A neat trick, that," said Fleet. "Moving on without moving anywhere."

Out of his old gang of four, it was only Stephen Payne who hadn't left town. Fleet knew because one of them had written to him. The postbox, fittingly: Nigel Sullivan. Five, six years ago now, this had been. In shockingly bad handwriting and with spelling that would have foxed the Forensics lads, Sullivan had not only revealed what his former friends had amounted to (Jimmy Cooper, the ringleader, was an accomplished housebreaker—or not so accomplished, arguably, given the amount of time he'd evidently spent in prison; Matthew "Morgue" Morgan was dead), he'd also apologized for everything he'd been a part of. He'd listed things Fleet hadn't even been aware had happened, though they didn't fundamentally alter the overall picture. Below the radar—below Fleet's radar, anyway—his little sister had suffered over a year of relentless bullying and abuse. She'd been made into a pariah at school, something else Fleet, in his dumb, dipshit existence, had failed to notice. To notice, or to take note of? Either way, he hadn't lifted so much as a fingernail to try to stop it, nor to attempt to understand the anguish his sister was going through. And he hadn't been there for her, either, when Stephen Payne and his cronies had followed Jeannie into the woods one day and subjected her to an assault that had only stopped short of rape by virtue of the fact she'd been having her period.

It freaked them out, apparently. Sent them running.

In his letter, Sullivan admitted to it all, and apologized for having denied it at the time. Which they all had, obviously, after Jeannie had admitted to her mother what had happened, and she in turn had insisted on taking the matter to the police. The problem, of course, was that it had come down to one person's word against four, and the boys' parents somehow managed to get the community on their sons' sides. They called into question Jeannie's character—did everything but put up posters declaring outright that she was a lying slut. They made out Jeannie had been obsessed with their boys, with Jimmy Cooper in particular, and that when he had rejected her advances, she'd concocted the entire story as a form of retribution. And so it had been Jeannie herself who'd paid the price for what had happened, while Payne and his buddies walked away scot-free.

Sullivan, when he'd contacted Fleet over a decade later, had offered to testify, but ten years into his career as a copper by then, Fleet had known precisely how much good that would have done. How insultingly slim the chances would have been of a conviction. Besides which, any charges that could have been brought against the three men who'd still been breathing would have fallen well short of the crime they deserved to answer for. Because in Fleet's mind, suicide wasn't the cause of Jeannie's death. The way he saw it, his sister had been murdered.

"Wasn't there something you wanted to say to the nice policeman, Steve?" said Lion, with an expression somewhere between a smile and a snarl.

Payne sniffed and wiped his nostrils with the side of his hand. Fleet could practically taste the cocaine dribble at the back of the man's throat.

"Yeah," Payne said, stepping forward—level with Lion but no farther, Fleet noted. Perhaps another pint of Foster's, another line of coke, would have carried him the extra few inches. "Leave my kid alone," Payne told him, pointing a finger. "He ain't done nothing and you know it. Not his fault some stuck-up bitch decided to take a swim and forgot to bring her armbands."

Fleet edged forward himself, far enough that Payne felt the need to withdraw a fraction.

"Are you offering to provide information that might be pertinent to an ongoing investigation, Mr. Payne?"

It was evidently too many syllables in quick succession for Payne to handle. "Huh?" he grunted.

"What I'm asking you," *you dumb, child-beating piece of shit*, "is whether there's something you'd like to tell me. Because it sounded just then like it might be worth my time hauling you down to the station. Asking what *you* know about Sadie Saunders's disappearance."

How dearly Fleet would have loved to do exactly that. To rattle Payne into believing he was a suspect. But Fleet already knew the man had an airtight alibi. The night of Sadie's disappearance, and following a brawl outside the boozer, Stephen Payne had been shut in a police cell. That was part of the reason Mason's alibi was so weak. He'd claimed he'd been asleep in his bedroom, but his old man being locked up meant there hadn't been anyone else in the house.

Still, it was worth putting the wind up Payne, just to see him rattled.

"Nuh-uh. Fuck you. You can't *do* that. You ain't pinning Sadie on me."

"Maybe I should just insist that you turn out your pockets," Fleet pressed. "You're looking a bit twitchy there, Steve. I wonder whether it's just cash you've got tucked away in your wallet. Or, if I searched you, whether I might find something a bit more . . . illegal."

Payne melted away, his skittering eyes landing on Lion in a plea for help.

Dismissing the men with a headshake, Fleet made to walk on, but once again Lion stepped across his path. Through it all, he'd been the only one of the foursome to hold his ground.

"All our mutual friend is trying to say," he said, his tone dangerously reasonable, "is that he thinks it would be a good idea for you to face the facts. You've been running around town shouting murder, accusing people left, right and center, when it seems blindingly obvious to anyone with half a brain that Sadie took a nosedive in the river. Just like your poor little sister."

Fleet's teeth clamped tight. Furiously, he held the man's eyes.

"And what you don't seem to appreciate," Lion went on, "is that when outsiders come along and start casting aspersions against the residents of this town, it affects the people who live here. Stand-up, honest people like our good selves." The irony was written in his smile. "Maybe it doesn't bother you now that you've set up home somewhere else, but for a town that relies so much on tourists, reputation is important. We want decent folks coming to visit. People with money to spend. Not fetishists and freaks, who only stay long enough to snap a picture for their scrapbooks before heading on to the next brains-spattered crime scene on their lists."

One of the hyenas tittered, as though his friend had described exactly the sort of pastime he might enjoy pursuing himself.

"Now, I'm not an educated sort," said Lion. "But from what I've heard, all sorts of nasty things start happening when there's a downturn, particularly in a community that's already on the edge. Crime goes up, apparently. *Nasty* crimes, like break-ins and burglaries, and assaults on little old ladies when they're walking home from church at night." He shook his head sadly. "It would be a shame indeed if that sort of thing started happening *here*. In the very place your mother lives. She's a churchgoer, I believe?"

Fleet moved so they were toe to toe, and allowed himself to flinch at the stench. The man reeked like a beer mat.

"Murdoch," he said. "That's your name, isn't it? Nathan Murdoch. Three counts of public disorder, four for the possession of class A drugs, and one for . . . what was the other thing?"

He watched Lion's smirk slip into his jowls. Almost the first thing Fleet and his colleagues had done when the Sadie Saunders investigation began was run checks on the local scumbags. It had taken him a while to place Nathan Murdoch, but now that he had, he found himself recalling the details in the man's file that had first caught his attention. Again, there was no suggestion of his involvement with Sadie's disappearance, but for a while Fleet and his colleagues had considered Murdoch closely—just as they had everyone within a fifty-mile radius who was on the sex offenders register. In Murdoch's case, the count Fleet had failed to mention was an indictment for distributing pornographic images involving minors. It was hard to say whether Murdoch had dabbled to satisfy his own proclivities or purely for profit, but Fleet doubted very much that Murdoch's associates, were they to find out, would draw a distinction either way.

From the expression on Fleet's face, it was obvious Murdoch was thinking the same thing.

Fleet shook his head. "It's slipped my mind," he said. "For the time being. But I could always give the local desk sergeant a call and ask him to refresh my memory? Seeing as we're standing around chatting and all, I'm sure it would make an interesting topic of conversation."

Now Murdoch was the one to bite down. His jaw bulged, as though he were attempting to swallow a shit sandwich sideways.

"No," said Fleet. "I thought not. Now, if you'll excuse me, I'll be on my way. Have a pleasant evening, gentlemen. Remember there's always a bed for you at the local nick if you find yourselves tempted to start any more trouble."

Fleet stood waiting, until finally Murdoch moved to one side. The other men parted, too. Grudgingly, as though they were being forced to watch a stranger queue-jump his way toward the bar.

Fleet kept his eyes on Stephen Payne's until he was through. And then he was walking alone through the rain, barely conscious of his strides, aware only of the torrents of adrenaline flowing within him. It was taking every ounce of his self-possession, every facet of his training, to stop himself from turning around and hurling Payne, Murdoch—the lot of them—headfirst over the railings and into the river.

His mistake was to assume it was over.

Such was the pounding in his ears, he didn't hear the sound of anyone behind him. He was focused only on the pavement at his feet, and he looked up in surprise when he realized he'd reached the hotel. The windows were dark, even in the guests' lounge, but the thought of inflicting his mood on Anne if she were still awake was enough to stop Fleet heading immediately inside.

And that was another mistake.

For it was as Fleet loitered in the darkened street that the hood came down over his eyes. From the stink of it, the dust that imme-diately clogged his throat, it was an old rubbish sack, something from a building site or a skip. It was the last thought Fleet had before the first blow impacted against his kidneys. It snapped his body one way, before a punch on the opposite side hinged it back again. Fleet managed to swing out an elbow, striking teeth, but he was outnum-bered, overpowered, and suddenly his feet went from under him.

He hit his head on something as he fell, and from that point on and until the darkness took him, there was only pain: sharp, intense, welcome, like an old, familiar friend.

DAY **NINE**

THE FIRST THING Fleet noticed when he woke was the scent. It was dizzyingly intimate, and at first he thought it was coming from the pillow that was unaccountably beneath his head.

But when he cracked an eyelid, he saw red lips, dark hair, and a face more familiar to him these days in his dreams. He blinked and, rather than disappearing as Fleet had half expected it to, the face only came into focus.

"I thought I told you to take care of yourself."

That voice. Jesus, that voice. As warm as the perfume she was wearing, and just as capable of stinging when applied to an open wound. Which . . . *ow* . . . his entire body seemed to be at the moment.

"Holly? What the . . . Where am I?"

Fleet tore his eyes from his wife and realized he was in a hotel room. Not *his* hotel room, but one very much like it.

"You're in room one," said another voice, and Fleet turned to see Anne standing near the door. "Ground floor," she explained. "You're not an easy man to move when you're only half-conscious, Detective Inspector. I've known cats that were easier to haul upright than you."

Fleet winced himself sitting. "You . . ." A flashing memory of what had happened, of those first few digs into his ribs, and the choking sensation from the dust that had been inside the bag. "You found me? Outside. Did you . . ."

"I didn't see what happened. I didn't even hear it. I only happened to go out to put the rubbish in the bin before I went to bed. Collection day tomorrow," she added with a shrug, then looked at her watch. "Today, I mean. In fact, it's probably been and gone."

"Why, what time is it?" said Fleet, moving suddenly and sending a jolt through his rib cage that was powerful enough that it might have been delivered by another fist. As for his head . . . Christ. He'd only once in his life known anything like it—the time he and Thomas Murphy had filched a bottle of gin from Tom's mother's drinks cabinet, and Tom had tricked Fleet into downing most of the bottle. When Fleet wasn't looking, Tom had been topping up his own glass with water, meaning Fleet had got the lion's share of the hangover, too.

"It's barely seven," said Holly, holding a hand against Fleet's chest to pin him. "And just so we're clear, you're not going anywhere anyway. Except maybe to A&E to get that bump on your head checked out." She turned to Anne. "Is there an A&E near here?"

Anne opened her mouth to answer, but Fleet interrupted.

"I don't need to go to A&E. I need . . ." He'd moved, and he winced again. "I need to get to the station."

Holly laughed, a single, bitter bark. "What did I tell you?" she said to Anne over her shoulder.

Anne smiled sympathetically, and Fleet couldn't tell whether it was aimed at Holly or him. "I think I'll leave the two of you to work it out," she said. "Just shout if you need anything."

She slipped into the corridor outside, closing the door quietly behind her. When she was gone, the room immediately felt smaller, the atmosphere within it thicker. Holly seemed to feel it, too, and withdrew a fraction from her position at the head end of Fleet's bed.

"She called you?" said Fleet, to test the silence. "That's how you're here?"

Holly's lips were in a pout, her arms folded across her chest. Fleet knew the signs well: his wife was braced for an argument.

"She got my number from your phone. Used your thumb to unlock it. She's a smart lady," she added, and to Fleet it sounded like an accusation.

"Very smart," he said. "Attractive, too, in case you didn't notice."

It was a risk, but it broke the tension. Holly tutted, unfolding her arms, and turned her chin to hide her smile.

Fleet shuffled until his back was against the headboard. "What did she say to get you to come down here?" he asked. It struck him that he hadn't said thank you to Anne—and immediately after, as he waited on his wife's response, that maybe he should be withholding judgment on whether Anne deserved his gratitude or not. Maybe she'd rescued him from a physical beating, but he could already sense that there was an emotional one still to come.

"She said you'd been hurt. She said she figured I'd want to know."

"And did you?"

The pout was back. Already. "I'm here, aren't I?" But rather than crossing her arms again, Holly exhaled, and dropped onto the foot end of Fleet's bed.

Fleet tried not to wince as the ripples carried through the mattress.

"What happened, Rob? You've obviously been busy making new friends."

"I was just getting reacquainted with an old one, actually," Fleet answered. Seeing the look that came into Holly's eyes, he held up a hand. "*He* found me. I didn't go looking. I promise."

Holly opened her mouth, then shut it again. She looked his way, studying him, and shook her head. "You're a mess. You do realize that, don't you? They spared your face, but your body's black and blue, and I really don't like the look of that bump." She reached to touch Fleet's forehead, and Fleet shied away. "I'm serious about A&E, you know. You need to get yourself checked out."

"I know. And I will," Fleet lied. "But not today."

Another pout. "The case?"

Fleet nodded. "Things are coming to a head. Roger's set on charging the girl's boyfriend, but . . ."

Holly waited. "But . . ." she prompted eventually.

This time Fleet was the one to shake his head. He regretted it immediately, and reached to test his bump with his fingertips.

"You don't think he did it," Holly said for him. "You think Roger's just trying to draw a line."

"I *know* Roger's trying to draw a line. The man's a walking Magic Marker."

Holly laughed. "Now there's an image," she said. "Personally, I've always pictured him as more of a ruler. You know, if we're comparing him to stationery."

"The ruler's just what he's got stuck up his—"

"*Rob,*" said Holly sharply, swiftly followed by another laugh.

You see? Fleet told himself, beneath his smile. *It's moments like this that are the problem.* How much easier things would be if he and Holly never accidentally got along.

"So what makes you so uncertain?" Holly asked him. "About what's his name. The boyfriend. Are you even sure the girl is dead? Because they said on the news—"

"Mason. The kid's name is Mason. And we're not sure of any-thing. That's the problem."

Once again Holly waited.

Fleet sighed. "I was never convinced, you know. About Mason. I mean, it all made sense. The idea that he killed Sadie was about the only theory that did. He had motive, opportunity, the temperament. But it just . . . it never *felt* right. You know?" Fleet glanced and saw Holly nod. "The only thing I was sure of was that Sadie's friends were lying to us. Holding something back. And as for Mason . . . he's basically his own worst enemy. Since the day Sadie went missing, all he's been doing is digging himself further into a hole. *That's* why we kept on at them. We *had* to. *I* had to. If I hadn't, I wouldn't have been doing my job. But I swear to God, Holly, it wasn't like people have been saying."

"What have people been saying?" said Holly, frowning.

"They think we—I—became fixated. Because of what happened to Jeannie. You see, Mason . . . he's Stephen Payne's son. He's the one who—"

"I know who Stephen Payne is," Holly interrupted. "Christ, Rob, we haven't been separated for *that* long."

From the moment Fleet had finally told Holly about his sister—about a month before they got married—she'd been almost as furious about what had happened as Fleet was. More so, actually, because by then Fleet had managed to bury his own fury deep inside him, whereas Holly's rage was righteous and raw. So he'd known she would hardly need reminding who Stephen Payne was. What he'd actually been about to tell her was that Payne was one of the men who'd jumped him. (*Allegedly*, the copper in him cautioned, reminding him that he had no actual proof. He hadn't even seen his attackers.) But Fleet decided that, on balance, it was probably better—safer—if he kept that particular piece of information to himself. Heaven knew what Holly would do if she found out.

"Anyway, the link with Stephen Payne is only part of it, I'm guessing. People see me as someone who's got it in for the entire community. They think . . . I don't know what they think. That somehow I've got it into my head that Sadie's friends are just like Stephen Payne's gang from back in the day. They got away with what they did, and I left town, but now I'm back and looking for revenge."

"But that's ridiculous!"

Fleet twitched a shoulder, and realized he'd found a part of his body that didn't hurt. "Maybe. Maybe not. But if I'd really wanted to get back at Stephen Payne by taking it out on his son, I could have had Mason in custody the day Sadie went missing. My team would have supported me. Roger would have given me a great big pat on the back."

"Exactly," said Holly, as though that settled it.

"But what I can't help thinking," Fleet went on, "is that maybe *that's* where I went wrong. Maybe the people round here are right after all."

"What do you mean?"

"I mean, maybe if I'd ignored that voice in my head—if I'd focused on following the evidence and taken Mason into custody at the start—the search party would never have happened. Because that part is unquestionably true. Sadie's friends only set off into the woods in the first place because we put them under so much pressure."

"Because they were lying to you! Because they're still lying, I'm guessing. And you just said, you don't think Mason did it."

"No, I know, but—"

"So there you go then! You said it yourself, Rob. If people lie to you, you *have* to put them under pressure. Getting to the truth is part of your job. Christ, it *is* your job. And if you're blaming yourself for the way things turned out in the woods, you can cut that shit out right now. You didn't want *that* to happen, did you?"

"No, of course not."

"And you're big enough and ugly enough to know that the whole world doesn't turn around you, right? That it's not just the decisions *you* take that dictate what happens to the rest of us. *Right?*"

Fleet couldn't help but smile.

"So are you done now?" said Holly. "Feeling sorry for yourself, I mean? So some people around town are talking shit. So what?" She exhaled angrily, shaking her head. "What does Nicky think? About Mason, about Roger. About what people around here are saying," she added scornfully.

"Nicky's loyal. Even if she thought I'd screwed up, she wouldn't—"

"Nicky's loyal for a reason, Rob. She's loyal because she knows better than anyone that you're a damn fine copper. And more important, that you're a damn fine human being. Honestly, Rob. You've beaten yourself up enough over the years, wouldn't you say? And as for that poor kid out there in the woods . . . surely you know by now that you can't save everyone. I know you want to. I know that's why you do what you do. But not everything is on you, Rob. Even Jeannie. *What happened to her isn't on you.*"

Fleet didn't respond. Mainly because he didn't know how to.

They sat in silence for a moment. From the expression on Holly's face, she seemed afraid that she'd gone too far.

"What's he like?" she said at last, her tone softer now. "The boyfriend. Mason. How badly screwed-up is he? I mean, Jesus. To have Stephen Payne as a father. Whatever that poor kid's done in his life, whatever he's guilty of now, you'd have to imagine he's already been punished enough."

Fleet didn't have to imagine anything to know that what Holly had said was true.

"Mason's angry. Stupid. Young." What Fleet didn't add, but he was thinking, is that Mason had come to remind Fleet of himself when he'd been Mason's age. Fleet had been just as disdainful, just as arrogant, just as insecure, deep down, in his sense of self-worth.

As was her knack, Holly appeared to have read between the lines anyway. "Sounds like someone else you used to know," she said.

Fleet returned her smile, then flinched at the pain in his head.

"Here," said Holly, reaching toward the bedside table. "Anne left a packet of paracetamol." She tossed the box onto Fleet's lap, and held the glass of water while he popped the pills from the blister pack. He swallowed two, shaking his head when Holly offered him the water.

She shuddered. "I don't know how you can do that. What if they got stuck in your throat?"

"It might help with the diet," Fleet said.

"Which is going well, I see," said Holly, nodding at the bulge where Fleet's belly was beneath the covers.

"You may mock," said Fleet, "but all this padding comes in handy when somebody's trying to kick the shit out of you."

"Oh," said Holly, ignoring him, "your cigarettes were in your pocket, in case you're wondering. If you're looking for them later, you'll find them in the bin."

Once again Fleet smiled, quietly.

They sat in silence for a moment, each of them lost in their thoughts.

"So what happened?" said Holly, after a moment. "If you don't think Mason did it—who did?"

"Jesus, Holly. Do you think I'd be sitting here if I knew?"

"But you have a theory. I can tell."

God, she could be annoying. Fleet didn't mean to be so transparent, but his wife could see through him as though he were a piece of glass.

"I have an idea," he admitted. "That's all."

"And?" Holly prompted.

"And I hope I'm wrong," Fleet said, sighing again. "I really, really do."

She helped him dress. Fleet possessed nothing she hadn't seen before, but even so, he felt uncomfortable at the echo of intimacy. Holly did, too, he could tell, though she disguised it better than he did, passing him his clothes and helping with the buttons with a brisk efficiency. In the end, the process took about three times as long as it should have done, though it would have taken far longer if Fleet had been on his own.

"You're serious about going to work today," said Holly, as she watched Fleet struggle to tie the laces on his shoes. He could bear the pain in his torso if he stood up straight and didn't breathe too deeply, but hinging at the waist brought on a sensation of a knife being thrust into his kidneys.

"I'll manage," he said. "Really. They weren't trying to kill me. Just to send me a message. I'd have been able to drag myself inside if I hadn't hit my head when I fell."

His fingers fumbled to loop the final knot. When he was done, he stood up straight, exhaling away his discomfort. He looked around the room, and Holly did the same. She'd already stripped the bed and cracked the window, and with Fleet superficially as good as new, there was nothing left to be done.

They lingered.

"So what now?" said Holly. And Fleet knew exactly what she meant.

He turned and took hold of one of her hands. Just lightly, finger-tips to fingertips. "I've missed you, you know," he told her. "Every day."

Holly brought her other hand abruptly to her mouth, as though to catch a sudden sob. Water welled in her eyes. "I've missed you, too," she answered, once she appeared able to trust herself to speak.

"And I'm glad you came," Fleet said. "Really. I'm grateful."

"Don't say it, Rob."

"But . . ." he went on, and Holly shook her head.

"I said, don't say it. Not yet. We'll talk. We will. But after this is over." She gave something between a sniff and a laugh, and used a finger to dam the water in her right eye. "Whatever *this* is," she said.

There was a knock, and like teenagers caught in an upstairs bed-room, they let go of each other's hand and moved apart.

Anne poked her head around the door.

"Sorry to interrupt, but . . ." She looked at Fleet. "There was a call for you. A DS Collins?"

"Nicky? What did she want?"

With an apologetic glance toward Holly, Anne allowed herself to cross the threshold. "She wanted to speak to you, but I said you were busy. Which she didn't take kindly to at all."

"No," said Fleet, with a glint. "I don't imagine she did. Did she leave a message?"

"She did. And she told me to deliver it right away. She said, and I'm quoting now, 'The kid's turned up.' And something about a busi-ness card? She seemed to think you'd know what it meant."

Fleet turned to Holly. He didn't have to say anything for her to start nodding. She'd read the sudden urgency in his eyes.

"Go," she said. Then, when Fleet spun away, "Wait, Rob. Here."

She snatched his car keys from the bedside table and tossed them toward him. As he caught them, Fleet was already moving for the door.

CORA

I'D ALREADY LOST sight of Luke as I crossed the stream. He'd disappeared into the darkness, chasing after whoever was out there. And I don't know why I was so panicked, but I just had this feeling that something terrible was about to happen. That Luke . . . that he was in danger.

"Luke? *Luke!*"

I tripped in the water, and landed knee-first on a rock. The pain shot all the way through me, like an electric current or something, like when you bang your funny bone, except way, way worse. And I can't be certain, but I'm pretty sure I screamed. In fact, I did, because someone must have heard me. Fash, I think, because it was definitely one of the boys who called my name. Except somehow whoever it was had got ahead of me, into the trees on the opposite bank. And that's when I realized that we'd all been separated, that everyone must have set off running in different directions. Which made that feeling that something awful was about to happen even worse.

When I got to my feet, I found I could only hobble. I almost fell again climbing the bank, but managed to use a tree root to haul myself up. On flatter ground the going was easier, but I was still only moving at half speed, and I didn't know in which direction I was supposed to be heading. In the dark, and with the rain . . . it was like running through static. Like floundering to get to the picture on the other side. And although I called out again, and thought I heard someone shout back, the sound out there was all messed up, too. Because of the rain. And all the trees, I suppose. I couldn't tell what was ahead and what was behind me.

"Luke! Wait, will you?"

I'd seen movement up ahead through the darkness, a shadow flashing between the tree trunks. And even though it was Luke's name I called, the truth is it could have been anyone. But I veered in that direction, limping as fast as I could to try to catch up. Because the other thing was, I kept thinking about Mason. I could picture him crashing through the undergrowth behind me—coming after me, in fact—and that just made me move even faster.

I don't know how long it all took. The five of us running through the trees like that. Probably not all that long, but at the time it didn't feel as though it would ever end. It was like being in a nightmare or something. A nightmare within a nightmare, where there's no way of telling what's really real. Which is why, when I heard it, I wasn't sure at first whether I'd really heard *anything*.

But what happened was, I tripped again. Over a root or something. And I landed on the very same knee. Which, even though the ground was softer, was so painful I thought I was going to black out. I couldn't even scream this time, because the pain was like a . . . like it had locked up all the moving bits inside me. I *wanted* to scream, and it was just right there, at the back of my throat, but that was as far as it could get. I couldn't yell, couldn't have talked, couldn't even *breathe*.

And then, when the pain subsided, I lay where I'd fallen, moaning. Crying, in fact. And my knee . . . I mean, take a look for yourself. See?

And now compare it to the other one.

Do you see what I mean?

Apparently all I did was bruise it, but it felt at the time as though someone had taken a hammer to my kneecap. It feels a bit like that even now, if I'm honest. Not that I'm complaining. They offered to give me a crutch at the hospital, but it's like . . . it's a bruise. You know? Like, big fucking deal. And, yeah, it hurts, but I'm not going to go around with the equivalent of a great big sign around my neck asking for sympathy. Not after . . . not after what happened.

So anyway, I'm lying there, my hands either side of my knee, and that's when I thought I heard it.

The voice.

I couldn't tell where it was coming from. It's like I said, for all I knew it was just my imagination. A trick of the rain or something. But it seemed as though it was coming from up ahead, from near where I'd seen that shadow. I couldn't see anything when I looked, though, and I couldn't make out what the voice was saying. But the thing was—the thing that made me listen so closely; the thing that freaked me out, if I'm honest—was that the voice sounded like it belonged to a *girl*.

And, no. Before you ask. It couldn't have been Abi's. Christ, I'd recognize her bleat anywhere. With Abi's voice, sometimes, it's like with bats. You don't hear it so much with your ears, as feel it in the back of your skull. And anyway, it turned out later that Abi had run in the other direction entirely. At least, that's what she claimed.

But it didn't sound like Abi's, is my point. And obviously it wasn't Mason's, or Fash's, or Luke's. I forced myself back onto my feet again, and tried to move closer, but the next time I stopped to listen, all I could hear was the rain. It was falling heavily, and the sound was like gravel coming down through the trees. But then there was another voice, deeper this time, and this one sounded more familiar. I strained to hear, but whoever it was seemed to be whispering, hissing almost. I caught a word or two—*home*, maybe. *Help. Hurry.*

And then both voices stopped. Instead, there was movement again, first on one side of me, and then on the other. There was a yell, a scream of pain, and this time I was certain it was Luke.

"Luke!" I called, stumbling forward. "Luke, where are you?"

He didn't answer, even though he'd sounded so close. I felt tree roots trying to snag around my ankles, and branches clawing at my face. And then, suddenly, I was in a clearing. It wasn't large, and it was almost as dark as it had been in the trees. But there was just enough light that I was able to see: Luke lying bleeding on the ground, and Mason standing over him looking down, his hand still clutching that broken bottle.

ABI

I MISSED IT all. Whatever it was that happened. By the time I found the others, they were in the clearing, arguing as though we'd never left the cave.

"You were standing right over him! And there was no one else here!"

"But you found us pretty quickly, didn't you, Cora? Meaning *you* couldn't have been very far away!"

"Guys. *Guys!*" This from Fash. "For Christ's sake, stop shouting at each other, will you?" He was crouched down for some reason, his torch on the ground beside him, and when he spoke I saw him glance out into the trees. Like he was afraid. Like he thought there might have been something out there, and he was worried all the shouting would bring it back.

"Cora?" I said, because even though she had her back to me, she was the one standing closest.

She spun and clutched a hand to her heart. "Abi, Jesus . . ." She lurched, then, and gave a wince, as though something was the matter with her leg.

"What's happening?" I said. "Why are you all—"

And then I saw Luke.

"Luke?"

I rushed forward. I was already out of breath from running, but seeing him on the ground like that, I felt my heart rate double.

"He's OK," said Fash, who was beside him. "Just a bit dazed. Right, mate?" He moved the torch so that the light was pointing at Luke's chest, close enough to allow us to see his face. He was propped up on his elbows, and his eyes were half-shut. Against the torch beam, I guess, and the pain, but also because of the blood that was dripping from his forehead.

"You're hurt!" I said.

"I'm all right," he said, kind of groggily. "Just got a bit of a headache, that's all."

He raised his hand to touch the cut on his head. It was hard to tell how bad it was, because the blood was mixing with the rain.

Mason and Cora edged closer, so that all five of us were in a sort of huddle. Fash was the only one with a torch—he told us later that he'd grabbed it from the floor of the cave before following the rest of us into the woods—and he kept lasering it out into the trees, first one way, then another. Cora looked even more jittery than Fash did. She was watching the woods, too, but she also seemed to have one eye on Mason. Even Mason kept glancing over his shoulder. He was still holding that bottle, I noticed, and when he saw me looking at it he tightened his grip.

"What happened?" I said to Luke. "Did you fall?" I looked around for something he might have tripped on, but I already knew from the way the others were acting that that wasn't what had happened at all.

"Yeah, Mason," said Cora. "What happened?" She half turned to face me. "He was standing right over Luke when I found them," she told me. "Just the two of them alone in the clearing."

"I told you," Mason said to her, his voice all angry and tight, "he was lying on the ground when I got here. And anyway, where the fuck have *you* been?" he added, and I realized he was talking to me.

"I was looking for you lot!" I said. "For *Luke*. I got lost, and . . . and I heard you lot yelling."

"You got lost," said Mason, making it sound like it was the most ridiculous thing he'd ever heard. "Which doesn't explain why you're so out of breath."

"I'm out of breath because I was *running*," I said. "Because I was scared. *OK?* To be honest, I'm still scared! I don't like any of this *at all*." I followed the beam from Fash's torch, but all I could see was the rain, and the tree trunks at the edge of the clearing. Past them there was just this *blackness*, hiding the eyes I felt sure were looking in.

Luke had hauled himself to sitting. He touched his head again.

"I didn't fall," he said to me, and I realized he was answering the question I'd asked him before. "Someone . . . swung a branch at me. Or . . . or something, anyway. I ducked, just in time, but . . . but I'm pretty sure they were trying to take my head off."

I felt my eyes widen.

"I saw someone," said Fash. "Out there. When I was stumbling around trying to find you lot."

"*Who?*" said Cora, but Mason interrupted before Fash could answer.

"So you happened to lose your way as well, did you?" Mason said to him.

"We *all* lost our way," Cora snapped. "In case you hadn't noticed, it's pitch-black out here, and Fash is the only one who's got a torch."

"Which is exactly my point," said Mason. "Fash has got a torch. So how the fuck did *he* manage to get lost?"

"I didn't say I got lost! I said I was looking for you lot!"

By this point I'd had as much as I could take. "Stop it!" I yelled at them. "Just *stop it*, will you? Stop *arguing*. It doesn't help *anything*."

Which seemed to do the trick. For the time being, at least.

"Who did you see, Fash?" said Luke, getting back to what actually mattered.

"I don't know. Just a shape, really. By the time I swung the torch they were gone."

Cora was frowning. "I might have seen someone, too. It was hard to tell. And I thought . . ."

"Thought what?" said Luke.

"Nothing, just . . . I thought I heard voices. That's all. Like, a girl's voice, maybe."

The rest of them turned my way. "Don't look at *me*," I said. "I wasn't talking to *anyone*."

"No, it didn't sound like Abi," said Cora. "It sounded like . . . I don't know who it sounded like. I fell, and hurt my knee, and it was hard to hear through the rain."

No one said anything for a moment. The rain wasn't as loud in the clearing as it had been under the trees, but there was still a constant hiss.

"So what are you saying, Cora?" said Mason. "I thought your theory was that *I* hurt Luke. That's what you seemed to think before."

"Well, what would you expect me to think?" Cora said. "You're the one standing there still holding that broken bottle. The same one you were threatening us with in the cave!"

"Don't start," I said. "*Please* don't start arguing *again*. Can't we just *go*? Whoever's out there just attacked Luke! And we're just standing here right out in the open. What if they come back?"

I looked again toward the trees. Fash, next to me, did the same.

"There are five of us," said Mason, raising the bottle. "And only one of them, from the sound of it. Assuming there's anyone out there at all."

"You don't think there's anyone out there?" said Fash.

"You're kidding," said Cora to Mason. "Right? Fash *saw* someone. I did, too. And we all heard someone when we were in the cave. That's why we're standing here now. *Remember?*"

"I heard something," Mason answered. "Not someone. *Something*. And all Fash saw was a shadow. As for you . . . you don't even know *what* you saw."

"So one of *us* attacked Luke? Is that your theory?"

"Let's just say I'm keeping an open mind," Mason snarled, and my eyes went again to that broken bottle.

"What about you, Luke?" I said, before Cora could answer back. "Did you see whoever it was who attacked you?"

Luke hesitated, as though trying to remember. "I didn't see a face," he said. "I had my back turned until I heard something behind me. And when I spun, the only thing I saw was that branch on its way toward my head." He touched his forehead again, then looked at Mason. "But whoever it was, it wasn't anyone standing here," he insisted. "I'm *sure* of it."

Mason was trying to stay angry, I could tell. But right then, when Luke said that, the only thing he looked was afraid.

With Fash's help, Luke got to his feet. "Come on," he said. "Let's get going. How's your leg, Cora? Can you walk?"

Which was typical Luke, you know? It's like, he was the one who'd just been bashed over the head. And yet the first thing he does when he gets back up again is ask someone else if they're OK.

"Honestly?" said Cora. "It's agony." She moved, testing her weight, and her right leg buckled beneath her.

"Fuck's sake," muttered Mason.

"We'll find you something to lean on," said Luke, ignoring him. "In the meantime, put your arm around my shoulders."

"No, wait," said Fash, stepping forward. "Hold on to me, Cora. The last thing Luke needs is to be bearing somebody else's weight."

"But where are we *going*?" I said, as Cora hooked herself on to Fash. "I swear, I am *not* spending the night in that cave. I'd rather sit here in the middle of the clearing. At least we'd have a chance of seeing someone coming."

"We can't stay here, Abi," said Fash. "We're already half-drowning as it is." He looked at the sky, scrunching up his eyes against the rain. I shivered, suddenly chilled. It was hard to believe that, twelve hours before, I couldn't have imagined feeling cold ever again.

"We should keep moving," said Luke. "Head home." And then, before Mason could argue, "We're done, Mase. The search party, if that's ever what it was . . . it's over. We're going back to tell the police what we saw."

And when Luke spoke like that, like a teacher would, or your dad or something, there was no sense arguing. Whatever he said was the way things were going to be.

But then he winced, as though at a sudden pain in his head.

"Mate," said Fash, "there's no way we're going to make it home in this state. You need to rest. Cora can barely walk. And we must be twenty miles from where we started." The torch he was holding flickered, and he gave it a waggle. When it was working again, he pointed the beam at the floor. "And what if someone else trips while we're walking along in the dark? What if you start feeling dizzy or something? You can't mess about with head wounds, dude. My mum must have told me that a million times."

Which all made sense, but I was serious about what I'd said before. "I mean it, guys. I am *not* sleeping in that cave. Because if that's what you're suggesting, Fash . . ."

He was shaking his head. "We should go the other way," he said. "The river's east, right? So let's head west."

"What?" said Cora. *"Why?"*

"Because however far it is to the river, the road has got to be closer. And if we get to the road, at some point there'll be a car."

"Wait," I said. "Why don't we just call someone?" It was so obvious, I don't know why none of us had thought of it before.

"Using what?" said Mason. *"Someone* stole our phones, remember?"

"We could use the one we found," said Cora, catching on to what I was saying. And I swear, it was the first time since Sadie had gone missing that, when Cora looked at me, she actually smiled.

"Right," I said, bobbing my head. "Exactly."

"Except there's no reception out here," said Luke. "We know there isn't."

"But if we head toward the road, get out from under these trees," said Fash, "maybe we'll get a signal on the way." He looked at me, Cora and Luke in turn. We nodded, all of us, and I couldn't help but feel a flicker of hope.

"And which way's the road, Fash?" said Mason. "You said west, right? So all we need is a sunset to show us the way." He turned his free hand toward the sky, palm up, and made a show of taking in the dark.

"My brother's compass," said Luke. "All we need is my brother's compass. It's in my bag. In . . . in the cave," he added. He looked at me, knowing how I felt about going back there.

The torch flickered again, and Fash gave it a whack. "I reckon we're going to need to get our stuff anyway," he said. "This torch is about to conk out on us. But look," he said to me and Cora, "why don't you two stay here. Me, Luke and Mason can—"

"Uh-uh. No way," said Cora. "We're not splitting up. Not again."

And as much as I hated the thought of going inside that cave, or even of going anywhere near it, I hated the thought of being on my own out there in the darkness even more.

"We'll all go," I said. "I don't see that we've got any other choice."

Which settled it, we figured. We had a plan. The only problem was, nobody seemed to know which way the cave was. And as we were standing there trying to work it out, that's when the torch finally died.

FASH

"WHAT WAS THAT?" said Abi.

The rest of us strained to listen.

"Seriously," Abi insisted. "I heard something."

"You're imagining things," said Mason, but he didn't sound convinced.

I looked out into the woods like the rest of them. I didn't hear anything . . . but then I did. Footsteps, maybe, or . . . To be honest, I don't know what I heard. But it was so dark all of a sudden, it could have been anything. And whatever it was, it would have been able to get right up close without any of us being able to see it coming.

I'd been trying to get the torch working again, but this time it had given up for good. "This way," I said. "Follow me." I wasn't certain, but I was pretty sure I knew the route back, or at least the general direction. And there was no sense us all just standing around, waiting for something to happen.

"*Which* way?" said Abi. "I can't even see where you're pointing!"

"Take hold of Cora's hand," I told her. "Cora, you latch on to Mason."

"No fucking way," said Cora. "Not while he's holding that bottle."

"I'm not exactly going to put it down *now*, am I?" said Mason, and even though he was trying to hide it, he sounded almost as scared as Abi did.

"Here," said Luke. "Take my hand, Cora. Mase, you grab on to me."

"I'll be fine," Mason snarled. "Just get moving, will you?"

We set off, blindly at first, practically having to feel our way with our feet. But gradually our eyes adjusted to the lack of light, and soon I could see the outline of the trees. Enough that I didn't lead the others right into them, anyway. Instead, what I did was, I led them all over the bank into the stream.

I didn't do it on purpose. One moment the ground was solid beneath my feet, the next there was nothing under them but air. Before I could pull myself back, I was falling, pulling Cora down with me. We were so wet by this point, it hardly mattered that we landed in the water, but the stream was low enough that it was mainly rocks, and I felt one of them jar against my spine. Cora must have hit her knee again, because she cried out, and I heard the others tumble after us, too. Luke was first on his feet, and he reached to give me a hand up. Abi, beside us, was doing her best to help Cora, in between sobbing and wiping at her eyes. Mason had stopped short of the stream just in time. His shadow was looming over us from the top of the bank.

He slid down the mud, and stood watching as the rest of us struggled to our feet.

"Everyone OK?" said Luke, looking mainly at Cora.

"Just fucking dandy," she replied.

I stood up and rubbed at my back. "Well," I said, through the pain. "At least we know we're heading in the right direction."

Even so, it took us long enough after that to find the cave. It was so dark out there without the torchlight, it's a miracle we found it in the end at all. By the time we did, Cora was limping worse than ever, and Abi's breathing sounded so panicked, I was worried she was going to pass out.

"I'm not going in," she said, when we finally spotted the shadow in the bank. "I'm *not*. I don't even care about my stuff."

"I'll get everyone's stuff," said Luke. "You lot wait out here. And . . ." He looked behind him, at the wall of trees, and raised a hand to the cut on his head. "And keep an eye out, will you?"

I swallowed, and turned to do as he'd said. Mason was the only one to go inside with him. They vanished the moment they took a step through the opening, and they were gone for so long I started to worry that something might have happened to them. I don't know what. To be honest, I found myself imagining all sorts of things. That maybe whoever was out there had got ahead of us, and was lying in wait inside the cave. Or that Mason had decided to use that bottle after all. He'd dealt with Luke, and next he would be coming for the rest of us. I even found myself wondering if he might have used something similar on Sadie.

But just when I was about to call out, a light flicked on in the darkness. There were footsteps, and Mason appeared through the shadows.

"Where's Luke?" said Cora, immediately, and I could tell she'd been having the same thoughts I'd had.

Mason seemed to realize what it was she was really asking. He sneered—and just at that moment, I felt certain that all of it was true. Everything everyone had been saying about him.

But then a second torch beam shone out through the darkness, and all at once Luke was standing at Mason's shoulder.

"Here," he said. He tossed me my rucksack, and Abi hers. His own bag was already on his back, Dylan's compass open in his hand. "You said west. Right, Fash?"

"Right," I said, with one eye on Mason. He was holding Cora's bag, I noticed. She snatched it from him without saying a word.

And then we were moving again. Luke had the compass, so he took the lead. Abi was next, and it was obvious she felt safest sticking close to Luke. Me and Cora were just behind her, Cora's arm still looped around my neck. Mason was on his own farther back. I'd caught him glancing once or twice over his shoulder, but mainly he seemed to be watching *us*.

The second torch lasted another hour. If we'd been smart, we would have used them one at a time, rather than having them both on simultaneously. Luke held one of them, obviously, seeing as he was the one acting as our guide. Mason had given the other one to me when we'd been outside the cave. Thrust it at me, actually. He wanted to keep one hand free, he'd said, and I guess he preferred to give up the torch than the broken bottle.

It was the torch I was holding that went out first. Not like the first one had, in stages. One moment it was working, the next it wasn't. I tried giving it a shake, but it didn't help. I kept hold of it even so, because it was old, which meant it was also big and heavy. It wasn't quite a broken bottle, but it was better than nothing.

We walked for ages. Hobbled, rather, in Cora's case. I guess the road was farther than I'd thought. I'd figured we'd reach it in a couple of hours—three, tops—but when my watch showed four o'clock in the morning, there was no sign we were any nearer where we wanted to be. We'd left the cave at just past midnight, meaning we'd been moving for four hours straight. Personally speaking, I was exhausted. Cora was doing her best to hold most of her weight, but every so often she'd stumble, and catching her was getting harder and harder each time. But it just goes to show how afraid we all were, that not even Abi asked for a break.

"Why do you reckon whoever's out there attacked Luke?" Cora said to me as we walked. Mason was still somewhere behind us, and Abi and Luke were up ahead.

"I don't know," I said. "Maybe just because he was there. Because he was the one who got closest."

I didn't know if that was reassuring or not. I didn't even know if I'd meant it to be.

We walked on, alert for any noises among the trees.

"Cora," I said, after a moment. "Those voices you heard. Back there near the clearing. Did you recognize them?"

Cora shook her head. "To be honest I'm starting to wonder whether I heard anything in the first place. Or, if I did, whether it wasn't just Mason and Luke."

"But you said one of them was a girl's voice."

"That's what I thought. At the time."

Which made it sound as though she might have changed her mind.

"I've been wondering," I said, after another pause. "About what Mason said before. I mean, you don't think it could have been *Lara*, do you? Her and one of those cretins from the river? And this is all their idea of a practical joke?"

Cora nodded toward Luke. "Some joke," she said. "Trying to decapitate someone with a tree branch."

"Or not a joke then. Maybe *they're* the ones worried about what we'll find. Maybe Luke almost *did* find something. Maybe *that's* why they attacked him."

"Maybe," said Cora. She thought for a minute. "Although . . . I mean, this is probably going to sound stupid. But if Lara were behind what's been happening, I'm pretty sure I wouldn't feel this scared."

She was wrong. It didn't sound stupid at all.

"*Shit.*"

It was Luke's voice, from up ahead.

"What's wrong?" I called to him, and he and Abi slowed down enough for the rest of us to catch up. Mason was hanging back, still keeping his distance from the group.

"This torch is running out of juice, too," said Luke. "It's not going to last much longer."

I'd noticed the light flickering as we walked, but had assumed it was something to do with the trees coming between us and the beam. But Luke was pointing it directly at our feet now, and I could see exactly what he meant. The light was weaker—rusty orange rather than bright white—and when Luke moved the torch even a fraction, the beam wavered.

"Turn it off a sec," I said.

"No, don't!" said Abi, panicking.

I was looking up at the sky. "Trust me," I said. "Try it."

When Luke did, the world went black. But only for a moment.

"You see?" I said. "It's getting lighter. The sun must be coming up."

"I wouldn't exactly call this *light*," said Cora, looking out into the gray.

"But we can see each other, at least," I countered. "Which is more than we could without the torchlight before."

"Jesus," said Luke. "We must have been walking all night."

"Do you think we're nearly there yet?" said Abi. "The road. Or the edge of the forest. Or wherever it is we're supposed to be going."

I felt the slight optimism I'd been feeling wane. It wasn't just the fact that we'd been walking for so long without any sign of progress. All of a sudden, the predawn light felt even creepier than the dark. It was like the difference between ducking your head under the covers at night, or daring to peer out into your bedroom. It *should* have been reassuring, being able to see better. But there were shapes out there in the shadows I didn't trust.

"We're still heading west," I said to Luke. "Right?"

"See for yourself," he answered, and he showed me the compass.

"Unless west is the wrong direction," said Mason. He was standing just far enough away that I couldn't see his expression, but I was fairly sure he was looking at me.

"Don't say that," said Abi. "*Please* don't say we've been going the wrong way. Fash? We haven't been, have we?"

"No," I said. "No, I . . . No. South would have taken us the way we came. North would have led us deeper into the woods. East would have taken us to the river." It sounded logical when I spelled it out like that, but even so, I found myself uncertain. It was because I was so tired, I expect. And not just from walking. Being on edge for so long, being afraid . . . It takes it out of you. I could tell the others were feeling it, too.

"I say we go back," said Mason, and the rest of us turned to him, incredulous.

"Go back?" I said. "Go back where?"

"Where we just came from."

"Are you *joking*?" said Cora.

But he wasn't. "Has anyone heard *anything*?" he said. "Since the cave, I mean. The whole time we've been walking. Any footsteps? Any *voices*, Cora? Anything at all apart from the rain?"

"Just because we haven't heard anything doesn't mean there's nothing out there," Cora said. "It doesn't mean we should be talking about going *back*."

"Guys, *look*," I said, interrupting. I pointed into the distance. The dark was definitely lifting, and I'd seen something through the gloom. Something that didn't belong.

"What are you pointing at?" said Abi. "I can't see anything."

Mason didn't even bother to turn his head. It was like, he was so convinced one of us was lying to him—that we *all* were, maybe—that he didn't dare take his eyes off us.

"There," I said. "See?"

"I see it," said Luke.

"Is that a *building*?" said Cora.

"*Where?*" said Abi. "Guys, show me! I can't—" And then I guess she could.

"Oh, thank Christ," said Cora.

I looked at Luke and grinned. He gave half a smile back. Mason was frowning into the distance, but I could tell he'd seen it, too.

"What are we waiting for?" I said.

Cora had been holding herself up against a tree, and she wrapped her arm back around my shoulder. Suddenly, somehow, she was half the weight she'd been before.

"Does that mean we made it?" said Abi. "Does that mean we're out?"

"It means we're somewhere," I said, glancing back at her. "Which is better than where we were before."

"Do you think they'll have Wi-Fi?" said Abi. "Do you reckon they'll let us use their password?"

I glanced at Cora, and all we could do was laugh.

It was Abi and Luke who got there first. They'd pulled in front of me and Cora as we'd started walking again, even though we were going as fast as we could. And right away, when I saw them stop abruptly up ahead, I could tell that something was wrong.

"Guys?" I called. "What is it?"

Luke turned to face me as we drew near. I looked over his shoulder.

"I'm pretty sure they don't have Wi-Fi, Abi," said Mason, who'd appeared by my side.

The entire place looked as though it had been abandoned decades ago. There were two barns, one of them basically a shell. And as for the cabin . . . Well. You know. You've been there. I suppose we shouldn't have been so surprised. I mean, we were in the middle of the woods, twenty miles from civilization. What were we expecting, a McDonald's drive-thru?

Even so, it was a blow when we already felt battered enough. It was like in a movie or something, when a group of people get lost in the desert, and the oasis they spot in the distance turns out to be a mirage.

"We should check it out anyway," said Luke.

So we started forward. But it didn't take long for us to confirm that there was nothing there. Nothing we needed, anyway. No sign of life. Nobody we could ask for help. After five or ten minutes' looking, we stood staring at the buildings in the rain.

"If . . . if there are buildings here," I said, "we can't be *that* far from the road. Right?"

"Unless the buildings were built before the road was," said Cora. Which, looking at the state of them, seemed entirely possible.

"But there must be a path or something somewhere," I said, searching the tree line. "Look, there. That gap. That looks like it goes in the right direction. What do you say we keep walking? We can't be that far now from—"

"No."

We turned, to see Mason standing on his own.

"Mase?" I said, and I could hear the uncertainty in my voice. "Mate, listen. We're almost out. I can feel it. Maybe . . ." I brightened, remembering. "The phone. Maybe we should try the phone. At least now, if we get through to someone, we can let them know exactly where we are."

"And where's that, Fash?" said Mason. "Because it seems to me all we are is further away from where we're supposed to be."

THE SEARCH PARTY   285

I frowned, not understanding what he meant. "They'll have maps," I explained. "That's all I'm saying. If we call, and tell the police we're near some buildings . . ."

"Call the police. That's your solution. Because that was working out so well before."

"What the hell else do you suggest?" snapped Cora. "Try it," she said, turning to me. "Try the phone. At least see if there's any signal."

I patted my pockets. "I don't have it. I . . ." And then I realized. We all did.

When we looked at him again, Mason was holding the phone in his hand. The one that wasn't gripping that broken bottle. And then he slipped the phone back into his pocket.

"The drinking water," he said. "The first night. Which one of you did it? And the phones. *Our* phones. Which one of you took them? Because one of you did, I know you did—and whoever it was also stole my knife."

"Your *what*?" said Cora.

"My knife! The one I brought with me! To *protect* myself!"

"You brought a *knife*?" Cora cast around at the rest of us. "What, a broken bottle wasn't enough for you?" She shook her head. "Luke was right. What he said to us all at the start. You *are* a psychopath!"

Mason looked at Luke, who swallowed. And Mason's smile . . . I mean, it wasn't really a smile. There was just a little curl to his lips, as though what Cora had just told him confirmed everything he'd been thinking all along. That we were all against him. That the world was.

"Wait," said Abi. "Does that mean whoever's out there has got a *knife*?"

"There's no one out there!" Mason said. "There never was! It was all just *lies*. All of it. Right from the start. Who here can prove they actually saw *anyone*? Even you, Luke. You told us. You admitted it.

You didn't *see* who attacked you. Meaning it could have been any one of the three people standing next to you."

"No, Mase, I told you, I'm certain it wasn't. One hundred percent! Just like I know it wasn't *you*. And what I said before, it—"

Mason dismissed what Luke was saying with a flick of that bottle. "Oh, wake up, Luke, for fuck's sake. Cora sees someone in the night. She hears voices that no one else does. Abi comes running because of a noise only she heard in the woods. Fash claims he saw someone, but surprise, surprise, nobody else is around to back him up." Mason scoffed, and shook his head. "At least one of them has been lying, trying to get the rest of us spooked. Like with the water, the phones, *my knife*. It was all a trick to send us running, our tails tucked between our legs. And when we didn't, they upped their game. Took a swing at you in the dark. Probably because by then we were getting closer."

"Closer to *what*?" I said.

"Closer to Sadie! To . . . to proof. Or something! Closer to the *truth*." Mason looked at me, Abi and Cora, one at a time. "How's that knee of yours?" he said to Cora. "Because I noticed you moving a bit faster when you saw the barn. When you figured you were free and clear."

"Oh, *piss off*," Cora spat at him. "You think I'm faking? You think I'm the one playing games? Take a look at yourself before you start accusing the rest of us, Mason! Remind yourself why we're even out here! Do you know, I actually meant what I said to you before. About believing you. About being certain you had nothing to do with Sadie's disappearance. But now . . ." She sniffed. "Now I hope they lock you up and throw away the key."

Mason took a step forward. He raised the bottle.

"Turn out your bags," he hissed. Then, when none of us moved, "I said, turn out your bags!"

I was closest, and he ripped my rucksack from my shoulders. I was helping Cora stand, and when Mason pulled me like that, she lost her balance and fell onto her hands and knees. She cried out, but Mason acted as though he hadn't heard. He'd wrenched my rucksack open, and was shaking it the way a dog would shake a rat it had caught between its jaws. I saw my Snickers bar fly off into the undergrowth.

"*Here*," said Cora, tossing Mason her bag. "Help yourself." He caught it and emptied it out the way he had mine. Next was Abi's. She held it out to him the way she would have offered a tiger a piece of meat. Luke turned out his own bag, then tipped it upside down to prove to Mason that it was empty.

When it was over, our belongings were scattered all around us. Mason checked one way, and then the other, swiping at the ground with his feet. But there was no knife.

"Mason?" said Abi. Quietly, tentatively. "Mase? It's not there. You can see it's not." She paused but Mason didn't respond. "Please, Mason. Just try the phone. *Please*. At least tell us if there's any recep—"

Now Mason spun. "Shut *up*," he spat. "Just . . . just *shut up*, will you? I told you already. I said to you. No one's calling *anyone* until we get this straightened out."

I don't think Mason realized how close he was holding the bottle to Abi's throat. I'm not sure he was really aware what he was doing by that point, nor what he planned to do next. And Abi clearly didn't know either. She started crying, whimpering really, as though she was genuinely afraid she was about to die. And I guess she realized there was no way she could get through to Mason. So she turned to Cora instead.

"Tell him," she said, through her tears. "Just tell him, Cora! He's not going to let us go until you do!"

I looked at Cora, frowning.

"Shut up, Abi," Cora hissed. "Just shut the fuck up, will you?"

But Abi wasn't listening. "Just tell him!" she said again. *"Tell him what you did!"*

Mason whipped his head toward Cora.

"Me?" said Cora, who was still only halfway standing. "What *I* did? What about you? *Both* of you!" She was back on her feet now, and her eyes, this time, landed on me.

And really, from that point on, all I can remember clearly is shaking my head. And a voice inside of me saying, *Deny it. They don't know. Nobody knows.*

But obviously, somehow, they did.

I sensed Mason turn to face me. I felt the others looking at me, too.

And then, after that, that's when it all came out.

The truth.

About what Abi did, about what Cora had done, about what I had. And the only reason I didn't tell you before—why none of the others told you either—was because we were scared of what you'd think. It was like Cora said to Mason: after the way it all ended, if you found out what we'd been hiding . . . you'd lock us up and throw away the key.

And maybe that's exactly what we deserve.

"YOUR *BUSINESS CARD?*"

"Yes, sir," said Fleet. "And I added a message."

"What message?"

"Just a few words," Fleet said. "Nothing consequential." What he'd written on the back of the card was: *I want to help you. And I want to help your friends.* But he had a feeling that, when it came to explaining to Superintendent Burton, it would be in everyone's interests for Fleet to keep the details hazy.

"I left the card on a tree stump near the barns," he said. "In a place it appeared likely someone had been hiding. Nicky here was the one who found the evidence."

Nicky seemed about to protest, to perhaps insist it was Fleet who deserved the credit, but there was no need. Burton didn't even glance in her direction.

"*Evidence?* I thought we'd searched that entire area!" Rather than worrying about assigning credit, Burton appeared more concerned with trying to decide who to haul over the coals.

"It's unlikely there would have been anything to find at the time of the search, sir. The truth is, it was more of a . . . feeling."

Burton made a face. He didn't have to say anything to make it clear what he'd come to think of Fleet's *feelings*.

The superintendent pianoed his fingers on the surface of a nearby desk. They were standing in the open-plan office at the station, the workspace full of officers trying to look busy, all of whom would have been following every word.

"It doesn't change anything," Burton announced at last. "The press conference goes ahead. The *arrest* goes ahead. You have him here, I take it? The Payne boy?"

"They're all here," answered Fleet. "And they all still have questions to answer. But I've got a feeling"—Fleet regretted the word the moment it escaped his mouth—"I've got a sense there's only one person's story now that matters."

"You're right, Detective Inspector," said Burton. "There is only one story that matters. The one that will appear on the front pages of tomorrow morning's newspapers."

"But, sir . . ." Fleet took a breath. "Sir, if I may. I agree that it looks bad for Mason. He's not going to come out of this with very much credit, however things turn out. He's reckless, unstable, angry . . ." *Which, given his provenance, is hardly surprising,* Fleet didn't add. "But I'd bet my career that he's no killer."

"But one of the others is? Is that what you're saying? Because if you take with one hand, Detective Inspector, you sure as hell better be giving with another."

"That's not what I'm saying, sir. However . . ." Fleet added hastily, before Burton's patience—and possibly one of his blood vessels—finally ruptured. "I believe we have a better idea now about what actually happened."

"A theory, you mean," said Burton, derisively. "If *I* may, Detective Inspector, the time for theories has passed. Theories aren't going to satisfy the two dozen journalists who are less than an hour away from gathering in the room next door."

"With respect, sir, *nobody* is going to be satisfied until we understand what happened to Sadie. Charging Mason isn't going to alter that."

Burton glanced around the room. Any eyes that had been looking in his direction immediately dropped away. Fleet could tell the superintendent was caught between looking like a fool in front of his troops, and making a bigger idiot of himself up onstage before the nation's media. Fleet had suggested they have this conversation in private when Burton first strode in, but Burton had blustered that there'd be no need. No doubt he was regretting that now.

"I'm listening," the superintendent said, grudgingly.

Fleet turned to Nicky, and gave her the slightest of nods.

"Well, sir," she said to Burton. "The first thing is, we've had corroboration from Forensics that the phone the kids discovered in the woods was likely to have belonged to Sadie. They haven't yet been able to draw anything conclusive from the blood traces, but what they did find was one of Sadie's fingerprints."

"A fingerprint doesn't prove ownership, Detective Sergeant. You're going to have to do better than that."

"You're right, sir. It doesn't. Except this print was taken from *inside* the phone's casing. On the battery, to be precise. And there was also a partial on the SIM card. Sadie's print was there, and nobody else's. Which, taken in the context of the circumstantial evidence linking the phone to Sadie . . ."

Burton had started nodding and was holding up a hand. "All right, all right. There's no need to labor the point. And anyway, I don't see how this changes things. I'd already said to you both that I accepted the phone was Sadie's."

Fleet blinked. He must have missed that particular conversation with his superior. The last thing he could remember Burton saying on the subject was, quote, *Fuck the phone.*

"The other thing we've had confirmed," said Fleet, "thanks to DC Dalton over there . . ." Fleet winced as he twisted. The paracetamol he'd taken back at the hotel had long worn off, not that it had done very much to numb the pain in the first place. Nicky noticed, and shot him a frown, but Burton was looking where Fleet was pointing. DC Dalton was seated at his desk by the window, and he turned the color of one of the fist prints on Fleet's rib cage.

"The Internet gossip," Fleet went on. "The rumors about Sadie that had been circulating over the summer. DC Dalton managed to pinpoint the account from which they originated. And by back-tracking a bit further, he's also managed to identify who owned them. The names of the accounts at first suggested they might have belonged to Lara Sweeney—either that, or someone who wanted to make it look like they belonged to Lara."

"And? Which was it?"

"The latter," said Fleet. "Dalton was able to establish a link between the accounts and an e-mail address owned by one of Sadie's friends. Abigail Marshall, to be precise."

Burton wore the expression of a man still waiting for the punch line. "So one of Sadie's friends got pissed-off with her for some reason, and decided to spread a few rumors to settle the score. So what?"

"As it happens, sir, I don't think it was Abi who started the rumors. It was her account, yes, but that doesn't mean the posts were hers." Again, it was just a feeling Fleet had, though he consciously avoided confessing as much. "But anyway, that isn't really the point. The point is, we believe the rumors were based on *fact*. That Sadie was unfaithful to Mason, and somebody somehow got wind of this."

"Sadie was unfaithful to Mason? Forgive me, Detective Inspector, but aren't you supposed to be trying to convince me that Mason isn't our man?"

Our boy, Fleet resisted saying. He had the distinct impression the superintendent had lost sight of the fact they were dealing with children here. Not adults. Not even potential criminals, by most international standards. *Children.*

"I hear what you're saying, sir," said Fleet, "but, taken together, it seems to me that these findings fundamentally alter the overall picture. There's the phone, to start with. The fact Sadie bought it three days before she went missing. There's the likelihood Sadie had been caught doing something she might have regretted, together with the possibility that she was pregnant. And remember her parents are Catholic, meaning abortion would at the very least have been problematic. And finally, there's the fact that Sadie was keeping back money she would ordinarily have paid straight into her savings account."

"I'm failing to see the connection, Detective Inspector."

"We think Sadie ran, sir," said Nicky, spelling it out for him.

"Ran? As in . . ."

"As in, ran away," said Fleet. "Maybe she didn't want to. Probably she felt she had no choice. But she'd bought a cheap phone nobody would have been able to trace. She had cash, allowing her to avoid leaving an electronic record, either of the fact that she was planning to leave, or—afterward—of where she'd gone. Because she knew full well that people would have come looking for her. She was smart, sir. Very, very smart. The only place she really tripped up was with her bag."

"Her bag? The one we found by the river?"

Fleet nodded. "Containing her phone, her wallet, her house keys—everything people would have expected her to have been carrying, unless of course she no longer needed them."

"It was a decoy?" said Burton, catching on. "To make it look like she'd fallen in the river? To make her disappearance look like an accident? *She* put it there?"

"That's what I'm guessing," said Fleet. "And that's why the bag was so close to the towpath: to make sure someone found it. And it was wet through, as though someone had dunked it in the river first, to make it look as though it had washed up after Sadie had theoretically fallen in."

"It was too high on the bank," said Burton. "That's what you said before. Right at the start."

"It was just a feeling, sir," said Fleet, unable to resist. Burton was too busy frowning to register the jibe.

"But if Sadie ran away—if what you're saying is true—why haven't we found her? Maybe she *was* smart, and maybe if her plan had worked and nobody had been looking for her other than out at sea, it would have been a different story. But in case you hadn't noticed, Detective Inspector, the search for Sadie Saunders has turned into the biggest missing-persons inquiry in the county's entire history. I know—I've been signing off on the bills you and DS Collins here have been busy racking up."

This time it was Fleet's turn to ignore the jibe.

"And what about her coat?" the superintendent went on. "None of what you've just outlined explains how or why we found Sadie's coat in the river, her blood all over the hood. Unless it's your contention that Sadie planted that as well. That, rather than an accident, she wanted her disappearance to look like murder."

Fleet shook his head. "No, sir. I don't think she wanted that at all. Quite the opposite. I believe she went to considerable lengths to ensure *nobody* would be blamed."

Burton was waiting. "Well?" he said. "How does it all tally up, Detective Inspector? Where does your theory lead now?"

Fleet glanced at Nicky. The truth was, they'd reached the point at which the evidence ran out. From here on in, it was all conjecture.

"All I can say, sir," Fleet said, "is that just because Sadie ran, doesn't mean she got away."

There was a silence which filled the entire room. There was no pretense now among the officers present that they were anything other than attuned to what Fleet was saying. Probably, like Fleet, most would have recognized a long time ago how slim the chances were of finding Sadie alive. But recognizing the fact and accepting it were very different things.

"So what we're dealing with here is a runaway *and* a murder?" said Burton.

As so often in recent days, a phrase echoed in Fleet's head. *More than one thing going on . . .*

"Yes, sir," he said. "You asked me about my theory, and that's basically what it boils down to. Sadie ran, and someone tried to stop her. Someone who didn't want her gone."

"But that's Mason!" said Burton. "And if Sadie was unfaithful, as you claim, that's all the more reason to suspect him. I'm sorry, Rob, but nothing you've just been saying to me does anything to change my opinion. Which was your opinion at one stage, too, I might remind you!"

Fleet didn't bother to correct him. The truth was, the superintendent had reacted exactly as Fleet had feared he would.

"The only thing I can say, sir, is that Mason wasn't the only one who loved Sadie."

Burton opened his mouth, then shut it again. He looked over Fleet's shoulder, toward the corridor leading to the interview rooms. After that, he checked his watch.

"The social worker's in there?" he said.

"She is. She has been for a while."

Burton's nostrils flared as he breathed out. "One last interview, Rob. Is that what you're promising me?"

"All I can promise, sir, is that it will be worth listening to. I don't know yet whether it will change your mind."

Once again Burton exhaled. "I suppose we had better find out," he said at last.

LUKE

YOU SAID YOU'D help. Right? You said you'd help my friends. So the important thing, the thing I want to begin with, is to say that none of it was anybody else's fault.

I'm guessing you know pretty much what happened out there in the woods by now. Because you've been speaking to the others, right? So what I'm saying is, please don't blame them. Not even Mason. Especially not Mason. They were just . . . they were scared. That's all. All of them. That's the reason no one told you the truth before we set off. Why they agreed to stay quiet after. Because they were worried about how things would look. Cora thought you'd think she did it. That she was the one who . . . who killed my sister. Because she figured you'd decide she hated her or something. That Cora hated Sadie, I mean. Which she didn't. I know for a fact she didn't. She only did what she did because of Mason. Because she was so in love with *him*. And Abi . . . Abi got herself in a mess. Which was partly Cora's fault, too. As for Fash . . . I mean, Jesus. I'd never have guessed. I really wouldn't. And I can see why he kept it a secret. He must have been terrified. Not just after Sadie vanished, but before. The whole summer. With Mason, and his mum, and then you lot . . .

Sorry, I . . . I'm getting ahead of myself again. It's so hard keeping everything straight in my head.

No, I'm . . . I'm just tired, that's all. Just really, really tired. My head's fine. It's just a scrape. It was only ever really a scrape. I made it look worse than it feels, I promise. What I want is for it all to be over. For everything to be out in the open. *Finally.*

So where was I? Where should I . . .

Yeah. Yeah, OK. That's the point it all came out anyway. When we reached the farm buildings and . . . and just before it happened . . . For all of us, that was when we finally realized what had actually been going on.

So we're outside the barn. And Mason's refusing to let us use the phone. The one we found. Sadie's phone. You know about that, right?

Right. So we're standing there arguing, and Mason's got the phone in his pocket, and the broken bottle in his hand, and Abi is so scared by this point, she can't keep it in any longer.

"Just tell him!" she said to Cora. "Tell him what you did! He's not going to let us go until you do!"

"Me?" said Cora. "What about what you two did? *Both* of you!" At which point, not only was she looking at Abi, she was also glaring at Fash. Who looked more afraid than either of them.

And what it all came back to, I suppose, was the night we went down to the sand dunes, right back at the start of the summer. We lit a fire, drank some wine, listened to music. At first it was all really chilled-out. But I think we got more pissed than we realized. In fact, I know we did. And there were all sorts of things simmering. Little . . . tensions. You know? End-of-term stuff. Stuff between Cora and Sadie. Because of Mason, which had basically been going on all year, and which made it kind of awkward for the rest of us. Particularly whenever Mase and Sadie argued. Which is what happened that night. I can't even really remember how it started. Sadie was anxious about exam results, and Mason was telling her to chill out, and she was going, *That's easy for you to say,* and it started building from there. And Fash . . . Fash was on one. On a mission, I mean. To get wasted. Because he was nervous about exam results, too—about what his mum would say if he didn't get all nines. About what she'd say if she caught him drinking wine in the sand dunes, come to that. And Cora wasn't helping. She was calling him a pussy, just joking around but also basically winding him up, getting him to drink more and more. As for me, I was worrying about Dylan, because he never liked it when me and Sadie were out of the house at the same time. So I wasn't planning on staying that long anyway. In fact, I left not long after Mason stormed off. I kind of took it as my cue. Maybe if I'd've stuck around, none of this would have happened. Maybe . . .

Maybe all sorts of things, I suppose.

But the woods. What it all led to.

"Tell them, Fash!" Cora was saying. "Go on! Tell them about you and Sadie in the sand dunes!"

It wasn't fully light at this stage, but the night was becoming grayer. We could see each other, basically. Meaning there was no more hiding in the dark.

"What?" said Fash. "I . . . I don't know what you're talking about."

But Fash has never been a very good liar. I mean that in the nicest way possible. I'm guessing he'd only managed to keep the thing with Sadie quiet for so long because it was the first time anyone had actually challenged him about it.

Mason had been pointing the bottle at Abi. His hand fell to his side. "What the fuck are you talking about?" he said to Cora, but his eyes were locked on Fash.

Abi, meanwhile, was crying and shaking her head, as though she was already beginning to wish she hadn't said anything. Or maybe that she'd had the guts to say something earlier.

"Mate," said Fash. "Listen . . ." He held up his hands, and his eyes kept flicking to that broken bottle. "Nothing happened, Mase, I swear it. It's just . . . What Cora's saying, it's . . ."

"Oh, for Christ's sake, Fash!" said Cora. "Grow a fucking scrotum, will you?"

"Me?" said Fash, rounding on her. "What about you? What have *you* been hiding, Cora? You—" And then I guess he must have realized. "Wait, you . . . you came back? That night. You *saw*?"

At which point, Cora looked at Abi.

You see, at the dunes, after I'd left, and after Mason had stormed off, Cora tried to catch him up. And Abi went after Cora because Cora had all her stuff. Which left Sadie and Fash on their own. And they were both pissed. A-bottle-and-a-half-of-wine-each pissed. Not to mention pissed-off. Sadie, in particular. Even before I'd left, she'd started bad-mouthing Mason. Him and Dad at the same time, actually. Our dad, I mean. Sadie's and mine. Again, it was all to do with it being the end of term, I reckon, and the pressure coming out of the exams, but what she said was, she was sick of being stuck on a fucking pedestal. Of everybody always expecting her to be perfect. And she said that sometimes she'd just get this urge to do something really awful, just to see everybody's faces. And all I can imagine is, somehow it went on from there. Fash agreeing, saying he was sick of the expectation, too. Of people like Cora calling him a pussy. And then the two of them maybe clinking bottles, saying *Fuck them*. You know? Fuck exams, and fuck being told what to do, and fuck always being fucking perfect. And then what I imagine is, they started laughing. Maybe they realized they were sitting too close. And maybe . . . Shit. I don't know. Maybe it was just like people say, one thing leading to another . . .

"I did," said Abi, still crying. "*I* saw. I'm sorry, Fash, I couldn't help it! I came back. After I got my phone and that from Cora's bag. And you and Sadie . . . you . . ." She looked at Mason, and didn't dare to say anything more.

"Tell them what you did *next*, Abi," said Cora. In a voice I didn't like at all. And then, when Abi didn't say anything, Cora answered for her. "She took a *photo*," she said. "Of the two of you *doing* it."

"I didn't mean to! It was like . . . like a reflex, that's all! I thought you were just messing around! And anyway, it didn't even come out! You've seen it. You all have. You can barely even see Sadie's face!"

"But you were more than happy to show me, weren't you?" said Cora. "When you came to my house the next day?"

"Which was the biggest mistake I've ever made!" Abi's face was blotched with tears, but now more than upset she looked angry. Furious, in fact. She pointed at Cora, her arm straight like a spear. "*She* was the one who shared it online. Using *my* account! The one I set up as a joke last year. The Lara one. I only didn't delete it earlier because it had so many followers. Because people thought it was genuinely her. And Cora was in my bedroom one evening, and when I went out of the room for like *five fucking minutes*, she swiped my phone and posted it! *More* than once! And she didn't even tell me!"

"*You* started the rumors?" I said to Cora. "You were the one spreading shit about my sister?"

Cora opened her mouth to answer, but Fash spoke up before she could.

"The photo," he said. "I thought . . . I thought it was fake. I mean, I figured *someone* had seen us. But I just assumed . . . Lara, maybe, or . . . someone who hated us. Who didn't really know us. Not one of our friends!"

Cora had the decency to look ashamed. "Why do you think I kept you out of it, Fash? To *protect* you. You and your friendship with Mason. And it wasn't *shit*, Luke. That was the whole point!" She looked at Mason, who was standing there trying to take it all in. "Everybody always thought Sadie was Little Miss Perfect. But she wasn't! I was trying to *show* you, Mase! To prove to you that she didn't love you as much as you loved her. The truth is, she didn't deserve you. You should have been with *me*!"

Mason looked appalled, disgusted. You name it.

"I would have stopped it, Mason," said Abi, pleading now. "I *did* stop it. I deleted the account. After Sadie went missing, Cora freaked out. She came to me and told me what she'd done. I didn't even *know* until then! I didn't even *use* that account! And what Cora said was, if I told anyone it was her—the police, she meant, because she knew how it would look if they found out how jealous she was—but what she said was, if I told anyone, she'd deny it. Tell them *I* did it. Which she said she'd be able to prove because the police would be able to trace the photo to my phone. And then she made me use another account to send *other* stuff. About Sadie's *parents*, this time."

"I didn't make you do anything!" said Cora. "You could have said no. You're not a fucking *sheep*." She turned to me. "And the stuff about your parents, Luke . . . I didn't think you'd even see it. You'd already told us you'd deleted your accounts. And I was only trying to stop the police blaming Mason. You see that, don't you? Both of you?" She looked at Mason. "I said to you, Mase. I told you I'd tried to help you . . ."

"Help me?" said Mason. "By spreading lies about someone *else*?"

"I swear," said Abi, cutting in, "none of it was my fault. It was all Cora. *All* of it. And I only didn't say anything because I was so afraid. I thought . . . I thought Sadie had killed herself. We both did! Admit it, Cora—that's what you thought, too!"

Cora didn't have to say anything to confirm Abi was telling the truth. And I could imagine exactly what they'd been thinking. At first, they might have figured Sadie had run away. Hoped she had, maybe. But then, when she didn't turn up, when there was no sight of her on any CCTV, and when you lot found her bag . . . Maybe they started to believe that Sadie had been so upset by all the gossip—the gossip *they'd* started—that she'd actually taken her own life.

It was no wonder they'd been so afraid of what they'd find out in the woods. And so ashamed, too. So terrified that one of them would betray the other.

"You lied," said Mason. "All of you—you all lied! I *knew* you were lying! And not one of you went to the police! All you cared about was trying to save your own skin!" He looked at Cora and Abi—and then his eyes settled on Fash. "And you. You let the police believe that Sadie was pregnant because of *me*!"

"Mate, listen, honestly . . . I didn't know anything about the pregnancy test! I swear on my life! On my mum's life! On . . . on . . ."

"On Sadie's life?" said Mason, and Fash's mouth clamped shut. Because it was clear he felt as guilty as Cora and Abi did. Not only for what he'd done, but for what it might have caused. Because if Sadie was really pregnant . . . I mean . . . Well. It was no wonder she ran.

Yeah.

Yeah, I knew about her running away.

And I'm getting to that, I promise. In fact, I'm almost done. Because then, after that, after the truth had come out, that's when it all kicked off.

"You fucked her," said Mason, and he took a step toward Fash.

"My *girlfriend*. And you didn't even have the guts to admit it. Not even when the entire town was ready to lynch me—my *dad* leading the way!"

"No, Mase, it wasn't like that. Honestly, mate, I—"

"Stop calling me that! Stop calling me *mate*!"

Mason still had the broken bottle in his hand. And right away I could see where things were heading. Because Mason . . . I mean, he's no murderer. I swear he isn't. What I said before we set off, about him being a psychopath—I didn't mean it. I just didn't want him being out there. I didn't want him being anywhere near where Sadie . . . where she . . .

I *never* thought he was capable of killing her. Of killing anyone. But you have to remember what he'd been through. The person he loved most in the entire world was gone. The police were accusing him of murder. And then he finds out that all his friends have been lying to him, and that his best friend slept with Sadie behind his back. So at that moment, after all of that, and after three days being out there in the woods . . . All I'm saying is, everybody has their limits.

He started forward. Fash started moving back. I made a grab for Mason's arm, to try to stop him from using that bottle, and then, the next thing I know, Mason's pointing the bottle at *me*. Snarling at me. *Raging*. And Abi's screaming, and Cora's yelling, and I can only imagine how it must have looked.

To an outsider, I mean.

To somebody watching.

And even though I'd known he was out there, I just . . . I couldn't . . .

I didn't expect it.

My brother. Dylan.

I didn't know he was still trying to follow us, and I didn't see him come rushing from the woods.

"Leave him alone!" he yelled, as he came charging toward us from the trees.

At first I'm not sure the others recognized him. He was in as bad a state as we were: his clothes wet through, his hair plastered to his head, and his eyes wild with fury.

"Let him go!" he shouted at Mason. "Don't you touch him!"

"Dylan? Dylan, no!" I reacted before the others did. When I called out, Mason spun, and I saw his eyes go wide. Before anybody knew what was happening, Dylan was standing right in front of us, his knuckles bulging around the handle of Mason's kitchen knife.

"Dylan? What are you—"

"I said leave him alone! Get away from my brother!" Dylan waved the knife, and Mason stumbled backward.

"That's . . . that's my knife. Where did you get that?"

"I found it! It's mine now."

"Dylan . . ." Mason said, but once again my brother slashed the air with the knife. The blade was as long as his forearm.

"Whoa," said Mason, "take it easy. Here, look." He tossed the broken bottle toward the trees. "It's fine. Everything's fine. Put down the knife, Dylan. You're going to get someone hurt."

"Do as he says, Dylan," I told him. "Put it down. You shouldn't have picked it up in the first place!"

"But it's his fault!" said Dylan. "All of it. It's all his fault!" The whole time, his eyes never left Mason.

There were too many people talking. Cora was saying Dylan's name, pleading with him, to try to get him to calm down. Fash and Abi were doing the same. And with me and Mason speaking, too . . . Dylan, he . . . he wouldn't have liked it. Everybody barking at him like that . . . I mean, they probably didn't even realize they were doing it. But nothing anyone was saying helped.

"Dylan, listen to me," I said, trying to make myself heard. "Sadie's fine. I told you already, she's fine. She's . . . she's coming back. Soon. We just have to wait a while. That's all. We have to be brave, and patient, and . . . and not do anything silly."

Dylan's eyes flicked toward me. He kept the knife leveled at Mason. There was only a blade's length between them.

"If she's coming back, why are you even out here? I heard what you said. I've been listening! You said you were looking for her. And *he* said Sadie was dead!"

"She's not dead, Dylan, I promise! She's just . . . She's gone away. But she'll be back!"

Dylan was shaking his head. "I saw him," he said, still glaring at Mason. "He was going to hurt you. The same way he hurt Sadie. I *hate* him!"

"Mason, don't!"

Everybody started moving at once. Dylan lunged forward, and Fash tried to grab him from one side. Abi was trying to pull Fash away, and Cora was struggling to help Mason. The only thing I had eyes for was that knife, and I'm guessing Mason was thinking the same. But it was just . . . it was like a bar fight. A brawl, where nobody knows what's happening. People were grabbing, pulling, just doing anything to try to stop anyone else getting hurt. And it . . . it . . .

It didn't work.

Dylan, he . . . he was so small, and . . .

And I don't know how it happened. One moment I thought I had hold of his arm, the next it was slipping from my grip. So I was flailing, basically. Grabbing anything I could. And all I know—all I really want to tell you—is that everything that happened is my fault. What happened to Dylan, what happened to my sister . . .

It was me. All of it. It was all me.

I'm the one who killed Sadie, and it was my hand around the knife when it slashed my little brother across the stomach.

THE RAIN HAD dwindled to a mist. With no breeze to disturb it, it hung in the air like a dying breath. When they'd driven past the harbor, the water had been like tar—dark and viscous—and in the fog the boats had looked like ghost ships. On the road, despite the hour, every car they'd passed had had its lights on, and all the traffic had been heading the opposite way. As though somehow the drivers all knew. As though instinct—discretion?—was calling them elsewhere.

Now, as Fleet and his companions continued on foot, nothing around them looked real. They could hear the rush of the river up ahead of them, but the water itself was shrouded from sight. Even the footbridge appeared half-dissolved. As though, when they came to try to cross it, the boards would simply vanish beneath their feet. Farther on, where the woods began, the trees seemed to be made of shadows.

Fleet didn't easily get spooked, but it was hard at this stage not to believe in omens. And there were five of them: Fleet, Nicky, a uniformed PC, the social worker and Luke. They were just the advance guard, and plenty of others were waiting to follow, but even so, the number felt significant.

From the way the rest of the group held their silence, Fleet could tell that the atmosphere was weighing on them just as heavily. Probably the only thing they were relishing less was the prospect of actually reaching their destination. Fleet glanced at Nicky, and she nodded. A small, tight movement that managed to also convey a grimace.

They crossed the bridge—the one the search party had crossed themselves, and where they'd had their encounter with Lara Sweeney. Then, the river had been low, but already it had been swelled by the rain, and the water flowed quick and cold.

It wasn't far after that to the trees, and once they were under the canopy, the sound of their footsteps somehow gave the place more substance. They still couldn't see more than twenty meters ahead, but out here they probably wouldn't have been able to anyway.

Fleet looked at Luke, who raised an arm and quickly let it fall again.

They walked on, in the direction Luke had indicated. Fleet could only measure in time, but it was barely half an hour later—half an hour since they'd broached the tree line—that Luke abruptly called a halt.

"Are we here?" Fleet asked him. He glanced around. Trees, leaves, fallen branches. Nothing unusual. Nothing distinct from the landscape they'd already passed.

Luke shook his head. "No, it's . . . further. Not much, but . . ."

"What's wrong, Luke?" said Miss Jeffries, the social worker. "Do you need a rest?"

"No, I just . . ." He looked around, at the others in the group, before his eyes settled on Fleet. "Can it be just you?" he said. "Just you and me, I mean. For the next part."

Fleet hesitated. Nothing they were doing was strictly by the book—although to be fair, the chapter on how to handle things in situations such as this hadn't actually been written yet. But the boy hadn't been charged. He wasn't in cuffs. Meaning they had no way of restraining him if he chose to run, other than by force of numbers.

On the other hand, could he be considered a flight risk if he'd turned himself in? And Fleet could understand completely why the boy was so reluctant to have an audience. His shame was palpable, to the extent he'd refused even to see his parents when they'd finally arrived at the station.

"We'll go ahead," said Fleet at last. "Me, you and Miss Jeffries. How about that? The other officers will follow on behind."

He looked at Nicky. *Drop back, but not too far back* was his silent instruction, and he could tell from the way she returned his gaze that she understood.

They walked on. Fleet had to moderate his pace to match Luke's, whose footsteps were heavy through the leaves. But with Fleet's colleagues distant enough now to be out of plain sight, and the social worker trailing slightly behind, it was obvious the boy felt marginally more comfortable than he had before.

"You were out here all this time?" Fleet said, glancing in Luke's direction. The area they were walking in was in fact a long way from where the search party had ended up. They were tracking the bend of the river, and were only just past the point the original search for Sadie had begun, before it had veered toward the estuary. Nevertheless, Luke seemed to understand what Fleet had meant.

"It didn't feel like I was out here very long," he said. "To be honest, I kind of lost track of time. Was it two nights in the end?"

"It was three. Not including the time you were out here with your friends."

Luke bobbed his head as he walked. Two nights, three, five—it was all the same to him.

"How did you stay hidden?" said Fleet. "Did you sleep in one of the barns?"

"I slept . . . I don't know where I slept. In the barn one night, I think, after the search had packed up. And after that first day, when they . . . when they took Dylan away, nobody was really looking around the clearing. They were out deeper in the woods. At one point I climbed that tree near where you left the card. I must have sat up in the branches for hours. I just . . . I went where you lot weren't. It wasn't hard."

Fleet didn't imagine it would have been. He knew from recent experience that it was difficult enough finding something static in woodland such as this. A mobile phone, for example. A body. But if the thing you were searching for was capable of moving, and didn't want to be found . . .

"Why didn't you come in earlier? Or even stay with your friends?"

This time Luke shook his head. "I couldn't. After it . . . happened, the others started panicking. Cora grabbed the phone from Mason and was trying to call for an ambulance. And then, when they realized there was nothing more they could do, they were all just slumped on the ground. Me, I . . . I was with Dylan. Trying to stop the bleeding." Luke looked down at his palms. The social worker had helped him get clean at the station, and had found him a fresh set of clothes, but it was as though Luke could still see the blood. "But it was too late," he went on. "I knew that, really. The others did, too. And I don't blame them for what they were whispering about after. I told you, they were scared. That's all. But I couldn't just sit there and listen. Not after what had happened to Dylan. Not when I knew what I knew."

"What were they whispering about?"

"Just what I said to you already. About what they'd say when the police arrived. They knew that if anyone told you the truth—about Sadie, about the search party, about all the secrets they'd kept hidden—they'd all be in even worse trouble than they were already. And nobody was willing to take the chance. Mason, in particular. I guess that's why he told the others to keep quiet, why he tried so hard to frighten them."

"What did he say to them?"

"He told them you'd twist things, the way he said you had with him. He told them no one would believe them, not after all this time— that not only would they be blamed for Dylan, they'd be blamed for Sadie, too. The important thing, he said, was to stick to the story. We were looking for Sadie. Dylan followed us. And after that there was an argument and somehow Dylan got hurt. If we all said we couldn't remember how it happened, nobody would get blamed, and nobody would be able to prove it wasn't an accident."

"And what did you think when you heard the others talking like that?"

"I didn't think. I couldn't. That's why I left. When the others weren't looking, I just . . . I ran. Into the woods. I couldn't face . . ."

He left the sentence unfinished. Not for the first time, Fleet felt a rush of sympathy for the boy.

"So they didn't realize it was you? The water that first night, the missing phones. They didn't know that you were the one who'd been trying to drive them back?"

Luke shook his head. "Cora still blamed Mason. For everything— including Sadie. She seemed to think he'd genuinely lost it. That he'd shown he was capable of anything, and that everything that had happened was all part of his messed-up game. Abi probably thought so, too, although she still had a bee in her bonnet about Cora. And the pregnancy thing . . . I think she had her doubts about Fash by the end of it as well."

"And Fash? Mason? What did they think?"

Luke rolled a shoulder. "Maybe Fash figured Dylan was the one who messed with the water, but he probably assumed it was just a prank. As for what happened to Sadie . . . You know what Fash is like. He doesn't want to believe the worst of *anyone*. After finding out that Sadie might have been pregnant, I think more than anyone he blamed himself. That was partly why he was so keen to help Mason in the first place, I reckon—because he felt so guilty from the start."

The woods were thickening, and for a moment they had to walk in single file. But then the trees parted again, and Fleet was back at Luke's side.

"I don't think Mason realized the truth either," the boy went on. "From what he was saying, the way he kept glancing at the others, as far as he was concerned, *nobody* was in the clear. Not for the water, not for the phones. And not for Sadie either. To be honest, I don't think Mason understood anything more by the end of it than he had on the day we set out."

Fleet suppressed a sigh. Such a waste. All of it. It was all such a waste.

For virtually the first time since they'd started talking, Luke glanced Fleet's way. "I tried to stop them, you know," he said. "From forming the search party in the first place. I mean, I don't think anyone actually *wanted* to come out here—other than Mason, obviously—but I suppose they felt they had no choice."

"Because the others were going," said Fleet. "Because they would look all the guiltier if they refused."

Luke nodded.

"But Mason . . ." said Fleet. "When we were speaking at the station, you said you didn't want him out here in particular. You kicked up a fuss when the others suggested asking him, called him a psychopath. Why was that?"

"Because you suspected him already. Everyone did. And if he went traipsing through the woods, spreading his, like, DNA or whatever all around . . . And if the others accidentally . . . if they . . . if somehow . . ."

"If they found her," Fleet said, finishing the thought, "you realized how it would look. So you were trying to protect him. That's why you didn't want Mason to go."

"I didn't want *any* of them to go. But when I tried to dissuade them, they told me they'd go without me. So then I didn't have a choice."

"What about Dylan?" said Fleet. "When did you realize he'd followed you?"

Luke dropped his head. "Too late," he said. "Just . . . too late."

Fleet thought he knew something of the way the boy was feeling. Not least because, when it came to Dylan, he and his colleagues had messed up, too. They'd made the mistake of assuming exactly what Dylan's parents had—that Luke had taken Dylan with him. That Dylan had been part of what had turned out to be the search party from the start.

"I should have realized earlier," Luke said. "Like, when Abi said she'd heard something. Or when Cora said she'd seen someone in the night. But I assumed they were imagining things. The fact that they all seemed so freaked-out was what gave me the idea in the first place."

"To scare them, you mean," said Fleet. "To try to drive them back."

"It was only when we got to the cave that I started to wonder. No, that's not true. I suspected before then, but it was at the cave that I finally realized. That's why I went rushing off into the trees. To try to find Dylan before the others did. To send him home. To tell him he wasn't being any help."

"And you did. You found him." Fleet thought of the voices Cora had spoken about, of how a young boy's voice might easily have been confused with a girl's. *Home, help, hurry . . .*

"Yeah, I found him. But when I heard the others coming, I just shoved Dylan off into the trees, told him to stay out of sight. I . . . I didn't have time to think. I just . . . I had this idea that . . . I don't know. That maybe it might actually help. You know, that if we all came home swearing we'd heard someone following us, and that if I said that person had attacked me, then maybe you lot would have to believe us. You'd think that maybe someone else *had* killed Sadie. Not Mason, not . . . not me."

Fleet gestured to the bandage on Luke's forehead. "What did you use? A branch? A tree trunk?"

"I hit my head against a tree, scraped it on the bark afterward to make sure it would bleed."

Fleet winced inwardly. A fist or two to the ribs, in comparison, didn't seem that bad. "That must have hurt," he said.

Luke shrugged.

"And the knife?" said Fleet. "How did Dylan get hold of the knife?" This time when Fleet looked Luke's way, he could see tears starting to build in the boy's eyes.

"I should have kept it. I found it while I was searching for Mason's phone. But at that point I didn't know Dylan was out there. And I didn't want to take the chance that Mason might find it in my bag. So I tossed it away. As far as I could."

I found it, Dylan had told the others outside the barn. *It's mine now.* Maybe he'd even been watching when Luke had hurled it into the trees.

Fleet dropped his eyes.

"Why did he even have to bring it?" said Luke, suddenly angry. "The knife, that stupid bottle . . . what the hell was Mason even *thinking*?"

Seeing the boy upset, Miss Jeffries edged closer and laid a hand on Luke's shoulder. He gave a start, as though he'd forgotten the social worker was even behind him.

They walked on, and for a while nobody spoke. Fleet stole a glance to check that Nicky and the PC were still with them, and spotted their yellow jackets weaving between the trees.

"We're not far now," said Luke, after another minute or two. "Up ahead of us is the stream. That way, over there—if you walk far enough you'll reach the place we spent the first night. And in the other direction, that way—that's where Abi found Sadie's phone."

Luke didn't alter his course. He led them straight on, toward a point midway between the spots he'd indicated.

"You walked right past it?" said Fleet. "When you were out here with the others?"

"Twice," said Luke, his voice heavy. "Once before we found the phone, once when we turned around again."

And no one saw. They were right there, searching, and still not one of them saw.

"What happened, Luke?" Fleet said. "With Sadie. Are you ready to tell me?"

"I . . . I killed her. I said to you already. Why do you need to know *how*?"

Fleet didn't respond. He knew Luke didn't really require an answer.

"She . . ." Luke started to say, but then he stalled.

"She was running away," Fleet prompted. "Did you see her go? Did you try to stop her?"

Luke continued walking for a moment, as though he hadn't heard Fleet speaking. But then he nodded, quick and fierce.

"I woke up," he said. "In the night. I wake up most nights. And when I do, I go to the bathroom, and on my way I check on Dylan. He has nightmares, you see. Not every night, but Dad gets cross if Dylan disturbs him and Mum. So I try to . . . I make sure Dylan's OK." He caught himself. "I used to, I mean. That's what I used to do."

"Dylan's bedroom is next to yours?" said Fleet. He didn't really have to ask. He knew the layout of Luke's house so well, he could probably have found the bathroom from one of the bedrooms in the middle of the night himself.

"All three of our bedrooms are together. Mine, Dylan's and Sadie's. The landing is kind of square. The bathroom's opposite my room. My parents' bedroom is up in the loft."

"So you woke up. The night it happened. Did you get as far as checking on your brother?"

"No, I . . . I noticed Sadie's door was open before I could."

"Her door was open," Fleet echoed, and Luke's eyes flicked his way.

"Yeah. Yeah, that's right."

"So you looked in Sadie's room instead?"

"Uh-huh. But she was gone. Her bed hadn't even been slept in. And her curtains were open. When I looked out of the window, I saw her. Squeezing through a gap in the fence at the bottom of our garden."

"And what did you do after that?"

"Nothing. For a minute. But then, I don't know. I just had this feeling."

"A feeling?"

"Like . . . a bad feeling."

"So you followed her?"

"I grabbed some shoes, put on a coat. By the time I had, I was almost too late. When I finally got outside, she was already at the end of our street. And she didn't turn left, toward Mason's house, which is where I thought she might be heading. She went right. Toward the river."

"Did you call out to her?"

"No, because . . . because it was so late. Like, two in the morning. And also I . . . I wanted to see where she was going. Which, after the river, turned out to be the woods."

Fleet was watching Luke carefully. "How long were you following her, Luke?"

"Not that long. Or maybe . . . maybe longer than I thought. But she walked quickly. In the end I had to run to close the gap. Again I almost lost her, because of the trees this time, but when we got . . ." Luke looked around, gestured loosely to a point somewhere behind them. "Here, pretty much. That's when she heard me coming after her."

"And what happened then? Did you argue?"

Once again Luke fell silent. Once again he could only nod. And then he abruptly stopped walking.

"It's just ahead," he said.

Fleet came to a halt by Luke's side. He looked, but could see nothing through the fog except the trees. He could hear the stream, but he couldn't see it. Unless the sound of the water was the river itself, which couldn't have been far away either.

"There's a . . . a tree," said Luke. "Just over there. An oak, I think. But it's old. Dying, maybe. And there's a hollow. When we were younger, playing out here, I used to hide there."

Fleet tracked the line from Luke's finger. There was indeed an old oak tree farther on. It bore no leaves. And unless it was a trick of Fleet's imagination, its trunk appeared darker than those around it.

"Luke," said Fleet, carefully. "Before I go on, is there anything else you want to tell me?"

Luke's head snapped Fleet's way—and just that slight movement was enough. It confirmed everything Fleet had already guessed. *I hope I'm wrong,* he'd told Holly, but now he didn't know which outcome would have been better. That he *had* got it wrong, and Luke had done everything he claimed he had? Or that Luke was lying—still—and that the truth was the only alternative explanation there was left.

"What do you mean?" said Luke, looking as afraid now as he had since the moment he turned up at the station. "I . . . I killed her," he said. "We argued, and I got angry, and when Sadie turned to leave—to walk out on us, on me and Dylan—I . . . I picked up a rock. I threw it. Hard. And it hit her. On the back of the head. I didn't *mean* it, I didn't *want* her to die, but she . . . she . . ." His voice trailed off. He was staring at Fleet, pleading with his eyes, but he'd registered the expression Fleet was offering back.

"What?" Luke said. "Why don't you . . ." He turned to the social worker, then back to Fleet. He shook his head, as though to clear it—or perhaps in denial of the unspoken accusation. "That's why I'm here," he went on, insistent now. "To tell you. To admit it." He gestured ahead of him. "To show you! And then, when you see, you'll be able to let my friends go." Even as he spoke, the tears that had been building in his eyes began to fall. "Please," he said. "Please. Why can't it be that? Why can't it be what I told you? What difference does it make to anyone now?"

Fleet sighed. He wasn't sure he'd ever felt so weary. "It wasn't Sadie's door you found open, was it, Luke?" he said, gently.

The boy let out a sound then, like wet fingers on a windowpane. His chin dropped toward his chest, and his shoulders began to heave. Miss Jeffries stepped forward, but Fleet raised a hand to hold her back.

"It's OK, Luke," he said. "Really, it's OK. I know you meant well. But I also know you wouldn't have let Mason shoulder the blame for as long as he did if it was really you who killed Sadie, not unless there was someone else you were trying to protect."

The only answer he received was the boy's sobbing. Fleet waited a moment, then nodded at Miss Jeffries to approach. He took a breath, steeling himself . . . and then turned to look at the oak tree.

He started forward.

Every step he took felt like a hammer blow against his heart, and it was nothing to do with the pain that was lingering in his ribs. Five strides away, he noticed the smell, although it struck him that in fact he'd noticed it sooner. He'd assumed it was the forest: dying plants and decaying leaves. But it was more than that. Sharper. More acrid.

Three steps away, Fleet spotted the hollow. It was no wonder none of the search party had noticed it. It was masked anyway by the shape of the tree trunk, the lumps and gnarls where the dying oak had turned in on itself. But the opening had also been blocked off with branches, most of which had now lost their leaves. There was just enough of a gap for Fleet to peer inside. The sound of the rain on the canopy above was like a constant murmur, but when he saw the girl's body lying crumpled in the hollow, the sight was one of devastating silence.

Before Fleet could properly react, there was a yell from behind him.

He snapped his head around, in time to see Nicky and the young PC rushing toward him. Miss Jeffries, the social worker, was holding herself up against a tree, and Luke . . .

Luke was nowhere to be seen.

"THAT WAY. HE went that way."

Fleet spun in the direction the social worker was pointing, and caught a flash of movement between the trees. His first reaction was confusion. Why was Luke running? How on earth did he expect to get away? He had a head start, yes, but there was no way he could hope to . . .

And then Fleet realized. A head start was all the boy needed.

No, thought Fleet. *No, no, no.*

He waved an arm frantically toward Nicky. "Go that way!" he called. "Both of you! Try to cut him off!" And then he was running himself, directly after Luke. Nicky and the young PC veered in the direction Fleet had indicated. There was no way any of them would be able to catch Luke before he cleared the tree line, but there was a chance Nicky would be able to outflank him. As for Fleet . . . all he could hope was that he'd be able to get close enough in time to convince the boy to change his mind.

As Fleet ran, he felt every bump and bruise from the night before. Every cigarette he'd ever smoked, too, and every spoon of sugar he'd ever added to his coffee. On top of which, Luke was twenty years younger than him. He was lighter, fitter, *faster*.

"Luke!" Fleet yelled, but either the boy didn't hear or he didn't want to. He continued to hurtle through the trees, as effortlessly as if he were sprinting across a field. Fleet, by contrast, sensed every root trying to trip him, every branch clawing to hold him back.

He stumbled, found his feet again, but when he looked ahead the boy had disappeared from sight. He cast around frantically, and once again caught a flash of movement.

Cursing himself for his clumsiness—not to mention his stupidity for giving in to Luke's wishes and instructing Nicky to hang back— Fleet redoubled his pace. They were heading parallel with the stream, Fleet guessed—and directly toward the river.

Not another one. Please, God, not another one.

Fleet tried digging his mobile phone from his pocket as he ran. It caught on the zip as he pulled it free, and almost somersaulted from his grip. Somehow he caught it, but when he finally reached a gap between the trees that allowed him to focus on the screen, what he saw almost made him hurl it away in frustration anyway. There was no signal. Of course there wasn't. He just had to hope that Nicky was having better luck.

It was only when Fleet burst unexpectedly through the tree line that he realized how close to the river they really were. It greeted him with a roar, which to Fleet sounded disconcertingly like laughter. And unless it was his imagination, the flow of the water appeared to be even faster here than it had been at the point they'd crossed earlier. But, of course, it wasn't how rapidly the river appeared to be flowing that really counted, Fleet knew. It was the currents beneath the surface that made the water so treacherous. The unseen hands that tugged you down with their icy grip.

"Luke! Lu—"

Fleet had been scanning one way and then the other, scouring the riverbank for some sign of the boy. But then he'd spotted him: not on the bank of the river yet, but running north, still clinging tightly to the tree line. Where was he going? There was only a short stretch of open ground between Luke and the river itself, and he was far enough ahead of Fleet that he might have crossed it in plenty of time to make the leap into the water. Unless he wasn't trying to reach the river after all. Maybe he—

The relief Fleet was feeling swan-dived when he realized where the boy was heading. He heard a shout, then, and turned to see Nicky and her colleague emerging from the woods, twenty meters farther downstream. There was a similar gap between Nicky and Fleet as there was now between Fleet and Luke. And Luke was getting farther and farther away. Closer and closer to the old pipeline bridge for which he was no doubt aiming.

The structure had long ago fallen into disrepair. It was nothing like the arched pedestrian bridge on the southern edge of the woods, which was broad and flat and made of stone. The pipeline bridge was little more than a steel truss girder lying sideways, held in place by suspension cables. There was an access ladder on each bank, of the type you saw on pylons. And the ladders rose almost as high. Unlike the pedestrian bridge, which sat relatively low to the water, the pipeline bridge crossed the river at least a dozen meters above its surface. Maybe the fall itself wouldn't be enough to kill someone, but there was every chance the resulting impact would snap a bone. After which, the currents would be waiting like crocodiles, ready to devour their injured prey.

"Call for help!" Fleet yelled to Nicky. "And keep your eyes open! Be ready if . . ." He had half a thought that Nicky might somehow be able to fish Luke from the river as the water bore him past—assuming it came to that, of course—but the channel was so wide, there was no way she would be able to reach him without risking being carried off by the undertow herself. "Just be ready!" Fleet called, knowing Nicky would be as ready as it was possible to be, even if she didn't yet know what for.

And then Fleet was off.

He could move more quickly now that he was out in the open, but the pain in his ribs hadn't diminished, and Luke was taking advantage of the clearer ground, too.

"Luke!" Fleet yelled as he ran. "Luke, don't!"

The boy had already reached the bridge. He'd clearly heard Fleet calling, because as he placed a foot on the ladder that would take him to the walkway, he turned his head. But he only paused for a second. He began to climb, swiftly and surely, and was already near the top by the time Fleet finally reached the ladder.

When he started climbing, Fleet made the mistake of looking up. Luke seemed impossibly far above him. In the fog, the walkway itself was almost lost to view. Worse, the rungs on the ladder were treacherously slippery, and the safety cage was mostly rusted away.

Fleet forced himself to focus on his hands, on the sturdiness of the freezing metal beneath his grip, but still he felt that familiar free fall in the pit of his stomach that told him he was no longer on solid ground.

About three meters up, there was a mesh guard that was supposed to deter members of the public. There was a hole, and Luke had managed to slip through easily, but Fleet was twice the boy's size, and the mesh caught on the fabric of his coat. It was all he could do to keep climbing. At first it was as though someone were attempting to pull him down, but then there was the sound of his jacket ripping, and all at once he found himself free.

The boy was waiting for him. It was the only explanation as to why, when Fleet reached the top of the ladder, Luke hadn't already jumped. He was out toward the center of the bridge, his legs hooked over the slender guardrail. Looking at him balanced there like that, Fleet's vision began to swim. He closed his eyes for a moment, then hauled himself from the ladder onto the walkway. He gripped the guardrail with his left hand, and kept his right firmly planted by his knees. Then he forced himself to clamber to his feet.

There may have been no breeze at ground level, but as soon as Fleet was upright, he found himself buffeted by a crosswind. In reality it probably wasn't all that strong, but to Fleet it felt like a gale. Even the bridge itself seemed to sway, and for one horrible moment, Fleet genuinely believed he was about to fall. He looked down, and saw the water churning far below him. There was no sign of Nicky. Wherever she was, she was shrouded by the fog.

He took a step.

"Stop," said Luke. He was standing—teetering—barely three or four meters away, but his voice sounded improbably distant.

"Luke, listen . . ."

"I came back to tell you what happened. So that you wouldn't blame my friends. That's all. If it hadn't been for them, I would have come here sooner."

"No one's blaming your friends, Luke. Not anymore. They made mistakes, yes, but we all do that. Please don't make another one now."

The boy shook his head. "I told you what I did. I killed Sadie. My brother, too. I killed them both."

"Luke, listen, we can—"

But Luke didn't wait. One moment he was standing on the walkway, the next he was gone—his fragile body plunging toward the water.

"*No!*"

Fleet lunged, but there was never a chance he would reach the boy in time. Even as he closed the distance there had been between them, there was a splash as Luke hit the water.

"*Shit*. Shit, shit, shit."

Fleet was already climbing over the handrail, fighting every instinct that was wrestling to hold him back. He looked down, all the way down, and saw only the water—cold and cruel, and gray like concrete. Luke appeared to have sunk like a piece of granite. There wasn't even a ripple discernible from the churn that showed where the boy had broken the surface.

Dimly, Fleet heard Holly's voice. *You can't save everyone,* she'd told him, and not for the first time in his life, he found himself wishing he would learn to follow his wife's advice.

And then he jumped.

His first sensation, strangely, was one of relief. The second was of time standing still. But then the world came rushing toward him, at a speed he couldn't have imagined. He barely had time to hold his breath before his feet impacted against the water, and pain coursed from his heel bones through his spine to the top of his skull.

He felt himself panic as he was swallowed by the water. He flailed uselessly, desperately trying to propel himself toward the surface. At first it had no effect. He was still falling, still plunging toward the riverbed far below. But then there was a moment of feeling in between, a sensation not dissimilar to how he'd felt when he'd been falling. He frogged his legs, the old muscle memory kicking in, and he found himself rising, rising, his lungs threatening to explode—until finally he broke the surface of the water.

He gulped in air, coughed it out again. He kicked against the current, rotating all the while as he searched for the boy. But there was nothing—just the cold and the rushing river. Dimly he found himself wishing he'd at least removed his coat before he'd jumped, because his clothes were suddenly as heavy as a suit of armor. He'd only been in the water a few seconds, and already his legs were burning from the effort of trying to keep himself afloat.

"Luke!" he called, whether out loud or in his mind, he couldn't tell. His mouth filled with water, and he spluttered. *"Luke!"*

He took a breath and then ducked beneath the water. Immediately the world went quiet, as though he'd dropped into a void. But he could see even less through the murk below than he'd been able to through the fog above the river's surface. He kicked for the sky, gasped as he stole another breath, then dived again—but as before, he saw nothing but a muddy swirl.

This time when he surfaced, he heard a shout. He whipped his head around in time to see Nicky and the young PC on the bank. Already the current had carried Fleet alongside them. Nicky was yelling, pointing. Fleet spun around, floundering to see anything but the spray of the water. Unless . . . *there.*

"Luke!"

It was only the boy's jacket and the back of his head that broached the surface. If Nicky hadn't shown Fleet where to look, there was no way he would have spotted him. The boy was right in the center of the river, and the current there seemed to be at its strongest, because the distance between him and Fleet was steadily increasing.

Fleet wrestled to free himself from his coat. Then he propelled himself forward, thrashing his way toward the boy in a messy mix of strokes. He was aware of a pain in his chest, which at first he'd assumed was coming from his lungs, until he realized it was the groaning of his ribs. He hadn't wanted to say anything to Holly that morning, but he'd been fairly sure that at least a couple of them were broken.

Ahead, Luke was still floating facedown. Fleet was struggling to close the gap. His shoulders were on fire, and his arms and legs felt as weak as ribbons. But then something in the river seemed to catch hold of him, and it was as though he were being funneled along a flume. He'd entered the same channel that had hold of Luke, and steadily

Fleet began to draw nearer. He was closer, closing . . . until at the last he felt certain he would be carried straight past by the current.

Fleet kicked again, trying to slow himself now, and flailed with an outstretched arm. He missed, flailed again, missed again, until—

Got you.

Fleet stopped kicking, allowing the water to carry them both on, and focused all his efforts on turning Luke over. From the angle Fleet had hold of the boy, it was like trying to flip a sodden mattress. But again, the current helped. The river kinked, and all at once the boy rolled onto his back. Fleet had to catch him to stop him rolling too far. He threaded an arm underneath the boy's armpit, hoisting his chin clear of the water. There was no way of telling whether Luke was breathing or not, and no way Fleet could administer mouth-to-mouth—not while they were both still in the water.

Doing his best to hold Luke steady, Fleet turned his head from side to side. They were right in the center of the waterway, a twenty-meter swim to either bank. With all his strength gone, and knowing it was probably useless, Fleet began kicking with his legs. His rib cage screamed at him, and when his body convulsed, his head whipped back and he found himself breathing in a mouthful of water. He coughed, kicked again, blind now, and kept on kicking until exhaustion threatened to overwhelm him. By the end, he couldn't be sure his legs were moving at all anymore, or whether he and Luke hadn't been turned back around and were being carried by the river straight out to sea.

But then he heard a voice, and felt something latch on to his arm. "I've got you," said the voice, over and over, and Fleet would have sworn in that moment that it was Jeannie's. His little sister, a ghost in the river, come to bear him back to shore. *Luke,* he tried to say, but he found himself gasping. And then the weight Fleet was bearing suddenly lifted, and after that he was aware of nothing more.

DAY TEN

HE SPOTTED HER the moment he stepped outside. She had on her raincoat, even though the weather was finally lifting. The rain had stopped, anyway, and a gentle breeze was stirring the puddles on the pavement. On the horizon there was even a streak of blue, approximately the color of Holly's eyes. On a good day, that is. When she was cross, or upset, her eyes turned darker, more like the clouds that still dominated the sky.

Fleet descended the steps, and checked quickly in both directions before crossing the road.

"I figured you must have left," he said, as he drew near. He hadn't seen Holly since he'd woken up to the sight of her the day before—the morning after his altercation with Stephen Payne. In the time since, and following his little swim in the river, Fleet had spent the night at the local hospital, before discharging himself first thing that morning and heading directly to the station. It was now late afternoon, and the investigation was as good as over, though the repercussions of what Fleet had uncovered were only just beginning to unfold.

"I've been spending some time with Anne," Holly said to him. "She gave me a tour of the local sights."

In all their years together, Holly had never seen the town in which Fleet had grown up. His choice, obviously—not hers.

Fleet looked at his watch. "I can't imagine that would have taken very long. What have you been doing for the other thirty-five and a half hours?"

"Shopping," said Holly, and she reached into her pocket. "Here. After what you've been through, I imagine you feel like you need them. And I felt bad for throwing yours away." She held out a ten-pack of cigarettes. "I couldn't bring myself to buy you twenty. You can think of these as being like a countdown. Ten more, and then you stop. Agreed?"

Fleet narrowed his eyes at her. He took the packet from her hand, then shook out a cigarette and planted it between his lips. "Thanks," he mumbled. He patted his jacket. "I don't suppose you brought a—"

"Agreed?" Holly repeated. This time she held out a box of matches, just out of Fleet's reach. She gave it a rattle.

Fleet smiled. He plucked the cigarette from his mouth, and fed it back into the packet. "In which case," he said, "I suppose I'd better make them count." He tucked both the cigarettes and the matches into his pocket. The truth was, he didn't feel much like smoking right now anyway. His lungs felt as though the insides had been scrubbed with sandpaper, and his throat was equally as raw. And with his ribs the way they were, it was hard enough breathing as it was, without adding carbon monoxide into the mix.

There was a low brick wall at the edge of the pavement, and Fleet moved to sit down. Holly propped herself beside him, so that together they faced the police station. As they watched, the building's doors opened, and one by one they began to file out. Abigail Marshall. Cora Briggs. Fareed Hussein. And finally, tentatively, as though he were expecting to walk into an ambush, Mason Payne. He was right to be wary, Fleet thought, although by now the press would most likely have lost interest in him. The story had moved on. And anyway, the hacks were for the most part otherwise engaged. Inside the building, Superintendent Burton was finally hosting the press conference he'd been obliged to delay, though Christ knew what the man was saying. Fleet made a mental note to avoid the evening news. Now that he knew the truth, he had no interest in how the superintendent chose to spin it.

"Is that them?" said Holly.

Even as she spoke, the kids spotted Fleet across the road from them. There were mutterings, Fleet sensed—and then Cora raised her middle finger.

"Yeah," said Fleet. "That's them." He returned Cora's salute with a nod.

"What's going to happen to them?" Holly asked him.

As he watched the kids walk off—Fash in front, Cora and Abi side by side, and Mason dragging his feet just behind—Fleet felt an urge to spark up that cigarette. He swallowed, to remind himself of the burn in his throat.

"In a legal sense, you mean?" he said to Holly. "Not a lot. A slap on the wrist all round. Mason—he's the one at the back. He's in the most serious trouble. Potentially. But there are mitigating circumstances. He'll be OK. I hope." Fleet queried himself, and found that he genuinely did.

"And the boy? The one you fished from the river?" Holly laid a hand on Fleet's knee then, squeezing it gently. Fleet turned and Holly looked down awkwardly, returning her hand to her lap.

"Luke's still in hospital. He'll be there for a few days yet. It was touch-and-go for a while. Nicky saved his life on the riverbank, you know. Administered CPR. And she'd already called for an ambulance."

"I know," said Holly. "I heard."

"You did?"

"Word travels quickly in this town. That's what I've gathered, anyway, from the little I've experienced of the place so far."

Fleet didn't know why he was surprised. The whole story was probably out by now. It wouldn't have taken long for the news to go around, not after the police were seen heading to the woods again, and reports had begun to emerge that they'd discovered Sadie's body.

"Do you know they changed their stories?" said Fleet, nodding toward Sadie's friends. "When we told them what Luke told us . . . when they heard that he'd confessed to holding the knife . . . from saying they couldn't remember what happened, every single one of them claimed *they* were the one holding the knife when Dylan died. Independently. Luke came back to protect them, and they decided to return the favor."

Holly joined him in watching the kids heading off in the direction of the harbor. Cora had an arm around Abi's shoulders, a sight Fleet would never have expected to see four days ago. Although when the lies had finally been stripped away, he'd been astonished by how much each and every one of the kids had changed. Even Mason. Particularly Mason. From a brash teenager, he'd morphed in Fleet's eyes into a terrified little kid. Telling him that Sadie was really dead was one of the hardest things Fleet had ever had to do. At first Mason had said nothing. Moments later, Fleet hadn't been sure the boy would ever be able to stop crying.

As he watched the kids comfort each other now, he marveled at how quickly indiscretions at that age were forgiven. He pictured them gathering on the quay one coming evening, passing around a bottle of cider and sharing stories about Sadie. Their friend. A girl they had loved in spite of their betrayals, and whose memory would haunt them for the rest of their lives. And afterward—after that final ceremony to say good-bye—it was likely their friendship would begin to crumble. Abi and Cora. Mason and Fash. Yes, indiscretions could be forgiven, but some could never be forgotten, and after Sadie things would never be the same. And of course there was Dylan—another ghost that would haunt them. This town was full of them, it turned out. Life was.

"So who was holding it?" said Holly, pulling Fleet from his thoughts. "The knife," she clarified. "Out there in the woods."

Fleet shook his head. "Who knows? To be honest, I'm not sure it even matters. Maybe to some people, but whoever it was, they didn't mean for it to happen. Officially, what happened to Dylan will go down as an accident."

"And Luke?" said Holly, hesitantly. "Will he be charged? I mean, is it true that he killed Sadie? That's what everyone seems to be saying."

Fleet gave in. He lit the cigarette. The smoke was fire in his throat, and he sucked it greedily down into his battered lungs. "It wasn't Luke," he told Holly. "It was Dylan."

"Dylan?"

Fleet left time for the sound of the name to settle. He knew he was breaking every rule in the book by confiding in his wife, but it would all come out soon enough anyway. Fleet would make sure of that. He knew Luke wanted nothing more than to protect his brother—even now, even after his death—but Fleet couldn't simply stand by and watch Luke throw away what was left of his life.

"Sadie was pregnant," he said. "I mean, that's not confirmed yet, but those tests . . . the ones you can buy? They're never wrong, are they?"

Slowly, Holly shook her head. "You can get a false negative if you take the test too early. It's rare to get a false positive."

"So Sadie ran away. We haven't worked out yet where she was going. Maybe she didn't even know herself. I suspect she had a plan of some sort, depending on what she intended to do about the baby.

But ultimately it hardly matters, because when she left her house in the middle of the night, her little brother heard her go. We've yet to get the full story from Luke about how it played out after that, but . . . Well. I doubt there will be any surprises."

In fact, Fleet thought he knew exactly how it had all played out. When Luke had got up to check on Dylan, just as he'd described, it was Dylan's door he'd found open, and his brother who'd been missing from his bed. Sadie would have made sure she'd closed her bedroom door behind her. A girl who went to such lengths to cover her tracks—with her bag, her bank records—wouldn't have taken the chance that one of her family would so easily discover she'd sneaked out in the middle of the night. And perhaps when Luke had crept downstairs in search of his little brother, Dylan had already returned. Either that or Luke had ventured farther, and when he'd found Dylan, his little brother had confessed what he'd done.

He'd heard Sadie leave, perhaps after waking from one of his nightmares, and he'd followed her into the woods, in precisely the manner Luke had told Fleet he'd followed Sadie himself. And when Dylan had caught up with her, or Sadie had realized he was there, they'd argued. Perhaps at first Sadie had tried to reason with Dylan, to explain why she needed to go away. Maybe she'd even mentioned Mason, which would have explained why Dylan was so angry with Mason at the end. But whatever she'd said, it hadn't worked. Dylan had insisted she come home; Sadie had refused. Maybe she'd even shouted at him, lashed out in an attempt to get him to leave. And if Luke had had conflicting emotions about his sister, how much worse must it have been for Dylan? He loved her, unquestionably, but how he must have hated her on occasion, too—not least when he saw his parents adoring her the way they had never adored him. And then for her to tell him she was *abandoning* him—leaving him and never coming back . . . It was no wonder that when Sadie turned away,

THE SEARCH PARTY   337

Dylan had felt such rage. And it was his rage—his sheer emotional turmoil—that had prompted him to pick up the rock.

Perhaps he never really meant the rock to hit her. Or, if he had, maybe he'd been aiming for her back. Certainly it was unlikely he understood how much damage a blow to the back of the head could cause. It would only have been after Sadie had fallen that Dylan would have realized what he'd done.

Except . . . Luke. Everything Luke did from that point on was designed to protect his little brother. He took Dylan back to his bed, telling him all the while it would be OK. And then he went into the woods himself, following whatever directions he'd been able to coax from his brother. When he found Sadie where she had fallen, at first he would have tried to help her. For some reason he had removed her jacket, perhaps to prop up her head. But when he realized he was already too late, he came to understand what he had to do. He concealed her body, in the best nearby hiding place he knew. He covered the hollow with branches, completely masking it from sight. Ideally he would have taken Sadie to the river, but there was no way he could have carried her that far—not by himself, and not while his brother lay waiting for him at home. But after Sadie was hidden, he realized he'd forgotten about her jacket. Perhaps he was reluctant to disturb the camouflage he'd constructed around the hollow, or perhaps he simply couldn't face going back, but either way, he decided to toss the coat into the river, going via the stream to get cleaned up on the way. At some point, Sadie's new phone had slipped from one of her jacket pockets, without Luke even noticing it had been there.

And then it was done. When Luke got home, there was only one task left: to convince Dylan that, when he'd got to the place Dylan had said he and Sadie argued, their sister had been OK.

She'd only been stunned, Luke told Dylan. *You didn't hurt her, Dylan. You* didn't. *I spoke to her and tried to convince her to come home, but . . .*

but she left anyway. The way she was planning to all along. But she'll come back. You'll see. One day, someday, she'll come home. I promise.

How desperately Dylan would have wanted to believe him. And perhaps, at first, he did. Except then people started saying Sadie had been murdered, and the entire town was looking for her body. But rather than blaming Dylan, they blamed Mason. Which meant . . . *what*? Dylan simply didn't know. By the end—by the point the search party had set off—he would have been no clearer on what had actually happened than Fleet had been at that stage himself. It was no wonder Dylan had followed Luke and his friends, the same way he'd followed Sadie. He would have been as desperate to know the truth as anyone.

It's the parents I feel most sorry for, Burton had said to Fleet, after Dylan's body had been found. But in Fleet's mind that was entirely back to front. Mr. and Mrs. Saunders wouldn't have wished for anything that had happened, certainly. And perhaps they couldn't have anticipated that their overwhelming love for their daughter would shape such radically different personalities in their sons. So yes, they deserved some sympathy—but not as much as their children did. Indeed, out of anyone, it was Sadie's parents Fleet held most responsible for everything that had happened. The same way he would have held himself responsible if he had been standing in their place.

"I hope they look after him," said Holly. "Luke, I mean. In hospital. I hope he gets the care he needs."

And that was almost the most tragic thing of all, as far as Fleet was concerned. Yes, he had pulled Luke from the river, but what sort of life was waiting for him now? What sort of *love*?

Fleet shook his head, and tossed his cigarette into the gutter. He glanced Holly's way, and smiled at her sadly.

"We said we'd talk," he said. "About what happens now."

Holly reached and took his hand. Her touch was warm and soft, and Fleet couldn't begin to comprehend how much he would miss it.

"I think I know what happens now," Holly said. "I think we both do."

"Listen, Holly," said Fleet. "I want you to know——"

"Rob, please. There's no need."

"Yes, there is. I want you to know that I didn't come back here to try to justify the way I was feeling. About having children, I mean. It was the opposite. I came back because I thought it might help. I thought . . . I don't know what I thought. That thing about confronting your demons." He thought of his mother, of the inscription on the bench. "And actually, if anything, it's helped."

There was a brief flash of hope in Holly's eyes, and for Fleet it was like a dagger to his heart.

"But it hasn't *healed*, Sprig," he went on. "If that's even the right word. I just . . . It wouldn't be fair of me. To you, because you'd always be walking on a knife edge, worrying that you'd made me do something I didn't want to. Anytime anything went wrong, you'd think it was *your* fault."

Holly was shaking her head, but Fleet could tell she knew he was right.

"And it wouldn't be fair to the kid, either," he went on. "Think about it, Holly. It wouldn't. How could it be?"

Fleet tried to continue. What he wanted to say was that his reluctance to have children was nothing to do with being afraid of the responsibility. Responsibility, he could handle. The thing he didn't think he could—the thing that terrified him about having children most of all—was the sorrow, the anguish, the sheer bloody heartache that would come if he were to fail them. It would destroy him, Fleet knew. And in turn it would destroy him and Holly.

They sat in silence, still holding hands. Holly used a tissue from her pocket to dry her eyes.

"You always said we sounded ridiculous," Fleet ventured, after a moment. "Robin and Holly. Like a cheesy Christmas card. Right? So maybe it's a blessing in disguise."

Holly gave a laugh that sounded like a sob.

She turned away.

"You're staying," she said, turning back. "Aren't you?" She moved her chin, loosely indicating the town.

"Not forever," said Fleet. "But for a while, I think. I've got some bridges to build."

Holly looked down at her lap. She freed her hand from Fleet's. When she looked at him, her eyes were the color of rain.

She rose, and it took all of Fleet's willpower not to stand up beside her.

"Look after yourself, Rob," she told him. "Please."

And then Fleet could only watch, as slowly his wife walked away.

He got up eventually. Holly had turned left, toward the center of town. Fleet went right—south—toward the harbor. He passed a litter bin and stopped beside it. He hesitated, but only for a second. He tossed away the packet of cigarettes and kept walking.

After a few moments he heard a car pull up behind him. He turned, and was only mildly surprised to see a marked squad car. The passenger-side window hummed down.

"Need a lift?" said Nicky.

"Thanks," Fleet replied. "But I could use the exercise." He patted his stomach and Nicky smiled.

Fleet raised his chin. "Off anywhere exciting, or are you just hitching a ride?"

Nicky's smile set harder. "We're off to pay a visit to Stephen Payne. Social Services are meeting us there."

As part of their final interview with Mason, they'd asked about his relationship with his father. About how often Stephen Payne hit him. That was another thing that had made Mason cry, though this time Fleet had at least taken some comfort from the fact that the boy's tears would ultimately offer him some release. Nicky, Fleet knew, would make sure of that.

"Send Payne my regards, won't you?" Fleet said.

Nicky nodded. "Will do, boss. Enjoy your walk." She pressed the button to raise the window.

"Oh, and Nicky . . ."

The window stopped moving.

"You might want to check the contents of his wallet," Fleet said.

"His wallet?"

"Right. And if you find anything, I'd start by asking him about his friends. The local dealer, Nathan Murdoch, in particular." *Lion,* Fleet thought. "A man like Stephen Payne . . . he'd throw his mates under a bus if it meant dodging a charge for possession. Particularly given everything else he's going to have to answer for."

"Gotcha," said Nicky, and she waved as the squad car drove off.

Fleet walked on.

He passed bait shops and greasy spoons and, on the corner where the road met the water, the Harvester where Sadie had worked since she'd turned fifteen. And ice cream vans. Half a dozen, at least. *Seriously,* came Cora's voice. *How many ice cream vans does one town need?* Only one was open for business, and Fleet half considered buying a can of something, purely out of sympathy. There wasn't another customer in sight, and he had his doubts there would be for months now. The weather might slowly have been improving, but the summer was definitively over. Already the town had the feeling of a place that had shut up shop. Like one of those villages in the Arctic Circle that, when the seasons reach a certain point in their cycle, don't see daylight until the following spring.

When he reached the harbor, Fleet spotted a light on in one of the rooms in Anne's B&B. Even without the rain, on a day in early September, it was gloomy enough that natural light simply didn't cut it. But the sun would be back, Fleet thought, looking at the horizon. The strip of blue was strengthening, and slowly extending the town's way.

He passed the fishing boats, and the spot he'd had his run-in with Mason's father. Compared to how it had appeared to Fleet last time, the promenade didn't actually look that shabby. Strange, how perceptions were influenced by the way you were feeling. For the whole of his adult life, Fleet had thought he hated this place. The promenade, the beachfront, the entire town. But really it wasn't so very different from anywhere else. It was tired, certainly, but at least it was trying. It was like with people: what more could you ask of them but that?

When Fleet was halfway along the walkway, he saw her sitting on the bench. Somehow he'd known she'd be there. He drew close, and waited for her to acknowledge his presence. When she didn't, he joined her in looking out over the sea.

"You found her, then," said his mother at last.

Fleet's eyes caught on the inscription on the bench. His mother still wasn't looking at him, and he found it hard to interpret who exactly she was talking about.

He sat down, at the opposite end of the bench from his mother.

"Are you staying?" she asked him, this time turning his way.

Fleet didn't know if she meant it the way Holly had, or if she was merely referring to his presence on the bench.

"I thought I might," Fleet answered, covering both bases, at which point he fully expected his mother to get up and leave.

But she didn't. Neither of them did. They just sat side by side on Jeannie's bench, waiting for the sun to break through.

ACKNOWLEDGMENTS

I am incredibly fortunate to have three people in my writing corner whose instincts I trust more than my own. The first is my wife, Sarah, who is also the first reader of anything and everything I write. I never fail to be humbled by her extraordinary patience and insight, not just into the craft of writing, but also into the human condition. It is for Sarah I write at all (though I imagine she sometimes wishes I wouldn't), and I could not write without her.

Next up is Caroline Wood, my agent now for over a decade. In all that time, Caroline's support has been unfailing, and her insights and instincts flawless. More than just a wonderful agent, she is also a wonderful person.

And then there is my editor at Viking, Katy Loftus. Everyone who knows her would agree: Katy has a gift for what she does. She knows instinctively when something works and when it doesn't—to the extent that I often feel two or three steps behind her in my thinking. It is a delight and a privilege to work with her, and to consider her a friend.

Without Sarah, Caroline and Katy, this book would have been

considerably poorer, and indeed would probably not have been written at all. So a heartfelt thank-you to them all, as well as to the entire team at both Felicity Bryan Associates and Viking. A huge thanks as well to Amanda Bergeron and everyone at Berkley, as well as to Gemma Wain.

Finally, thank you to my friends and family, in particular to my three children, for their love, forbearance and support. You make it worth it.

Photo © Justine Stoddart

SIMON LELIC is the award-winning author of numerous crime novels, including *A Thousand Cuts*, *The New Neighbors*, and *The Liar's Room*, as well a highly acclaimed series of books for young adults. His writing is inspired by a lifelong love of both Alfred Hitchcock and Stephen King. Simon lives with his wife and three children.

CONNECT ONLINE

SimonLelic.com